HOLLIS
and Gray

HOLLIS
and Gray

J.P. Zeigler

Serafina Gray Mystery: Book One

Hollis and Gray

Copyright © 2023 by J.P. Zeigler

All rights reserved.

This novel is a work of fiction developed from the author's imagination. While some names, personality types, facts, places, and events may actually exist, they are used fictitiously to create the world of the author's imaginary characters. Any resemblance to real persons, living or deceased, is wholly coincidental.

Editing and Summary by Sara DeGonia/DeGonia Editing
Cover and interior design by David Ter-Avanesyan/Ter33Design LLC
First Edition: 2024

www.jpzeiglerbooks.com

Publisher's Cataloging-in-Publication data

Names: Zeigler, J. P., author.
Title: Hollis and Gray / J.P. Zeigler.
Series: Hollis and Gray
Description: South San Francisco, CA: J. P. Zeigler, 2024.
Identifiers: LCCN: 2023922580 | ISBN: 978-1-962983-05-1 (hardcover)
978-1-962983-04-4 (paperback) | 978-1-962983-00-6 (ebook)
Subjects: LCSH Private investigators--Fiction. | Detroit (Mich.)--Fiction. | Mental illness--Fiction. | Murder--Fiction. | Family--Fiction. | Detective and mystery stories.
BISAC FICTION / Mystery & Detective / General | FICTION / Friendship
FICTION / Family Life / General
Classification: LCC PS3626 .E55 H65 2024 | DDC 813.6—dc23

This book is dedicated to J.W. whose encouragement back in 2004 kicked off this whole adventure. To my husband Steve for all his support. And to actors Tommy Lee Jones and Morgan Freeman who were the inspiration behind characters Frank Hollis and Levi Nestor, respectively.

Chapter 1

Frank Hollis already had another crisp twenty out for the bouncer when he exited what might have been the sleaziest strip club he'd been in yet. Few could fare worse than the first he'd entered back in July 1970—the one that had turned a blind eye to his underage drinking on the day he'd been drafted.

Many had been sympathetic about him having to fight a war nobody wanted, but not many were willing to risk their liquor license over him—only the one with the reputation for "anything goes." It wasn't surprising they'd closed down months later. Him having a few beers was the least shocking thing to go down in that establishment.

Hollis held the twenty out so the bouncer could see. He wasn't required to tip him, but he'd learned over the years to always take care of the bouncer.

The muscular man pocketed the twenty and motioned to the valet attendant in the parking lot that Hollis was leaving. The scrawny fellow nodded his acknowledgment and walked toward them.

Hollis had already tipped the valet attendant well for the parking space closest to the entrance. There was no need for exchanges of any kind. Still, the guy made his way over.

It had to be close to midnight, Hollis thought, but he didn't care enough about the time to check his phone. He just knew it was late and that he needed to rest.

The streetlights were dim, casting foreboding shadows around the entrance to the bar. Hollis walked over to his Harley, parked under a pink neon light in the shape of a topless woman.

"She's a beauty." The valet attendant motioned to the motorcycle.

Hollis wasn't much for small talk, but tonight he felt even less talkative. "Sure is."

Mist clung to the streets from rain earlier in the evening. Hollis took in a deep breath of the crisp air as he prepared himself for the long ride home.

It wasn't really motorcycling weather by Michigan standards, but the smell of wet dirt always put him in the mood for riding. And since his diagnosis a few weeks ago, he wasn't sure how many more opportunities like this he would get.

The temperature had definitely dropped since that afternoon. Hollis zipped up his leather jacket and put on his helmet, keenly aware of his surroundings.

In the daylight, it had been a desolate scene, but now it was a deeper level of despair. The only other businesses in that less-populated area of southwest Detroit were a *taqueria* and a *supermercado*, but they were both closed now. The people he'd seen there earlier that day were now gone.

Hollis's uneasiness signaled him to take the quickest route out of there and back to a more populated area.

As Hollis drove down Dix Street, past Central Avenue, he considered taking Waterman Street down the equivalent of eleven or so blocks to Fisher Freeway / I-75. It would be quicker after all. But if he did, he'd be heading toward Delray, and that was rumored to be motorcycle gang territory.

He decided it was probably safer for him to stay on Dix Street since it would turn into Vernor Highway, which was basically Main Street for Mexicantown. He could just take that through the center of it all and get on the freeway near the Ambassador Bridge. It wouldn't be a significant difference in distance or time either way. Maybe a mile shorter, a minute longer. A straight shot up to Rochester Hills once he got to the freeway.

If he felt like he couldn't make the fifty-minute drive home, he could always crash at the agency in Royal Oak and slash twenty minutes off the trip. It wasn't what he wanted to do, but he reassured himself that he had that option. He couldn't trust his body these days, and if his exhaustion suddenly worsened, that extra twenty-minute drive might feel like torture.

Hollis resisted thinking about the last time he had crashed at the agency. It had to have been at least ten years ago. He'd spent most of that Sunday trying to clean out the loft above the agency once and for all. But just like the times before, he would pick up one of those photographs or letters, try to lay those dark places of his past to rest, only to find himself transported back as if it all happened yesterday. No amount of tequila could wash down the bitter taste of his self-loathing when he succumbed to the painful memories.

He couldn't let himself spiral out like that anymore. He decided that if he did end up going to the agency that night, he wouldn't go up to the loft to sleep. He'd just stay on the couch in the agency instead.

But then he imagined Datson waiting patiently at the front door for him to come home. He'd installed a doggie door awhile back so Datson could let himself out, but he always came home at night, no matter how late.

What would happen to Datson when he was gone for real? That wasn't something he'd really considered until now. He owed it to Datson to make sure he was well taken care of, especially in his senior years. He'd been more than a dog to him—Datson was his guardian angel.

Hollis thought back to when Datson came into his life, compartmentalizing it from the parts he didn't want to recall. He was quite good at not allowing feelings to come in that he didn't want to feel. He had been functioning like that for far too many years. And when the noise of those feelings became too loud, he would just muffle them with whatever hard liquor was available. Thankfully, the noise had lessened over the years, becoming more like the low-setting whir of a box fan.

As he allowed himself to recall that particular night, Hollis was careful not to become too relaxed in his thoughts. Not to let his mind sink into the past like a heavy head on a pillow. He knew too well the danger in that comfort. He wouldn't get caught up reliving regrets anymore. If he thought about anything involving his past, he'd make himself an outsider looking in, watching a movie about someone else's pathetic life.

Hollis saw himself as a random man waking up in the parking lot of some random bar. It was all random, definitely not him.

$$\bullet \ \bullet \ \bullet$$

A man was passed out where he'd tripped while exiting the back door of a bar. The spinning in his head had kept him from getting back up, and now, it was likely he would be there all night.

A tri-colored Australian shepherd came out from the darkness, walked right up to the man slouched against the wall, and started licking the man's face.

The man swatted the air around his face, insistent on continuing his drunken slumber. The dog grabbed hold of the man's pant leg and pulled repeatedly, as if trying to move him.

The man didn't budge. The Australian shepherd relentlessly kept on without a moment of pause. A depiction of futility if there ever was.

The man's eyes opened slightly, revealing the wandering gaze of his pupils. The canine persisted, urgently nudging the man to get up.

The man pulled himself up to stand and clumsily walked to his truck. The Australian shepherd remained close to the man's heels.

The man opened the truck door, and the shepherd immediately jumped inside, as if no invitation was needed. One look at that mangy coat and emaciated rib cage, the man had no doubt the dog was a stray. Not putting too much thought into it, the man took the dog home.

• • •

Hollis hadn't realized the significance of what Datson had done for him until the next night when he went back to that very bar. There had been caution tape in the parking lot and patrons saying that someone got robbed and stabbed to death the night before.

If there was such a thing as reincarnation, this dog was Datson, for sure.

At the Junction Avenue stoplight, Hollis zipped his jacket up more and looked around for signs of activity.

Aside from the gas station and liquor store he'd passed earlier, the only other business open was a McDonald's.

Along Vernor Highway, as far as he could see, were dilapidated homes and businesses. The signs in the storefronts were all written in Spanish, reminding him of his time in Texas—a familiarity that unnerved him. He did not want to be reminded of Texas.

When Hollis realized Clark Park was on his right, he slowed down, astonished at how unrecognizable it was at that late hour. Earlier that day, it seemed the whole community had gathered at the park for some sort of festival. This was no small park either. From his early years of farming, he guessed it to be about thirty acres.

Now, it was a very dark place to be.

He looked to his left and up ahead, noticing the gang graffiti claiming the walls of local businesses. Instinctively, he felt for his firearm on his side and became alarmed when he realized it wasn't there.

Hollis remembered that he intentionally hadn't carried that night on account of being in a strip club, a restricted area for carrying a firearm whether he was drinking or not, and he wasn't about to risk losing his Concealed Pistol License.

His uneasiness lingered. Maybe it was a Texan thing, but he'd been carrying a firearm for so many years, it was almost unnatural not to carry.

He passed 25th Street and 24th Street. The smell of authentic Mexican food still swarmed outside the Mexican restaurants. He looked to his right, wishing Xochimilco or El Zocalo were still open.

As he approached the overpass for Fisher Freeway / I-75, he saw orange construction barrels blocking off his route. He would need to find another entrance ramp onto the freeway—one that wouldn't have him accidentally driving over the Ambassador Bridge to Canada over on his right. He'd done that only once, many years ago, back when a driver's license was all he needed to return. He didn't want to make that mistake again. Not when a mistake like that would delay him getting to the agency, or home—he hadn't decided yet which it would be. He slowed down to think through what action he should take.

He could zigzag his way along I-75 to find another entrance. Or maybe it was better to just go back to Clark Street where he knew there was an entrance. Either way, he needed to go somewhere other than straight ahead.

With little thought, he turned his bike left and went down a side street that seemed to go the same direction as the freeway. Almost immediately, he questioned his decision to do so.

On the corner to his left was a two-story wooden house in serious disrepair. The gable roof above the porch was leaning as if it could fall any minute. A tattered blue tarp covered a section where the gable roof met the actual roof. Logs were stacked on the corners and all along the edges of the tarp, holding it in place.

The streetlights barely projected any light, but he could see a few more old houses farther down beyond the vacant lots where other houses used to stand. The lots were overgrown with weeds and littered with tires, various car parts, and trash.

Hollis slowed his pace, carefully avoiding the potholes and broken glass on his path.

Halfway down the street, he decided Clark Avenue was the way to go after all, so he slowed down even more to turn his bike around.

At that moment, a car turned the corner onto the barren street, so Hollis rode on a little farther than he'd planned.

The car slowed down.

Hollis looked back once more to get a better description of the car, but when he did, the driver sped up.

Hollis didn't have time to think on his reaction. He just accelerated as fast as he could.

Loud pops reverberated the booming of what Hollis first thought were tire blowouts.

Forceful blows pushed him forward, and he flew off his bike, landing on a wet patch of dirt next to the curb. His bike skid farther down the street.

The car continued its pace down the street and vanished.

Hollis felt a rush of indescribable pain come over him, something he'd not felt in years. He was pretty sure he'd broken a rib. He reached down to touch that area and felt wetness on his fingers. Then he made the connection. He'd been shot.

Hollis called out for help, but the pain of doing so was more than he could bear.

He lifted his head to see what was in view.

There wasn't much of anything around. A house halfway down the block appeared to be lived in. It had a light on in the window.

He rolled onto his hands and knees, gathering his balance to stand, and managed to take a step before falling onto the palms of his hands.

He tried again, lifting his right knee up, and then his left knee. He attempted to walk again, this time standing only slightly up before his right foot gave out, taking the last bit of strength he had.

Blood started to pool around him. He looked up once more to the house with the light. Although the house seemed to be farther away, the light itself shone brighter than before, and he became fixated on it. His mind drifted to another point in his life, and this time, he didn't resist.

• • •

It was an autumn night in Texas. He was walking down the old dirt road where he'd walked a million childhood steps, this time with pieces of gravel under his boots. The house at the end of the road was the house he'd always known, but the years he'd been away could be seen, like the wrinkles on the face of an old friend.

He only half-expected to see Samuel on the front porch rocker when the porch came in view, but it didn't keep him from looking. The lamp was on, and it was still in the front window just like Daddy had always had it.

Samuel must be home, he thought. And then, there he was. Samuel walked into sight inside the front room just beyond the light. Hollis felt panic set in. Samuel would be happy to see him, wouldn't he?

Samuel walked farther into the room where Hollis assumed the television would still be. He imagined Samuel watching a program on fishing or hunting. Then he imagined Daddy sitting in the room too. But Daddy wouldn't be there—he was with Momma now.

As he approached the farmland adjacent to the house, he could see the oak tree that had once stood as the lone guard to a vast acreage full of crops. The tree seemed to slump over, like a tired old man who had lost everything. There was nothing to harvest anymore. Guarding the barren land now was a tall post with a sign nailed to the front of it. He looked closely at the sign. It was for a property development company. Hollis looked back at the light, which seemed to fade away.

. . .

Hollis had lost a lot of blood and he knew he didn't have much time. He needed to call someone. He needed to call 9-1-1.

His phone was tucked away in the inside pocket of his leather jacket, and he was lying on his right arm. He tried to free up his hand, but his body had suddenly become very heavy, making it difficult.

Hollis pushed his body to the left with all his strength while pulling his right arm out from under his body. It wasn't working. He rolled back and forth, ending up on his back.

He unzipped his jacket and fumbled inside it for the phone. His hand, now covered in blood, retrieved the device. In a matter of moments, he would have someone on the phone. He would be saved. He just needed to . . . *hang in there.*

. . .

"Hang in there," Datson said as he rushed up and kneeled beside Hollis.

They'd been ambushed. Casualties lay scattered all around them, and with every bomb that exploded throughout the Vietnamese countryside, cries for help rang out.

Everything had happened so fast. Hollis had been shot in the shoulder, and his leg looked mangled up from what could be seen. Datson ignored the bombs, quickly assessing the situation like the soldier he was trained to be.

Datson grabbed hold under Hollis's arms and tugged. He was a much smaller man than Hollis, but he was determined as hell. As he pulled, the blood seeped out more from under Hollis's jacket.

The ground exploded again, this time even closer. Datson was struggling to hold up Hollis's weight, and they were running out of time.

"Go," Hollis directed Datson. "Git on."

"Not without you, Hollis."

"I'm serious. Go! I'll be right behind you." Hollis sat up.

Datson looked around in a movement that could've been missed in a blink. "I'll git some help." He turned away and ran a few steps before the ground exploded where he stood. Shrapnel embedded into his face and throat. He ran almost in circles with his hands covering his face, and then fell to the ground.

The shrieking and thundering sounds around them were closing in. Hollis used all the strength he had to turn onto his knees and crawl to Datson.

"Datson! You hold on."

Datson's injuries were extensive, and it was critical that he get medical attention.

"I can't."

"Yes, you can!" Hollis insisted.

Datson took a handwritten letter out of his jacket pocket and put it in Hollis's hand. On the front, it was written in cursive, "If I die."

"Give . . ." Datson coughed. "Give to her."

"But . . ." Hollis started to argue.

Hollis could hear footsteps heading his way. Someone yelled, "There! Over there!" It sounded like Nestor.

"Please." Datson started to close his eyes.

Nestor and Platt rushed to Hollis, each pulling an arm of his over their shoulder. In moments, Hollis was carried away from the danger, away from Datson.

• • •

Hollis opened his eyes and looked at the numbers on his phone, unable to make any of them out. The digits were blurry, and he felt dizzy. He stared at the numbers, hoping they would come into focus.

The urge to go to sleep was getting stronger. He placed the phone down and unstrapped his helmet. He pushed it off his head, and it rolled a few feet away. Unable to make out his surroundings anymore, he became fixated on the helmet. His eyes felt heavy, so he closed them.

• • •

Next to his head was a terracotta flowerpot. The leaves of the plant had long withered away from the October air.

Lizzie opened up the screen door and stood over him as he lay on the front porch. The coolness of the wooden planks felt good against his throbbing head. Normally she would say something when he came home drunk, but this time, she just stood there in silence. Was she waiting for him to say something first? He waited.

Hollis groaned. The spinning had begun, and he was regretting that last shot of whiskey.

He knew that at any moment Lizzie would help him inside, lay him on the couch, take off his boots, grab him a blanket, and shut off the light. And shut off the noise. And shut off the pain.

She would let him wallow in his self-pity and be there in the morning acting as if the sun never stopped shining.

The minutes dragged on and still she said nothing. Just hovered. That wasn't like her.

The screen door opened. Lizzie stepped into the house.

She must be preparing the couch, he convinced himself.

Hollis fixated on the terracotta flowerpot again. He had never before noticed the intricate design of leaves sketched into the pot.

The screen door opened again, and as Lizzie passed through, something hit the flowerpot. It rolled away toward the front porch stairs, making a loud thud with every step it hit on its way down.

That's when he saw it. In her hand was a suitcase.

Halfway down the steps, he caught a glimpse of his sweet baby girl fast sleep, nestled against Lizzie's chest and neck.

Lizzie became a blur as she walked away. He tried with all his will to focus on her, but he could see nothing.

Hollis closed his eyes and listened for the car door to close. It closed. He listened for the car engine to start. It started. He listened for the tires to hit the gravel. He waited. Nothing. Just the sound of an engine running.

Could she have changed her mind? She wouldn't leave him drunk on the front porch, would she? Lizzie may have been a wild horse in spirit, but she was always one you could count on to be there.

The tires hit the gravel and Lizzie drove off.

• • •

One raindrop and then another began to fall around Hollis as he lay on the damp ground. With each drop that came down, another came down faster than before. He watched them hit the dirt in front of his helmet and become wet spots. A few droplets landed on his face and trickled down the side of his cheek.

Hollis stretched out his right hand, which had tightened from the bitter cold. The joints ached as he opened and closed his hand. He patted the damp ground for his cell phone. It was there a minute ago.

This wasn't how he was supposed to die.

Did it really matter though? Either he would die here or in six months. The look on his doctor's face had said it all before she even had a chance to give him the best-case scenario. "There have been many successful medical advances," she'd stated at one point. But then, as if to keep him realistic about the prognosis, she almost immediately followed that up with the standard, "There are no guarantees with treatment."

By the time she wanted to discuss treatment options, he'd already come to terms with his fate. He'd thanked her and explained that it wasn't worth it to him to spend his last few months invested in a slim chance when he could be out—his eyes teared up with the irony of the thought now—*enjoying the smell of wet dirt*.

Ever since that diagnosis, his focus had been on Serafina. He needed to find answers for her, and that's not something he could do while puking into a toilet.

From the very beginning, when she started at Planet Janet as a cocktail waitress, he knew he wanted better for her. How he ended up taking on that fatherly role, he wasn't quite sure. It just kind of gradually happened. His first impression of her hadn't been that of a daughter at all though.

He could still remember it so vividly. It had started off like any other visit to the club. The lunch crowd had just left and there would be a few hours of stragglers before business picked up again. During that lull, the dancers would typically congregate at his booth for appetizers and drinks, occasionally making their rounds for dances. He preferred company over dances, so the cost of providing such amenities had been a small price to pay.

On that particular day, he had been sitting at his normal booth with the typical drop-ins. As usual, Paige had been waiting for her exclusive regular, Tony, who was there practically every day. Likewise, Kristin and Breanna had also been waiting for their regulars, while complaining about the twins, Hailey and Harley. Ariel had been waiting to be called onstage for her set. Chanel had just come over to sit down and needed to pull the table out to move it away from the booth. But as she did that, her wine spilled. Hollis had offered to order her another one. That's when Serafina had appeared.

Serafina looked like a Brazilian model straight out of a Victoria's Secret catalog. In all his life, he'd seen only a handful of women so beautiful that time seemed to stand still when he looked at them. Serafina ranked at the top of them all.

As he got to know Serafina, he realized there was so much more to her. She was classy. And witty. She had a good head on her shoulders and a lot of potential. For whatever reason, though, she worked as a cocktail waitress, and she didn't belong there. That's why he offered her a job in the first place. He needed an assistant, and she needed to be elevated from the life she was living.

What he hadn't known at the time was that Serafina had already elevated herself from a rough childhood. She'd been a foster child since age four and had grown up in Detroit. He didn't know a lot of details, but what he did know provided enough glimpses to spark interest.

Maybe that's why he'd started this investigation in the first place. Sure, he was curious. And yes, he wanted to make sense of it all. But none of that changed the fact that he wanted to help her. He loved her.

He acknowledged what he'd just said in his mind.

He mouthed the words, "I love her."

He hadn't allowed himself to love anyone for years, and then came Serafina. He'd always expected to die alone, after pushing everyone he'd ever loved away. Now he had someone to love, and he was still going to die alone. This was how it was going to end.

Hollis stared as far out as he could. His vision strained, failing to see anything clearly, so he focused on the rain that pelted him. It was as if he were being whipped for his sins. Or was God washing his sins away for him? Maybe that was why the rain was pelting him so hard—the sins weren't washing away so easily.

• • •

The rain eased up, becoming steady and rhythmic. Frankie Hollis stood a few feet right of Sammy, with Daddy all the way left of them. The three of them were suited up, each holding a white rose. The reverend was speaking about the life of Genevieve Hollis, wife of Samuel Hollis Sr. and mother of two, Samuel Jr., age ten, and Frank, age five.

Sammy reached down for Frankie's left hand. Frankie switched his white rose to his right hand and took Sammy's hand in his.

The reverend stopped speaking and motioned for Daddy to come forward. Sammy and Frankie stayed behind, allowing Daddy to say his piece. Daddy walked up to the black casket and stood there quietly with his back to them. He spoke a long time to Momma, and then gave in to crying.

Church women stood behind Sammy and Frankie talking to one another. "Vivi's sure gon' be missed," one of them proclaimed.

Sammy led Frankie to Daddy. As they approached the casket, though, Frankie let go of Sammy's hand and stood back as Sammy continued on.

"Frankie." Sammy motioned Frankie to the casket, but Frankie remained where he stood, as if frozen.

Daddy put his arm around Sammy's shoulder. Sammy said some words to Momma and then started to cry. Daddy looked back at Frankie standing there alone, and then beckoned to him.

Frankie crept up to where they were standing. He stared a long time at his mother's face. The person in the casket didn't look like his mother.

The makeup hid her freckles, making her face look unnaturally tan. Blue eyeshadow coated her eyelids. The lipstick was a coral pink shade she'd never worn before. Frankie just stared, a part of him hoping it wasn't his mother after all. A big mistake someone had made. But deep down he knew the truth. It was a truth he wanted to deny. Yet, he couldn't.

Daddy and Sammy headed back while Frankie lingered there.

Frankie knew he should be saying something to Momma, but all he could do was stare.

Little Stevie Lawson came over and stood next to him. Their mothers had always been close, so they'd been best friends since birth.

"It's okay, Frankie." Stevie put his hand on Frankie's shoulder and tried to guide him away.

Frankie resisted, freeing his shoulder from Stevie's nudging hand.

Stevie understood and let him be.

Was this really his mother? He needed to be sure.

• • •

Hollis shivered as the rain came down faster. He tried to curl up for warmth, but he felt something poking at his side when he did. With little energy left, he reached under his side and pulled out his missing phone where it had somehow become lodged.

He was going fast, becoming too weak to even hold his phone. Any minute, calling someone would be impossible.

Hollis held the phone less than a foot from his face and tried to make out the numbers. Without his readers, he struggled to see the numbers. After identifying what he believed to be the number 9, he extended the phone out an arm's length and tried to select it.

His fine motor skills were going now, and he couldn't seem to get his finger on the number just right. He squinted and kept trying to adjust the distance of the phone from his face.

Hollis's arm fell to the ground, still holding the phone in his hand the best he could. His hand slowly released its grip on the phone.

It was no use. He was going to die before any ambulance came.

How would Serafina react to him dying there? He didn't want her to be upset over him dying like that. Whatever this unnamed bond was between them, he knew she'd be devastated to learn how he died.

He cared about her very deeply. He hoped she knew that. But then, how could she really know? He'd never told her. He never said that she was important to him.

Maybe she could tell by the way they bantered. She was always joking about how he put the "age" in "agency." And she'd mock him for his Boomer ways as she flaunted her technological savviness.

Hollis remembered how she used Siri on her own phone. She would just hold down the home button and give a command to Siri.

A sense of urgency rushed through him. He could call for an ambulance, but by the time they found him there, it would be too late.

It wasn't too late, though, to tell Serafina all that he felt.

He held down the home button on his phone and forced out the words, "Call Serafina."

The phone on the other end started to ring.

Hollis needed to let Serafina know so many things. He needed to tell her that she was the best daughter a father could ever want, that he was so grateful to her for all the times she'd been there for him. He needed to tell her that he was very proud of her for finishing all her courses, that he was so very sorry that he wouldn't be able to attend her graduation coming up. He needed her to know that he was going to die anyway, that he was diagnosed with cancer and had made peace with it all. He needed to explain why he withheld it all from her, that he didn't want to burden her with it during her finals.

"Hi, you've reached Serafina Gray. Sorry I can't come to the phone right now . . ."

His hand weakened and he dropped the phone. It landed to the side of him, somewhere in the dirt.

· · ·

Frankie poured lemonade into a glass and carried it outside to Daddy, who was tending to the crops. Daddy took the glass, drank every last bit, and handed it back to Frankie.

"Do you like it, Daddy?"

"Sure do, Buckaroo." Daddy tousled Frankie's sun-matted hair, and then crouched down to Frankie's level and grabbed at some dirt with his left hand. "You see this, son?"

"Yes, sir."

"Do you know what this is?"

"Dirt, sir?"

"Not just dirt, son. This is land."

Frankie stared at the land in Daddy's palm.

"This is the land your Papaw bought many years ago."

Daddy took Frankie's hand in his and poured the contents into it.

"When I'm gone from this world, son, you and your brother will have it to pass on."

Frankie looked down at the "land" he held in his own palm. He only saw dirt.

· · ·

The phone! Hollis focused every bit of remaining strength into his right hand. Having a sense of where the phone fumbled, he frantically grabbed at the dirt until he found it.

Time was running out. He needed to leave his message now or she would never know that she mattered to him. That he wished her a wonderful life. That he hoped she would get everything in this world that her heart desired.

As if fighting against a magnetic pull, he gave all he had left to bring the phone to his ear. The message had already beeped, and if he wanted to say anything, he had to be brief and he had to say it now.

"I love you."

Blood had pooled into his lungs, and he was gasping for air. He knew that his time had run out.

Beep. "If you are satisfied with your message, please . . ."

Hollis's arm gave way. It fell to the ground with a thump, causing his hand to release the phone from his tender grip.

• • •

"Daddy!" Frankie yelled, struggling to steady the fishing pole.

"Sammy, get the bucket," Daddy said in his usual calm voice.

"Daddy?" Frankie looked at his father and then back at the fishing pole.

"You got it, son. Reel'er in nice and easy."

Frankie slowly reeled in the thrashing fish.

"Keep on, son. Almost there." Daddy motioned for Sammy to hand him the net.

Daddy put the net underneath the fish just as Frankie pulled the fish out of the river. Together, they lowered the fish into the bucket.

"Look at the size of that one!" Sammy said, handing Daddy the net.

"Looks like you caught yourself a blue catfish." Daddy patted Frankie on the back.

Just as Daddy removed the hook, the fish thrashed, causing the bucket to wobble.

Frankie reached out to try to stabilize the bucket, but it wobbled more. Then it tipped over, dumping out the fish and splashing water into the hull of the boat.

Daddy quickly picked up the bucket, and then scooped river water back into it from the outside of the boat.

The fish frantically flopped and gasped. Its eyes stared out at Frankie as if begging him for mercy, pleading to be thrown back into the river. Frankie stared back.

Daddy held out the bucket for Frankie.

Frankie knew what needed to be done. He needed to reach down and pick up the fish.

"Come on, Frankie. Don't be scared. Jus' pick'm up," Daddy said, inching the bucket closer to Frankie.

Frankie wasn't scared to pick up the fish. He just wasn't sure if he wanted to put the fish back in the bucket.

The fish continued to gasp, but its flopping had just about stopped.

Frankie crouched down to the fish's level and with both hands, gently picked up the fish and stood.

Daddy held the bucket out for Frankie.

Frankie looked at the river water splashing up against the exterior of the boat's hull. He looked at the fish. He looked at the river water again.

It would be just as easy to throw the fish back into the river, he thought.

He stood a moment more, contemplating that thought, and then put the fish back in the bucket.

Chapter 2

Four hours earlier

Serafina had just spent the whole afternoon—and evening—trying to get whatever video footage she could for one of the agency's clients. She'd never stayed on an assignment this long, and she was restless.

Her idea of a fun Friday night was not this. It did not entail sitting in the agency's old Explorer outside a Quiznos in Canton. Although, what else would she be doing? Again, not this.

Serafina had a considerably small circle of friends, and none of them were the Friday night hangout type. Maybe some of that was done intentionally on her part, distancing herself from people, like Hollis often claimed. Although, he should talk! He had even fewer people in his life than she did.

And as if her job description included being his grown child, Hollis would pester her regularly about getting out more so she could meet a nice guy and settle down. She wasn't really sure if she ever wanted to settle down. The whole family concept had always been what separated her from others. She wasn't sure if she knew how to be like everyone else. Hell, she wasn't even sure she wanted to. Sometimes being normal seemed lame.

Hollis just seemed to have Levi and Datson, which included Levi's family too, she supposed—but who would want to go have a family Thanksgiving gathering with Suong?

That woman, Levi's wife, was scary, with her soulless demeanor, devoid of any emotion.

Serafina hadn't met their grown kids, Brian and Michael, but maybe that was a blessing if they were anything like their mother.

Serafina liked Levi, although he made her nervous too. Maybe because he looked so damn much like Morgan Freeman that when he spoke to her, it was like having a conversation with God.

She used to have an app on her phone that would show who a person's celebrity lookalike was, based on a photo. She had tried it out by uploading a JPG she had of Hollis, and it turned out he looked like Tommy Lee Jones, but much older than when he did in *Men in Black*.

He hadn't been amused when she said he might be related to Tommy Lee Jones somehow, both being from Texas and all. Sometimes she was able to make him laugh, but Texas seemed to be an off-limits topic.

Anyway, if she thought about it, this circle of friends could also be referred to as a circle of family.

That thought resonated with her. Were they friends or family? The lines were blurred in that regard. Maybe they were both. They were fami-riends. Friend-amily. She mumbled the Pillow Pets song lyrics to herself, as she thought of more ways to blend the two words. She hadn't seen that commercial in a while. Did they still make Pillow Pets?

She was starting to feel agitated. The urge to end the assignment and leave was becoming stronger. But did she have enough to write up a report and satisfy the client? That was the question.

She didn't want to leave prematurely and have anyone upset with her. The dude had been in there for hooooouuuurrrrrrs though. And unless he slipped out the back door or something, it was probably safe to assume that he was inside working, just like the HR manager of their client had suspected. Damn, should she stay, or should she go?

The Clash song "Should I Stay or Should I Go" entered her mind, and she sang a few of the lyrics.

Hollis would have the answer on when she should leave. She picked up her phone and was ready to place the call but realized she only had Hollis's old cell phone number.

"Now, what is your new number?" she asked aloud, stretching out the words as she said them.

She thought about it for a second and then remembered she'd written it down on a sticky note at work. Only problem, she hadn't actually saved it under his contact information yet.

She thought about it some more, still holding her cell phone. Hollis might have set up the agency's landline to forward calls to the new number like he did with his last number. Worth a shot.

As the agency's landline rang, she wondered what the longest time was that he'd ever stayed on a job assignment.

And why did he need to get a new cell phone number anyway? Did he not know that you can keep your old cell phone number when you get a new phone? Or was he trying to avoid talking to someone? That's probably what it was, she laughed. Hollis did *not* like to talk. He was the best listener in the world, but not a talker.

Knowing how Hollis was so technologically inept, he probably didn't know he could block people's numbers. She shook her head and gave up on trying to guess why he changed his number. She chalked it up as one more thing to wonder about Hollis, the mystery that he was.

The voicemail for the agency picked up. She wasn't sure what to say, or if she should even leave a message since he wasn't physically at the agency and probably wouldn't be for the rest of the night. But maybe he would check the voicemail? She quickly decided to leave a message asking him to call her back.

Serafina still wasn't sure if she should end the assignment. She continued to look out the windshield toward the Quiznos entrance. It was increasingly difficult to see through the windshield, which had gradually become foggy. She rolled the driver's side window down slightly.

The brisk air funneled in, and she was starting to feel chilled. Hollis never wanted to have the heat on. He thought idling the engine would attract attention. The whole point is to be inconspicuous, he'd say.

If Hollis had been there, he'd lecture her about dressing appropriately for the job. But Hollis wasn't there, now, was he? Defiantly, she decided that if she wasn't going to leave the job assignment just yet, then she would at least blast some heat on her feet.

Whether from curiosity or boredom, she decided to have another look at this Raj fellow, the employee the agency wanted surveilled.

She picked up her phone and opened the email attachment the client had sent over. Then she zoomed in on Raj's picture to get a close-up view. He looked like a normal, husky set, Indian guy.

Raj had been scheduled to work the 3:00 p.m. to 11:30 p.m. shift that day. When he called the attendance hotline to report his absence, the company's HR manager had immediately notified Serafina. That's when she'd put a tail on him and ended up at that Quiznos.

The notes Serafina had written down earlier that day didn't reveal a ton of information. Just that Raj had a tendency to use his FMLA leave on Fridays. Apparently, that's what initially drew suspicion. But then they heard rumors that he was working the same shifts at his relative's Quiznos in Canton. There were no real specifics beyond that.

She had taken some camera shots of Raj going into the Quiznos earlier, but that didn't really prove anything nefarious. He was dressed in street clothes. For all anyone knew, he was just going in for a bite to eat.

Hours later, though, he was still in there, and she was still sitting in the agency's vehicle, watching people going in and out of Quiznos.

Years ago, when Hollis had first asked her to quit her waitressing job and come work for him, she thought the whole investigation job was something else. Maybe asking people questions, like where they were on some specific day between such and such times. Like one of those private eye shows her foster mother Wanda always used to watch—*Matlock* or *Columbo*.

Or that she'd be infiltrating a company's workforce like a spy or a mole, getting intel on drug smuggling or something just as dangerous. She would use her seductive looks to manipulate men, like a female James Bond. Something about that just sounded so exciting. She wouldn't sleep with any of them though. Unless they looked like some sexy celebrity. She could make some exceptions.

Hollis had made sure to set her straight on the expectations of being his assistant. While any of those scenarios were entirely possible, his bread and butter were companies investigating workers' comp claims and FMLA abuse. Folks who falsely stated they had physical restrictions at work but would be moving heavy furniture into their house on the weekend. Folks who would use their FMLA leave for a condition like migraines or vertigo, but then they'd be at Cedar Point for a day of riding roller coasters. Those types of investigations. The sitting and waiting and watching kind. She'd had no idea how boring it would actually be.

Serafina had been apprehensive about Hollis's job offer at first. She didn't know him well enough back then to completely trust his intentions. Ultimately, the promise of a steady paycheck convinced her to take a chance. Now she trusted him wholeheartedly, but even still, it never really made sense why he chose her to be his assistant. Why her? He could have chosen anyone.

She had once asked Hollis about the reason he wanted her to come work for him, but his response didn't really answer her question. He had said something about how he couldn't be in two places at once with some of these job assignments.

When she'd pressed for more explanation, he'd said that this wasn't a "9 to 5" job, and he didn't get to dictate when the job assignments started or ended. Sometimes there was little notice on when things would go down. If he had any kind of conflict with taking the job, he risked the company using a different agency. Once that happened, he'd risk losing more than just that particular job assignment; he'd risk losing the client altogether. Especially if he made a habit of being unreliable. He couldn't afford to lose his client base.

So, she knew why Hollis needed an assistant. As for why he had asked her, specifically? Probably no reason except that she had been available.

Serafina's legs were begging to be stretched out. She straightened them out the best she could, and when that didn't seem to help, she began bobbing her torso, as if keeping rhythm to some imaginary music. She picked up her phone to check for any missed messages. None.

Why hadn't Randy texted her yet? She wouldn't have thought him capable of going a day without texting her.

In many ways, they were more like best friends than foster siblings. He was always the one to contact her first, though, usually with some nonsensical observation he'd made, and he'd enlighten her with just how wrong in the world it was. He thrived on passing along the latest gossip he'd read. Like what so-and-so celebrity was doing now. Honestly, she couldn't understand how Nick managed to live under the same roof as them.

Nick was so calm and patient. Very much not the description of Randy. They say opposites attract, and that was one perfect example.

Should she worry? Nick would have told her if something happened to Randy, like if he was in the hospital. She didn't make a habit of reaching directly out to Nick, but she knew he cared about her because Randy cared about her. He was loyal like that.

Randy was all that and a bag of chips when it came to personality. He had his ups and downs, for sure. Sometimes his moods were roads she wished she traveled less.

She couldn't put her finger on it, but Randy seemed moodier than normal.

She'd been waiting for the right time to tell him about their foster brother DeMarcus. That she'd done a search on his whereabouts and was close to locating him after all these years. She hadn't told anyone yet. Not even Wanda. The excitement was getting harder to contain.

So many feelings flooded her. Mixed feelings. Mostly based on memories. Although, how much of what she thought were memories actually were memories? Were they just her mind piecing together disjointed remnants of confusing encounters? How much of it could she trust to be accurate and true? Maybe the feelings she'd had at that time? The feelings of a four-year-old girl whose life had just changed in an instant.

Strangers, all of them. That's what she recalled—being introduced to people she didn't know. But she had felt safe. She knew that to be true. That day when the social worker had taken her to live with Wanda Price, there had been an ambiance of comfort. Of stability. Of home.

· · ·

The social worker parked between two other cars, on the right side of a one-way residential street. Looking out of the window from her booster seat in the back, Serafina saw a giant maple tree outside her door. It took up the whole space between the sidewalk and the curb, its roots pushing up the concrete slabs in front of a light-yellow house. She waited to be helped out of her seat by the social worker, a roly-poly, middle-aged, white woman with short, wavy brown hair cut like a mushroom on her head.

Serafina held onto the social worker's soft hand, and they walked up to the light-yellow house. As they ascended the wooden stairs leading to the front door, Serafina grabbed hold of the decorative iron handrail for support. It rocked back and forth with unsteadiness, squeaking as she pulled herself up onto each individual step. First her right foot, and then her left foot. Each thud echoing beneath her feet.

Three boys watched from the top of the porch. Serafina hadn't noticed them until she approached the top step. They couldn't have been but a few years older than Serafina.

One of the boys—a white boy—was sitting on a swing on the right side of the porch by himself, brushing a Barbie doll's hair. He watched blankly, no reaction.

The other two boys were African American, and they were on the left side of the porch, playing with a collection of Matchbox cars. They looked like they could be brothers, one being older, like in the second grade. The older one smiled brightly and came right over to say hi.

An African American woman came to the screen door and opened it. She wore yellow latex gloves, the kind Serafina's mother wore when handwashing dishes. Serafina thought about how she'd wear gloves like that when she grew up.

"You must be Serafina." The woman leaned downward and smiled gently at Serafina.

When Serafina smiled back, the woman refocused her attention on the social worker.

"I'm Wanda. Come on in. I was just trying to get some cleaning in before you came."

She removed the gloves as she held the screen door open with her back.

As Serafina and the social worker stepped into the living room, the woman, Wanda, abruptly stopped them. "If you don't mind, hold on a second."

Serafina and the social worker stood at the front window of the living room and awaited instructions. Serafina looked around.

The room was bright from the sun that shone through all the double-hung windows on the right. The furniture wasn't old, but it wasn't new either. Just a few couches. Several coffee tables with some lamps. A television in the corner, turned off. No knickknacks. No toys. No clutter.

"You boys getting hungry yet? Want me to make you up some peanut butter jelly sandwiches?" Wanda looked at the African American boys.

"No thanks, Grandma," the older African American boy politely responded to Wanda.

"Such nice manners," the social worker said, taking a moment to apply some Chapstick on her lips.

Wanda smiled proudly.

The younger African American boy jumped up and announced, "I want mac and cheese!"

Wanda firmly said, "I'm not making mac and cheese right now, DeShawn. Would you like a peanut butter jelly sandwich?"

DeShawn smashed two cars together, ignoring her question.

Wanda didn't give in to DeShawn. She turned to the white boy on the porch swing. "Randy? You want one?"

Randy turned his head in Wanda's direction but avoided eye contact with all of them. "No, thank you, Mrs. Price."

"Ms. Price, dear. Not Mrs. We say Mrs. when the woman is married."

Randy just nodded, still not looking her directly in the eyes.

"It's okay, dear. I don't mind making you a sandwich if you're hungry. Are you hungry?"

Randy nodded but didn't say yes.

"Is that a 'yes'?"

Randy sat silently, and then whispered a quiet, "Yes."

Serafina was confused why Randy said, "No, thank you," when he was hungry. She was confused about the woman saying her name was Wanda, yet the African American boys called her "Grandma," and the white boy called her "Ms. Price." Or rather, he called her "Mrs. Price."

That was confusing too.

Serafina wanted to call the woman Wanda. To her, it sounded like the name of a mermaid. A mermaid princess. She closed her eyes and listened to her mind saying the name. *Wanda.*

Wanda led Serafina and the social worker through the long living room toward the back of the house.

"Sorry about the mess," Wanda said modestly.

Serafina looked around to find the mess, but she couldn't locate it.

The living room had a hallway opening to the left. Serafina tried to look down the hallway as they walked past it. She hoped she would be able to get a glimpse inside a bedroom or a bathroom, but the social worker unknowingly hindered her view with each step.

They entered the large kitchen through a doorway at the back of the house.

"Have a seat. Make yourself comfortable." Wanda motioned to the kitchen table.

Serafina sat in the chair nearest the living room, hoping the boys would come inside and play with her. The social worker sat in a chair near the back door.

Wanda stood at the kitchen table. "Can I offer you anything to drink? Coffee? Water? Juice? Milk?"

Serafina looked at Wanda's smile, her teeth perfect and white. Her eyes were bright, as if smiling also. Her skin looked flawless, yet natural. Maybe this woman actually was a mermaid princess. But older. Like the mother of one, not the younger daughter one.

Maybe she, Serafina, could be the daughter mermaid princess, she thought. Looking at her legs and feet, she imagined them the shape of a mermaid's bottom half.

"Nothing for me. Thank you. I just had some water in the car on the way over." The social worker then looked at Serafina. "Milk okay?"

Serafina gave a wide smile and nodded happily at her.

Unlike Wanda, the social worker was not a princess in any way—for many reasons. The one that stuck out the most for Serafina was that no princess she knew of wore glasses, and this lady wore big, round glasses that made her look like an owl. Like a human owl.

Serafina imagined a reality where the social worker was actually an owl that some witch had turned into a human. Even though she was an owl lady now, deep down, she was still an owl. And Serafina had special powers to recognize those owl-like attributes. Mermaid princess powers.

Serafina thought of how the magic spell might be lifted. A true love's kiss? No, she was an owl lady, not a princess.

Then, Serafina figured it out. Maybe finding homes for children weakens the spell's power. Placing Serafina in Wanda's care would turn her back into an owl. Did the social worker know that would happen, or would it be a surprise to everyone in the room when it did?

Part of Serafina expected the social worker to turn back into an owl any minute. Wanda would then release her through the window at the kitchen table, and they'd watch her fly away.

Wanda placed a short, plastic cup of milk in front of Serafina, and then went back to the counter where she'd taken out peanut butter, jelly, and white bread to make sandwiches.

"So, those are your grandchildren?"

"Yes, the younger one is DeShawn; the older one is DeMarcus."

"And they live here with you?"

"Yes, I have temporary custody while my daughter, their mother, is in rehab."

It looked like Wanda was holding back emotion as she stopped short of saying anything else about her daughter.

Wanda placed the first sandwich she'd made in front of Serafina, not asking her whether she was hungry.

"And the boy . . . Randy was his name?"

"Yes, Randy came to me a few months ago. He's probably going to be here for a while. His mother and her boyfriend . . ." Realizing she had the audience of a four-year old, she said, "He suffered a lot of trauma."

The social worker seemed to understand and just shook her head in disbelief.

"Oh!" Wanda blurted out, rushing to the kitchen table. "She's not allergic to peanut butter, is she?"

The social worker grimaced as she realized Serafina was already eating the sandwich. "I don't believe so. I guess we'll see."

"I'm so sorry. I should have asked."

"It's okay. I didn't think about it either."

They both stared at Serafina as she overstuffed her mouth with another bite from the sandwich. They sat waiting, occasionally breathing in and exhaling deeply. When Serafina appeared to be unaffected, they continued their conversation.

"I want to thank you again for your willingness to take on another. Four little ones can be a handful."

"I handle way more than that on any given day."

"Oh?"

"I'm a teacher here in Detroit."

"What do you teach?"

"English and Language Arts. Middle School."

"Okay, so then you should be fine."

Wanda gestured with her head as she looked at Serafina. "I was told she was living in Mexicantown?"

"That's right."

"I don't speak any Spanish. That would be my only concern."

"I'm not sure she'd understand you if you did speak Spanish to her. We thought we'd need a translator, so we got one just in case. She didn't seem to understand a word spoken to her."

"But she does speak?"

The social worker chuckled. "Yes. She's slow to warm, but once she feels comfortable around you, she is very talkative. Trust me on that."

"What does she say?"

The social worker looked at Serafina as she answered Wanda. "Just lets you know when she wants something. Like milk. She loves milk, as you can tell."

Wanda and the social worker laughed as they looked at Serafina holding the plastic cup with both hands. The milk was flowing faster than she was drinking, and it was giving her a milk mustache.

The social worker paused and then added, "Mostly though, she asks for her mother and father."

"So, she doesn't know then?"

"She knows, but she doesn't quite understand."

"Oh." Wanda stood in place with a sandwich on a plate, about to head into the living room.

"We're hoping it won't take long for us to locate some relatives. Maybe an aunt or uncle somewhere."

Wanda accepted this information as if it meant something more to her. "I'll be right back."

"No problem. I've got this pretty girl here to keep me company." The social worker smiled at Serafina.

Serafina had eaten most of her sandwich; only a few bites remained on her plate. She finished off her milk, fully aware that the social worker's eyes were fixated on her. Studying her.

Wanda returned without the plate. "Looks like the other two are hungry now," she said, and then headed over to the peanut butter, jelly, and white bread still on the counter.

The social worker hesitated to speak, but then continued, "The boy,

Randy? He called you Ms. Price. Is that what Serafina should call you?"

Wanda stopped and turned toward them sitting at the kitchen table, no longer spreading peanut butter on the slices of bread she had out for DeShawn and DeMarcus's sandwiches. She looked embarrassed.

"Oh. No. I guess I've been teaching students so long that it's just a habit to refer to myself formally like that. They're welcome to call me Wanda too. Or Mom, even. You know, it's really about whatever makes them feel comfortable." Then, she smiled warmly at Serafina.

• • •

Serafina imagined Randy and Nick sitting on the living room couch back at the house in Ferndale. While Nick might be asleep at this hour—he was an early riser—she knew Randy would be up.

On the weekends, especially, Randy had a tendency to get caught up on a Netflix series and then binge-watch it until all hours of the night. There had been many times she'd gone into the kitchen for something to drink and been surprised that he was still awake in the living room, having almost completed a whole season in one night.

There was a point where Randy had started making a habit of falling asleep on the couch too, but then Nick made an issue about it. She'd heard them argue behind closed doors one time when she was in the hallway headed to the restroom. Randy didn't fall asleep on the couch anymore after that.

She decided to text Randy.

7:22 p.m.

Serafina: *Hey, what are you and Nick up to tonight?*

As she sent the message, she wondered how lame she sounded, sending a question like that. Randy responded quicker than she had expected.

7:23 p.m.

Randy Staszak: *Nothing. Just relaxing.*

Serafina wondered if that was code for "Leave me alone." But then he continued.

Randy Staszak: *What are you up to?*

Serafina: *Been on a job all day. So boring.*

Randy Staszak: *This late?*

Serafina: *Yeah. Sucks.*

Randy Staszak: *Where's Hollis?*

Serafina: *Had another job to do so he asked me to cover this one.*

Neither texted for a moment. Serafina wanted to tell Randy about DeMarcus, but she wasn't really sure how he would react. He was all over the place sometimes when it came to emotions. Especially when it involved Wanda.

There was no way of ever knowing what to expect. She'd have to just throw it out there. Just let the coin land and prepare herself for both sides of that toss.

7:24 p.m.

Serafina: *I did a search the other day, and I am so close to finding DeMarcus. Kind of exciting, huh?*

She waited for Randy to respond, but nothing.

7:25 p.m.

Serafina: *I thought you'd be happy to hear that.*

Still nothing from Randy.

She started to text more, but then she could see text bubbles on Randy's end, an indication that he was texting something. She waited and waited. The text bubbles stopped at one point, but then they started up again.

What the heck was he writing that was taking so long?

She was beyond antsy now. She was tired of waiting for Raj. Tired of waiting for Randy. Tired, period. Her stomach was hurting from hunger. And she needed to use the restroom something fierce.

Randy's text came through.

7:26 p.m.

Randy Staszak: *Why would I be happy to hear that? Did you forget about last time he came around? I'm sure Mom hasn't forgotten. I don't know what to tell you except you just opened Pandora's box. I hope you know what you're doing. Good luck with that. Just please don't get me or Mom involved in this. We didn't ask for our lives to be upended again.*

Serafina didn't know how to process Randy's response. She hadn't planned for this sort of antipathy from him. What she had been expecting was closer to maybe . . . ambivalence? Recognize the good with the bad?

She wasn't asking him to forget the past, but if he was going to hold onto the past—to hold a grudge or whatever—then he needed to remember the whole past. Not just the parts convenient to remember.

Part of her wondered if Randy's disdain for DeMarcus went deeper than that. Like a rivalry for Wanda's love, as if she only had so much to give, and that DeMarcus coming back into the picture would somehow take this limited supply from him that he felt entitled to.

He was being possessive. That's what this was really about. It was all a guise, this display of overprotectiveness for Wanda.

This elephant in the room that she'd been tolerating for years was becoming harder to ignore. He couldn't be more blatant about his close relationship with Wanda, rubbing it in that his mother-child bond was stronger than Serafina's. Just being around their love fest annoyed her.

Mom this, Mom that—gimme a break! Cut the apron strings already!

Serafina held her cell phone, attempting to text back. She made several attempts and then angrily flung the phone onto the passenger side seat. It slid and landed somewhere between the passenger seat and the door. She hadn't meant for the phone to end up on the floor, but she was too upset to retrieve it at the moment.

That's it, Serafina thought. She was going to go inside, if for nothing else to at least use the restroom.

She clipped on two camera pins, one to the lapel of her jacket and another on her purse strap. They weren't the best on the market in terms of spy gear, but they were what she could find online with the limited budget Hollis had given her to spend.

As soon as Serafina entered Quiznos, she made a beeline for the restroom in the back. She took a quick glance at the person working behind the food counter, and lo and behold, her guy was serving up food.

Before leaving the restroom, Serafina turned the camera pins back on and readjusted them to make sure she could get footage from several angles just in case one didn't capture him as well as the other.

She got in line and faced the cameras in the direction she knew would get the best view of Raj.

He looked like a nice guy, like someone she'd want as her neighbor to say good morning to as he watered his lawn and she got into her car to go to work. That was the part that made her feel bad about her job.

"Welcome to Quiznos. Would you like this for here or to go?"

Serafina considered her options. On one hand, she hated eating alone in public. For whatever reason, it just made her more self-conscious. On the other hand, it would be her opportunity to ensure extra video footage, give her more to report on maybe.

But it was kind of chilly in there, and she really disliked eating in cold restaurants. It was a huge reason she avoided restaurants altogether in the summer. They always blasted the air conditioning to an uncomfortable setting. But then again, it would be easier to eat what she'd ordered at a table and not in the driver's seat of a dark vehicle.

"Here's fine."

Raj grabbed a tray and set it in front of himself, preparing to take her order. "What would you like?" Raj asked.

"Um," Serafina responded. She hadn't really thought about what to order. She had been too focused on getting the video footage.

"One of those." She pointed to the picture of something that had guacamole in it. She loved guacamole to no end. Not just because of the taste but also because it was probably the one thing—albeit non-Hispanic—that made her feel a connection to her Hispanic roots.

At the register, she made use of her proximity to Raj. To get good angles on her camera pins, she moved around, pretending to fumble in her purse for a credit card.

"I'm sorry. I had it just a second ago."

"No worries. Take your time," Raj said.

When she was sure she'd sealed the deal for the job assignment, she miraculously discovered the credit card. "Oh, there it is."

As Serafina ate her meal, she captured each transaction Raj had with the several customers who came in after her. She was just going through the motions though. Her mind had gone on autopilot, and she was no longer focused on the job assignment.

Randy's last text had struck a nerve with her. She was trying to move past it, but it wasn't easy. It was right there at the forefront of her thoughts, right next to breathing.

Did Randy have a valid point about the whole Pandora's box comment? Did she know what she was doing by seeking out DeMarcus? Not that she was any expert on family rules and codes of conduct, but shouldn't they extend an olive branch instead of holding decade-long grievances?

DeMarcus was family. Period.

It wasn't like he'd killed anyone or committed some horrific crime. Addiction is a disease, a sickness. What he stole could be replaced. Shouldn't they at least try to seek treatment for him? With what DeMarcus went through, what he endured, of course he'd be changed after that. How could family not understand that? They all knew what happened when DeMarcus and DeShawn went back to live with their mother. Why DeMarcus had burn scars on his face and why DeShawn was dead.

She still saw DeMarcus as that sweet boy on the porch. At his core, he was a good person. She just knew it.

When Serafina first thought about doing a search on him, she'd assumed Wanda would be supportive of the idea, especially since—aside from cousins far removed—DeMarcus was the only blood relative for Wanda. He was it. She would want this.

Now she wasn't so sure anymore.

She so badly wanted to respond to Randy's text, but she knew it was better if she didn't. Their relationship was a dance, and she knew the steps. Tomorrow would be another day. Tomorrow he would be normal Randy, going on about the latest celebrity gossip.

The second she was done eating, she headed home, exhausted.

Chapter 3

Serafina woke to the smell of coffee brewing outside her bedroom door and couldn't ignore it any longer.

As she opened her door, Randy could be heard complaining. "Is the coffee done yet? My God, it's taking forever."

Randy and Nick were in the kitchen doing Randy and Nick things. Nothing ever changed with those two.

"Mailman just came," Nick said, looking out the kitchen window as he rinsed egg off a whisk in the kitchen sink.

"I'll get it in a sec." Randy sat at the kitchen table cutting coupons and organizing them into piles.

As far back as Serafina could remember, this was part of Randy's weekend routine. It dated all the way back to their childhood, when he'd help Wanda cut and sort coupons at the kitchen table. Saturday morning cartoons would be on, and no amount of coaxing could pull Randy away from their Randy-Wanda weekend activity.

Randy's pure enjoyment in that activity had once convinced Serafina that she was missing out somehow. When she tried to join them, however, she soon realized it wasn't as much fun as Randy made it seem. She couldn't seem to cut as steadily as Randy, and she didn't understand his sorting. Eventually she had lost interest and gone back to watching cartoons.

Whenever Serafina felt a twinge of jealousy about Randy and Wanda's connection, she'd quickly remind herself that sharing coupons and comparing grocery bill savings was a weird activity she wanted no part of.

"I'll get the mail," Serafina said, standing in the doorway of her bedroom. "I need to go out anyway. I left my phone in the Explorer last night."

Serafina grabbed keys out of her jacket, slung over the back of a kitchen chair from the night before.

"Where's your Jeep?" Nick flipped the omelet he was tending to at the stove.

"It's still at the office. I was too tired to get it last night." Serafina started out the back door.

"You know that's not the place to hang jackets," Randy said, peering at the kitchen chair from his peripheral view.

Serafina was used to Randy's tone and constant regulation of her actions. Often an apology was enough to calm the beast.

"Sorry," she said, poking her head through the opening of the doorway. "I'll hang it up when I get back."

Serafina returned shortly thereafter with the mail tucked under her arm, listening to the last bit of a message on her voicemail.

"Yeah, I love you too," she chortled, mocking the caller.

Nick gave her a questioning look, while Randy carried on with his coupons.

"Oh, some drunk whack job left me a message last night, saying 'I love you.' Probably drank himself so silly he didn't know who he was calling."

She slung the mail on the table, the sudden gust causing some of the coupons to scatter.

"Hey!" Randy sneered at Serafina, recategorizing the coupons that had been swept out of place.

Serafina stood still, watching Randy straighten the mail into an orderly pile. "Sorry, I didn't mean for that to happen."

She promptly took her jacket off the chair and hung it up on one of the coat hooks behind her on the wall.

As if Serafina was no longer in the room, Randy scooted his chair out from the kitchen table and went to the cupboard where the coffee supplies were kept.

Yes, coffee.

Serafina placed her phone on the table and went over to where Randy was standing. She took a mug out of the cabinet and waited for Randy to get his coffee poured.

Randy continued to be standoffish, ignoring her presence.

She stood patiently as Randy methodically measured out two precise spoonsful of cream and then two precise spoonsful of sugar.

Although Randy had always been so exacting about order and perfection, this sort of stringent measuring was on another level, almost ritualistic.

Nick and Serafina exchanged wide-eyed looks while continuing to observe Randy, now slowly pouring his coffee.

Serafina maintained her composure all that she could, but she really wanted a cup of coffee, and this was taking way longer than it needed to.

As all her patience was nearly depleted, she neared the coffee maker to make her own coffee, despite Randy still occupying that space.

She poured the usual guesstimate of cream and sugar straight from the containers right into her mug, and then poured the coffee. When she did, it came out too quickly and spilled droplets onto the counter.

"Do you think maybe you could pour your coffee without getting it everywhere?" Randy snapped at her.

He'd admonished Serafina for similar things before, but rarely were his reprimands so aggressive. Even Nick stopped to witness the hostility.

Both Nick and Serafina knew what the other was thinking when they looked at each other. Randy's stress level was exceptionally high.

Randy was fastidious by nature, but when he was excessively stressed, one would swear that he had obsessive-compulsive personality disorder. His need for perfection would come out in full force.

She'd read enough from her psychology courses to realize that it was Randy's coping mechanism for when things felt chaotic. That's why she tried not to react when he got like that.

He was just trying to gain a general sense of control by controlling his surroundings and the people in those surroundings, she reminded herself. It isn't personal.

But what had him that agitated? Was he still upset from last night?

Serafina calmly picked up the dish rag from the sink's divider, wiped up the coffee spots on the counter, and then carefully laid it back on the divider.

"Seriously? You're just going to put it back without rinsing or wringing it out?" Randy asked, getting feistier.

Before Serafina could retrieve the soiled dishrag, Randy grabbed it and rinsed it out himself.

Serafina exchanged looks yet again with Nick, who seemed equally stunned. Her heartbeat started to race, so she took several deep breaths, picked her coffee mug up from the counter, and calmly headed to the table to sit.

When Randy joined her at the table, he proceeded to put the organized coupons away in a coupon organizer, acting as if Serafina wasn't next to him.

Serafina looked at Randy, waiting for him to notice.

"So, what's going on, Randy? Why are you so irritable this morning?" she asked him in the most nonthreatening way possible.

"I'm not irritable. I'm just asking for some consideration. *Others* live here and don't want to clean up messes *others* make."

Scandalized, she scowled. "And who are these *others*? Me?"

Randy didn't respond, just finished putting the last few coupons away.

"Is this some kind of code-talk for the whole DeMarcus thing?"

"No. You do whatever you want with that. You always do anyway." He grabbed the mail he'd neatly piled on the table.

"What's that supposed to mean?" Serafina immediately regretted reacting so quickly and tried to regain her composure. "Randy, where is all this coming from?"

"Where is all *what* coming from?" He closed the coupon organizer and pushed it toward the center of the table.

"This. Obviously, something has you upset." Her self-control was wavering.

Nick flipped an omelet onto a plate and brought it over for Randy. "Did you want me to make one for you too, Serafina?"

"Oh." Serafina was caught off guard. Clearly, he was trying to distract her, to calm the storm that was brewing. "No, thanks, Nick. You know—"

"I know, you don't eat breakfast." He finished her sentence and smiled.

"Thanks though." She smiled back politely, knowing that what he'd done worked. It stopped the momentum of pending doom.

Serafina turned to Randy and was about to get to the bottom of why he was being so harsh, but Nick spoke up first.

"Just figured I'd ask. Let me know if you change your mind." Nick continued with his diversion tactic.

Nick noticed Randy wasn't touching his omelet yet. "You're not eating?"

"I lost my appetite."

Serafina rolled her eyes at his comment. She leaned back farther in her chair, now crossing her arms defensively.

"Do you not want it then?" Nick asked.

"I'll eat it in a minute. Go ahead and make yours."

"You sure? It's gonna get cold."

"It's okay." Randy began sorting out the mail into piles designated as junk or important.

The first letter on top of the pile of mail was addressed to Serafina. Randy slid it over to her, which she promptly ripped open, mangling the envelope as she pulled out the invoice. She gave it a quick glance over, aware of Randy's movements in her peripheral view.

Normally, Randy would judge her with her eyes—so *uncivilized*, he'd be saying with them—but he was doing his best to give her the cold shoulder.

Randy preferred mail to be opened with precision. That's why he always used the vintage letter opener he'd bought at one of the bed-and-breakfast inns he and Nick had stayed at a few years ago.

This silver knife with an ornate handle, in Serafina's opinion, was not worth what he'd paid for it. But it was almost like unwavering religion to him. He was incapable of opening mail any other way.

As if a surgeon, he would stick the sharp-pointed end inside the corner of the envelope and meticulously slide it through the top crease. Then he'd remove its contents like a delicate organ.

One time she'd used his precious letter opener, not to open an envelope but to dig out clumped-up hair from the bathtub drain. He would have lost his mind had he known. She'd forgotten to return it, and when Randy asked her about it, she definitely did not want to admit to using it—for either reason. Her response had been that he was the only one who used that thing, and he probably left it somewhere.

Even then, he wouldn't open the mail without it. He had been like a hound sniffing for a lost person. She had felt so guilty watching him search in desperation that she stuck it under some papers when he wasn't looking.

Serafina was about to continue where she'd left off with their quarreling when Randy held an envelope in awe and exclaimed, "It's here!"

Never in a million years would she think Randy would attempt to open an envelope without his trusted mail scalpel, but he did. He ripped it open. And Nick was also there to bear witness.

Serafina's interest was piqued. She wanted to ask what it was.

Randy just scanned the letter for the information he was looking for. Then he got up in a hurry and waved his arms around as if he couldn't make up his mind what to do next.

"So?" Nick waited.

"Baby!" Randy cried out.

Serafina hadn't seen Randy act like this in years. It was actually kind of disturbing.

And what did he mean by "baby?" He always called the dog "Baby" instead of its actual name, Muffin—the name he fought long and hard over, despite everyone's objections. Did he mean Muffin?

They didn't need another dog in the house. Muffin was quite enough, Serafina thought, as Muffin came around the corner to find out what the commotion was all about.

Muffin, or Mutt-fin as Serafina often called the little dog, was a mixture of a lot of breeds. Some sort of a terrier, maybe?

Serafina thought of the afternoon Randy had brought Muffin home. It had been beyond shocking to see a puppy *that* neglected. So frail and undernourished.

Randy had immediately gone into his typical download mode, explaining how he was at the "Joseph Campau" shelter getting Patches his medication because Mom couldn't get the time off work and it couldn't wait—"God, how old is that cat anyway? I swear he's gonna outlive us all"—and how he offered to do it because Mom's always been there for them, and it was the least that he could do. And how it was really no imposition since Hamtramck's not even twenty minutes away, just a few exits down I-75, and "Boom, you're there." And how he was sitting in the lobby to see the vet when one of the workers came in with this puppy.

The worker said they just got a call that some kids were throwing rocks at a little puppy on the nearby playground—"You know, that one we always pass right around the corner from Mom's house?" And how they really needed to do something better with that space, that it wasn't fit to be called a playground anymore. And how he was just in shock when the worker said they'd be euthanizing the puppy—"Can you believe that they were going to put this sweet baby to sleep? And how everyone in the waiting room was like, "Why? That don't make no sense." And how the worker said they don't have the resources to provide her the care she's gonna need—"But really, she just needs a little extra care and to put on some weight." And how, when he heard that, he just about exploded off his seat and was like, "I'll do it! Let me have her." And how that witch of a lady that works at that front desk in the lobby—"You know, that one with the nasty attitude?"—how she was like, "No, we can't adopt out sickly animals." And how he had to get the vet involved because he wasn't about to let her make that call. And how the vet made an exception to their policy because Mom's been taking Patches there since the beginning of time. "Isn't she so precious? Look at her."

After riding out the Randy waves, three main thoughts had come to mind.

First, it was actually called the Michigan Anti-Cruelty Society. The *street* was Joseph Campau. Why correct him though? Anything she would have said in that moment wouldn't have registered anyway.

Her second thought had been that of relief. *Thanks, Randy, for volunteering to be the martyr on that one!* Visiting that animal shelter as a kid had never been a pleasant experience. She'd always felt claustrophobic, waiting for what seemed like hours in one of those uncomfortable chairs that lined the wood-paneled walls of that dank lobby—and that weird, indescribable smell! It would permeate her nostrils so much that she swore she could still smell it long after she'd gone home and washed off the stank. *Yep, never be jealous of their special bond.*

Her third thought had begun as, Does Nick know? But then she answered her own question: Of course he doesn't know! So then, her thought quickly morphed to: What will Nick say? He definitely wouldn't be as excited as Randy. That was for sure. Although, that was true with a lot of things in their relationship.

It wasn't that Nick didn't like animals. She'd seen him interact with plenty, and he had always seemed so affectionate to them. If she had to peg down a reason for his apathy, or rather reluctance, it would be because he was noncommittal about plans that affected the future. Hell, they were going on nine years together and still weren't married. Granted, they weren't even allowed to marry until five years ago, but still.

Muffin wasn't a puppy anymore. She was now toothless, deaf, partially blind, and severely obese. Her breath stank badly, and for some odd reason, she preferred breathing that foul breath on Serafina's leg. ALL. THE. TIME.

"Baby?" Serafina asked, closely taking in their facial expressions, assigning possible meanings to what she was observing. Somehow, she knew that they weren't talking about Muffin.

Both sat down at that moment and looked at Serafina without speaking. The intensity of their reticence was tormenting her.

She wondered if this was the feeling kids experienced when their parents sat them down for the divorce talk.

They looked at each other, and Nick broke the silence first. "We wanted to wait to tell you until we knew for sure."

Nick briefly looked back at Randy for encouragement, and then took a moment to gather the rest of his words. "Remember awhile back when we said we might one day want to adopt?"

She remembered Randy saying he wanted to adopt. She remembered Nick saying, "One day."

"It's time." He looked at Randy, confirming that his words spoke for them both.

Randy, no longer able to hold back his emotions, put his hands over his eyes and wiped at his tears.

Nick held Randy's hand in his. Randy just nodded.

Serafina's processing capabilities were stalled. A million questions exploded in her mind, but she couldn't grasp any to ask.

Nick's intuition kicked in, and he tried to reassure her. "Serafina, there's no rush."

"Yeah, there's no rush," Randy chimed in. He took a bite of his omelet and looked in the direction of Serafina's bedroom.

Rush? Serafina looked at her bedroom door connected off the kitchen.

The intention was to convert it into a den when she eventually moved out, but there was never any hurry on that happening. Randy only hinted at it on occasion, like when they passed office furniture in OfficeMax or wherever.

"What's on your mind?" Nick asked Serafina on his way to the stove to make his omelet. "Do you have any questions? Any concerns?"

Yes, they were zooming around in her head. Part of her wanted to congratulate them, but she was too hurt to express anything positive.

With his back to Randy and Serafina, Nick said, "We thought about putting an extension on the house, but the cost was just too much. Plus, the layout of the house here on the back end would require some reconfiguration. We just don't have that kind of money. We barely have enough to make the adoption happen."

Serafina thought about where an extension would be put on the house if it wasn't too expensive.

Before taking another bite of his omelet, Randy added, "And we've been here like seven years. It's our home. I don't want to move."

Now, she was *really* hurt.

Nick scowled at Randy for his insensitivity. It had also been her home for seven years and she didn't want to move either—but, she didn't seem to have a choice in the matter.

"Sorry," Randy said unapologetically.

Nick looked at her with the remorse Randy should have displayed.

"I really need to get myself going," Serafina said, expressionless. She took her mug of unfinished coffee and headed for her bedroom door.

"Hey . . ." Nick stopped her before she got too far. "This isn't how we'd planned to tell you. I want you to know that your feelings do matter to us."

Serafina turned to listen to what Nick had to say. She didn't want to make a big deal out of her feelings, so she just stared at the coffee maker, avoiding eye contact as much as possible without being rude.

"Talk to us." Nick examined her overall facial expression, especially her eyes.

Nick—or Dr. Nick, as his patients called him—was an excellent pediatric dentist. But his habit of being a self-proclaimed "excellent listener" got under her skin. She didn't need him to be her therapist. She needed him to leave her alone and let her process everything in her own time.

Besides, what was the point of talking? Nothing would change the fact that she didn't belong there anymore.

"Are you okay?" Nick asked.

"Uh, yeah. Just looking at the time."

"Sure?"

"Yes, I'm sure. I've just got a lot at the agency to get done before

Monday, and I don't need Hollis riding my ass about stuff not getting done on time."

She immediately felt bad about portraying Hollis so inaccurately. Hollis wasn't one to ride her ass on anything. He was actually very laid-back. If something was truly important to him, he'd let her know, but other than that, he trusted her enough to manage her job assignments.

She saw in Nick's face that he wasn't buying it; he knew she was hurt. And after all, she should be. They didn't clue her in that they were even trying to have a baby. All these years together and everything they'd been through—this is what she got? *There's no rush.*

She closed the door to her bedroom before Nick could say anything else.

On the other side of the door, she could hear Randy. "That went pretty well, don't you think?"

Chapter 4

Serafina had blubbered all her tears out in the shower and was better equipped to cope when she reentered the kitchen. But she was conscious of her strained eyes when Nick noticed her.

Nick had just entered the kitchen from the living room with his photography bag slung over his shoulder.

"Off to a wedding?" Serafina asked, trying to convince him that she was fine.

She already knew he was off to photograph a wedding. It's what he did just about every Saturday in spring. What had started off as a favor for some friends years ago was now his side gig.

"Yeah, actually, I am," Nick said, and then smiled reassuringly, as if to say everything was going to be okay.

Randy was sitting in the kitchen chair, nearest to the back door, talking on the landline phone. He made a slight gesture to say goodbye to Nick.

Nick leaned down to Randy's level, and they quickly kissed before he headed out the back door.

"Yeah, in two weeks," Randy said into the phone, and then looked up at Serafina and handed her a note. "I know, isn't it great news?"

Serafina looked at the note. It read "Levi Nestor" with a seven-digit phone number underneath. Why was Levi calling for her?

She thought about how Levi would have even got her landline number, but then she remembered giving the number to Hollis as an emergency contact some nine or so years ago when she started working for him. Maybe he shared it with Levi? After all, Levi was his silent partner and owned a portion of the agency.

"Is this a 313 area code?" Serafina asked Randy, who was busy saying, "Uh-huh," and, "Mm-hmm," and, "Exactly," to the person he was conversing with.

Randy kept talking to the person on the other end of the phone call. "No, we'll find out once she gets here."

Serafina clenched her jaw and began to grind her teeth as she stood there waiting to get an answer from Randy.

Why didn't Randy ask for the area code when he took down the phone number? Was he purposely going out of his way to upset her? Was she supposed to guess which metro Detroit area code it was? 313, 810, 248, 734, 586? Seemed like every decade another one was added. Remembering Levi lived in Southfield, she'd have to start with those area codes first and go from there. *Great.*

Randy motioned to Serafina about talking on the phone. He knew Serafina had an extreme aversion to talking on the telephone.

Guessing that it was probably Wanda on the other end of the line, Serafina immediately shook her head "No."

"No, she's in the shower right now. Yeah, I'll tell her you called. Of course. I'll keep you posted. I love you too, Mom." Randy hung up the phone.

"You're just plain mean," Randy scolded Serafina.

"Why is that *mean*? Just 'cause I don't want to talk on the phone right now?"

"What do you mean by 'right now'? You never want to talk to Mom. She's your mother. She deserves better. Oh, and by the way, she agrees with me about DeMarcus. You should let sleeping dogs lie."

"First of all, Wanda Price is not my mother. She's my foster mother.

Second of all, why'd you have to go tell her if you didn't want her involved?"

"So, then, I'm not really your brother. I'm just your foster brother? Got it. Thanks for clarifying."

"You know what I mean."

Serafina stood there focusing on the note, careful not to look Randy directly in the eyes. She wasn't even sure if she knew what she meant.

How could Wanda say to let sleeping dogs lie? If she even said those exact words. It sounded more like something Randy would say.

Wanda was more likely to say something a little less hurtful, like, "What's done is done." Not something that compared her grandchild to a dog.

Yes, that's probably what Wanda had said before Randy filtered and adulterated her words, before he Randalized them, making them insensitive and void of any compassion.

They *were* family. But then so was DeMarcus. Maybe they shouldn't be so quick to act otherwise.

Serafina's rationalizing didn't produce any viable excuse for what she'd said to Randy, and she felt instant regret.

Randy crossed his arms. "No, I don't know what you mean. How could you say that? She's the closest thing to a mother you've ever had—*we've* ever had."

Serafina took her keys off the kitchen table she'd left there from that morning.

"I don't have time for this," she said as she left the house, closing the back door behind her.

That was a stupid thing to say, and she knew it the second it came out of her mouth. She had nothing but time today. It was Saturday and, except for the report she had to write for last night's job assignment, she had no plans. Which equated to no life. Soon she'd have no home too.

It was a sunny day, which normally equated to a good day. But it wasn't a good day. Far from it.

Serafina's whole world was teetering on its foundation, and she wasn't so sure whether it would hold up under the pressure. She just sat there, hands on the steering wheel, inside the agency's Explorer, thinking. Her mind was sending all the signals to start the engine, but it was getting caught up in her mental queue.

Also stuck in that queue was the task of calling Levi back.

What did he want? He probably just needed to get a hold of Hollis and didn't have his new number.

A couple years back, Levi had called her, frantically trying to get a hold of Hollis. He'd accidentally locked himself out of his house, and everyone was at work.

"Hollis should still have a key," he'd said.

Distraught with the whole situation, Levi then divulged something Serafina hadn't known, that Hollis had stayed with him and his wife, Suong, for a short time.

After that call, she couldn't stop obsessing over this new information she now knew about Hollis. He had always been so private. Sometimes it seemed like he had this whole secret life.

It had also been mind-boggling to her to think of Hollis living under the same roof as Suong. Why would anyone volunteer to do that?

She'd thought of all the possible scenarios. Maybe his house was getting remodeled? That didn't seem likely. Maybe fumigation? From termites or something? But even so, why not just get a hotel or stay in the loft upstairs from the agency?

She'd wondered about the timeline as well. When did Hollis stay there? Was it before she knew him? Was it before he had Datson? She couldn't imagine him staying there with Datson. Suong was far too uptight to allow that.

Serafina started the engine and began driving down her residential street toward Woodward Avenue, slowly committing herself to navigating in the direction of the agency. She'd be able to get Levi's number there from Hollis's Rolodex. She also needed to exchange the agency's Explorer for her Jeep. Plus, the agency was the next best thing to home, even more so than Wanda's house.

By the time she got to Woodward Avenue, her decision to go to the agency was locked in. She'd call back Levi, change out the vehicles, and write up her report there.

From Ferndale to Royal Oak, it was a ten-minute drive, just a straight shot up Woodward Avenue, with a turn onto Main Street just before crossing over Walter P. Reuther Freeway/I-696.

Along the way, she passed nail salons, smoke shops, barber shops, liquor stores, pay advance loan offices, auto repair shops, gas stations, and the gamut of family-owned and predatory businesses. They all blended in, one block looking like the last. Maybe that's why her mind drifted into autopilot mode.

. . .

"So, you're really doing this?" Randy flung himself on Serafina's bed and comfortably watched her take clothes off their hangers and pack them into a large cardboard box. "Can you even afford the place on your own?"

"I've been saving. And why are you hating on my plans all of a sudden?"

Randy tightened his lips, as if scandalized.

Serafina continued to pack.

"Okay, so then, I'm never going to see you?"

Serafina paused and looked directly at Randy. "You'll see me. Just not that often."

Randy situated Serafina's pillow under his head and continued to watch her pack.

"Why don't you just leave them on the hangers? Or get a special wardrobe box?"

"Those wardrobe boxes are expensive," Serafina said, placing a folded sweater into the box.

"Are they?"

"Uh, yeah!"

"I wouldn't know. I've never had to move." Randy held up one of the shirts Serafina had placed on the bed, admiring it.

"Well, I don't have to move either. I choose to. And they break when you do that."

"Huh? You lost me." Randy looked bewildered.

"The hangers." Serafina pointed to a several broken hangers in a pile on the floor next to her garbage can. "They break when I stuff them in the box with the clothes still on them."

"Well, just don't stuff them in there, silly!"

Serafina smiled, her long brown hair cascading into her face as she closed the cardboard box.

Silence found space between them as Serafina taped down the seams of the flaps. She grabbed another cardboard box and assembled it.

What was *that* all about? "I've never had to move . . ." Did he think she had to move? What a weird comment. Sure, she and Wanda didn't always see eye to eye on things—actually, a lot of things—but there was no push for her to leave. Was there? Serafina briefly questioned her own sense of reality. She could stay if she wanted to. She just wanted to move. She just wanted a place of her own. What was so hard to understand about that?

Then, as if it were steam finding an open window, the silence dissipated.

"Hey, why don't you just move in with me? We could totally share the place. It's a two-bedroom. I'd let you have the bigger room?" Serafina asked nonchalantly, hiding her eager want.

"I don't know." Randy hesitated.

It wasn't a full-on "No," Serafina thought.

"Maybe. I mean, I really need to think about it." Randy reached for a celebrity magazine placed an armlength away from him on the bed.

Serafina knew when she asked that he'd be reluctant to move out of Wanda's house, but it was worth a try. He had a much deeper connection with Wanda than her—always had been that way, always would be that way.

"You still gonna go into teaching?" Serafina grabbed a hair tie from her nightstand drawer and pulled her hair up.

"Yeah, that's kind of always been the plan." Randy flipped through the pages of the magazine. "What makes you think I would have changed my mind?"

Nothing. She knew he wouldn't be changing his mind on teaching. It was as if there had never been any other choice in the matter. For as long as she could remember, he'd been saying he was going to be a teacher just like Mom.

As Randy briefly scanned the articles in the magazine, Serafina thought of all the various projects and school-related activities Randy had worked on with Wanda. And how he would proactively point out the usefulness of random items anyone else might throw away—sometimes even taking discarded items out of the garbage. Wanda would always pull him in close, kiss the top of his head, and tell him what a great teacher he would make someday. It was always in the cards.

. . .

Randy had ended up moving in, just not right away. He had waited until he had a reason to. A Nick reason.

How differently things could have turned out, Serafina thought, as she remembered the night of her twenty-first birthday that December 2nd.

• • •

"Please no," Randy insisted.

"Oh, come on!" Serafina persisted.

"Seriously, Serafina. I'm exhausted. It's been a long week at work. Can't we just go out tomorrow night instead? You know I like to spend Friday nights at home."

"Can't you make an exception to that? I mean, it's my birthday, for God's sake. My twenty-first birthday! I'm looking forward to having my first drink."

Randy laughed so hard he started choking on his drink.

"I'm serious, Randy."

"You act like you never drank alcohol before. Give me a break."

"Sure, but your twenty-first birthday drink is special. It's legit. It's a rite of passage, a milestone. It's not gonna be the same doing it on Saturday."

"Why not?"

"Because it's not!" She had begun pouting.

"Fine, but I don't want to be out late."

After getting Randy to agree to go out, there was still the question of where to go.

"Menjo's?" Serafina asked.

"You sure? We always go to Menjo's."

"Not on a Friday night. We've only ever gone on Saturday."

"Doubt it's any different. It's okay, we can go to a straight club if you want," Randy conceded.

"No, I'm feeling like Menjo's tonight." Serafina felt the need to explain. "I really just want to dance tonight, and I'm tired of having strange dudes grinding up on me all the time."

Randy tilted his head to the side and looked up, thinking about it. "Hmmm."

"I'm being serious." Serafina laughed.

Randy laughed also.

It was a short, eight-minute drive south on Woodward Avenue from Serafina's apartment to Menjo's. Serafina grabbed a table while Randy went up to the bar for drinks. When Randy returned, he brought back someone he had just met at the bar to introduce to Serafina.

"This is Nick," Randy said, blushing and giddy.

• • •

She didn't belong there anymore. That was clear. They couldn't have made it clearer. When did it happen? How did she go from inviting Randy to live with her to Randy disinviting her to live with him?

Having noticed the change of scenery, now boutiques and coffee shops, she resurfaced from her somber thoughts.

It was hard to imagine what downtown Royal Oak must have been like when Hollis had purchased the agency's building back in the '70s or '80s, before it became popularized as a weekend hotspot. Back when folks called it "Royal Joke."

He must have paid a tenth of its current worth, she thought. Now that whole area was prime real estate, right where the two Walters meet—Walter P. Reuther/I-696 going east and west and Walter P. Chrysler/I-75 going north and south.

She turned right onto Fourth Street and continued past the park on the right. She focused her eyes on a low-profile business sign on the front lawn of a two-story brick building just beyond some other brick buildings to the left before the side-by-side duplexes started farther down.

She knew what the business sign looked like since she'd been the one to design it years ago when other business signs started to sprout up in the area. It still made her smile with pride whenever she pulled up in the driveway. *Michigan Investigative Services Agency*.

Hollis had left the design up to her. His concern had only been the cost. She was glad she'd convinced him to pay extra for the higher quality sign. It still looked just as new all these years later.

Serafina pulled into the driveway and drove to the rear of the building where her prized possession was parked: a yellow 2006 Jeep Wrangler Rubicon Unlimited.

She'd wanted one ever since they came out in 2004, but she hadn't even been old enough to drive at the time. Once Hollis had hired her on, and she had what would be considered a steady income, she had been determined to find one. It had taken a little bit of searching, but she had managed to find a used one in Ohio.

She'd needed someone to drive her the three hours there and the three hours back to get it, but she'd decided not to ask Randy after he'd been so vocal about the absurdity of paying so much for a used Jeep instead of getting one of the newer models. She'd tried explaining that 2006 was the last year the two-door Unlimited models with the longer wheelbase were made, and that it was also the last year Jeeps actually looked like Jeeps. But no matter what she said, nothing was going to sway his belief that new is always better.

Hollis had understood, though, which is why she'd asked him to drive her there instead. Being old school and all, he could appreciate her preference for the old-school Jeep look.

Prior to their road trip, she'd asked Hollis what her actual job title was for the online loan application, and he'd said whatever she wanted it to be, that the pay was still the same.

Private Investigator, Investigations Specialist, Surveillance Agent, she'd considered others also. In the end, he was right; it didn't matter. She'd be paid the same. What mattered was that Hollis considered her his right hand on all things MISA-related.

MISA was the nickname she'd given Michigan Investigation Services Agency before "the agency" had become its default. Hollis hadn't commented either way when she started calling it that, and even referred to it as MISA on occasion. But that was Hollis. He didn't have much of an opinion when it came to the small stuff. It was as if he already had more than enough on his mind.

When Serafina stepped out of the Explorer, she nearly plopped her right foot down into a puddle. Water had pooled on the pathway to the back door, and the ground surface was too spongy for her to attempt walking through.

She scooted along the side of the Explorer's black exterior to avoid getting her shoes soaked, and then proceeded to walk around the building to the front door.

Normally, Hollis would arrive at the agency before her, so it was strange to see the inside so dark. She immediately opened the vertical blinds to let the morning sunlight shine in through the large front window.

After making a break for the restroom and starting the Keurig in the kitchen, she came back to the front office area and sat down to listen to the messages on the office phone.

The first two voicemail messages were work-related, and she'd already called them back. *Delete. Delete.*

"Call me back" was the third voicemail message—clearly another dancer, Serafina presumed. There had been less of those types of messages ever since Hollis started giving out his cell phone number instead, but every so often, one would come through. *Save.*

The fourth message was Serafina from last night calling to see if Hollis was at the office since she hadn't put his new cell phone number in her contacts yet and had a question. She couldn't remember what she had wanted to ask him now. *Delete.*

The last message was Levi Nestor. He was asking for her, and his voice sounded troubled. It didn't sound like the kind of call where he might have locked himself out of his house or car, rather it seemed grave and solemn. *Delete.*

She should call.

Serafina sat at the front desk staring at the phone. It was an old-style phone—not rotary, thank God, but it had big buttons. Hollis would always comment that she'd understand when she got to be as old as him.

Serafina was about to pick up the phone to call Levi when the front door chimed open and a tall, blonde-haired, blue-eyed man her age walked in. She was aware that he was handsome—his looks would have captivated anyone—but something about the way he carried himself made him less attractive.

She hung the phone back up.

He looked around the room and in the direction of the hallway. "Is Frank around?"

No one ever called Hollis by his first name. It was somewhat comical when people did. She'd always known him as Hollis, and most people who knew him called him Hollis.

"No, I'm afraid he's not. Is there something I can do for you?" Serafina tightened her lips after taking a deep breath and holding it.

"Do you know when you can expect him in?"

She crossed her arms. "No, usually he's in by now. Would you like me to leave him a message?"

He seemed hesitant to divulge any information, and his nervousness made Serafina keenly aware that something was amiss.

"Do you mind if I wait for him then?" He nervously asked, standing irresolute in the middle of the front office.

There was very little Serafina didn't know about Hollis's business affairs. As his assistant, she'd been involved in just about everything.

"Sure, I guess." Serafina sat stiffly.

She thought about calling Levi, especially since he'd sounded so serious, but figured she'd wait a moment in case the guy decided to leave. Instead, she checked her email.

Occasionally, when Serafina would look up, she'd see him just sitting there, staring at his phone, checking email or whatever he was doing. This time, she caught him checking the time on his watch.

"He sometimes doesn't come in at all." She hoped he would take the hint and go. When he looked up, she asked, "Was he expecting you?"

Again, the guy hesitated in saying anything. "Actually, yeah, I needed to drop something off for him."

"I can give it to him. I'm his assistant." She leaned into her left leg as if standing there waiting for him was an imposition.

"Can you tell him Cole stopped by?" He avoided eye contact.

"Yeah, sure."

"And do you have an envelope I could use?"

Serafina gritted her teeth and responded, "Yeah, I'm sure I have one here somewhere."

She walked over to her desk and fumbled through her bottom drawer where she always kept envelopes. She grabbed one and held it out for Cole.

Cole placed what looked to be a report inside the envelope and then sealed it well.

"Do you happen to have a pen?" he asked.

Serafina grabbed a pen off her desk and fully extended her arm out to hand it to him.

He wrote something on the envelope. Realizing Serafina was glaring at him, he hesitantly held the envelope out to her to take.

Serafina took the envelope in her hand and waited, silently looking at Cole.

Cole remained in place, like a deer frozen by headlights, and then awkwardly left out the front door.

Serafina looked at what Cole had written on the envelope. It read, "To: Frank Hollis, From: Cole McDermott." *How infantile*, she thought. She whirled the envelope onto her desk and headed to the kitchen. She needed a moment to settle her nerves before calling Levi, so she went to get herself coffee.

As she finished stirring her coffee, she heard the chime ring on the front door.

"Hey, Hollis!" She started walking down the hallway toward the front office area, careful not to spill the coffee in the mug she was carrying.

When she entered the front office, her eyes were still on the coffee sloshing inside the mug she was carrying. "Hey, I tried to reach you last night."

As she approached the front desk, she looked up to see that it wasn't Hollis after all.

Chapter 5

Serafina jolted back, surprised to see Levi sitting in the chair on the other side of her desk.

"Oh!" she exclaimed. "I thought you were Hollis."

She reached for a Kleenex on her desk and used it to wipe spilled coffee off her hand.

"Sorry, I didn't mean to startle you," Levi said, getting up to stand, as if greeting her in an old-fashioned kind of way.

Even though Levi had his own key and a vested interest in the agency's business affairs, he never just stopped by. *Ever*. In fact, he didn't seem to be involved at all. He was a silent partner in every sense of the term.

She fidgeted nervously, wondering what he would say. What was it that he so urgently needed to speak with her about?

"I was just getting ready to call you," she said, hoping to speed him up on speaking.

Levi just stood in awkward silence.

In that moment, Serafina noticed how much Levi had aged since the last time she'd seen him.

"Maybe we should have a seat," Levi said, sighing heavily and resuming a seated position.

Serafina lowered herself into her desk chair, her brows furrowed with worry.

Levi sat quietly, as if formulating how his words would come out.

Serafina stiffened. "Did you need to talk to Hollis too?"

"No, dear, just you."

She looked into his deep brown, grandfatherly eyes, seeing that he was close to speaking. She concentrated on controlling her breathing, as her heart pounded in her chest.

"Serafina, I received a call last night." He looked down, preparing to say something.

Levi's eyes closed as if gathering strength. He then continued. "I received a call last night that Hollis was in an accident."

He lifted his gaze and looked directly into Serafina's eyes.

"Wh . . ." Her throat was suddenly dry. She coughed hoarsely, and then quickly sipped her coffee and tried again. "Was he badly hurt? When can I see him?"

He wavered his head back and forth. "He's at Beaumont Hospital. We can head over in a bit if you'd like to see him."

Like woven threads, Serafina felt herself starting to unravel. "What happened?"

Levi read her eyes and must have seen she could handle the truth. "He was shot." He stopped as if that was enough information.

Serafina mentally rewound what he just said, freeze-framing on the footage where he said Hollis was shot.

Within seconds, she was ready to take action—any action. That meant she needed answers. Where was he when it happened? How long was he there? Were there any witnesses? Who found him? What was he doing at the time?

She didn't want him to pull back, so she took a deep breath, something she practiced all the time in her dealings with Randy. "Can you tell me anything else that would be helpful?"

"Helpful for what?" He responded more quickly than she had expected.

"Helpful for me to look into. Any leads?"

Obviously, it wasn't an accident. She knew from looking up what it would take to get a Concealed Pistols License that when people said someone was shot accidentally, that wasn't the case. Someone was negligent for it to happen, or it was intentional.

"Dear, I don't think this is anything you should be following up on. The police have it handled. They're doing an investigation."

Levi had been a detective for the Detroit Police before retiring. Of course he felt that the police had it handled.

Levi's phone rang. He immediately grabbed it when he saw the number of the caller.

"I'm sorry. I have to take this." He stood up and walked across the room for privacy.

Levi never seemed to take Serafina seriously. She could only guess what assumptions he was making about her.

It wasn't a secret that Hollis frequented strip clubs, so for all Levi knew, she'd been a stripper—and not just a stripper but a stripper at some sleazy strip club on Eight Mile where bouncers look the other way. Of course Levi would think that. He only knew what he'd seen on television, some inaccurate portrayal that he applied to all strip clubs. Cocaine and blow jobs sorts of assumptions.

She'd always wanted to set him straight on the facts: that she worked at Planet Janet, one of the higher-end strip clubs on Eight Mile. And that she had been a cocktail waitress, not a stripper. And to further set him straight, it was "dancer" or "exotic dancer." No one she ever knew called themselves a stripper. At least not at Planet Janet.

She was protective of her story, her narrative. Not he nor anyone else was going to have the rights to it. He didn't know a thing about her, and he certainly didn't know Hollis the way she knew him.

She sat watching Levi on his phone. He stood very still listening to the person on the other end of the call. Occasionally he would say something while pacing, but then he would stop again, biting his lips, looking serious and inquisitive.

Serafina thought back to that pivotal moment in time when she was put on the path to being Hollis's assistant.

• • •

"Oh my God! Serafina—is that you?" A familiar voice came from behind Serafina as she stood waiting for the Starbucks barista to make her order.

Serafina turned around, immediately recognizing her friend from high school.

"Oh wow, Shelly!" Serafina said, looking Shelly up and down. "Look at you!"

Shelly was dressed so sophisticated, nothing like how she'd looked in high school. She flaunted a large, skin-tone-colored Henri Bendel purse over her shoulder. She wore long slacks that elongated her legs and accentuated her curves. Her toes peeked out from heeled sandals, displaying well-pedicured toenails. Her blouse was fit and classy, obviously made from some material more expensive than cotton. But the thing most noticeable to Serafina was Shelly's breast size, which had gone from an A cup to a D cup. Clearly, she had had breast-augmentation surgery.

Serafina tried not to gawk, but Shelly's breasts ostentatiously formed cleavage at the opening of her shirt. It was hard to miss.

"How've you been, girl? You look great!" Shelly said, taking a step back to get a full view of Serafina.

Jealousy started to surface within Serafina, but she contained it. After all, Shelly had been a decent friend and was deserving of whatever success she had.

The barista placed a coffee drink on the counter. Written on the label was the name "Sarah F," their version of Serafina.

"Did you just get here?" Serafina picked up her drink.

"Oh no, I just came out of the restroom." Shelly walked over to the counter where her coffee drink was waiting for her. It was labeled with the name "Michelle."

"You go by Michelle now? I remember how you would insist on being called Shelly back in high school."

Shelly laughed. "I do remember that. I guess I've grown into it over the years."

Shelly and Serafina sat down at a table and caught up on each other's lives, as well as the lives of their mutual acquaintances from high school. Folks who had average grades in high school were now a year away from graduating with their bachelor's degree. Shelly was one of them.

Serafina realized as they talked, as it all sank in more and more, that others were getting ahead, passing her by. It just didn't seem fair. She had been the one with good grades, the one with a promising future. But here she was three years later with little to no progress. It was as if life stopped when she graduated high school.

"You ever think about going to college?" Shelly asked.

"Every so often, yeah. The student loan debt scares me. I thought about joining the navy as an option."

Shelly held back something she wanted to say.

"What?" Serafina asked, coaxing her.

"Don't do that. Look, there's another way." She stopped to look around, making sure their conversation was private. "Have you ever thought about dancing?"

Serafina was confused by the question. She considered herself a good dancer, but she didn't see how to make money doing it.

"That's what I do. I'm a dancer. An exotic dancer."

Serafina's eyes widened.

"It's what's paid my tuition, so when I graduate, I won't have any student loan debt."

Shelly waited a second, watching Serafina's response, and then she continued. "Because of dancing, I can afford to have a nice car too. It's nothing fancy, but it gets me where I need to go."

Serafina nodded as she processed this information. She needed a reliable car. Hers was on its last leg. Every day driving it was a gamble.

"It's very good money." Shelly smirked, coaxing her.

"Like how good?" Serafina asked.

"On average, maybe three to five hundred a shift."

Serafina couldn't find words. She thought about how her minimum-wage job as a cashier at Rite Aid compared.

"Think about it. It's an option." Shelly opened her purse and took out a pen, and then fumbled for some mail she'd put in there. She tore a corner piece off an envelope and stuffed the mail back in her purse.

"Here's my number." She wrote her number down on the piece of torn paper.

"If you want to come by and check out where I work, let me know. It's the best of all the clubs. I'm sure you've passed it before on Eight Mile. Planet Janet?" Shelly handed Serafina the piece of paper.

"Oh, yeah," Serafina said, nodding.

"I work almost every day. I go by Coco."

"Coco?"

"Yeah, that's my stage name."

Serafina shot her a questioning look.

"All the dancers have a stage name. No one uses their real name, for obvious reasons."

"That makes sense."

"Best time to stop by would be after 2:00 p.m. The lunch crowd should be gone by then, so we can sit up at the bar and talk."

"They're open during the day?"

"Oh, yeah! That's the best shift to work. Believe me. Same money, less work."

"How so?"

"It's businessmen during the day. Guys who want to have affairs without the commitment. They spend a few hours with their dancer, pay them a couple hundred, and then go home to their wives and family. On the other hand, the night shift? You've got obnoxious bachelor parties and young guys looking for girlfriends. They can be exhausting."

"Makes sense."

"Serafina, you would totally clean up in a place like that. Look at you! You're gorgeous without even trying."

A week later, Serafina walked through the doors of Planet Janet. The room was large and dim. String lighting bordered the stage, bar area, and the railings. It took a moment for Serafina's eyes to adjust.

Most of the women were topless, either on stage or giving a customer a dance. Serafina immediately met eyes with Coco, who was sitting at a private booth with an older man in a business suit. Empty lunch plates still occupied space on their table.

Coco let Serafina know with her eyes that she noticed her, but she kept smiling and nodding at the customer, pretending to be engaged in what he was saying.

Serafina went up to the bar and ordered herself a pinot grigio. Shortly after, Coco's customer said his goodbyes, and Coco joined Serafina up at the bar.

Coco got the bartender's attention. "Hey, Joey, can you put her drink on my tab?"

"Oh, she's with you?"

"Yeah."

"No worries. On the house."

"Thanks, Joey," Coco responded.

"Yes, thank you." Serafina nodded in agreement.

"You want another?" Joey pointed to Coco's wineglass, which still had a couple of ounces left in it.

"Not yet. I have to pace myself."

Joey tapped his hand on the counter, a confirmation that he had them covered.

"So, what do you think?" Coco turned to Serafina.

Serafina wasn't sure what to think. It looked like all the dancers did was prance around seductively on stage. But, on the other hand, they were topless and wearing thongs. Not to mention, she wasn't sure if she'd be able to walk in four-inch heels without falling flat on her face.

"Okay, I can see from the look on your face, it's terrifying you. It terrified me too when I first started."

A businessman walked through the door, signaling to Coco where he would be sitting. She gestured with her finger that she would be a minute.

"Eh, sorry," Coco said to Serafina. "My regular came in early."

"It's okay," Serafina said. "I know you're here to make money."

"Okay, well, listen, if you decide you want to try it out, you'll have to audition. This would actually be the best time to do it too because there's hardly anyone here. I have outfits you can borrow too—if you decide to."

Coco looked back over at her regular and noticed another dancer was walking over to him. "Oh, that fucking bitch, she better not."

Serafina and Coco watched the dancer stop at the customer's booth, place her wineglass on his table, and proceed to sit down. The customer and the dancer exchanged words, and then the dancer got up from the table and left.

"That's right, bitch. Better step off. That's my regular," Coco said, and then refocused her attention on Serafina.

"Thinks she can try to steal my regular right up from under me. She needs to get her own customers instead of trying to steal everyone else's.

That's why no one can stand her. Anyway, what was I saying?"

"About auditioning?"

"Oh, yeah. So, what I was saying was the first couple times going on stage are the hardest, but then you just get used to all of it. Eventually, none of it phases you anymore."

The DJ called Coco's name as the next dancer on the Main Stage, so she excused herself. During those two songs Coco was on stage, Joey talked to Serafina. He told her how he had seen dancers start off with the best of intentions to pay for college tuition but become too used to the money to ever get out, how being a dancer changed them. He told her the next best thing was waiting tables there instead. The money was significantly less, but it was still more than she'd ever make waiting tables anywhere else. By the time Coco returned to the bar, Serafina was already filling out the waitress application.

• • •

Joey had no doubt saved her from the dog-eat-dog politics of dancing. Over time, she would learn that dancers were an endless source of drama. Not only were they possessive and territorial, as she had witnessed sitting with Coco, but they were cliquey and ruthless.

It had been exponentially worse during the daytime lull that hit around 1:30 p.m. after the lunch crowd went back to work. That was when the catty behavior would come out in full force, waning around 5:30 p.m. when business picked up again.

For those four hours, dancers would either be on stage, in the dressing room calling in their regulars, or sitting up at the bar hawking the front doors for the next straggler to walk through them.

Serafina would be at the bar getting drinks for her customers or simply talking with Joey and overhear the "hawks" talking with one another. She would observe how each time the doors would open, the light from the outside world would flood in and be momentarily blinding. And how for those few seconds it took for everyone's eyes to adjust, there would be hope. "It only takes one customer," they often reassured one another.

More times than not, that hope would be squashed. It would just be the valet guy coming in to use the restroom and grab a fountain pop. Or it would be the bouncer, bored and in want of new scenery, now coming back inside. One by one, regulars who were called in would start to show up, making the desperation worse for the dancers who remained perched at the bar. When a new customer finally did walk through the doors, those hawks would waste no time being the one to claim him, sometimes before he had even had a chance to order a drink.

With nothing else to talk about up at the bar, the hawks would spend hours fueling each other's jealousy, commenting on the dancers who were getting dances.

No one had tolerance for the new dancers, especially those from less-classy strip clubs where "no touching" policies were not enforced. The hawks made it their business to keep the new dancers in check, swiftly handling any evidence of unfair competition. They'd have the bouncer interrupt the dance and direct the dancer to see the manager at once. The hawks would all then congratulate themselves.

Sometimes, a dancer would just be sitting with the customer, not getting dances. The hawks would complain that she should move her ass along and let others have an opportunity if she was just going to sit there.

Sometimes, a dancer would "win the lottery" with a new customer who had come in on a day that dragged on for everyone else. If she started getting dance after dance after dance, the hawks would reassert how "it only takes one customer," presenting it as evidence to continue hoping. If no other new customers came in, though, the hawks would make hypocritical assertions, like how that dancer should give other dancers an opportunity to make money from the customer too instead of hogging the customer for themselves. Never mind that none of them ever thought twice about sharing when the shoe was on the other foot.

Typically, a dancer would spend no more than fifteen minutes with a new customer before asking him whether he would like a dance. If he said, "No, thanks," the dancer would be on her way. If he said, "Yes," the dancer would try milking him for at least two dances before he wanted a break. That usually set the cycle. She'd wait out another fifteen minutes and try again, until he no longer wanted dances.

Eventually, the dancer would have to go on stage. If her instincts told her he had a few more dances in him, she'd leave her wineglass on the table, signaling to others her intention of returning. Whenever a dancer claimed a customer like that, most dancers respected the boundary, like an unspoken rule. But desperate times often called for desperate measures, so that's where drama flourished.

Oh, and the rules they held for one another! Such double standards. Dancers were more forgiving of those in their cliques than those who were not. They were also less inclined to respect boundaries with those who were not in their cliques, especially new dancers whose peers considered them third rate.

Serafina felt bad for some of the new dancers. They had to hustle nonstop to make what the others earned because they hadn't yet built up a clientele of regulars. They had to depend on the new customers who came through the door. The problem was in not knowing whether the guy was another dancer's regular. Everyone else knew of course. Dancers had excellent memories. They could remember who was fair game to other dancers and who was exclusive to whom. Not that that ever made a difference. If there was ever an opportunity to take another dancer's regular, they took it.

Serafina recalled how upset Coco had been after finding out Paige had made money off Coco's regular, Dave. Coco had left work early that day for an appointment, so when he came in and she wasn't there, Paige took the opportunity before anyone else could.

Serafina got to hear all about how "that fucking cunt" stole Coco's money. Even though Paige technically earned the money, and even though the regular was a willing participant, Coco felt entitled to that money. Really, it was kind of dumb to be upset, Serafina had thought. If it hadn't been Paige, it would have been someone else. It might have even been a new dancer. It wasn't like the regular should be expected to sit alone or leave if she wasn't there. Nevertheless, Serafina listened with compassion as Coco went on and on about it.

It didn't end there though. Coco bitched about it every single time Dave came in, because after that, he was no longer exclusive to her. He would spend half the money he used to with her and save the rest for Paige.

Eventually, Coco did shut up about it, but only after she became the target of gossip for doing the exact same thing to another dancer. The whole thing made Serafina want to shake her head in disbelief.

Serafina was glad to have trusted her instincts to be a cocktail waitress instead of a dancer. She'd seen enough drama play out in that bar that she could have easily written a book about the politics of dancing. She mused about the title being *The Politics of Dancing*, or something like that.

If she ever did write that book, she'd have to dedicate a whole chapter to the one customer who seemed to have defied the rules of engagement. That customer had been Hollis. Not knowing anything about him at the time, she just knew what she had observed. This customer, he never got a dance. Ever. Yet, dancers would hang out at his booth for hours on end. None of it had made sense. Serafina thought back to when she had asked Coco about it.

• • •

"Why does that guy come in if he doesn't want to get any dances?"

"Who? Hollis?" She looked in the direction of Hollis, sitting in Serafina's section.

"Yeah. Him."

"He says it's more enjoyable talking with us instead."

"But then how does anyone ever make any money?"

"Oh, he pays us for our time."

"All of you?"

"No, no, no. He only pays one of us. The others can get drinks, plus he buys food for the whole table to share."

"How does he decide who gets paid?"

"Oh, he alternates us."

"Alternates you?"

• • •

"Sorry about that," Levi said, walking back from the corner of the front office after ending his phone conversation.

"Everything okay?" Serafina asked.

"Uh," Levi paused, as if distracted. He shook off his thoughts and refocused.

Serafina wanted information, but it didn't seem that Levi wanted her involved. Did he not trust her? How was she to get Levi to recognize that she was competent and completely professional?

What would Hollis do in that situation? She imagined Hollis standing there next to her, talking to Levi. She imagined how calm he would be, how calm he always was. Hollis was the epitome of calm. Like Hollis had obtained some kind of inner wisdom or something. He rarely spoke, and when he did, it was important. People took notice. He smiled too, which made people naturally feel comfortable and at ease. After nine years of learning from the master, she tried on calm.

With a modest facial expression, she asked in the calmest way possible, "What kind of information was Hollis able to provide?"

"Not much, I'm afraid," he said.

Serafina was confused. Hollis may not be the talkative sort, but he was always observant. He was able to pull information out of all sorts of situations. "Nothing?"

Levi closed his eyes as if to blink away the despair they now revealed. He took a deep breath, slowly shook his head side to side, and then exhaled as if controlling his emotions. With a shaky voice, he finally spoke. "He's on life support."

Chapter 6

At the hospital, Serafina walked through the revolving glass doors and stood in the lobby looking at the directions from Levi she'd written down. She approached the security desk for clearance, and then followed the signs down the hallway, turning left just past the waiting area, heading down halfway, and taking the elevators on the right up to Hollis's floor.

From behind the nurses' station, a young woman in scrubs noticed Serafina looking at the room numbers. "May I help you, miss?"

"It's right down this way, dear." Levi's hand touched Serafina's right shoulder.

Serafina instinctively turned her head to the right, in the direction of the unannounced touch, and noticed the other elevator door behind them close. *Levi must have been on the other elevator.*

"Frank Hollis's room," Levi informed the nurse, who then nodded and smiled warmly with approval.

Down the hall, Serafina could see an older Korean woman on her cell phone leaving a room on the right. She knew in an instant that it was Suong Nestor, Levi's wife, and that Hollis would be inside that room. Her stomach churned in anticipation.

Suong wore her usual ensemble, an A-line skirt, fitted blouse, and block-heeled pumps, looking proper as ever, like a member of the Queen's royal party. She strode over to the windows at the end of the hall with an inconsistent, sporadic pace, her obnoxious click-clack sounds echoing with each step.

Suong began pacing but stopped at one point to meet eyes with Serafina's, lifting her left eyebrow in condescending recognition.

It wasn't often that Serafina was around the Ice Queen. Just a few times that had made a lasting impression, like the first time she met Suong, when Suong stopped by MISA unannounced looking for Levi.

. . .

The front door to the lobby opened unexpectedly. No knock or notice. Serafina looked up from the report she was working on at her desk. There at the door stood a Korean woman in a dark green trench coat, looking around with an air of disdain and annoyance.

"Can I help you?" Serafina asked.

"Who are you?" the Korean woman asked, ignoring Serafina's question.

"I'm Serafina. I work here. Is there something I can help you with?"

The Korean woman grumbled under her breath, and then, with exasperation, asked, "Is Levi here?"

Serafina must have had some sort of look on her face, because the Korean woman then blurted, "I'm his wife."

"Oh, you must be . . ." Serafina struggled to remember the woman's first name. "Mrs. Nestor."

Mrs. Nestor just nodded.

"Um, no, Levi doesn't ever really come around here. Was he supposed to stop by today?"

Mrs. Nestor ignored Serafina's question again. "Is Hollis here then?"

Suong! Serafina remembered Mrs. Nestor's first name. Suong hadn't offered up her first name—or corrected her when she said Mrs. Nestor, so . . . should she keep calling her Mrs. Nestor?

Feeling out of sorts, Serafina said, "Sorry, no he's not."

Suong huffed, and then eyed Serafina as if Serafina were hiding something. And she *was* hiding something, but not what Suong thought she was hiding. It felt like Suong thought Serafina was being disingenuous about knowing where Levi was, like Levi and Hollis might be together doing something a wife might not want her husband doing. Such as going to the strip club. Which is exactly where Hollis was. Planet Janet's, to be specific. But was Levi with him?

"Did you try Levi on his cell phone?"

"Well, of course I did!" Suong snapped back.

Serafina took a deep breath. "Hollis too?"

"I called and got his voicemail. That was hours ago though. He can't find time to return a phone call?"

Serafina knew Hollis wouldn't take a call at Planet Janet's. Not with the loud music.

"Hollis usually responds to texts if he can't take a call. Let me text him real quick." Serafina picked up her phone and texted Hollis that Suong was there looking for Levi and thought he was with him.

Hollis responded right away that Levi wasn't with him, that he hadn't spoken with Levi in quite some time, and that he didn't know where Levi was.

Serafina relayed the message.

Suong stood up, scanned the room as if looking for clues, and then left.

It was an uncomfortable exchange—one that Serafina hoped she'd never have to experience again. Later, she had asked Hollis about it. "You think Levi's cheating on her?"

"Levi? No." He took a moment as if he needed to think about it more, and then followed up with, "No, not Levi."

• • •

Luckily, Suong was on her cell phone as Levi and Serafina approached Hollis's room, so Serafina was able to avoid any interaction with the Ice Queen.

Serafina's knees immediately buckled at the sight of Hollis intubated with a ventilator to help him breathe, hooked up to machines monitoring his vitals. She grasped for the nearest chair to sit at Hollis's bedside.

Distressed, she held her hands together against her mouth and nose like a face mask, and then turned her head downward. She couldn't bear to see Hollis like that. It all felt so wrong. She shouldn't be there. He wouldn't want people watching him sleep, invading his space, violating his privacy.

Levi stood silently across from Serafina, allowing her to process and grieve.

Neither spoke in that moment. Serafina focused on the swirly pattern on the carpet. The rhythmic whirring from the machines was both soothing and stressful. In the hallway, Suong's click-clacking slowed steadily to an occasional clack.

Serafina finally broke the silence. "Where'd it happen?"

"Hmm?" Levi turned toward her as if he had been concentrating on something far away in his thoughts and was suddenly pulled back into the moment.

"Where was Hollis when he got shot?" Serafina rubbed her hands together, holding onto her own fingers.

Levi inhaled, readying his response.

"I'm just curious," Serafina stated matter-of-factly. She pulled her hair back and out of her face, trying not to seem overly consumed with what Levi had so blatantly made off-limits to her.

"I know, dear." Levi walked over to the window and stared outside.

"It happened on the southwest side of Detroit, near Mexicantown."

Serafina eyed Levi at the window, waiting for him to continue, but he just stared outside.

Serafina's mouth was dry, so she moved some saliva around in her mouth and swallowed. "He was working on an investigation last night. I don't know any specifics though." She remained focused on Levi, unsure if he was listening.

She continued. "We don't really do anything dangerous when we're working. Just surveilling, really. It's actually kind of boring."

Serafina leaned back in her chair and looked at the ceiling. "Maybe it's connected to whatever investigation he was working on."

Levi turned around and faced Serafina. "I was able to call some friends at the station and right now they suspect it was gang related."

"Gang related?" Serafina sat up straight.

"I suspect it as well."

"Oh?" Serafina's eyebrows shot up.

"Unfortunately, it's probably a case of being at the wrong place at the wrong time."

He began to walk away from the window and past Serafina, toward the pitcher of water on the rolling tabletop. He poured water into an extra clear, plastic cup stacked next to it, and then took a drink.

He continued. "The southwest side of Detroit is known for being gang infested. I'm sorry, but you probably won't find out much more beyond that."

Suong's voice encroached Hollis's room, and then silenced as she stood at the doorway, no longer on her phone, just waiting for Levi's attention.

"Excuse me for a moment, dear," Levi said upon seeing Suong beckoning him, and then promptly exited the room.

Serafina heard them whispering with one another in the hallway.

It sounded like a serious discussion, but she couldn't make out what either of them were actually saying. It didn't matter to Serafina though. Nothing really did in that moment, as she began to process seeing Hollis like that. Their voices became background noise, just like the sound of the machines.

Serafina eyed the pitcher of water on the rolling table and decided to pour herself a plastic cupful as well. She took a few sips while looking at Hollis lying there, this time taking more notice of the machines keeping him alive.

The IV solution was getting low and would need to be changed soon, she thought. Beyond that, all the other machines were just that—other machines. She examined all of their parts, taking it in that these machines were very important. Life-saving machines. She walked slowly to his bedside.

First, she looked at Hollis's aged hands. Then, she watched the rise and fall of his chest as he inhaled and exhaled. Then, Serafina willed herself to look at Hollis's face. As she did, she began to notice things, like his sunken-in cheeks and pale skin. Was that a result of being shot? Had he looked like that before, and she was just now noticing?

She stared closely at the large pores on his nose, and then at his greasy hair, in need of a wash. She realized how much older he actually was than how she saw him in their day-to-day interactions. Glances, where the whole picture was taken in, not the zoomed-in, close-proximity details such as pores. In that moment, his mortality became real, and she couldn't look away.

The nurse from the nurse station came in and checked his vitals. "Are you his daughter?"

Serafina didn't know how to respond. Was she not supposed to be there? Was it family only? Instead, she just moved her chair back, away from the nurse to give her more space, and then sat down.

The nurse looked at Hollis and then Serafina and smiled. "You look like you could be related."

Serafina thought about saying she was Hollis's business partner, or even his assistant. But as his assistant, shouldn't she know more? Shouldn't she know where he was last night? Or what he was investigating? Shouldn't she know who the hell that Cole McDermott guy was and what he wanted with Hollis that was so secretive that he had to put whatever he had, a report of some sort, in an envelope?

The moment had passed, so Serafina chose not to respond.

The nurse was marking notes on the clipboard at the end of the bed. "He's doing much better than when he came in. Stay positive."

"Yes. I will." It occurred to Serafina that the incident happened in Detroit, a good forty-five minutes to an hour away, yet Hollis was taken to the hospital in Royal Oak.

"Shouldn't he be in another hospital?" she asked the nurse.

The nurse looked confused.

"I mean, he was shot in Detroit, right?"

The nurse reluctantly answered. "I'm sorry. I don't know the details of his intake. He came in early this morning before my shift."

"Oh, right." Serafina looked back at Hollis. "Thank you anyway."

The nurse shifted her attention back to Hollis, checked a few more things, and then walked out.

Serafina wanted to talk to Hollis. She had so many questions, and she needed his advice. But it was too weird for her to talk aloud, with him lying there like that. It would be like talking to someone while they're sleeping. How could she know for sure though whether he was asleep or awake? He was heavily sedated, so, in her mind, he probably wasn't conscious enough to comprehend anything she might say. But then, what about those people she heard about who remembered conversations while in comas?

Serafina decided that on the off chance that Hollis was aware of his surroundings, she should talk to him. She felt self-conscious about what she might say. It would be easier to say what she wanted to say with thoughts, not words. Was it possible for her to communicate her thoughts to him telepathically?

The thought of him hearing her thoughts caused her concern. What if she thought something inappropriate? Would she be able to control her thoughts just enough to tell him what she wanted to say? And what did she want to say, really? That she missed him. That she needed him in her life, so he needed to get better. He needed to not die. She focused on that word: *die*. The thought that he could actually die was more than she could handle. She quickly shook that thought from her head. The nurse told her to stay positive and look, she was already failing at that. Already thinking the worst. And if he did die, would it then be her fault for not staying positive? And if Hollis could hear her thoughts, then he'd know it was her fault. Was he trying to communicate to her telepathically, too, like *stop thinking negative thoughts so I don't die*? And was she just not hearing him because telepathy didn't work that way? Or maybe because she wasn't listening correctly, the way one needs to listen in order to receive telepathic messages? Or maybe she was just a failure at that too?

Serafina realized how tense she'd become. Her muscles ached and she was holding her breath again, just like she often did when she was anxious. She took a deep breath and exhaled.

"Hollis," Serafina whispered. She wanted to let him know she was there but didn't want Levi, Suong, or anyone else in the hall to hear her.

Serafina looked intensely at any changes in Hollis's breathing. His chest expanded the same. His chest deflated the same. No movements in his fingers like they did in the movies when they tried to communicate back. One tap for yes, two for no. None of that.

"Hey, I'm here," she continued. "I don't want you to worry about anything. I'll hold the fort down until you get better."

Hold the fort down? She thought how strange that sounded. Should she have said, "Hold down the fort" instead? And what did that even mean? Were forts known to blow away or something?

Serafina thought hard about what else she might want to say in that moment. Should she mention that some guy named Cole stopped by with an envelope? Some guy who mistakenly called Hollis "Frank"? Some guy who was hired for something that she didn't know anything about? Would that stress Hollis out if she mentioned Cole? She deserved some answers about Cole, didn't she? But, okay, maybe not in that moment. But later, yes, later . . . He should explain what that was all about. But then, would that be the moment he told her he didn't need her as a partner anymore? That she'd been replaced by Cole? No, why would he do that? She was like a daughter to Hollis, wasn't she? That whole thing about their relationship was kind of confusing at times. What the hell was she thinking? Hollis would never replace her. Was it something serious that she shouldn't be involved in? But then, why keep it a secret? Why not just tell her? Did he not trust her? No, he trusted her—that was her insecurities talking. She knew he trusted her. So, then what? He was protecting her? Was she not safe?

Levi entered the room without Suong and stood where the nurse had been.

"Levi? How did Hollis get here to this hospital if he was shot in Detroit? Shouldn't he be in a Detroit hospital?"

Levi kept his eyes on Hollis. "I had my eldest son, Michael, get him transferred here this morning from Detroit Receiving, so he could be closer to us all."

Serafina thought through how that was possible.

"Michael's an oncologist here," Levi added.

"Oh," Serafina responded, having more clarity.

She thought more as they remained there looking at Hollis. "How did you find out?"

"Friend on the police force contacted me. He recognized Hollis from Michael's wedding and Brian's college graduation party. Thought maybe I would have contact information for any of his relatives."

Serafina waited to find out whether Hollis had any relatives since he never spoke of any and seemed to shy away from discussing matters of family. That never bothered her before because she certainly didn't want to discuss "family" either. It was like an unspoken rule between them to not ask. But now she was curious. *Did he?*

Levi didn't offer up any additional details. He just stood in silence.

Serafina folded her arms. "That's good."

Levi's taciturn demeanor had Serafina on edge. "I've got to get going." She grabbed her purse off the back of her chair and stood up.

"Yes, of course, dear."

Levi held his arm out as they walked toward the door, inviting Serafina to head out first. "If you don't mind, I'd like to ask you something."

The hallway was still, the fluorescent lights humming above them. Levi stood in front of Serafina with his jacket folded over his right arm.

Hesitatingly, he asked, "How would you feel about taking care of Hollis's dog for him while he's . . . here?"

"Datson?" Serafina didn't know how to respond.

There wasn't anything she wouldn't do for Hollis. And to be honest, she always got along well with Datson. He was a good, old dog. She knew he wouldn't be any trouble at all. Her stomach turned with anxiety at the thought of what she should do.

There was no way she could take Datson home. Not that Randy or Nick would mind. They loved animals. And she knew that their dog Muffin would be fine. They'd been known to watch friends' pets from time to time. But she just couldn't. Just didn't seem right to. She wasn't even welcome there, let alone Hollis's dog. No, she just couldn't. She wouldn't feel good about taking any more space than she had to for the time being. She wouldn't be around much anymore either, so letting Datson out would be an issue. Taking care of Datson wouldn't be fair to anyone. She just couldn't.

"Is there anyone else, you know, who could take Datson? I live with my brother and his partner, and they already have a dog. She's not good with other animals." Serafina felt guilty for saying the last part, knowing it was a lie.

Serafina wanted to take care of Datson, not just for Hollis but because she could actually use the company of someone right now, even an old dog. Those new feelings furthered the complexity of how she was already feeling.

Levi's shoulders fell slightly. "I understand."

"I'm really sorry."

"It's okay," Levi said.

Serafina wondered if Datson was still at Hollis's house. "Where is he right now?"

"My son Brian went to get him this morning and took him to my house."

Maybe it was the look on Serafina's face in that moment, but suddenly Levi became defensive.

"Suong has a bichon frise, Mimi, and she's terrified of other dogs. We have them separated for the time being, but it's not a good plan, long term."

He left the conversation assuring her that he'd figure something else out and told her not to worry. She couldn't help but worry though. This was Hollis's beloved dog. Could she live with whatever Levi figured out instead? And what did he mean by "separated?" Was Datson alone in a room or stuck in a crate? She knew Hollis wouldn't want either for Datson, but what choice did she have? She couldn't take Datson. *Could she?*

Chapter 1

The world outside seemed to disappear as Serafina sat in her Jeep at the hospital entrance. She started to zone out while waiting for the influx of cars to pass. So much was weighing on her mind that she couldn't seem to focus on anything anymore.

Autopilot took over, and at some point, she had turned onto Woodward Avenue. Traffic was light so she continued to go deep into her thoughts, unaffected by her surroundings which seemed to blend and blur.

Although she was traveling southbound on Woodward Avenue, she was uncommitted to any particular destination. She just knew she needed to drive somewhere other than the hospital.

Driving around aimlessly was always an option. But the stress of everything was starting to take its toll, both mentally and physically. Instinctively, she continued driving in the direction of home.

Although home was the logical choice, it wasn't her first choice. That morning, it had felt as though she were being pushed out of her home. Now? It was different. It was like she had already moved out. Just like that, she had become an unwelcome visitor dropping by unannounced.

Her uneasiness intensified with every stoplight. She half-wished the drive would take longer, but at the same time, she half-wished to already be there, sheltered in her bed. As she continued down the avenue, she eyed parking areas—or any place, really, so long as she could park there and take a nap in her Jeep.

It was too cold for that though. How would she stay warm? By keeping the Jeep running while she napped? That would surely draw attention— "Some lady knocked out in the driver seat of a running vehicle." There would certainly be a call to the local police station from a concerned citizen if she did that. She imagined how it would play out, her waking up to tapping on the window.

Oh, sorry, Officer, I had to pull over and . . . rest my head. Yeah, I was starting to feel dizzy . . . Oh, no, I'm fine now. Thank you for asking . . . No, I'm okay, Officer. I think I just need to eat something . . . Oh, yeah, I'm heading home right now. I can grab something to eat there . . . Thank you, again, Officer.

Her subconscious kept track of her general location. Royal Oak on the left, Berkley on the right. The Detroit Zoo water tower just ahead on the right, with its shadowed animals against the backdrop of mulberry shades. Over the Walter P. Reuther/ I-696 Freeway. Ferndale ahead.

Where else could she go? She certainly wasn't going to stay with Wanda. The plight of that old neighborhood had worsened over the years. It wasn't worth the risk of her Jeep getting broken into. Not to mention, staying at Wanda's house was in many ways worse than staying at Randy and Nick's. Like a major step backward. There weren't many other choices, so she resolved to go home.

As she approached the corner of her street, she hesitated about turning. It occurred to her that she could always go back to the agency. There was nothing to eat there except for Hollis's Hot Pockets in the freezer. Plus, what would she do there, besides sleep? She was too mentally exhausted to work on her report. She was almost home anyway, so she'd have to turn around and go back the other way.

In a last-minute decision, Serafina turned down her street. Her angle was too wide, though, and she almost hit a gray car pulling up to the stop sign at the other corner. The white-haired man driving glared at her as she quickly corrected her turn.

Halfway down the block, Serafina tried to regain her composure. She inhaled slowly and consciously relaxed her grip on the steering wheel.

On her right, crossing the side street, stood the elderly woman who was always out walking her dog. Serafina must have passed her a million times. Only this time, Serafina was just now realizing the dog was an Australian shepherd, like Datson. How was it she'd never noticed that before?

That thought sunk in deeper as she drove down her neighborhood street, with its many mature trees lining the curbs. Tall maples with large trunks canopied the rows of updated Dutch Colonials on either side.

Some homeowners had opted for wood-finished siding. Others had insisted on using fresh paint as an attempt to preserve historical elements. Each home had character and stood out in its own unique way, all testaments to the community's improvement initiatives. *So many changes*, she reflected.

Maybe noticing the dog being an Australian shepherd was that effect where a person buys a car and then starts noticing cars with the same make and model everywhere. She remembered there was some science behind why people did that, which was probably why she couldn't remember what that was called.

Science had never interested her; she blamed Randy for that. Every chance he could get, he would school her on something science related.

Damn, what was that called? It was going to bother her not knowing, so she'd have to look it up. *Or ask Randy.* She laughed at her own joke.

Just a little farther down after the first stop sign was "the" house, the one with white siding and dark green shutters. In her mind, she could no longer refer to it as "her" house; it was now "the" house.

She parked in her usual spot past the driveway, next to the tree they had planted back when Randy was hired as a science teacher at the nearby school. Nick had said something about planting roots in Ferndale, and Randy followed up with something sciencey for them to do, something that symbolized planting roots in Ferndale.

The tree was budding leaves, a welcoming sign for the newness of spring. The season of new beginnings. Serafina wanted to yell at the tree for mocking her predicament. Sure, it was a great new beginning for Randy and Nick, but what did it mean for her? She took a moment to consider that question. What *did* it mean for her?

She couldn't answer that question. Everything felt so obscure. The only thing she knew for certain was that she wouldn't be parking next to this tree much longer, and she mourned that loss.

She pulled out her phone, still interested in why she was just now noticing the breed of that elderly woman's dog. Her search revealed that it was called the Baader–Meinhof phenomenon. Good thing she looked it up. She would have never recalled that one.

Had she just experienced the Baader–Mein-whatever phenomenon? Was that what had just happened? Or could it have been something else, like a sign? Forces of the unknown telling her she should take Datson?

Serafina shivered abruptly. The chill in the air was permeating through the Jeep's exterior. Soon the temperature outside would drop twenty degrees, as it typically did in the evening hours. That was Michigan spring weather, temperatures fluctuating like the callout of lottery numbers.

It didn't make sense to start up the engine again, just for the heater. And the hoodie she was wearing wasn't enough to provide warmth—not the kind of warmth she'd need if she wanted to stay in the Jeep much longer.

She thought about what her evening would entail if she went inside. Soon, Nick would be making dinner. Probably something carb-loaded, like his eggplant parmesan. A tribute to his Italian heritage. She could really go for that right now—actually, any of his Italian dishes.

But she decidedly couldn't. It gnawed at her to think of them feeding her out of obligation. More evidence of what a burden she was. She wasn't even sure if she was ready to sit in the same room with them, let alone humble herself like that.

And if they were seeking redemption, Serafina wasn't about to give it to them so easily. *Sorry to kick you out, but here's some comfort food to help with that.*

She dreaded going inside—not just a little—but a lot. To the extent that each muscle in her whole body ached from tension. And she felt a dull headache coming on. She couldn't continue sitting in the Jeep though. At some point, she would need to accept that it was time to go in, dread or not.

Serafina climbed out of her Jeep and walked around the rear of the Jeep. In an instant, her arms tingled, as if she were preparing for actual pain. She rarely experienced that sort of involuntary self-defense mechanism. Only when her body recognized a need to guard itself. In this case, it was protection from an onset of emotions—emotions that would undoubtedly make her implode.

She trudged down the long driveway, each step heavier than the last. To the right, she noticed grass creeping from the neighbor's lawn onto the driveway. Normally, she'd enjoy pointing those things out to Randy, knowing he'd be outside in an instant to edge the lawn. He couldn't resist fixing things that were out of place, and she couldn't resist pointing them out to him. But today, it wasn't happening.

On the left, a walkway led to the front door where a bronze mailbox was posted into the ground. Out of habit, Serafina headed down the walkway. Partially down, she realized she'd already grabbed the mail that morning. She turned back around—annoyed—and proceeded toward the rear of the house.

No one ever used the front door. It was too much of a hassle. Without a foyer or entryway, there was no place to stand, except on Randy's precious carpet. That was never an option.

They could always just take their shoes off before going inside, but then they'd have to carry their shoes—along with everything else they were carrying—to the back of the house. It was just easier to enter from the back door.

Randy had established rules for storing everything, including shoes and jackets. The designated area for outdoor clothing and other gear, like umbrellas and gloves, was a small nook near the back door. It had once been a built-in pantry, but Randy had converted it to what he deemed more practical.

Jackets were to be hung up on the wall-mounted coat rack using one of the "many available hooks," as Randy put it. Shoes were to be placed in one of the many "nifty" shoe cubbies provided in the massively tall, espresso-colored shoe storage cabinet, designed to accommodate thirty-six pairs of shoes.

It was all part of some sort of system he'd dreamed up. The layout of the unit was three cubbies across in length and twelve cubbies in height. Each member of the household had been allocated a column, so they each had twelve cubbies: the first column was Randy's, the middle column was Nick's, and surprise, the last column was Serafina's.

Randy would be annoyed if thirty-six shoes were actually stored in the unit though. Anything more than six pairs in a column was expected to be moved to the person's individual closet at a "hopefully soon" time. "Those cubbies are only for temporary use," Randy would say. It wasn't worth arguing about how a smaller unit would have been more practical. *Just accept*, she'd tell herself.

Serafina was immediately greeted by Muffin when she stepped inside the house. After closing the back door behind her, she bent down to rub

Muffin's happy spot behind the ears.

"You're a good girl. Yes, you are," she softly whispered baby-talk to Muffin.

Serafina stood back up to put her shoes away, and then glanced down at the table, the mail still neatly stacked there. So was the letter. Serafina let her feelings surface in that moment.

Here she thought she was part of the family, but clearly, she was just a tenant renting a room from them. Had Wanda known all along? Randy had to have said something. There's no way he could keep that kind of news from his precious "Mom." How callous of them, waiting until the last minute and then so nonchalantly kicking her out! Randy could be a lot of things, but Nick too?

Fuming, she huffed out angrily. *There's no rush.*

She shook off her exasperation and walked lightly across the kitchen toward her bedroom, not wanting to draw attention.

Muffin started to follow behind, panting as if a snail's pace was completely overexerting her, and then made a beeline for her water bowl.

Serafina heard acoustic rock music coming from the front of the house. It sounded unmistakably like the Coffee House station on Sirius radio, although she knew with almost 100 percent certainty that they did not have Sirius radio.

The only time Randy and Nick ever had Sirius radio was whenever they started a new vehicle lease, and it would come with the free, limited subscription. As soon as the subscription's expiration date would near, there would be a whole discussion on the cost versus value of paying to continue the subscription. She couldn't care less what they decided, but they always managed to pull her into their debate. Like a broken record, she'd remind them of their phones' unlimited data plan and how streaming on Pandora was free.

Serafina's jaw ached from clenching it. She was bitter, thinking about how she wouldn't be around anymore for any of their dumb debates. What were they going to do then? Call her? Text her?

Her eyes teared with anger. *They don't get to just throw me away and then call me up over some stupid shit like that.*

She wasn't some sort of doll on a shelf that they could just take down for their amusement whenever they wanted. Amenable Serafina, the doll with the pull-string that repeats phrases like, "Okay, Randy."

Nope, if they contacted her about their dumb stuff, they were going to get the This-Is-What-You-Asked-For Serafina doll that says, "Figure it out on your own," or, "Are you serious?" Better yet, she'd ghost them— ignore their texts, ignore their phone calls. She'd go dark.

Serafina squinted her eyes several times to stop the burning from tears being held back.

She glanced to her left through the opening into the living room and saw a huge cardboard box with a picture of a crib on the side. The contents were laid out neatly with the Styrofoam packing material already put in a large, clear, plastic bag.

Whenever they ran out of room in the recycle bin, they would use those bags for the overflow. That was rare though.

No, he wasn't planning to recycle the Styrofoam; it wasn't recyclable. She could only surmise that Randy intended to store and repurpose the pieces for some school-related projects, much like he did with other items that normal people throw out.

He often did that with items like toilet paper rolls, paper towel rolls, Kleenex boxes, shoeboxes, plastic milk jugs, and egg cartons. He'd go through a phase of, "Don't throw any of those away," and later it would turn to, "Oh, yeah, I don't need those anymore."

He was also known to take up requests for other teachers, too, especially kindergarten through second grade teachers. They were constantly engaging students in crafts projects. Serafina remembered how Wanda had saved items too. Must be a teacher thing, she thought.

"Oh, hey, you're home," Nick said, as he opened the door from the basement.

Serafina turned around to see Nick step into the kitchen with the electric drill in one hand and the drill bit case in the other.

"Yeah," she said, and then turned back around and kept walking.

Randy came in from the living room and blithely headed to the refrigerator. "I can get dinner started if you want to keep working on the crib," he said to Nick.

Nick—still behind Serafina—didn't verbally respond.

As Serafina passed Randy, he gasped with astonishment in the direction of Nick, as if he'd been shot a scolding.

"No rush, right?" Serafina said, walking straight into her bedroom and closing the door.

Someone knocked on the door twice. It was probably Nick. Serafina debated on responding. She wanted to answer if it was Nick, but she was emotionally spent. Instead, she put on her headphones and lay in bed listening to music.

· · ·

Serafina woke to the scent of garlic and onions. Whatever Nick was cooking smelled fabulous. Staying for dinner was extremely tempting.

She slowly opened her bedroom door and peered out. Aside from the overhead light above the stove, the kitchen was dark.

Chillout lounge music floated in from the living room like an invitation. She walked over to the entryway and leaned against the opening.

Nick was leaning over the assembled crib, admiring the finished product.

Randy was lying on the chaise sofa, with Muffin nestled beside him. He had his cell phone up to his ear, giving an occasional, "Uh-huh."

Nick caught Serafina in his peripheral view. "You're awake."

Randy looked curiously over at Serafina, inspecting her for short-comings.

"Looks nice, Nick," she said.

The crib did look nice. Nick deserved to hear some recognition. Any more than that, though, was asking too much of her.

Nick beamed with pride. "Thanks." A few moments later, he added, "Food should be ready in about twenty minutes."

"I'm heading out tonight."

Randy laughed insufferably. "Of course, Mom."

Nick locked eyes with Serafina. "You're not staying for dinner?"

Serafina didn't want to be there any minute longer than necessary. The idea of suffering through "family dinner" with Randy was more than she could bear. Going around the table and discussing the best and worst parts of their day—a handed-down tradition from their childhood with Wanda—was both laughable and cruel.

"I can't tonight. Thanks anyway."

She needed to come up with an excuse fast. Nick could be tenacious at times, especially when it gave him the opportunity to test out his self-proclaimed "excellent listener" skills, the ones he learned in fake therapist school.

"Covering Hollis again tonight?" Nick took a sip of his wine.

Serafina realized she hadn't said anything to them about Hollis. Neither of them knew Hollis had been shot or that he was now in the hospital.

"Hold on, Mom, let me ask him," Randy said into his phone, and then turned to Nick. "What was the name of that place we went to in Traverse City that we said we wanted to go back to?"

"Which one? There was a lot we visited there." Nick turned to face Randy, inquisitively.

"The place where we said we wanted to go back to. Remember? It was closed when we went there . . ." Randy snapped his fingers three times, and then rested his index finger against his top lip. "Never mind, I'll think of it in a minute.

"Oh, Mom, it was so quaint. You would have *loved* it," Randy said, obnoxiously emphasizing the word "loved."

Nick blurted, "That wasn't Traverse City, silly. That was in Grand Haven."

"Oh, yeah! You're right. That was Grand Haven. But what was that place called?"

Their conversation faded into the background as Serafina headed to her bedroom. She immediately grabbed items for an overnight bag and hurried for the back door.

Remembering her work bag, she went back to retrieve it as quickly as possible. As she walked past the opening into the living room, she could see Randy and Nick still engrossed in the same dumb conversation.

She couldn't wait to get out of there.

Chapter 8

The first thing Serafina noticed when she pulled up to the agency was how dark and eerie it appeared at night. She'd only been there a handful of times that late, but from what she could remember, it had never been that ominous.

Come to think of it, she recalled it as somewhat inviting on previous visits that late. The porch light had been on. The interior of the agency had been lit up. And Hollis had been there.

That's right, she reminisced, thinking of Hollis.

Hollis would call her—never text, until recently, that is—and it would be because he had a question or needed her for something. Always starting off with, "Are you busy?" At one point, she had suspected that he was just coming up with reasons to have some company, even if for a brief visit.

Some calls for assistance were legitimate, though, like the time he had needed a special camera lens that she still had. Or there was the time that she had installed a new software program on their desktops, back before they switched to laptops, and he had needed help trouble-shooting an issue.

As Serafina drove farther down the driveway, she realized she couldn't see anything in the backyard. It was pitch black. She imagined some wretched soul with a sinister plan lurking back there.

Too creepy, too creepy. Nope. Nope.

Serafina shifted the gear into reverse and parked closer to the front door. Before turning off the engine, she grabbed her purse, her overnight bag, and her work bag, ready to race to the front door. She hadn't been that creeped out since she was five years old running up the basement stairs to escape the Boogie Man.

One . . . two . . . three. She turned off the engine and in seconds was at the front door, keys in hand with the office key positioned to be inserted for quick entry.

After locking the door behind her, Serafina made it her mission to turn on as many lamps as possible within the first ten seconds. The front window still had the vertical blinds open from when she was there that morning. She instantly closed them and scanned the room for anything she might need to defend herself against.

Once her adrenaline subsided, Serafina's stomach reminded her that she'd failed to adequately fuel herself for the day. She ventured to the kitchen to microwave a Hot Pocket and grab an iced tea. They were Hollis's, but she knew he wouldn't mind.

She walked back to the front room to eat, looked at her desk, and then rerouted herself over to the sofa instead. A few bites later, her plate was empty, and she was ready to settle in for the night.

From a seated position, she reached down to her overnight bag and dragged it closer to where she was sitting. She pulled out her phone charger and the comfy clothes she'd packed—yoga pants and a fitted T-shirt.

After plugging in her phone, she did a full scan of the room for any camera devices she might not know about.

That's silly, she thought. Hollis wouldn't have security cameras inside the agency. Although, that wasn't a bad idea. Something to think about. Like a Smart Home system that she could log into from her phone to check on intruders and turn lights on in advance. She made a mental note of that.

Deciding it was too weird to change into her comfy clothes there in the main office area, she made her way to the restroom.

When Serafina came back into the front room, with worn clothes stuffed under her right arm and shoes clutched in her left hand, she stood there mesmerized. The dim lighting, with its cozy ambiance, had transformed the front room office into a living room with two desks.

Serafina felt the tightness of every muscle in her body. Her head ached. Her jaw was clenched. Everything hurt.

Brrrr. Serafina shivered. She rubbed both arms for warmth.

Serafina checked the thermostat on the wall. She started to adjust the temperature to a Hollis-approved temperature, but she felt cold to the bone. She needed to stop the shivering, or she would continue to feel horrible. Hollis wasn't around to question the temperature, she thought. She adjusted the temperature higher, feeling guilty as she did so.

Before going back to the sofa, Serafina grabbed Hollis's throw blanket off the armchair. It was a luxurious hue of taupe, made from the softest plush fleece imaginable. Hollis kept it on the main floor for whenever he needed to "rest his eyes," which seemed to be more and more often lately.

She smiled knowing how the whole "resting his eyes" would play out. She'd be sitting at her desk working, and then seconds later, sounds of deep slumber would emerge from his region of the room.

Strange, she thought. Hollis had a private loft upstairs, yet he chose to sleep on the sofa.

For the longest time, she'd thought the upstairs to the agency was just one big storage area. They never had a reason to go up there, so she had just assumed that's what it was. Until the day Hollis had changed out the restroom faucet, she hadn't been given a reason to think otherwise.

. . .

"Dad gum it!" Hollis swore from the restroom.

Serafina looked down the hallway in his direction, and then got up from her desk where she had been typing a report to go check on him.

She stood in the doorway of the restroom looking down at Hollis on the floor. He was on his back, reaching up under the sink.

"How's it going?" she asked.

With his arms still extended upward, Hollis said, "Ain't no hill for a stepper, that's for sure."

"What's wrong with the sink?" Serafina took note of all the tools spread out around Hollis.

"I was fixin' to remove the sink faucet, but this nut's too flush to the retainin' plate, and I can't seem to git enough grip to . . ."

He proceeded to try loosening the nut, grunting with each effort given. Exasperated, he declared, "I swear this thang's got me madder'n all git-out."

"What's the problem with it?"

"Looks like the bolt's rusted on. I'm seein' some corrosion."

He pulled himself out from under the sink and sat up, holding a strange tool he'd been using to access the tight space up under the sink. It was a long, cylindrical rod, with a smaller metal rod inserted on one end to form a *T*, and some sort of clampy-wrench thing on the other end.

He was a mess. Hair disheveled. Sweaty and flushed. He smacked his dry mouth, quenching it.

"Think you might could grab me one of them Dr. Peppers from the icebox?"

Serafina walked a few steps over into the kitchen and opened the refrigerator door. "Sorry, I just had the last one."

"Make it a Coke then."

"Sorry, there's no Coke."

"Already? I just bought some Sprite."

"Sorry, I thought you meant Coke, like Coca-Cola," she called from the refrigerator, still holding its door open.

Hollis chortled. "Pop's what y'all raised on concrete call it. We Texans call it a Coke."

She shook her head, smiling with amusement as she grabbed a Sprite and walked back to hand it to him. "Yeah, but you've been here in the city for how many years?"

"No matter. Raised a Texan. I ain't never gonna call it a pop. This here's a Coke." He held up his Sprite and gulped it.

"Then why don't you call Dr. Pepper 'Coke'?"

He guffawed. "Because it's not a Coke, it's a Dr. Pepper."

In that moment, she noticed something different about Hollis's eyes. They were smiling. Genuinely smiling. Time stood still as she witnessed this rarity. It was as if his soul had swum up for air and a day in the sun.

She nodded her head toward the sink. "Are you gonna have to call a plumber?"

"Oh, no. I'll git-r-done, come hell or high water. Nut joint just needs some grease, that's all. I got some right here. I'll just slap some on, and it might oughta soften right up, you'll see."

Serafina just nodded. What else was there for her to say?

He sat looking at the long tool he had been using. "This basin wrench is as sorry an excuse of a tool if there ever was. Grip's bad. Ain't got much torque. Can't believe I wasted my money on it. Thang's about as worthless as teats on a bull."

Serafina smiled to see that side of Hollis, talkative and feisty.

"You're all piss and vinegar today, aren't you?" Serafina teased him in jest, humored by his Texas variant of English coming out in full force.

He wiped sweat off his forehead with his sleeve, not recognizing her banter until he looked up to see her grinning ear to ear. "You mockin' me?"

"Maybe?" She laughed. "You sure are throwing out a lot of metaphors and figurative speech. You only go this Texan on me when you're in a mood."

"Oh, I'm in a mood all right. This is turnin' out to be about as easy as puttin' socks on a rooster."

She laughed. "You're too much. I'm going back to finish up my report now."

"Wait, you think you might could do me another favor?"

"Yeah, what do you need?"

He wiped more sweat off his forehead. "In the front drawer of my desk, there's a keychain with a few keys on it. Can't miss it."

"Okay, hold on."

When she came back holding the keys, he asked, "You think you might could git me my socket wrench and whatever other tools you find upstairs?"

"The attic?" She looked over at the door in the corner. The one mirroring the back door on the opposite wall. The one that had hid in plain sight and gone unnoticed until just then.

Hollis furrowed his brow with puzzlement. "Sure."

Serafina turned back to Hollis swigging his Sprite. "Do you know where it is up there?"

"Should still be in under the kitchen sink."

Her eyes widened. *Kitchen sink?*

• • •

Serafina had grabbed the tools for Hollis so quickly that day that she couldn't remember much about the loft. Just that she'd stepped into a huge open room with hardwood floors, exposed brick walls, and lots of large windows.

Immediately to her right had been an open kitchen, and next to it in the corner had been an enclosed restroom, which, from what she could see inside, had appeared to have a shower.

The rest of the space to her left had been set up like a living room on the side closest to the exterior wall and a bedroom area with a queen-sized bed closest to the interior wall.

But ask her what color the walls were painted or the even the color of the furniture and she couldn't say for sure. Gray? Beige? Off-white? Tan?

Lots of space, that's what she remembered most. And lots of stacked boxes—many of which were opened with various contents spilled out onto the floor, as if they were in the process of being sorted. It had looked mostly like paperwork from where she had been standing, but she couldn't be sure. Overall, it had felt kind of homey up there, like . . .

Like a place to live.

The heat had kicked in fast. It had got to a tolerable temperature, one where Serafina started to feel a calmness take over. She cozied up into the sofa, starting to relax. She felt the easing of tension in her body as muscles loosened and her mind cleared. It was as if her troubles had been uncaged, released to wreak havoc elsewhere.

She resituated herself on the couch to a more reclined position. As she lay there facing the front door, she pictured Hollis walking through, returning from some errand.

She closed her eyes and pretended Hollis was there at his desk working on something. He was usually silent anyway, so it wasn't difficult to imagine.

Oftentimes, though, it would get too quiet in the room, with Serafina working on her reports and Hollis being his normal taciturn self. She would start to notice his breathing, and it would distract her. Whenever that happened, she'd go to the Pandora app on her phone and stream music for them to listen to.

Serafina had created several stations for them by brainstorming songs they liked. Both really liked Van Morrison's "Brown Eyed Girl," so Van Morrison had become the first station they created.

They would venture into other genres occasionally, depending on whatever mood they were in, but the one station they always seemed to fall back on was that one.

Still lying on the sofa, Serafina reached behind her, splaying her fingers out to pick her phone up off the end table. She quickly found the Pandora app and selected *their* station.

The first song Pandora selected was Van Morrison's "Just Like Greta." She set her phone on the ground, and at the same time, imagined Datson lying there on the floor. She put her hand down to where he would be, within reach, close enough to pet. She imagined the feeling of his fur.

It wasn't often that Hollis would bring Datson to work, but when he did, it had always had such a soothing effect on her. Especially when Hollis needed to step out to run an errand and would leave Datson behind. It would be the two of them, and somehow, it just felt comforting. She wasn't completely alone, feeling vulnerable with every strange sound she'd hear. Sometimes she even talked to Datson. Held full-on conversations.

Just then, it occurred to her that she could have Datson stay there with her if she stayed at the agency. There was a complete loft upstairs she could use. Temporarily, of course. "Yeah?" she questioned her own suggestion. *No one's using it.*

Impulsively, Serafina picked up her phone, paused the song playing, and called Levi. It was close to ten o'clock on a Saturday night. If she called that late, he might be sleeping. She paused the music station and called anyway, committing herself before she could change her mind.

After several rings, a man younger than Levi answered. "Hello?"

"Hi, this is Serafina Gray. I'm not sure if you know who I am, but—"

He interrupted. "Hollis's partner, right?"

Partner. She liked the sound of that. "Yeah, I'm sorry to be calling so late, but—"

"You need to talk to my dad, right?"

"Yeah. Does he have another number? Like a cell phone number? This was the only number I had," Serafina said apologetically.

He laughed. "Yeah, he's got a cell phone. My dad's old school, but not that bad." He laughed some more. "Let me go get him so you can exchange numbers or whatever."

"Okay, thanks."

That must've been Levi's son Brian, Serafina thought. Michael was the older one. Michael was the doctor at Beaumont, she recalled.

Serafina became tense; she instantly questioned having called. Was she doing the right thing by calling about Datson? She was nervous about what Levi might say.

"Who is this calling?" the voice of an older Korean female asked on the other line.

It caught Serafina off guard. "Hi, Mrs. Nestor. This is Serafina."

She never really felt comfortable calling her by her first name, Suong, after that first time meeting her.

Before Serafina could say more, Suong asserted, "It is a late hour to call."

"I know. I'm sorry. I—"

Levi spoke on the other line. "Hello? This is Levi."

"Hi . . ." Serafina paused. "Sorry about calling so late, sir."

"You're fine, dear." Levi consoled her. "Is everything okay?"

"Yes, sir." Serafina said respectfully. "I'm calling because I would like to make a proposal."

Levi listened on the other end.

"Well, I can't have Datson stay with me at my house, but . . ." Her heart raced inside her chest as she prepared herself for his reaction. "What would you say if I watched him here at the agency?"

Levi was silent on the other end.

Serafina continued. "I came by the agency to get some work done tonight and got to thinking that there's that loft upstairs I could stay in, if you didn't have a problem with that." Serafina listened for breathing or acknowledgement on the other end. "Datson stays here enough already when Hollis brings him by, so he's used to it here. He likes hanging outside in his doghouse. I would just have to close up the gate to the backyard, is all, but that's no big deal." She paused, allowing Levi to respond.

"Are you sure, dear?" Levi proceeded to speak. "Who knows if Hollis will improve, and if so, how long until then? I'd hate to see you uproot your whole living situation. I mean, I appreciate it, don't get me wrong. Just want to make sure you're really okay with this commitment."

"Absolutely, sir." Serafina reassured Levi. "It's the least I can do."

"You said you're at the agency now?" Levi asked.

"Yes. Just here working on some reports." It was easier to say that than explain her living situation. Plus, she actually did need to complete the reports, although that would be in the morning.

"Are you okay with me dropping him off tomorrow morning, or would that be too soon?"

"Tomorrow morning would be perfect," Serafina said, holding back her nervous excitement.

"Okay, I'll see you then, unless you can think of anything else."

Serafina thought, and then said, "I don't think there's anything else."

"All right then. Good night."

After hanging up, Serafina played the remainder of "Just Like Greta" and leaned back, taking it all in.

Damn, she thought, realizing she'd forgotten to get Levi's cell phone number. She made herself a mental note to get it from him in the morning.

Serafina wondered how the business arrangement would work out now. Would Levi be more involved? Would she need to keep him informed about things?

With Hollis in a coma, so much was uncertain about the future of the agency. So much was uncertain about her future—*period*.

Chapter 9

The first knock was just a random, unrecognizable sound, jolting Serafina half awake. Her subconscious quickly tried to incorporate that sound into her dream, but by the second knock, there was no chance of that happening. She was now fully aware that someone was actually at the front door.

She instinctively looked at the clock on the wall next to the front door. Had she really just slept until 10:37?

She quickly sat up on the sofa, scrunching her eyes and rubbing out the crust of yesterday's mascara. Then, she licked the tip of her middle finger and wiped off what residue from under her eyes she could before answering the door.

"Figured I'd knock going forward," Levi said as he entered with Datson.

Serafina wasn't fully awake, so it took her a moment to give any type of reaction beyond a yawn.

Levi handed Serafina the leash, adding, "Just thinking that with you staying here, you'll need privacy."

Serafina knelt down to Datson's level and unclipped the leash from his collar. As she stood back up, Datson abruptly took off, sprinting down the hall to the kitchen and back to the front room several times.

"He's probably searching for Hollis," Serafina said.

They stood in the center of the room in awkward silence, watching Datson until he settled down in his usual spot near Hollis's desk.

"Oh, shoot!" Levi said, snapping his fingers. "I forgot to bring his bag of dog food. It's back at the house. I can bring it by later."

"Whenever is fine," Serafina said. "Hollis stocks a whole cabinet full of canned dog food here."

"Okay, great," Levi said, sighing with relief.

They both looked at Datson again—their only commonality besides Hollis and the agency.

"He looks pretty content," Levi said.

"Yeah." Serafina nodded.

With Datson doing nothing more than just lying there, Serafina shifted their awkward conversation to the topic of Hollis. "Any news about Hollis? How's he doing?"

Just then, Cole knocked lightly at the screen door.

Datson lifted his head off the floor briefly, and then laid it back down, attentively watching the interactions in the room.

Serafina motioned Cole inside.

"Are you expecting somebody?" Levi turned his head slightly toward the sound and then back at Serafina for a sign of recognition.

"No, he's an acquaintance of Hollis." *Unfortunately.*

"Oh?" Levi said. His eyes widened.

Cole entered, and then immediately scanned the room for signs of Hollis.

"I was just wondering if Frank is around," Cole said. "I haven't been able to get in touch with him for a few days."

Frank. Serafina did her best not to roll her eyes in that moment.

Cole stretched his neck out to the side, tilting it for a better view down the hallway that led to the back of the building.

Levi and Serafina glanced at each other to determine who would be the one to report on Hollis's condition. Levi readied himself to speak, but Serafina made sure to put Cole in his place first.

"*Hollis. . .*" She emphasized the name. ". . . isn't here right now."

She turned to Levi for him to elaborate.

Levi took his cue. "I'm afraid he's been in an accident, son."

Cole's expression turned to concern.

Levi continued. "He's been in the hospital since early yesterday morning."

Cole suspiciously eyed Serafina, as if she'd hidden that golden nugget of news when he had stopped by the day before.

"I just found out myself," Serafina said, instantly feeling defensive. "Levi told me right after you left yesterday."

Not that she owed him an explanation, she thought.

"Is he okay?" Cole directed his concern to Levi.

Serafina caught herself rolling her eyes—mid-roll—so, she played it off as if something was in her right eye by blinking and rubbing at it.

"He's improved greatly since he first went in, but he's still unresponsive," Levi said.

The room fell silent as Cole pondered the news.

"You're an acquaintance of Hollis?" Levi asked.

"Oh, sorry, I'm Cole McDermott. I was doing some work for him."

Work for him? Serafina's interest piqued. She glared at Cole with distrust.

It then occurred to Serafina that there was no mention of Hollis still being on life support. She needed clarification. "Wait, you said he's unresponsive? Is he still on life support?"

"Thankfully, no." Levi exhaled a deep breath and continued. "Michael . . ." Levi turned to Cole and explained. "Michael's my son. He's a doctor on staff at Beaumont where we were able to get Hollis transferred."

Cole nodded, as if processing this information.

Levi then turned slightly to include Serafina. "Michael called this morning with an update. He said that Hollis is recovering nicely from his surgery and is now breathing on his own, but that he's still not awake."

Why was she finding out an update on Hollis's condition at the same time as Cole? After all, who was Cole? Nobody! She was Hollis's assistant—not him!

And what was up with that whole interaction? Levi's body had faced Cole more than her when giving that update. She hadn't even been informed as an equal! She felt slighted, like an afterthought.

Serafina stewed with indignation. Her jaw tightened.

"So, what happened? With Hollis, I mean." Cole probed Levi, excluding Serafina from any consideration.

Did he think he could just wedge himself in between her and Levi, like he was already trying to do with her and Hollis?

Levi began to reply, but Serafina interjected with a curt response. "Someone shot him."

Levi briefly studied Serafina, perplexed by her tone.

Serafina noticed Levi's look of bewilderment. She also noticed Cole carefully observing them, as if just discovering weakness in their relationship. A place he could target and erode.

Was her umbrage toward Cole that obvious? Did they catch her playing off the eye roll? She probably grimaced. She never did well at hiding her emotions. She was always an easy card to read. She needed to do her best to play nice or else risk being shut out altogether. What's that saying about keeping your friends close but your enemies closer?

Serafina smiled courteously at both Levi and Cole. "I'm sorry. I didn't mean to interrupt. As you were saying, Levi?"

Levi turned to Cole and responded in a cordial tone. "He was on the southwest side of Detroit. The consensus is that it was a gang-related incident."

"How do they know it was gang related? Because of the location?"

Cole hypothesized.

"Because of the location?" Serafina internally mocked him, restraining her imminent eye roll.

Cole didn't need to keep asking questions. Like, what was he going to do—solve the case? If Levi didn't think *she* should be getting involved, then this dude *definitely* didn't need to be.

"Not so much the location as the weapon," Levi said.

That was news to Serafina. Did they find the weapon?

Levi caught Serafina looking at him. "I was able to get more information this morning from some former colleagues at the police station."

"You worked for the City of Detroit police?" Cole asked Levi, excitedly.

"Yes. I was a detective there. Retired about seven years ago," Levi said proudly.

Cole grinned from ear to ear. "I'm an officer for the city. It's an honor, sir."

Serafina shifted her stance, glancing back and forth between them. What the hell was she witnessing?

Levi responded, "Likewise."

Great. Serafina clenched her jaw.

"So, you were saying, the weapon?" Cole encouraged Levi to continue.

"It was connected to another murder where the main suspect in that case was a known gang member," Levi said.

"How does gang affiliation of a suspect equate to it being gang related?" Serafina asked Levi, purposely avoiding eye contact with Cole.

Cole jumped in. "Gangs often have an individual commit a crime such as that as part of their initiation into a gang." He turned to Levi for an attaboy.

Serafina couldn't help but roll her eyes that time.

Levi concurred. "Yes, exactly."

Cole perked up.

Serafina clenched her jaw tighter.

"So, you're an officer. How many years you got in?" Levi asked.

Blah, blah, blah. Whatever.

Datson gave out a quick bark at the back door, his signal for wanting to be let out.

Even though it pained Serafina to watch Levi and Cole carry on like that, she didn't want to leave them there to carry on without her. It was unavoidable though.

"I have to let him out. I'll be right back," she announced.

Neither of them acknowledged that she'd even said anything, an act that would have required pulling themselves away from their bro-fest long enough to notice.

Outside, she hurriedly closed the gate and latched it, reminding herself that the longer she stayed out there, the more she'd be missing of their conversation. For all she knew, Levi could be telling Cole information that he didn't want to tell her.

She glanced over at Datson at the back end of the yard doing his business. She assured herself that it would be good for him to be outside for a bit, and then raced back inside and sped down the hallway. She slowed her pace as she entered the front room from the hallway, trying to appear as if she were casually walking in.

Levi and Cole were still discussing mutual acquaintances when she approached them. She tried to stifle her heavy breathing so as not to be obvious about hurrying back.

"What'd I miss?" Serafina interrupted their get-to-know-you session.

Levi appeared to be blushing. No doubt Cole stroked his ego while she wasn't in the room. *Such a suck-ass.*

"So, do either of you know why Hollis was down there and what he was doing?" she asked.

"Beats me," Levi said candidly.

Serafina presented the facts as she knew them. "Is it possible he was investigating that other case? The one that connects the gun to a gang member—what's the story with that?" Serafina asked Levi.

"I don't think they're related, dear." Levi looked at his watch, as if Serafina's questions were boring him.

"Why not?" she insisted.

"For starters, it's not the typical kind of case we investigate— 'we' being the agency," Levi said.

"How so?" Serafina asked.

"The other one was a store robbery committed back in the '90s," Levi said matter-of-factly.

Serafina noticed Cole was avoiding eye contact. He looked tense, as if he knew something but was resistant to say anything.

"Do you know anything about why he was there or what he was doing?" Serafina asked Cole squarely.

Cole looked consternated with that question. He simply shook his head no, and then evasively turned to his new friend Levi to change the subject. "Okay, well, let me know any news on Hollis's condition?"

Serafina kept her eyes on Cole the whole time, her gut telling her something was amiss.

"Of course, son." Levi looked at his wristwatch. "I'll be heading over to the hospital later today. I'll let you know if there is a change if you'd like."

"Okay, yes, if you don't mind. I'd appreciate that," Cole said.

Levi took out his cell phone. "What's your number? I'll send you a text and then you can save it as a contact."

Cole stopped him, and said, "You know what? It's probably easier if I just enter it in."

Serafina watched Levi so willingly hand over his phone to Cole, and Cole so assuredly handle Levi's phone as if it were his own, exchanging contact information and then handing the phone back to Levi. She watched Cole hold out his hand to Levi for a handshake. She watched Levi take Cole's hand in his and appreciatively shake it.

"Nice to see you again." Cole flashed his hand to say goodbye to Serafina like an afterthought, not really looking her in the eye.

"Yeah," Serafina said unconvincingly. Her eyes narrowed and steadily followed Cole as he left out the screen door.

"I must get going, too, unfortunately." Levi turned to pull his jacket off the seat behind him. "Thank you again, dear."

"No problem. Just please let me know whatever you find out about how Hollis is doing or even the case. Yes, I know the police have it handled. I would just like to know." She gave him her most genuine *I'm serious* look.

Levi looked reluctant. "I'll give you an update tonight when I visit the hospital."

"Maybe we should exchange cell phone numbers as well?" Serafina held her phone in anticipation of taking his number.

Levi acquiesced to Serafina's suggestion.

She sent a text message to the number he gave her. "I just sent you a text."

Both of them saved each other's contact information, and then Serafina waited self-consciously as Levi put his jacket on.

"Oh, there's something I wanted to ask you." She waited for Levi's full attention, and then continued once his eyes met hers. "Since you're a silent partner here, should I be including you in business affairs now? With Hollis being in a coma and all?"

Levi paused briefly. "I'm okay with keeping things as is. If you need my assistance on anything, I'm always available. But it looks like you have things covered. If you don't mind assuming the day-to-day issues of running the agency, then less headache for me. Sound good?"

She agreed to that arrangement as she led Levi out, eager to resume her morning wake-up routine.

. . .

The blinking cursor on Serafina's computer screen served as an incessant reminder that she needed to continue typing. Instead of heeding its nudges, she reclined in her desk chair, letting out what had to have been the hundredth sigh since she'd first sat down.

She'd spent most of the afternoon writing up her weekly reports and was now beyond antsy about having the last one complete.

Normally, that number of reports would have taken her half the time. She'd written reports enough for it to be second nature. They all had the same cadence, the same type of information. She'd already created a Save As off another report she typically used as her template. She just needed to plug in relevant facts and make a few modifications.

Why was she having such difficulty focusing?

She knew why. Cole's sealed envelope. It was there, still on her desk, waiting to be given to Hollis. It had caught her eye the second she had sat down. She had tried to ignore it, but that was proving to be impossible.

Cole had said he was doing some work for Hollis. Was that the work he was referring to?

She stiffened in her chair and fixated on the envelope.

Why hadn't Cole mentioned it when he had stopped by that morning? Shouldn't he have asked for it back? Knowing that Hollis was in a coma, wouldn't he want to make sure whatever job he had handled received their report?

Without haste, Serafina picked up the envelope and held it up in the light that was beaming through the front window.

Datson lifted up his head and watched her as she attempted to see through the envelope. She looked back at Datson.

"What?" Serafina asked him defensively. "It might be something urgent that needs my attention."

Datson enjoyed the conversation as much as any dog would.

"What do you mean he would have said something? Whose side are you on anyway?"

Datson just stared at her, panting.

"Okay, well, technically speaking, Levi *did* put me in charge of the agency."

She held the envelope up for Datson to see, and then put her finger on the preprinted return address on the top left corner of the envelope and said, "There. Does that not say Michigan Investigative Services Agency?"

She waited for Datson to respond, knowing he wouldn't.

"Care to argue that one?"

Still no response from Datson.

"Okay then."

Although Serafina would normally just rip open the envelope, she decided to open the envelope with the precision of a letter opener, as if doing so made it official business of the agency.

Randy would be so proud.

Serafina retrieved the letter opener out of Hollis's desk drawer and sliced through the top crease. She sat there looking at the perfectly opened envelope, and then, preparing herself with a deep breath, she slipped the paperwork out and unfolded it with shaky hands.

At last, she would know what the big secret was all about with Cole. Why he was hired. Why she wasn't told about Cole, or whatever Mr. Brown Nose was investigating. Maybe why Hollis got involved with gangs? Questions needed to be answered. She wasn't doing anything wrong. Not at all! She deserved to know. She was Hollis's business partner, his right hand.

Serafina wavered. Maybe she shouldn't open it.

Well, it's a little too late, she thought. She already opened the envelope. It wouldn't matter if she put the paperwork back in without reading it—they'd all assume she did. And then they'd act differently around her, but she wouldn't know what they were thinking because she wouldn't have any context. Context that the paperwork would tell her.

Fuck it. She shouldn't be made to feel like this. That was on them for putting her in this position. She needed to think about herself. If Hollis was planning to replace her, then she needed to plan accordingly. Find a new job. Oh, and now find a new place to live!

But she did agree to watch Datson. And Datson was such a good, old dog. He deserved to live out the rest of his life in a familiar place, surrounded by people who cared about him. And, well, she did care about him. And she cared about Hollis. How could Hollis do this to her? Just replace her?

Serafina stopped herself from spiraling. She reminded herself that a lot was going on and she just needed to breathe. There was probably a very good explanation for Hollis having Cole do some work for him. No more questioning Hollis's intentions. He had always been good to her. Why would he stop now? She was going to read the contents of the envelope and that was that.

Chapter 10

Serafina unfolded the contents from the envelope and began to read them. In the header, it stated Cole McDermott's name, along with his contact information.

Interesting, she thought, noticing the Berkley address. He lived just on the other side of Woodward Avenue. Maybe five minutes away, if that.

Underneath the header, it was formatted like a report, only more professionally written than her typical reports.

Biting on her bottom lip, she started scanning the report for its details.

"woman and man killed in a robbery"

" dead on arrival "

" gunshot wounds "

Serafina was baffled by its contents—*theft, murder, guns*.

Even Levi had said that the investigations they typically handled were the corporate type, nothing inherently dangerous.

Was the agency not making enough money from their corporate jobs? Were they starting to branch out? Was that why Hollis hired Cole? Because Cole was a police officer and could protect himself better than Serafina? But why keep it from her? Unless . . . Was Hollis planning to replace her?

Not that again. Serafina stopped herself from spiraling.

Datson startled Serafina with a bark, and then waited intensely for her to respond.

"Outside?" Serafina asked.

Datson backstepped, giving Serafina space to stand up.

The investigation seemed interesting, but the report was lengthy. She would need a break before reading through it in its entirety.

As Serafina placed the report down on the desk, Datson positioned himself to show her the way to the back of the house—even though she knew where it was. She walked to the kitchen and opened up the back door to let him out.

While Datson did his business outside, Serafina grabbed an iced tea from the refrigerator and gulped down a third of the can. She waited a few minutes for Datson to decide if he wanted to come back in, and then decided to check out the news on her phone.

As she took out her phone from the pocket of her hoodie, she felt it vibrate. The message was from Randy.

4:32 p.m.

Randy Staszak: *Didn't come home last night. Everything okay?*

Serafina didn't know how to feel about Randy texting her. A part of her questioned his motive for texting. Was it compassion? *Unlikely.* Curiosity? *More likely.* Phishing for information, like whether she was out looking for a new place to live? *Probably, perhaps, and most certainly!*

Serafina decided to be aloof but not mean.

4:32 p.m.

Serafina: *Just busy.*

Serafina wanted Randy to feel some sort of compassion for her predicament, but she knew enough not to expect it from him. He had entered his Randy World—the one where he was the center of the universe and everyone else was some sort of exoplanet in another distant galaxy. She knew from experience that there would be no use in getting him to care like she needed him to.

4:32 p.m.

Randy Staszak: *Where are you?*

Why would he care where she was? Serafina squinted her eyes, masking her hurt feeling with mild annoyance. She quickly texted out the shortest, to-the-point response she could think of in that moment.

4:33 p.m.

Serafina: *Work.*

Serafina watched the text bubbles appear, stop, reappear, and stop several times, as she waited for Randy's text response to come through.

4:32 p.m.

Randy Staszak: *Dinner? Nick's asking.*

What. The. Fuck. Serafina's hurt feelings had intensified, and she was fuming. *So, Nick's asking, but not you?*

She thought hard about what to type next, trying several times to respond but kept deleting and retyping. Exasperated, she decided she'd keep it short, like her earlier message.

Datson barked to be let back in, startling Serafina. She hadn't seen him come to the door. Impulsively, she pressed the send button.

Enough of that conversation.

4:33 p.m.

Serafina: *No, thanks.*

Serafina put her phone back in her hoodie pocket. Another text vibrated through the fabric of the hoodie, but she ignored it. Instead, she grabbed her iced tea and headed back into the front room.

When Serafina reentered the front room, she noticed that the letter opener was still out on Hollis's desk, so she put it back in his desk drawer. As she did, she caught a glimpse of keys on a keychain, right in the front corner of the drawer, next to the set of business cards she'd ordered for Hollis that he never used.

Oh, yeah, the loft.

Serafina grabbed the keys and headed back to the kitchen, eager to unlock the door to the loft and settle in up there.

Datson pushed past her and galloped to the top of the stairs as she unlocked the door. Serafina trailed behind, wondering why the door was even locked to begin with.

Serafina's phone vibrated again. She knew it would continue if she didn't check the message, so she took it back out of her pocket and looked at the missed message. As she suspected, it was the last text Randy had sent.

4:34 p.m.

Randy Staszak: *Okay.*

Serafina shook off her mild annoyance from his "Okay." Standing at the top of the stairs, she flipped on the overhead lights and immediately scanned the open space to determine a plan of action.

Aside from years of accumulated dust and scattered paperwork, the loft was relatively clean. If anything, she just needed to contain everything into a box and stack it with the others in the corner. Then she'd get a bucket of hot water, add some Murphy Oil Soap, and wipe everything down, including the hardwood floor.

This shouldn't take too long, she thought.

Serafina went over to the stack of boxes in the corner to see if any of them were empty. One of the first boxes she pulled out was about the size of a microwave. She wondered about its contents as she pulled it out to look inside. It seemed light enough, so she hadn't expected to find a wedding dress, a bridal veil, white, lace flats, and a dried-up bouquet when she opened it.

Why would something like that be stored up there? Unless it was there when Hollis bought the place? People leave stuff behind all the time when they move. Although, that seemed like something a person wouldn't want to leave behind.

Regardless, Serafina didn't want to mix Hollis's belongings up with a previous owner's, which meant she needed to find another box. She folded the box's top flaps under one another and pushed the box to the side.

One by one, Serafina tested the weight of the other boxes, slightly picking up each one off the ground. They all seemed somewhat full, so she gave the room another scan to see if there were any other boxes she might not have noticed. Unable to spot any, she resolved to find a box later.

Serafina made her way over to the living room area rug where paperwork had been haphazardly strewn about. It looked as if Hollis had begun sorting items and given up early in the process.

Standing over the large area rug, she debated on how to proceed without a box. After a few moments, she decided to just push all the items into a center pile that she could easily scoop up once she did find a box.

She knelt down to position herself for pushing the items but then realized that the paperwork wasn't just paperwork and sat down for a closer look.

There, intermixed with the paperwork were photographs and personal letters, opened and on display for anyone to read.

Datson plopped himself down at her feet and rested his chin on her leg. Serafina reached over to pet his head, thinking about whether to take a peek at any of the letters.

No one would know if she read them. Except her. She would know. Could she live with that? Knowing that she'd violated Hollis's privacy? His trust?

Hollis wasn't one to open up about his past, so all she really knew was that he'd grown up in Texas and that he had been in the army with Levi. This was her chance to find out more.

From what Serafina could tell, the letters all appeared to have the same cursive handwriting. She glanced at the return address on several of the envelopes next to the letters. They were all from someone named

Samuel Hollis Jr. with an address in Texas. Could Samuel be a relative of his? Her curiosity was piqued.

One by one, she picked up the personal letters to "Dear Frank" and skimmed them to get the gist of their contents. Some were written as early as February 1989, others as late as January 1990, and they were laid on top of one another in what seemed to be chronological order.

The first letter on top of the small stack, dated February 26, 1989, was Samuel breaking the news to Frank about "Daddy" not doing well. Near the end of the letter, Samuel asked Frank to come home. He said they needed to discuss how to keep the farm running and that he would need help if any crops were to be grown that year. From the way the letter was worded, Serafina wondered if Samuel might be Hollis's brother.

The next letter she looked at, dated March 18, 1989, was Samuel letting Frank know Daddy's health was diminishing. The tone had a sense of urgency, and again, Samuel asked Frank to come home.

The letter after that was dated March 28, 1989. In that one, Samuel pleaded with Frank to come home on account of Daddy being hospitalized. She must have read the word "please" a dozen times in that letter alone.

After that, there was a letter dated April 6, 1989, with Samuel informing Frank that Daddy was released from the hospital and that hospice care would be taking over. It said things like, "He doesn't have much time," and, "Say our goodbyes." He also expressed concern over the farm facing foreclosure, pleading Frank to reconsider, "for Daddy."

The last few letters seemed to be out of order. One was dated January 10, 1990, and the one underneath was April 17, 1989. The January one was Samuel letting Frank know that the bank had foreclosed on all their acres of farmland, that it was just the farmhouse property now. The April one was Samuel letting Frank know that "Daddy went home to be with Momma."

As Serafina placed the letters back down into a neat pile, she noticed an obituary underneath some of the envelopes. She pulled it out and examined the name—Samuel Hollis Sr. She stared at the photograph, recognizing bits of Hollis in the face of the elderly man. At the bottom, it read that he had been survived by his sons, Samuel Hollis Jr. and Frank Hollis.

Serafina rested her back against the couch, thinking.

Hollis had a brother? Is this why Hollis had never mentioned his brother? Was this Samuel guy still alive? Why did Hollis avoid going back to Texas? Did he actually miss his father's funeral? If he did miss it, then why?

Downstairs, the office phone rang.

By the time Serafina had descended the stairs and got to the office phone in the front office, the ringing had stopped. Noticing the half-read report from earlier, she took a seat and decided to take a quick look at the rest of the report before putting it away on Hollis's desk. Maybe she'd find something interesting.

Nothing really riveting left on the first page. Serafina turned the page, scanning for any facts or details that might add to her understanding without her having to read the whole thing.

Nothing much on the second page. She turned to the third page and proceeded in the same manner.

"Xavier Palo"

"suspect in case"

"eighteen years old at the time"

"never officially charged for the murders"

"deal made on other unrelated charges"

"left during investigation"

"not investigated further on the murders"

She turned the page and began reading the fourth page, again homing in on key details.

"store owners"

"Alma and James Gray"

"no known relatives"

"southwest Detroit"

"four-year-old daughter placed in foster care"

Instantly, Serafina was thrust into a montage of hazy, disjointed memories.

• • •

Serafina looked up at the policeman holding her hand in his. He towered over her. His hand felt dry and rough, and it was bigger than her father's. The policeman was walking her down a hallway. The walls were concrete blocks. The floor was laminated with tiles. They entered a big room. Other police officers, all sitting at their desks. A lady police officer with dark skin smiled at her. She was pretty, like one of Serafina's dolls. She had red lips and long fingernails. The lady talked to Serafina. She asked Serafina questions. The words made sense, but Serafina couldn't find her words. A tall white policeman gave Serafina something to eat from the vending machine and a coloring book with some crayons. After a while, a woman who looked like a younger version of Serafina's mother came over. She spoke with the red-lipped lady. ". . . not speaking." ". . . understand English?" ". . . Mexicantown." ". . . Spanish?" The social worker began speaking to Serafina in the language her mother used. Serafina understood some, but she still couldn't find her words.

• • •

Serafina pushed the report away and leaned back in her chair, her hand covering her mouth. She tried to think back further in time, to before she'd been brought to the police station.

Alma and James Gray. Those had been her parents. She'd always known that from her birth certificate. She just hadn't *known* known them. Not the details like this.

And she'd always known they'd been killed. But she didn't know the specifics, or that they had a store.

How come she didn't remember anything about the store? Or where she lived? Or anything about her parents? Or anything before being taken to the police station?

There was so much to process, so much to sort out. Her hands trembled with adrenaline. Her heart raced. She felt immobilized. Confined.

Overwhelmed by so many emotions coming at her, Serafina left out the back door and got in her Jeep. She backed out of the driveway and then drove down the side street to get on the freeway. She got on Walter P. Chrysler/I-75 southbound and then immediately took the exit to get on the Walter P. Reuther/I-696 eastbound. Instinctively, Serafina knew where she was going. She stayed in the far-right lane and cruised, not wanting to speed while she allowed herself to release all that she was holding inside.

Serafina put the radio on scan, allowing it to play ten seconds of a song before moving to the next station. She barely paid attention to the songs as each played. She couldn't really handle much more than ten seconds anyway. She was too antsy for anything more.

One song after another played as she contemplated how she would get through it all. She wanted to cry. She wanted to scream. She wanted to run as far and as long as she could. She wanted to be held. But she didn't want to be confined. She felt angry. Yes, definitely angry. But most of all, she felt sad. And alone. So alone.

Who was in her corner? Who could she call to comfort her? No one.

Serafina noticed that the radio had stopped scanning and was stuck on a station. She was about to select scan again when the next song came on—Coldplay's "Yellow." She paused herself in mid-action.

The lyrics spoke to her. Not in the way that translated anything she was feeling. Not in the way that made sense. It was as if her heart knew. The melody, the message—it soothed her. Tears receded back into her strong heart. She breathed in deeply and let out a long exhale. Calmness began to set in.

As Serafina drove the remaining twenty minutes to the Nautical Mile in St. Clair Shores, she thought about the first time she'd been there. Back when she'd followed Hollis there and watched him walk along the dock behind Jack's Waterfront on Lake St. Clair.

Not often, but every once in a while, something would inevitably put Hollis in a funk. He'd become withdrawn and just leave. Serafina would wonder where he went during those times, so she began following him. Nothing she was proud of. Her curiosity had just got the better of her.

The first time following him had been extremely difficult because she had no clue where he was going. She had needed to keep a close distance without being conspicuous.

The several times after that, she had an inkling of where to go and what to expect. She knew he wouldn't be going there to meet up with anyone. He'd find a parking spot near Jack's Waterfront, and then walk the dock, looking out, as if talking to the lake. Looking for answers. Each time became a repeat of that instance. Nothing ever changed. Eventually, he'd leave, and she'd just remain in her office chair, completing her report.

Serafina arrived at the parking lot where Jack's Waterfront used to be. It was under new ownership now. She could see Lake St. Clair just behind the building—the "lake of answers" to Hollis. It was time that she got answers too.

Serafina parked her Jeep close to the dock alongside the canal where boats would come in for waterfront service at Jack's. She began walking out.

Why would Hollis investigate her? It just didn't make sense. Did he not trust her? Did he not believe her? Did he know something she didn't?

Serafina stood at the end of the boardwalk and watched the waves gently roll under the dock. A few pigeons wandered around the garbage can close by. She leaned up against the rail and looked out.

There had always been parts of her life she had questioned. Like why she had gone into foster care instead of living with a relative. Wanda had told her no relatives could be found, but that seemed hard to believe. *No* relative? *None? No* cousin twice removed or whatever? *No* distant aunt from Connecticut? *No* grandmother from the old country—wherever that was? *No one?*

Those were all things that she'd lain in bed at night and thought about back when she was younger. Back when she'd fantasize about the life she could have been living, instead of the life she had. But she'd long ago accepted her circumstances. She no longer sought out those kinds of answers. So why was Hollis doing so now?

A gust of wind from the northwest swept across the dock where Serafina was standing. She pocketed her hands into the front compartment of her hoodie and shivered.

Those were questions she wouldn't get answered from the lake. She needed to find them out from Hollis.

Chapter 11

Serafina was finding it difficult to focus that next morning. She sat at her desk trying to type up the last investigative report for work but kept getting distracted by the thoughts still reverberating within her from Sunday's events. It was as if her mind had become an overcrowded room and the cacophony was so loud that she could barely make sense of her thoughts and feelings, each competing to be voiced. Having Cole's investigative report on her desk wasn't helping. She picked up his report and placed it back inside the large envelope, hoping that would quiet the noise.

She looked over at Datson, lying in his usual spot under Hollis's desk. Her internal nagging system reminded her that she really needed to finish typing up that last report, but she convinced herself that giving Datson the attention he deserved was just as important.

"Wanna go for a walk?"

Datson's ears perked briefly, and he slightly lifted his head, as if waiting for Serafina to move from her position.

Serafina stood up and retrieved the leash from its hook on the wall near the front door. Normally, that would send Datson into a frenzy, running down the hall and back, but Datson just laid his head back down.

"Come on, boy," Serafina said in her high-pitched voice, showing him the leash in her hands.

Datson closed his eyes and continued resting.

Serafina crouched down beside him. "Don't you want to go for a walk?"

After a few moments of watching Datson breathe, she stroked the top of his head with her left hand. "I know, boy. I miss him too."

Serafina put the leash back in its place. She sat back down at her desk and willed herself to focus on the last report.

It was unusual for Serafina to have residual reports hanging over her head beyond Sunday night. In fact, more times than not, she wouldn't have any to complete on Sunday at all. Her preference had always been to blast through them by Saturday afternoon and have the rest of the weekend to hang out and do whatever. She thought about everything she'd experienced over the past few days, likening it to treading water out in the ocean as one wave after another pummeled her in the face, barely able to take in air before another round engulfed her. First wave: Randy and Nick preparing for their adoption. Second wave: having to move. Another: Randy's weird relationship with Wanda constantly rubbed in her face. Another: Hollis on life support. Again and again, they kept coming. Hollis in a coma. Levi and Suong judging her—mostly Suong. *Bitch*. Datson needing to be cared for. Cole working for Hollis. Cole investigating her. Hollis investigating her. And now—as if that wasn't enough—she was behind on work too.

Serafina shifted in her chair restlessly. She looked at the calendar on the wall next to her desk. The new work week was here, whether she was ready for it or not. Soon, research and investigation requests would start to trickle in from their clients. Without Hollis there to help, how would she be able to tackle them? *One way or another*, she resolved. What else was there to do?

Serafina struggled through the next thirty minutes of typing up the last report. She composed an email to her client, attached the file, and sent it off. *Why didn't Cole just email his report to Hollis?* she wondered as she closed her laptop, and then finished her thoughts aloud. "That's what a normal person would do. Clearly, he's not normal."

Serafina leaned back in her desk chair and stretched out her back. She lowered her head to stretch out her neck muscles, holding the position. After a few moments, she rose slowly from her chair and started stretching out her lower back, thinking about her plans for the day.

She'd need to follow up with the HR Manager for one of their top clients today, a manufacturing plant in Westland. But that would be a quick email. Aside from that, there wasn't much of anything else pending. There were quite a few items Serafina could put on her agenda—items Hollis had mentioned more than once for her to look into or follow up on—but she really only had one item on her mind.

She sat back down in her desk chair and took out Cole's report, turning to the page where it addressed the suspect who was never charged on the case for her parents' murder.

"Xavier Palo"

Serafina mentally sounded out the name. She sat still in her chair, processing her thoughts, her mind still weighing in on the findings from Cole's investigation.

Her phone dinged as a new message came in from Randy. She took a quick glance at what he wanted.

9:54 a.m.

Randy Staszak: *You don't need to be so dramatic, ya know? Stay somewhere else at night if that's what you want. Just know that's by your choice.*

Serafina didn't have the fight in her. She replied with little thought to her response.

9:55 a.m.

Serafina: *Not dramatic. Taking care of Datson at agency until Hollis gets out of the hospital.*

Serafina opened her laptop and began searching on the Google browser for whatever information she could find about Xavier Palo. Without too much effort, she found a somewhat recent article about Friends of Clark Park, a community center in Mexicantown where he worked as a volunteer for their youth programs. It had been published a few months prior, so she figured it was worth a shot. She wrote down the address, and then looked at the time on her watch. "Yeah, I think we have time for a visit today."

Serafina looked over at Datson, still sleeping peacefully. She debated whether to wake him. *It's probably best to have him stay outside so he's not waiting on me to return.* She assured herself, *He has his doghouse to keep out of the elements if it rains.* "Come on, Datson. Let's go outside." She coaxed him to follow her.

Datson rose in a way reflective of his age, unlike the full-on puppy power he'd produced the other day when Levi had dropped him off. He walked slowly behind Serafina as she went to the back door to let him out.

• • •

Serafina parked in front of a duplex on Clark Avenue and looked over at Clark Park to her left.

That must be it, she thought, spotting a brick building that resembled a community recreation center. Her phone rang just as she unbuckled her seatbelt. She glanced quickly at the incoming caller before answering. *Randy.*

"Yeah? What's up?" Serafina asked, distantly.

"I only have a few minutes between classes, so I have to be quick. You were saying Hollis is in the hospital?"

"Yeah."

"What for?"

"He was shot." Normally, she'd elaborate, but . . . *whatever.*

"Oh, wow, is he okay?"

"Yeah, I suppose. He was on life support, but now he's breathing on his own. Still in a coma though."

"A coma! What happened? Do they know who did it?"

"No, not yet. Someone shot him on his motorcycle Friday night, or rather, Saturday morning."

"Wait, when did you find out about it?"

"Saturday morning."

"WHAT?" Randy yelled. "It's Monday, and you're just now telling us? Don't you think Nick and I would want to know if Hollis was in the hospital?"

Like I would want to know you and Nick were planning to adopt a baby and making me move?

"Figured you both had a lot going on," Serafina said, intentionally being obstinate.

"Seriously?" Randy retorted on cue.

They were both silent on the phone.

Serafina spoke up. "I've been thinking lately . . . I should probably start clearing my things out so you can have the room to set up the nursery."

Serafina didn't want to start clearing out her things, but she figured that was what Randy wanted to hear. She just needed to be sure.

The silence continued.

Was he ready to discard their bond so easily? She didn't blame him for wanting to adopt, to have a family. She, of all people, knew how he felt. To watch others with their families. To feel like an outsider looking in. To not have a sense of belonging. But that's why they were so close. They'd been through similar circumstances. Sort of. Different forms of trauma, but trauma just the same.

Serafina broke the silence. "I'll grab a load next time I'm there."

Randy remained silent on the other line.

"Okay, well, talk to you later." Serafina hung up before Randy could get in his usual "Mm-hmmm."

As Serafina entered the community center, she noticed a display on the wall holding various pamphlets. She grabbed one that read "Friends of Clark Park" on the front cover. It was thicker than the others and appeared to highlight their programs. She read an excerpt on the first page and was immediately impressed by its mission to provide all sorts of services for the community.

Serafina heard the ding of a text message come from her pocket. She closed the pamphlet and took her phone out to check the message. It was just Nick.

12:13 p.m.

Nick Rigatos: *Hey, Randy just told me that Hollis is in the hospital? Is he all right? Is there anything we can do to help?*

Without hesitation, Serafina silenced her phone and put it back in her pocket.

"Is anyone helping you?" a man asked from behind her.

Serafina turned around to see a gray-haired, Hispanic man coming in from outside. He wore wire-rimmed glasses with a squared-off frame. His transition lenses were still somewhat darkened from being in the sun.

"Hi. I read an article about your mentoring program and was interested in talking with that particular speaker. Xavier Palo?"

Serafina quickly started thinking about the answers she would be providing when asked who she was and why she was there to speak with Xavier Palo.

"Ah. He's one of our volunteers for the mentoring program." He smiled and nodded. "His hours vary, but he is actually expected here later today around three o'clock to speak with a group, if you care to come back."

Serafina looked at her watch. It was going on 12:15 p.m. She looked back up and smiled politely. "Yes, that would be great. Thank you."

The man simply nodded his head and walked away, disappearing into an office down the hallway.

The sunlight seemed brighter to Serafina as she exited the building. She squinted her eyes, doing her best to shield them with her right hand while she looked around. *Hollis was shot somewhere in this area*, she thought, looking at her surroundings with intensity. There wasn't much going on at Clark Park. Just an elderly woman walking her Pomeranian.

Serafina had wanted to take her Jeep, but the yellow would have stuck out too much. Not a good idea if she wanted to keep a low profile. Disgruntled about her choice, she got in the Explorer and started driving down the side streets, making her way up to Vernor Highway.

All along the highway, parked cars lined each side of the street, with only one lane to drive for either direction. Brick buildings—mostly restaurants, barber shops, and resale boutiques—lined each side of the street, one after another. Most of the buildings had upstairs apartments, or at the very least, a floor for storage above them. Some had big picture windows, others small double-hungs.

A person on a scooter rode past her on the left as they both drove down Vernor Highway toward Junction Avenue. Up ahead, the scooter slowed down at the stoplight. As Serafina pulled up to the right of the scooter, she looked over at the young man riding. The light turned green. The man on the scooter drove off quickly and then turned left onto a side street a few streets past Junction.

Those things were so small compared to actual motorcycles, Serafina thought. You'd get crushed in a collision. And the scooter! No fixing that. Might as well send it to a scrapyard.

Serafina continued to drive a few more blocks and then immediately pulled into a parking space on the side of Vernor Avenue. She was never going to find the place where the accident happened by going up and down random streets.

The repair garage. That was the answer. The repair garage that left a message that morning for Hollis was the one that picked up his motorcycle from the crash site. They would know where the crash site was. What was the name of the garage again? *Think, think, think.* Unable to remember the name of the shop, Serafina took out her phone and began putting in key words to search on Google.

repair garage Detroit [search]

repair garage southwest Detroit [search]

motorcycle garage southwest Detroit [search]

None of the search results stuck out to her. She would have to wait until she got back to the agency that night to relisten to the messages on the desk phone. Hopefully, she hadn't deleted the call.

As Serafina pulled up to the corner of Junction Avenue and Vernor Highway, she felt a strong sense of déjà vu. Across the street, on her left, was a huge Catholic church attached to what looked to be a school, its presence taking up more than a block. She immediately parked the Explorer and walked across the street to the entrance of the church. Etched into a concrete slab on the brick exterior were the words, "the Church of the Most Holy Redeemer," with the date, "July 10, 1921." Why did this seem so familiar to her?

Serafina turned around with her back to the entrance, scanning the area for clues to her sudden sense of familiarity. She quickly looked both ways on Vernor Highway and then crossed the street.

Serafina stood outside a Coney Island restaurant on the corner, allowing her instincts to guide her next steps. Could she be experiencing memories? Was it possible her parents' old convenience store was nearby? Something told her that she was close.

She started walking down the sidewalk, but then something clicked in her mind. She instantly turned around and headed back to the corner. There, on the other side of Junction Avenue, Serafina recognized a convenience store. *Was that it?* She walked over to it and stood at the door, entranced with a vivid moment from her past.

• • •

Serafina was twirling around on the sidewalk in her yellow sundress, watching the fuzzies blow off the dandelion she held in her hand like a wand. She'd spent most of the afternoon coloring on the sidewalk with chalk, and now she was finding other ways to amuse herself. She picked up her big, speckled-blue ball and began bouncing it off the brick exterior of the building again. She knew not to allow the ball to go into the street, so she was careful to catch it before it rolled past her. A lady she recognized walked up to the screen door and waved to her before opening the screen door to go inside. *Butterfly*, she thought. Just then, the ball bounced past her. Serafina ran quickly after it to keep it from going into the street, tripping on her chalk in the process. She fell forward, her knees hitting the ground first, and then the palms of her hands. The ball rolled into traffic and disappeared. She cried out.

• • •

Serafina wondered why she associated that woman with a butterfly. She tried to think about it more, but nothing came to mind. Maybe she'd seen a butterfly in that moment. Whatever the reason, Serafina wasn't going to continue thinking about it when her curiosity was telling her to go inside. Someone from her past might be in there. She held her focus on the screen door, intensely waiting for a familiar face to appear.

The smell immediately stopped Serafina where she stood upon entering the store. It was as familiar as any smell could ever be, yet she couldn't name the source. She stood in place breathing in deeply. Everything around her seemed to fade away in that moment as her mind transported her to another time. All of a sudden, she felt lightheaded.

"Are you okay, miss?" asked an elderly Hispanic woman in a loosely fitted green dress.

A middle-aged Hispanic man with a mustache came rushing to Serafina and took her by the arm over to a chair against the wall.

"Get the girl some water," the elderly woman told the man.

"Sí, Mama." The man left Serafina's side to go get her a bottle of water.

The elderly woman approached Serafina curiously.

Serafina tried to stand up.

"Rest." The woman coaxed her to stay seated and then patted Serafina's shoulder.

The man returned with a bottle of water and handed it to his mother who then handed it to Serafina.

"Thank you." Serafina took a drink of the water and then drank more until it was three-quarters empty. She hadn't realized how parched she was. She looked at the elderly woman's face, whose kind eyes felt soothing, and then she looked at the middle-aged man's face, who seemed concerned.

Serafina swept the room with her eyes and prepared herself to speak. "I used to come here." She knew it was an odd thing to say as soon as she said it. But it wasn't really said for their benefit. It was more like an admission to herself.

The elderly woman and her son looked at one another.

Serafina slowly shook her head side to side in disbelief. She was *really* there—in her parents' store. She knew it with every fiber of her being that this was the store. She thought how many years had gone by since she'd stepped foot in that place. She barely had any memories, just spurts of memories that would come out of nowhere on occasion and, in an instant, be gone just the same. So many of her memories didn't always make sense either. She'd found it easier to just suppress them over the years. But now, maybe things would finally start to make sense.

The elderly woman shifted her stance. Her son motioned to her that he'd get her a chair, but she shook her head to indicate she was fine. "Me and my late husband—bless his soul—purchased this place about twenty-five years ago. Did you know the previous owners?"

Before Serafina could respond, the elderly woman recalled, "It was such a sad thing to happen. Nice people."

Serafina looked at the elderly woman and then at the middle-aged man looking questioningly at his mother.

The elderly woman turned to her son. "Remember they had that sweet little girl? Such a shame."

He seemed to be thinking about it. "Yes." His voice crackled when he started to speak. "Sad, indeed. It was all over the news back then. They said so many things; nobody ever knew the truth of what really happened. They said it was a robbery; then I think they thought it was a gang thing."

Serafina took another drink of her water.

The elderly woman interjected. "Such a horrible thing for those kids too."

Kids? Serafina was frozen by that word.

The elderly woman turned to her son. "I wonder what ever happened to them."

"Maybe went to relatives?" her son conjectured.

"Maybe. The older boy must have stayed local because I still see him from time to time. Heard he is in a wheelchair now too. So sad."

"Ma, isn't he that guy in the wheelchair up at Clark Park?"

"Yes, I believe it is. I have seen him up there a few times come to think of it.

"Yeah! I know him. I mean, I don't *know* him, but I know of him. He comes in here every so often. Nice guy."

"Do you know his name?" Serafina blurted out.

"I'm not too sure," the man said.

The elderly woman touched her son's arm. "His name is Guillermo . . . from his license. Don't you remember me saying that one time that he's got the same name as your great grandfather?"

The man gestured that he didn't. "Oh wait! Yeah, I remember. But he doesn't go by that name. His friend called him Gill."

The elderly woman turned to Serafina. "How did you say you knew them?"

"The little girl was me."

The elderly woman and her son looked shocked, but before either could respond, Serafina stood up. "Thank you so much for the water. I need to be going now."

Outside, Serafina looked back at the store before crossing the street. *Do I have an older brother?*

Chapter 12

Serafina looked at her watch as she stood outside what had been her parents' convenience store. It was already more than a half hour past two o'clock. If she wanted to catch Xavier Palo before he started speaking to the youth group, she'd need to get there by three o'clock. Actually, before three o'clock, she thought, since she wanted time to speak with him. Time to get a sense of what he knew or didn't know about her past—or even what happened to Hollis. She hurried over to the Explorer and started it up, looking for the best way to turn around to head back down West Vernor Highway toward Clark Avenue.

As she parked the Explorer out front of the community center and readied herself to go inside, she noticed that the park was no longer empty as it had been earlier. At the baseball field, grade-school children were gathering with their teams for a game of softball. To the left of the field were the basketball courts where young men dodged one another and tested out their hooping from a distance. Serafina exited the Explorer and began walking toward the entrance to the community center when she spotted a man in a wheelchair at the edge of the basketball court, situated under a tree near one of the picnic tables. It stopped her in her tracks. *That could be Gill.*

She looked at her watch again: 2:47 p.m. There was no guarantee the man in the wheelchair would still be there when she was done speaking with Xavier Palo. Not wanting to chance it, she firmly decided to head over to the direction of the man, taking the most direct path so as not to draw unwanted attention from the men on the basketball court. The grassy field was still spongy from the recent rain showers, causing her shoes to sink slightly into the soil with each step. She strategically avoided dirt patches that might be deceivingly slippery as she mapped out her path to him. At one point, she looked back up to gauge the remaining distance she'd need to walk and realized one of the basketball players—an older one in his forties—had walked over to a rust-colored 1978 Chevrolet Impala parked at the curb. Both he and the driver were watching her. She didn't get a good look at the driver, but he seemed to be in his forties as well.

Serafina half-expected to be catcalled with the usual, "Hey! What's your name? You got a boyfriend?" or, "Hey! If I gave you my number, would you call me?" But none of that came her way this time. The ballers continued dodging and hooping. The driver and the older baller at the curb resumed their conversation. But now the man in the wheelchair was looking back in her direction. She held his attention until they were within hearing distance.

The man squinted his eyes and stared hard at her. He was older than Serafina for sure. Maybe in his forties? She couldn't be sure when it came to age guessing. She just knew all these forty-somethings were older than her by about ten years.

"Hi, I believe we may know each other. Gill, right?"

The man leaned his head to the side, continuing to squint as she neared him. "Since the day I was born."

"Wow, I . . ." Serafina pulled her shoe out of a spongy spot that she hadn't paid attention to. "I don't know where to begin."

"Usually at the beginning is a good place to start," Gill joked, stroking his stubbled face.

Serafina hesitated for a quick moment and then gave into blurting out, "I'm Serafina."

Gill's eyes widened. He moved his head backward, getting a better look at Serafina.

She continued. "I was just at the store. My parents' old store? And they told me—the owners, I guess? They said they remembered us from back then and that you were sometimes over here at this park. They said you were in a wheelchair, so that's how I knew it was you. Well, I didn't know, but I thought it might be you." Serafina gleefully laughed. "Wow. I can't believe I've found you after all these years."

Gill smiled softly, his eyes following Serafina's facial expressions. "Yes, it has been a long time."

"Have you been here this whole time? Not here at the park, I mean, here, in general. This area?" Serafina felt the questions tripping out of her.

Gill laughed. "Kind of, I suppose."

Serafina processed her own question and his answer. "Wait, so you've been here the whole time? You didn't get sent away too?"

Gill looked confused.

Serafina found herself confused as well. "You didn't have to go live in a foster home too?"

"No?" Gill answered questioningly.

"Then where did you live all these years?" Serafina asked.

"At home?" Gill continued to show confusion. "I guess I'm confused."

"But . . ." Serafina sorted through the confusion, "So, wait . . ." She continued to think.

Gill filled in the blanks as best he could. "After what happened to your parents, I stopped working at the store."

Your parents?

"You were just working there?" Serafina asked.

"Yes?" Gill responded cautiously. "Why? What did you think?"

Serafina felt embarrassed. "I'm sorry. I feel stupid now."

"What?" Gill coaxed her.

"I, okay, when the guy said . . ."

"Guy?"

"Sorry, the guy at the—actually, it wasn't even the guy. It was the old lady, his mother. She said . . ." Serafina hesitated, averting her eyes from looking at Gill. "Well, she made it sound like you were . . ." She stopped short as she returned her eyes to his.

"Were what?"

"Were . . ." She bit her bottom lip. ". . . my brother."

Gill blushed. "Oh."

"I feel silly now."

"No, don't." Gill quickly absolved her. "You were so young, and I kind of was like an older brother to you back then. Your parents . . ." Gill stopped mid-sentence and then apologized. "I'm sorry."

"It's okay. What were you going to say about my parents?"

Gill's eyes met squarely with Serafina's, as if he was looking right into her soul. "Your parents were very good people. They treated me like I was family. They didn't deserve what happened to them."

Serafina teared up, pursed her lips together, and nodded.

Gill motioned for her to come over to him. Serafina complied. He reached his arms out to embrace her in her sorrow, and she welcomed the gesture from this man she knew as family, if only for an hour. She leaned into him at his wheelchair, closed her eyes, and accepted the embrace, and then awkwardly moved away from his wheelchair, careful not to fall over onto him.

"Sorry," Serafina said, as she stepped on his foot instead.

"It's quite all right." Gill took her hand and lightly squeezed it.

"Hey!" A woman's voice called from the other side of the basketball court.

Serafina looked over to see a young woman in her twenties—most likely in her third trimester of pregnancy—walking toward them, holding a bag of Doritos and a Mountain Dew.

"Hey, long time no see. Girl, you 'bout to explode!" Gill let out an eruptive laugh.

"You have no idea." She rubbed her belly. "This kid needs to hurry up already!"

She turned to Serafina, sizing her up inconspicuously.

Gill quickly introduced them. "Tammy? Serafina. Serafina? Tammy. Serafina and I—we go way back."

Tammy held her hand up and gestured a side-swipe wave to Serafina. "Cool." She then redirected her attention to Gill. "Hey, have you seen Manny 'round?"

"He was around earlier. I see he caught up with Renzo."

Tammy shot him a questioning look.

"They was here just a bit ago."

"Yeah, I know all about that." Tammy seemed annoyed.

"You don't sound too happy about it."

"Well, yeah, it's all right, but like for real, though, how'm I supposed to get a baby seat in that car?" Tammy shook her head as she put another Dorito chip in her mouth.

"No idea," Gill said. "Everything else okay?"

"Hm." Tammy licked Dorito seasoning off her fingers. "Depends on what you mean by 'okay.'"

"Not good?" Gill inquired.

"Just funny how Manny's not answering his phone and all. Better not be hookin' up with no other girls an' shit. He lucky I took him back the last time."

"Aw man. Girl, I hope that's not the case," Gill said sympathetically.

Their cryptic and sensitive conversation was making Serafina feel uncomfortable, like she was being forced to invade someone's privacy. She interrupted their conversation. "I gotta head out."

Gill and Tammy both turned to Serafina as she continued. "I'm taking care of a friend's dog, and I gotta let him out. Plus, I need to stop inside the community center real quick."

Maybe she didn't need to mention letting Datson out—which wasn't even true since he was still outside in his doghouse—but she wasn't sure if just mentioning the community center would be enough to justifiably escape Tammy.

"Yeah, no problem. I understand. Make sure you come around again. Love to catch up, 'kay? You still gotta fill me in on what you been up to all these years." Gill threw up two fingers sideways, a symbol of peace.

Serafina smiled back. "Absolutely." She then turned to Tammy. "It was nice to meet you."

"Yeah," Tammy said coolly.

Serafina briskly walked over to the community center, worried about missing out on her chance to speak to Xavier, even though logic told her that he'd still be speaking to the youth group.

At the entrance, she thought how she should have exchanged contact information with Gill but quieted her angst with the knowledge that Gill frequented the park and was well-known.

Inside the community center, a few people lingered around in the main hallway. One boy around twelve years old was tying his shoe while a younger boy around eight years old nagged him for something in the older boy's bag. A teenage boy disappeared through a door farther down the hallway. Serafina wondered if that might be the room to find Xavier speaking to the youth group.

As she walked toward the door, she could hear a speaker inside. She was debating on whether to go inside when the gray-haired Hispanic man with the wire-rimmed glasses she'd met earlier came out from the room. He motioned his head toward the room, which she took to mean she could find Xavier in there. She nodded her head in acknowledgement and thanked him with a smile.

The meeting room was relatively large, the size of several classrooms that had been opened up by a retracted divider. Serafina stayed at the back of the room near the coffee and cookies as the speaker presented his message to the mentorship program participants.

The speaker—who she presumed was Xavier Palo—was a medium-sized Hispanic man with a shaved head and a goatee. His demeanor gave the impression he had a lot of life experience to share, like that of an old man. But he couldn't be much older than Gill, she thought. He wore black jeans and a plain black T-shirt untucked. His arms were muscular like someone who turned wrenches for a living, and they were adorned with various tattoos, none of which Serafina could make out from where she stood in the back of the room. Serafina noticed him looking over to her as he spoke to the group, giving her a welcoming smile.

Xavier took in their attention and became dramatic as he spoke. All the teenage boys sat entranced, listening to the stories Xavier was telling them.

"I still remember the last time I was pulled into court like it was yesterday. Me and my boys had just boosted a ride and were looking at doin' time. I could tell that lady judge didn't like me none. She took one look at me and my long-ass record, and she was ready to lock me away for the maximum time she could. I already knew I was goin' away 'cause I heard my boys weren't so lucky in court and all. I was thinking no way she gonna give me one ounce of mercy. What happened to me was short of miraculous, really. I had Mother Mary on my side that day, for sure. 'Cause I should have got locked up that day, but instead I was released to my abuela on the count that I agreed to enlist in the army." He elicited some reactions from the group and then continued. "Yeah, my abuela—sweet but tough woman, she was—she begged that lady judge to spare me on the count of me being all she had left in this world.

I don't know where I'd be without that woman. Y'all remember that. Your folks want the best for you, so you gotta listen to 'em."

One of the teenage boys raised his hand to be called upon, and then asked, "Is that what you wanted? To go into the army?"

"Naw. In fact, that day, I remember thinking how it wa'nt any different from going to prison. Lost my freedom to go run around. But what I didn't know at that time was that I was getting so much more in return. I'll tell you what I got. I got my self-respect. I got my confidence. I got an education. I got trade skills now and can make a good, honest living using those skills. I pretty much got myself a life worth living. I thought I needed that gang I ran around with. Most are either dead or in jail now. Those that are still around, I feel sorry for. They done wasted their lives on nothing. No one never had my back like those I fought with in the military."

Serafina's phone began to ring. Xavier and the group of young men in the room all stopped and looked her way. Serafina grappled for her it inside her jacket pocket in the midst of leaving the room entirely.

The call had been forwarded from the office phone and was a recording from the phone company reminding her that the bill was due. She needed to remember to pay the bill, especially since Hollis was unable to and Levi had put her in charge of those business affairs.

The door to the conference room flung open, and the people within dispersed. The hallway instantly flooded with people. She put her phone away and looked up just as Xavier Palo approached her.

"I was told you were here earlier looking to talk with me about the mentorship program?"

Serafina looked at Xavier's face. The hard lines on his face showed he'd had an eventful past, whether it had been with the gangs or the military. But there was softness in the way he spoke and looked at Serafina. Serafina couldn't make sense of this guy. He was neither good nor bad in her assessment. Even if the weapon could be found that matched both her parents' murder and the attack on Hollis, as the evidence seemed to point to, Xavier had only been a suspect in her parents' murders. He had never been charged in the case. And like he admitted, he ran around with the wrong crowd. Could have been one of them.

"I read an article about the mentoring program, and you were the speaker—"

"Oh? Which one?" Xavier asked with intrigue. "I've been in several."

Serafina continued nervously. "I don't remember which one. I was just in the area and thought I would get some more information."

"You're not from around here?"

"No, just visiting. I have a nephew who could use some mentoring. Thought I'd get some information." *Was that a dumb reason to give?*

"Do you have time now?" Xavier asked hesitantly, as if more were to come.

Serafina could see where this was going and began thinking of how to make an exit.

"Maybe we could talk over dinner? Have you ever been to—"

"Oh wow. I didn't realize how late it is," Serafina said abruptly while looking at her watch. She looked at Xavier apologetically. "I'm so sorry, but I have to run. I'll have to stop by another time when I'm not in a rush."

Xavier brushed it off. "Oh, yeah. No biggie. Do whatcha gotta do."

As she proceeded to exit the building, she could sense him watching her every step.

• • •

The streetlights had just turned on when Serafina arrived back at the agency. She pulled into the driveway and sat silently in the Explorer a moment before turning off its engine. It had only been three days ago that Hollis had been shot—and almost taken completely from Serafina's life. As the thought of not having him in her life seeped in, she met it with heavy resistance. She was determined to remain hopeful to the very end.

She entered through the back door since she figured Datson would be eager to come inside.

"Come on, boy," she called to him after she unlocked the back door and opened it.

Datson continued to rest in his doghouse. She held the door open for him for a moment and then decided to coax him inside with food.

"You hungry, boy?" She pulled out a can of dog food from the cabinet and poured it into his bowl, and then rinsed out the can and placed it in the small bucket of recyclables they kept under the kitchen sink.

Datson was motivated enough to come inside, but apparently not motivated by the food. He took a couple sniffs of his bowl and then proceeded down the hallway to the front office area.

Serafina joined him after turning on the lights under the kitchen cabinets. In the front room, Datson had already plopped down in his usual spot under Hollis's desk and was now watching Serafina's every move as if patiently waiting for something. She walked over to the corner tables next to the sofa and turned on the lamps, and then closed the blinds in the front and side windows. She turned around afterward and looked around the room. It felt so empty without Hollis. She looked at her watch. It was close to seven o'clock. Too late for a visit to the hospital. She wasn't even sure she could stand to see him like that again anyhow.

She listened to the voicemail messages on the office phone, which were all old except for one new message that she promptly saved: the auto repair shop that had towed Hollis's motorcycle. *I'll need to call them back.*

She thought about taking Datson for a quick walk, but he gave no indication that he'd be moving from his dog bed any time soon. It was just as well. The temperature had cooled off considerably, and she just wanted to settle in for the night. She headed up the stairs to the loft, leaving the door open behind her for Datson to follow.

After a quick scan of the open loft, Serafina checked off her to-do-list: turn on lamps—*check*; close the blinds—*check*; blast the space heater—*check*. It was time to get comfy now. She changed into some yoga pants, a loose-fitted top, and some thick-soled no-show socks, and then threw her hair up into a ponytail. Her stomach growled something fierce, so she headed back downstairs to the kitchen to see what she could muster up from the fridge.

There had always been an endless supply of Hot Pockets that Hollis kept on hand, but they were starting to dwindle down in supply. She'd need to start grocery shopping for the agency if this was to become her new home. She took out a Philly steak and cheese Hot Pocket and micro-waved it. Behind her, Datson had started to eat. *Finally*, she thought.

"Good boy!" He didn't eat it all, but it was something. "Not that hungry? You must be missing Hollis, huh? Me too, boy."

After taking her Hot Pocket out of the microwave and grabbing an iced tea from the fridge, she headed back upstairs with her plate of food in the other hand. She plopped down on the floor where stacks of newspapers, letters, and photographs were waiting to be moved. Datson followed her over to the rug and lay next to her while she scarfed down the last bite. She placed the plate on the end table, stretched out her legs, and began sifting through the contents on the floor, which had piqued her interest. Datson rested his head on her lower leg. Instinctively, she petted him while she began sorting out the photographs from the newspaper clippings and letters.

The first photograph she held was a Polaroid of a very young Frank Hollis fishing with another little boy with whitish-blonde hair. They looked like they could have been best friends. On the bottom, it was written "Frankie and Stevie." She set that photograph aside and held up a heavily creased envelope labeled "Datson." Its age showed in the yellowed tape that concealed its letter inside. She set it in a pile separate from the photographs and continued to sort through the stack.

Serafina located another photograph in the stack and pulled it out for a better look. This one showed Hollis with the same young boy, only both must have been teenagers or in their early twenties in this one. They were standing in front of a slate-blue Dodge Charger, next to two young ladies wearing sleeveless tops and skirts that stopped mid-thigh. *Girlfriends?* She set that one in the photograph pile and picked up a stack from the main pile to move closer for sorting.

A small photograph fell out of the stack and landed upright to the side of her leg. She immediately noticed Hollis's familiar face in a five-year old's body. She picked up the Polaroid and held it up to examine. *Hollis was so young.* He was dressed in a suit as if he were going to church. She set it in the photographs pile and took a sip of her iced tea.

The last photograph in the pile showed a young adult version of the tow-headed boy, Stevie, only with a darker shade of blonde hair, wearing a cowboy hat, white T-shirt, and blue jeans, leaning up against the side of a tractor, holding a bottle of Dr. Pepper in one hand and a Texas State Bobcats jersey in the other, and grinning ear to ear. At first glance, he reminded her of a young Kevin Costner. Kind of, but not really, she thought after inspecting the photograph more closely. More like the younger brother of a young Kevin Costner. Underneath the photograph was an announcement for the graduation of Steve Lawson, Southwest Texas State University, commencement on May 19, 1973. She thought about the date. 1973—was he not drafted?

Chapter 13

Serafina opened her eyes, surprised to find herself lying on the cold, hardwood floor from the night before and Datson, an armlength away, patiently waiting to be let outside. She positioned herself into a sitting position, extended her arms above her head to stretch out her back, and rubbed her eyes. Her mouth felt incredibly parched, which she figured was from sleeping with her mouth open. She did that occasionally when her sinuses would act up. Probably from the dust up there. She looked around the loft, determining all the likely places dust had accumulated. She moved saliva around in her mouth to moisten the inside and licked her lips to wet them, making smacking noises in the process.

"Wanna go outside?" Serafina asked Datson as she got up from the floor.

Once Datson realized Serafina was going downstairs, he got a head start to the back door. When she opened the door, she saw the bag of dried dog food that Levi had promised on Sunday to drop off. She pulled it inside as Datson headed out.

She poured some kibble bits from the dog food bag into Datson's food bowl, changed out his water, and then went to the Keurig to make a cup of coffee. She smiled thinking of how Hollis had insisted that they didn't need a Keurig but eventually gave in. She had tried to get Nick and Randy to get one, too, but to no avail. Randy had insisted that with how much coffee they all drank, it would be less costly to just stick with making a full pot at a time. Was it really that much cheaper though?

Part of her suspected that the real reason had more to do with getting Wanda's approval. "It's not *that* much cheaper," she grumbled to herself.

After getting her cup of coffee made, she checked on Datson and then headed to the front office where she noticed on the office phone that she'd missed a phone call and there was now a voicemail waiting. She put down her coffee mug on the desk and listened to the voicemail.

It was a corporate client requesting the agency to surveil one of their employees—a "frequent flyer" they'd suspected for some time of abusing his intermittent FMLA. She remembered the last time the client had them investigate this particular employee. She had spent hours recording video footage of him playing golf immediately after calling off work and had thought for sure she'd given them evidence for proving abuse. But it was later alluded that his FMLA leave was for stress and that his doctor had recommended he engage in stress-reducing activities—e.g., golf—whenever he had an episode.

She wrote down the information for the job and deleted the message, convinced that anything she provided them wouldn't catch this guy abusing his FMLA.

The first saved message was supposed to be the auto repair shop, but it was the message from Ms. Call-Me-Back. That's what Serafina decided she'd call her, as she saved the call again.

The next call was Levi. She thought she'd deleted his message on Sunday. *Delete*. She continued to listen, expecting to hear the message from the repair shop, but it wasn't there anymore. "Fuck," she said, realizing she must have deleted it by mistake.

Out of habit, Serafina checked the time by looking at the clock near the front door, rather than her phone. She recalled how she'd razzed Hollis about putting a clock on the wall in the era of cell phones. He had made some good points though.

. . .

"Could it be any bigger?"

"What?" Hollis looked at the clock he'd just put on the wall. "That's not that big."

"Why even put up a clock? It's not like you need one, really."

"What if you need to keep track of the time, but you have a client sitting at your desk talking away?" Hollis motioned to the seat in front of his desk where a client might sit.

Serafina picked up her phone and showed him the time on it.

"Naw, that'd be rude."

"And the client sitting there just talking away isn't rude?" Serafina gestured her hand to open and close as if it were talking.

"Doesn't matter. You should always avoid looking inattentive. Especially with clients."

"But isn't it just as rude to look up at the clock?"

"Certainly . . . there's a right way to do it and a wrong way to do it."

Serafina laughed jovially. "Wrong way?"

"Yeah," Hollis insisted. "If you're doing it noticeably and often."

"So, show me how you'd do it then," she chortled as she sat down in the client's chair at his desk and started talking nonsense. "I noticed that the sky is blue, and, oh, here's a pen on your desk, and I ate breakfast this morning, I wonder what I'll have for dinner, so please investigate it right away . . ."

Hollis, already sitting at his desk, focused his attention on the nonsense Serafina was saying, occasionally nodding. Then, without moving his head, he blinked, looked at the clock, blinked again, and then looked back at her and kept eye contact until she broke character and started outright laughing.

"Notice how I didn't move my head?"

Serafina continued laughing.

"Takes less time too." Hollis picked up his phone and proceeded to put in his passcode, slowly, as if he'd just aged another fifteen years. "See how much time it took me using my phone?"

"It's not that much longer!" She laughed heartily, now wiping tears from the corner of her eyes. "You're intentionally touching the numbers slow!"

Hollis looked up and grinned.

. . .

Serafina held her mug firmly in her hands, comforted by the heat it gave off. She breathed in the moist, warm, coffee-scented air infiltrating her nostrils, and then took a sip of her coffee, savoring the taste in her mouth before swallowing it. She thought for a moment as she did so. Her half-baked plan was to quickly get dressed and head out so she could get to the house of the employee who called off before he left—assuming he was planning his day around another stress-relieving activity. But first, before she forgot, she'd need to set the office phone up to forward to her personal cell phone. *Done.*

Serafina came downstairs from the loft with the five-minute version of dressed and ready to go. She poured the remainder of her coffee into a thermos and grabbed her jacket, purse, keys, and equipment bag.

After taking the items out to the Explorer and setting them on the passenger side seat, she turned back and looked back at Datson. *Should I leave him outside or take him back in?*

Datson was enjoying himself, but he needed his bowls of dry dog food and water to get him through the day. Serafina quickly grabbed them from the kitchen floor, opened the door with her elbow, and placed the bowls on the ground outside the door. She looked at Datson looking back at her questioningly. *Probably could use a rawhide.* She went back inside and grabbed a rawhide for Datson. "There you go, boy."

Datson took the rawhide in his mouth and then dropped it. He continued to sit in place, looking at Serafina.

"I'll be back, boy." Serafina knelt down and hugged Datson. He sniffed at her face for a moment and then picked up the rawhide and walked over to his doghouse. She stood up, wiped the dirt from the palm of her hands, and then went to unhook the gate so she could get to the Explorer in the driveway.

As she proceeded to reverse down the driveway, she noticed the mail lady walking to her building next, so she stopped to let her pass by.

The mail lady walked over to Serafina with mail in her hands. "Great morning, huh? Finally got some good weather." She held the mail out and asked, "You want it?"

"Thank you, yes," Serafina said courteously. "Yeah, it's about time. I'm so tired of the cold."

"You and me both! Have a good one." The woman continued to walk down the sidewalk to the next building.

"You too." Serafina put the stack of mail on the passenger side of the Explorer, along with her equipment bag.

$$\bullet \ \bullet \ \bullet$$

Serafina sat outside the house of the employee she was hired to investigate, readying herself to watch the most boring show ever. That's truly what it was when she thought about it. A really boring show with a lot of one-star reviews and a horrible Rotten Tomatoes rating. Like a reality show where the contestants do normal stuff that isn't remotely interesting. Yup, that show.

Serafina took out the equipment from the bag on her passenger seat, and in doing so, dropped the mail on the floor of the passenger side. She didn't have time to pick it up. She needed to set up the recorders. One for monitoring movements and zooming in; the other, a stationary one for following the subject. That was basically all she needed. She reminisced about pestering Hollis years ago to buy a variety of spy gadgets and wearables.

· · ·

"How about a . . . ?" Serafina slowly enunciated every syllable and then stopped to see the look on Hollis's face.

Hollis just gave her the look. The one where he had no expression and just blinked once or twice. That look.

"Okay, I'll stop." She turned the page of the spy magazine. He'd been tolerating her incessant pestering about various spy gear long enough and had been a good sport about it, mostly shaking his head and smiling. She knew when he gave her the look that it was time to stop.

There on the next page, though, were various wearable cameras, which made her instantly regret badgering Hollis unnecessarily, because she really wanted some of them and she didn't want him to think she was still messing around. One was an HD 1080P video recorder in the shape of a black button, like the one that would be on a jacket, with one center hole and four surrounding it.

Cool, she thought, looking at the smiley-face camera pin and black baseball cap with the hidden camera that was about the size of a dot on the other side of the page. She inspected the picture closer to determine how detectable it would be.

Another item on the page was a necklace. She spent a few minutes longer with that one trying to determine if she'd actually wear it since it kind of reminded her of a car fob, only smaller. In some ways, it even looked kind of like a cockroach, come to think of it.

A pair of black spy camera glasses caught her eye near the bottom of the page. They somewhat reminded her of the Groucho Marx glasses, minus the large plastic nose, big bushy eyebrows, and thick mustache that stopped at the edge of one's mouth. She imagined wearing Groucho Marx glasses as a disguise for getting close-up video footage, and it made her laugh out loud, especially when she took the visual a step further and imagined herself holding a cigar and talking like she was from that era.

Hollis glanced her way for a quick second but then resumed the research he was doing at his desk. The black spy glasses were actually kind of normal looking, she supposed. Nothing too obvious, even the extremely small video camera imbedded into the center of the frame, between the two lenses, was discreet. She smiled, thinking of how she'd get good video footage with them though. Would she have to uncomfortably stare at the suspect until they called the cops? She laughed, which sounded more like a quick huff from her nose. Hollis glanced over again, holding his attention on her just a little longer this time before resuming his research.

The last item on the page looked like a Fitbit or a knockoff of the Apple Watch, but it also had a hidden camera the size of a small dot embedded into it. She wondered how she'd get video footage with that though. Wouldn't it have to face outward to get footage of the suspect? She'd be like those newly engaged women who try to inconspicuously show off the large sparkly gemstone on their ring finger, failing miserably. She shook her head as if to indicate that she wouldn't even attempt such a thing.

But she did like the idea of a wearable. Even if Hollis didn't think all those gadgets were necessary. She decided she'd buy something in the twenty-to-fifty-dollars range, just not now. Next paycheck.

• • •

As Serafina kept her eyes glued to the subject's house, she thought about all the various spy gear she'd purchased over the years. Nothing too expensive. She'd even intrigued Hollis enough with a few to have him go out and purchase some for himself. He'd offered numerous times to reimburse her for her purchases, to write it off as a business expense, but she'd always declined. She knew the business was profitable, just not that profitable—not profitable to where they could, on a whim, just go out and purchase the latest and greatest technology on the market. Some things had to be old school, and she was fine with that.

Serafina's phone dinged just as the subject came out the front door of his house. There was no time to check the text message, although she could guess with all certainty that it would be from Randy. It was always Randy. Nick didn't care about the current celebrity gossip—not that she did, but at least she gave Randy the responses he needed to feel a connection. "Oh wow!" "That's hilarious!" "Seriously!?" and, "IKR?"—which she had to Google to find out it stood for, "I know, right!?" Basically, all the standard girl-talk responses. Nick didn't seem to understand girl talk at all. His responses were often centered around trying to understand the point with a bunch of questions and offering advice. She knew Randy wouldn't talk to Wanda about those things either. First, Wanda didn't even know who half those celebrities were, and second, she and Randy tended to talk instead of text. Sure, they texted, but it just wasn't their thing.

Serafina grabbed the camera and began to track the subject's movements to his red Ford Edge. She placed the camera on the passenger seat and quickly turned on the stationary video recorder hooked to the visor to record the subject backing out of his driveway. When the subject pulled onto the street, Serafina turned the Explorer's engine on and followed him down several side streets and onto the main street.

The subject pulled into a Burger King and stopped in front of the large menu display to place his order. Serafina followed behind him, into the parking lot, and backed into a parking space to wait for him to get through the drive-thru lane. She was about to check her text messages when she noticed the subject had pulled away from the speaker and was proceeding to the first window. With him nearly out of sight, Serafina had no choice but to pull out from her parking space and follow at a safe distance, staying as inconspicuous as possible while she waited for him to pay for his food.

Serafina's phone dinged again, but she continued to keep her eyes on the subject as he pulled out onto the main street again. She could see him eating small hashbrowns from the bag as he drove, which made her crave some.

As her subject went through the intersection up ahead, the traffic light turned from green to yellow. By the time Serafina approached the traffic light, she had a split second to decide whether to brake or floor it. The debate ended when she noticed an old, dark blue car in her peripheral vision to the right, on the street perpendicular to her, pulling into the intersection to make a left turn onto her street. She slammed on her brakes and came to an abrupt stop at the traffic light. The equipment bag and her purse fell onto the floor of the passenger side. "Damn it!"

Serafina instinctively looked in her rearview mirror, mentally preparing to have someone slam into the back of the Explorer. When she looked back up at the subject's red Edge, it was so far ahead that there was next to no chance of catching up. She wasn't going to give up the chase though. She waited as patiently as she could for the traffic light to turn green, and then she proceeded to speed just a tad faster than traffic.

Up ahead, she could see the red Edge coming up to another traffic light that turned yellow. She watched to see if the subject would slow down to a stop or go through the yellow light. "Slow down and stop," she said, as if her coaxing would impact the outcome. She smiled to see the red Edge start to slow down. But it didn't stop. The light remained yellow up until it was in the intersection and then changed to red.

"Fuck." Serafina lightly hit the steering wheel with the palm of her hand.

She continued to drive up to the red traffic light with her eye on her subject. Up ahead, her fortune changed for the better. The subject was slowing again, and his left-turn signal was on to turn into the parking lot of a Home Depot.

When Serafina pulled into the parking lot, she immediately scanned the parking lot for any red vehicle. The first red vehicle she noticed was the Edge. She positioned herself in a spot that was at a distance but within view of the subject.

The subject exited his vehicle just as Serafina was grabbing her camera off the passenger seat. "What you gotta get from Home Depot? Hmm?" She zoomed in on him walking into Home Depot. *Probably going to do some doctor-recommended woodworking for stress relief.*

Once the subject was inside the store, Serafina picked her purse up off the passenger side floor and placed it on the seat next to her. Then she grabbed her equipment bag off the floor and placed that on the seat as well. She reached down to pick up the mail, too, but could only go so far with her seat belt on. She unbuckled the belt and then leaned down to grab the mail and put it in her lap. Even though the subject was inside, she alternated between looking at the Edge and the entrance to the store.

It was time to see what Randy wanted, so she pulled her phone out of her jacket pocket and checked the message from Randy.

9:22 a.m.

397737: *EXPRESS: An exclusive offer, just because we <3 you: $15 off $30, $30 off $100, $40 off $120 or $75 off $200. Use code: 2157 in stores or 1165621197002158 online. Add to wallet: bit.ly/3ySdQcb. Terms: bit.ly/3RoYpRU. Shop Now: but.ly/3revts6*

She hadn't expected to see a text message from Express. Sure, she typically received sale notifications from them regularly, but in that moment, she had been so convinced that it was a text message from Randy. It was always Randy! Always. And now, he had just moved on? Who else might he be texting instead of her? God knows he needed to text someone if it wasn't going to be her. Nick? Wanda? Good luck with that! He'd grow tired of their responses eventually. He'd realize he needed her after all. And where would she be when he came to his senses and realized that he threw away their relationship? Would she be available? To be like some sort of doll sitting up on a shelf that he could take down whenever he needed a friend? *Nope.* She deserved better than that. If he couldn't be there for her when she needed a friend, then maybe he needed to see how that felt. Maybe she needed to repay the favor!

Serafina felt a stinging as tears began flooding the corners of her eyes. She wiped a few with her middle finger, but they continued to flow at a heavier pace. She reached into the center console for a travel pack of Kleenex and pulled a tissue out to use instead.

As she thought more about it, she wondered if maybe Randy wasn't texting her because she hadn't told him about Hollis being in the hospital. Was *she* the asshole here? Even if she were, how many times was Randy hurtful and insensitive to her? And she just had to take it? She gave him all kinds of grace with how he treated her half the time, and here he was just going to reject her over not telling her about Hollis? *That's bullshit!* If he wanted to be like this, then he better make sure that's what he wanted, because there was no going back.

Even as Serafina consoled herself with her angry thoughts, she knew she owned some responsibility for how their relationship was going. She thought back to when things started to go sour between them, and it was when she told him about her looking into the whereabouts of DeMarcus—which he *should* want! He didn't get to dictate which family members got to be part of the family. Demarcus had every right to still be part of the family. She did too! What—did he think she didn't have a right to be upset over how quickly he was ready to have her move out on Saturday? Acting like he couldn't wait to get her out of his life. Screw him!

Serafina looked at the subject's Edge again, sensing the tightness of her jaw and furrow of her brow. She distracted herself with the mail on her lap. There was a flyer for Bed Bath & Beyond and a phone bill for the agency. Serafina held the envelope in her hands, debating whether to open it. Levi had put the agency's responsibilities in her hands after all, right? She opened up the envelope and pulled the phone bill out. Just then, her phone dinged again.

Chapter 14

Serafina had just been deflated by a text message from Express that she'd expected to be from Randy. She didn't want to set herself up for more disappointment by even guessing who it might be texting her now. Still, she was curious.

She looked at the subject's Edge again, ensuring he was still in Home Depot, and then proceeded to look at the text message.

10:07 a.m.

Michelle (Coco): *Hey*

Serafina: *Hey, Michelle, what's up?*

Michelle (Coco): *Just wanted to see if you and Hollis wanted to stop by the club this Friday for my birthday.*

Serafina really didn't feel like going to Michelle's birthday party at Planet Janet. Not that she didn't want to see Michelle. Okay, part of it was that. Some of the drama *was* entertaining, as long as she wasn't caught up in it, but that's what seemed to happen on a consistent basis when she had worked at the bar. And even, still, to some degree when she'd drop in to see everyone for a short visit after quitting the bar and working for Hollis instead. They'd all be up at the bar with her asking all sorts of personal questions, and then she'd hear about it later on, usually from Michelle, that they had this or that to say about it—behind her back, of course. Never through Hollis though. Either they didn't tell him gossip, or he didn't care. Or maybe he didn't want her to get hurt by any of it. Yeah, that was probably the reason.

Regardless, the main reason she didn't want to go to the bar—okay, one of several main reasons—was because Michelle turned into a different persona under her stage name, Coco. Maybe it was the several glasses of wine Coco paced herself on throughout the day, or the dog-eat-dog conditions they worked under, but the cattiness could be a real downer at times. So much negativity.

Another reason was that Coco would be busy with the influx of all her regulars who would certainly come in and vie for her attention on her special day—even if it wasn't her real birthday. That's right, it wasn't even her real birthday. Serafina knew from a birthday app on her phone that Michelle's birthday was this upcoming Sunday, a day when the bar was closed. But who could blame Michelle for wanting to cash in on it that way?

The more *reasonest* reason was that Serafina just didn't know who should know about Hollis. That he had been shot. That he was in the hospital. That he was in a coma. Knowing that Hollis was a private person, would he want them knowing that about him? Should she tell Michelle that Hollis was sick? Or maybe out of state right now on a business trip? Or visiting relatives? On vacation? Maybe she should tell her the truth? No, not the truth. But then, all the other reasons were just as personal, in terms of information giving. Would Hollis want to have to continue with the lie once he was out of the hospital? Unless he didn't get better and didn't get out of the hospital. She couldn't bear the thought. This *one* text was causing Serafina so much angst. She typed out a vague, upbeat response.

10:09 a.m.

Serafina: *Oh cool. That's right, your birthday is coming up. Happy birthday! We'll definitely try to stop by.*

"Try" was the operative word. *Send.* Serafina certainly wasn't going to be going, but leading Michelle to believe there was a chance seemed to be the least complex way to respond.

Serafina looked at the subject's red Edge and then at the Home Depot entrance. With the subject still inside, she proceeded with her text conversation, waiting to see what Michelle's response would be. There was no response for a few minutes. Best guess, Coco was carrying on multiple text message conversations with customers about coming in for her birthday, or she was giving a customer a dance. Then, Coco's messages came through.

10:11 a.m.

Michelle (Coco): *Sorry, customer wanted a dance. So yeah, please do! I miss you guys.*

Michelle (Coco): *Oh, btw I texted Hollis too but he hasn't me texted back yet.*

Serafina took pride in having been right about the reason for Coco's delayed response. That last text, though, kind of seemed like she expected a response back. Serafina didn't want to divulge anything about anything, so she simply liked the text and waited to see if that response would suffice.

There were no other texts from Michelle after that, so Serafina picked up the phone bill off her lap and prepared to pay it online using her corporate card. It shouldn't take that long, she thought. Would be nice to knock it out and not have to worry about it later.

She took her iPad out of the equipment bag and pulled up the Verizon website. The login most likely for Hollis to use, the one it almost always was: "Hollis." She knew this from experience. The password would be trickier. Hollis was known to use "Datson1971," and when a character was required, he would use "Datson@1971." When it was a pin, well, it was just "1971." Hollis was predictable in many ways, yet a mystery altogether in others. She made several attempts and then, just like that, she was in.

There were two sets of online phone records: one for the agency and one for Hollis's cell phone. Serafina looked up at the subject's red Edge quickly and then glanced at the features for the online account. One option she didn't know was available anymore was the detailed call history. She clicked on the call history, which opened up a detailed record of incoming and outgoing calls. Immediately recognizing the call from the repair garage from the other day, she hurriedly wrote down the number on the envelope of the phone bill, knowing the subject could come out of the store any moment. As she looked up in the general vicinity of the subject's red Edge and the Home Depot entrance again, this time, the subject was walking toward his vehicle holding several plastic Home Depot bags, which appeared to be heavy. She would have to find time later to pay the phone bill.

Serafina hastily closed up her iPad and grabbed her camera. She took a few pictures and then reached up to turn on the stationary camera on her visor to capture the subject's movements.

She followed the subject to a nearby duplex apartment building and then parked in the street with the Explorer positioned so that she could capture a full shot of his Edge in the street and the front door to the duplex apartment building. Serafina recorded him on the visor cam as he exited his Edge with the plastic Home Depot bags and walked up to the door. She picked up her camera and photographed him knocking at the door. Was he the landlord of this duplex apartment? Or was this some kind of side hustle? Like was he a plumber, or electrician, or something? She didn't have those specifics about his position with the company. Worth noting in her report, however.

She took a few more photographs of him waiting outside the front door, and then watched him through her camera lens as he took out keys and unlocked the door. *Interesting. Must be the landlord,* she thought, as she took a few more photographs of the subject before he disappeared from view inside the duplex apartment.

Serafina sat in the Explorer as inconspicuously as she could, waiting for the subject to return into view. But the minutes turned into one endless fog. She looked down to where she put the envelope for the phone bill on the passenger seat and decided to call the number she'd written down, hoping it was for the auto repair shop. She needed to find out where the crash happened. She needed to have a better understanding of what happened—and maybe find some clues. She could always try to obtain the police report for information, but then she risked news getting back to Levi that she was going against his advice to stay out of it. Better to do it on the sly.

The phone rang on the other end. It rang once more and then a man's voice answered on the other line.

"Springwells Auto Repair Service."

Serafina wasn't sure how to broach the topic. Should she explain that she was Hollis's employee? Partner? Would that just create more questions . . . and resistance? Daughter?

"Hi, I'm calling about my dad's motorcycle."

"Brought in early last Saturday morning?"

"Yeah, Frank Hollis?"

"Okay, can you hold for a moment?"

"Yeah, of course."

Serafina occasionally glanced up at the front porch of the duplex as she sat waiting patiently for the man on the other end to return.

"Hello. Are you still there?"

"Hi. Yeah, I'm still here."

"The bike wasn't too damaged when it was brought in, so it didn't need to have anything really repaired. Just has some minor paint scratches. Nothing major though. Nothing a body shop can't fix. It can be picked up at any time."

"Actually, it's kind of hard to pick it up right now because, um, well, my dad . . ." She had a difficult time finishing her words. Why was that? Why was she so emotional all of a sudden? She held her breath and then tried to breathe in deeply. "He's in the hospital."

"Oh, wow, I'm sorry to hear that. I hope he's okay."

Serafina held back her emotions. Hollis wasn't okay. He may never be okay again.

"Look, it's okay, hon. We're not in a hurry. Your dad can pick it up when he's ready. How about we check in on you in about a week or so?"

Serafina wiped her runny nose with a napkin in the pocket of the door that she remembered getting last Friday night when she investigated the other subject at Quiznos.

"Thank you." She steadied her quivering voice and continued. "Can I ask you something?"

The other side of the line was momentarily silent and then the man responded, "Sure."

"Where did it happen?"

"I'm sorry?"

"The accident."

"Oh, we had the bike towed to our yard early Saturday morning. I'm not sure exactly where it was picked up. I'd have to ask the tow driver. He won't be in until later. Would you like to call back in a few hours? Or I could call you?"

"Yes, please."

"Is this a good number to call you back on?"

"Yes, please. Thank you so much."

• • •

It had been several hours with no activity from the subject inside the duplex apartment building, so Serafina had called the corporate client to get guidance on whether she should continue monitoring the subject's activity beyond the hours she'd already put in for the day. After the corporate client made the decision for her to cease surveillance for the day, she ended the call. She sat up in the driver's seat and adjusted her back and then started the Explorer to head home to the agency.

The sound of a phone call coming through on Serafina's phone took her out of autopilot. She recognized the phone number as the number for Springwells Auto Repair Shop, so she immediately answered the call.

"Hello?"

"Hi, this is Tony at Springwells Auto Repair Shop. Is this . . ."

"Frank Hollis's daughter," Serafina interjected. "Yes?"

"I was able to get hold of the driver who brought in your father's motorcycle," he said, and then paused.

"Yeah?" Serafina encouraged him to continue.

"I'm so sorry about your father, miss. I had no idea when we spoke earlier, no idea that . . ." He was searching for the words.

Serafina reassured him. "It's okay. I understand."

The service repairman continued. "I was told he was shot? Is he okay?"

"Mmm . . ." She wavered. "He's been unconscious since the incident but is stable now. Thank you for asking."

"Yeah, of course. No problem, miss."

It had started out to be a ploy for getting information about the crash site, but as Serafina spoke in terms of Hollis being her father, she started to believe her own story. The more she accepted Hollis as her father, the more she felt the loss. She felt emotions bubbling inside, and the sudden urge to cry caught her off guard.

"So, you wanted to know where the accident happened, right?"

Serafina took a deep breath in and regained her composure. She wiped tears that had reached her lips and said, "Yes, please."

He gave her detailed directions that weren't too far off from Clark Park. "I hope that helps."

"Yes, thank you." Serafina slowly recovered from the burst of emotions.

"Sure thing. Let me know if you need anything else. And again, no rush on getting the bike. We can hold it as long as you need."

"I really appreciate it." She felt the emotions stir briefly and then settle again.

• • •

At the crash site, Serafina sat in the Explorer and took in all the surroundings. The condition of the two-story wooden houses was questionable. Many of them should have been condemned. Broken windows patched with cardboard and duct tape. Dangerously leaning porches. Roofs protected by tattered tarps. And those were the few houses on the street. Most of what she saw were overgrown vacant lots with scattered items that no doubt had been intentionally dumped. A mattress. Some toddler toys. A bicycle missing its tires. Probably some dirty syringes too. With both caution and curiosity, she got out of the Explorer and walked over to where she thought Hollis's motorcycle had skid on the ground.

Serafina imagined how the incident might have happened. She envisioned Hollis riding his bike toward her and the Explorer from the street near Vernor Highway. The vehicle with the shooter probably followed him here from that street, so . . . the shooting probably happened around here. She looked at the markings on the cement, staring hard at the ground for remnants from the bike. She thought she saw a piece of a reflector but wasn't sure. She knelt down and looked at the pieces and then walked over to the field where there were scuff marks in the dirt and briefly examined the trail. *He must have fallen off the bike there.*

She looked around at the distant surroundings. Across the field, near the street where the shooter must have followed Hollis, was a bank. It was a small branch serving the local community but nonetheless an actual business in that desolate area. She was about to turn around and get back in the Explorer when she noticed that the bank had an ATM on the side facing the side street.

Wait! ATM machines have surveillance cameras built into them. She followed the view of the surveillance camera for the ATM machine outward to get an idea of what might be captured as evidence. The area of the incident wasn't in the direct view of the camera, but she was hopeful she could get a lead from it if only she could see what was on the video footage.

Inside the bank, there was no one in line for the bank tellers, so Serafina walked up toward the counter and waited to be called. One teller was helping a customer; another was getting reorganized after a customer had just completed their transaction. A woman came out of an office and walked over to a central station and sat down. Serafina just wanted to see the manager about the footage, so after a brief debate on whether she should remain in line or go speak with that woman, she decided on the latter.

"Hi. I was hoping I might speak with the manager about a matter."

The woman looked up from where she was sitting. "Sure. I just need to get some information from you first. Are you looking to open up an account or loan?"

Serafina shook her head. "No, sorry."

"Are you interested in making a change to an existing account or loan?"

"No, just need to speak with the manager."

"Is it a matter I might be able to assist you with?"

"I don't believe so."

The woman seemed to expect Serafina to elaborate, but Serafina was not in the mood to have to explain things twice. When she realized that Serafina was not going to continue, she stood up and motioned Serafina over to a set of chairs against the makeshift wall. "Okay, if you'd like to have a seat, I'll see if he's available."

After about five minutes of waiting, a short white man came out from a room in the back. He wore a short-sleeved, light yellow, button-down dress shirt tucked into a pair of khakis that barely came to his ankles, exposing white socks that noticeably contrasted with his black shoes. As he approached the counter where the bank teller stood guard over Serafina, she noticed how his shirt was tucked in in the back but barely made it over his stomach. Although Serafina tried not to look, it was almost unavoidable. She found it both disgusting and intriguing at the same time.

"You needed to speak with me?"

The odd voice that came with his body caught Serafina off guard. As she looked him in the face, preparing her words, she noticed his greasy hair. *Does this guy ever shower?*

Serafina hadn't thought out exactly what she would say ahead of time. The sympathy card got her further with the auto repair shop than she had anticipated. Deciding she'd go with that, she stood up and stepped forward to shake his hand.

"Hi, I'm so sorry to bother you." She really wasn't, but that was the polite thing to say.

"No bother at all. What can I do you for?"

Do you for? That alone was nails on a chalkboard to Serafina. Right up there with "Yeppers" and "Cool beans!" *Just say it right, dude. It's, "What can I do for you?"* She mentally emphasized the last two words and then shook off her annoyance.

"Well, I'm not sure if you heard about the accident the other night?"

He looked confused.

"The shooting?" Serafina clarified.

"Ah, yes, last Friday night?"

"Yeah, technically Saturday morning, but yes."

"Yes, we heard about it the next day. I'm not sure how I can help you with that though."

"The person shot was my father."

The other customer had left, and the bank tellers were now watching out of curiosity.

The man interrupted. "I'm sorry to hear that, but the bank was closed when that happened. As far as I know, there weren't any witnesses."

"Yes, you're right about that, but I'm hoping the ATM machine's camera might offer something to help with the investigation?"

"Oh, the police already asked about it and, er, well . . ." He stumbled on his words a bit. "It's not facing where the shooting happened. I doubt it would show you much of anything."

"Actually, I understand it isn't facing where the shooting happened. But it faces where a car would have left that area. I'd still like to see it if you don't mind." She was hoping he wouldn't mind because her next plan of action would be to cry. Whatever award-winning performance she needed to do to see that video footage, she was prepared to do.

"The police seemed to be handling the investigation though. I'm sure if there's anything out there as evidence, they'll find it."

This was Serafina's opportunity to rebut, but she was at a loss for words.

"I'm sorry I can't be more helpful. Good luck with your father."

If this was her last chance to change his mind, it was time to bring out the tears. She felt inside the pocket of her jacket for the travel pack of Kleenex she'd taken out of the center console of the Explorer that morning. *Yes, still there!* "I'm sorry." She pulled out a tissue from the travel pack and held it up to her face, sobbing. "It's just . . . it's just . . ."

She acted as if she were hyperventilating. "It's just my dad's not doing well. He was on life support up until the other day, but he's still in a coma." She sobbed some more.

The manager stood there uncomfortably, unsure of how to react. He reached out with his hand on her shoulder and patted her. "There, there."

Gross. He was definitely the type of guy who didn't wash his hands after using the restroom. Serafina didn't stop crying though.

The manager finally gave in. "Well, I probably could make the time if you want to wait right here."

Serafina sniffled and nodded. She resisted breaking character by looking around, but she could sense the two tellers looking her way.

Within a few minutes, the manager returned. "Ma'am?"

Serafina looked up and followed the manager through a door to a room down the hall that appeared to be a storage room of some sort with storage boxes and various IT equipment. The manager walked her over to a small table in the corner with a monitor screen showing four camera views, all streaming live. He pulled up an extra chair for her from behind a stack of boxes, and they both sat down.

The manager clicked on the camera view for the ATM machine and adjusted the date for the previous Friday. "Around what time would you say we should view?"

"They believe it happened some time on Friday night or possibly Saturday morning, so can we try from like 11:00/11:30 p.m. Friday night and go from there to maybe 3:00 a.m. Saturday morning?"

Without verbally responding, the manager adjusted to Friday's date and set the time for 11:00 p.m. They awkwardly sat with one another in silence, viewing the video in real time, until finally the manager broke the silence by clearing his throat. "Maybe I can speed up the pace a little." He adjusted the speed, and they continued to watch the screen for any movements.

The time went by much quicker than real time, yet nothing changed on the screen.

The manager adjusted the pace again such that the time went by even quicker, to where she had to pay close attention to any changes. The view remained the same, despite the rapid time-warping taking place. Then, at 12:22 a.m., a car appeared in the video.

"Stop! Right there! Did you see that?" Serafina's adrenaline kicked in.

The manager stopped the video and rewound the time slowly. Although the surrounding area beyond the ATM machine was pitch black, there was definitely movement in that area of the screen.

"Is there a way to lighten it up, make it not so dark?"

The manager messed with a few options and then rewound the video to play it again.

The video showed what appeared to be an old, '70s, rust-colored Chevy Impala, like the one she'd seen at Clark Park the day before—the one where an older basketball player was talking to the driver. *Yes, that was the car! Or was it?* She wasn't exactly sure, but if she had to place a bet on it, she'd put her money down on it being the vehicle.

"Do you want me to keep going?"

Serafina was still processing this new information but didn't want to risk losing any other information by prematurely ending the viewing. "Yes, if you don't mind."

The manager remained silent as he let the video play in a slightly faster pace than real time. They reached 3:30 a.m. with nothing else showing up on the screen, so he attempted to turn off the video.

"Wait, why didn't we see the ambulance or the tow truck? Wouldn't they have come from that direction too?"

Instead of turning the video off, the manager paused it. "Not necessarily. They could have come up from the other direction. There's a side street over there that also goes up to Vernor."

"Oh." Serafina sat and thought about what to do next.

"Do you want me to keep going?"

"No. That's okay. Thank you." Serafina wavered on whether she should change her mind, even as she said no. "I appreciate all you've done already. I'll be going."

The manager turned off the video and reset the monitor screen to the four-camera view again. "I'm sorry there wasn't much to see on the video."

Ah, but she saw enough. At least now she had a suspect. If only she could get the license plate for that vehicle and look it up in the registry program. "Yeah, me too."

The manager walked her to the main lobby where the bank tellers were now helping several customers with a few others waiting in line for assistance. "Good luck with your father."

Standing at the bank's entrance, Serafina's phone rang as she thanked the manager. She exited the bank while retrieving it from her jacket pocket. Outside, she recognized the caller as Levi.

"Hello?"

"Hi, dear. This is Levi . . ."

Serafina jumped at the opportunity to hear what Levi had to say, pressing the phone closely to her face so she didn't miss a word. "Yes?"

There were other voices in the room with Levi, and he seemed distracted.

"Hold on," he said as his attention was diverted to another person in his presence.

The waiting was tormenting Serafina. Levi wouldn't call for no reason. She just needed to know whether it was something good or something bad. She began walking in the direction of the Explorer. As she neared the area of the field where Hollis most likely would have been shot, she looked over in the direction of the ATM machine to get a better idea of the proximity where the old, '70s, rust-colored Chevy Impala would have been, and where Hollis fell, and determined that it most definitely would have been within shooting distance.

She needed to locate this mystery car. She could head over to Clark Park and just hang out there until it showed up again. Maybe Gill would be there, and she could find out more about her past. She unlocked the Explorer, ready to step into it.

"Sorry about that. Are you still there?" asked Levi abruptly.

"Hi, Levi. Yeah, I'm still here. Is everything all right?"

"Hopefully, yes. I wanted to let you know that Hollis is awake."

Chapter 15

Am I in the hospital? Hollis tried to look around the room with as much concentration as he could muster, but he felt weak, and lifting his head required great exertion. He soon succumbed to the heaviness of his head and rested it back down.

Hollis listened to the sounds around him, unsure of so much.

"He's awake again!" Levi called out from across the room.

A nurse came into view and briefly stood over Hollis's hospital bed. Then she was gone from view.

Levi spoke again; this time his voice seemed closer. "Serafina should be here any minute. I called her when you woke up about an hour ago."

Hollis tried to respond, but it was as if his mouth was stuffed with cotton, making it challenging to form words let alone have them come out coherently. Mostly what came out were sounds of groaning and wincing with every effort he made to get comfortable. His body ached, and there was a dull, throbbing pain emanating throughout his whole upper torso.

The nurse came into focus again. "I'll get you something for the pain in a moment. But let's just see if we can't make you a little more comfortable by fixing this pillow here." She began adjusting his pillow and repositioning Hollis in the hospital bed. Then she went over to the machines that were monitoring his vitals. It was quiet in the room for those few minutes.

A familiar female voice came from the room's entrance. "How's he doing? I got here as quickly as I could." *Serafina*.

Serafina came up to Hollis's bedside and held his hand in hers—a first for them. It felt oddly natural. He could see her beautiful face, concerned and exhausted, her eyes starting to tear up, and all he wanted to do in that moment was console her. He patted the top of her hand with his, letting her know everything was okay, which only made her tear up more.

"Hey," Serafina said with a shaky voice and a steady flow of tears filling her eyes. "You had us worried." She unlatched her right hand just as a few tears began their descent to her chin. "You had *me* worried." She wiped away those tears and the others forming out of the corner of her eyes.

Hollis squeezed her hand and started to tear up too.

The nurse finished monitoring his vitals and turned to those in the room. "I'll be back in a moment to administer his pain medication. The sedative will make him drowsy, so he will need to rest again soon."

After the nurse left the room, Levi said, "I think that was her nice way of telling everyone they will need to leave soon to let Hollis sleep."

Hollis was okay with that. He was fighting to stay awake and coherent as it was.

"You need to rest up so you can get better, okay?" Serafina said to which Hollis silently nodded.

The nurse had returned right away with his pain medication and was already pushing it into the tube in his IV with the syringe when he looked up. Almost immediately, Hollis felt his head start to spin and his body become increasingly heavy. He closed his eyes and allowed the medicine to take effect. Levi and Serafina began talking to one another after the nurse left, but it took too much out of him to discern what they were saying. A few words stuck out to him, like "agency," "Datson," and "Cole," but other than that, it was a meaningless exchange of many words, nothing that made much sense.

With each breath Hollis exhaled, he sank more and more into a deep state of relaxation.

He heard Levi's voice: ". . . asleep . . . get going now . . . walk down together?" and then he heard Serafina's voice: ". . . stick around . . ." and felt her hands pull away from his. He couldn't resist slumber any longer.

Chapter 16

When Serafina opened her eyes that Wednesday morning, she felt off, like her mind had just come off autopilot. She tried to straighten out her right leg to stretch the muscles but found it difficult. The bottom half of the bed was taken up by Datson.

"Bed hog," she called out to Datson.

Datson lifted his head and proceeded to rest it on Serafina's lower leg.

She thought back to when Levi had left her at the hospital the night before. She had been sitting there, deep in her thoughts, watching Hollis rest for who knows how long, when all of a sudden, she had been jolted back into the present with a hand on her shoulder. She'd looked up to see the nurse talking to her, but the words hadn't taken on meaning until her mind came back up for water and it registered to her that visiting hours were over.

She remembered walking down the halls of the hospital toward the elevator, and she remembered walking to the parking lot. She remembered driving the short distance down Woodward Avenue to the agency. She even remembered greeting Datson and pouring him some food. But the in-betweens? Not so much.

Serafina's phone began to ring from the nightstand slightly out of reach on her right. She reached for it but had to pull on the charger to move it close enough to grab without disturbing Datson.

She didn't recognize the phone number and was about to let it go to voicemail when she remembered that she had forwarded the calls for the agency to her phone. It could be one of their clients, she thought.

"Good morning, Metro Investigation Services Agency," she greeted the caller, feeling self-conscious about sounding like she just woke up.

"Good morning, Serafina. It's Larry Parson."

Oh, shit! Serafina sat up quickly, disrupting Datson's rest.

He continued, "I know this is short notice, but we got a call-off this morning from one of our frequent flyers. How is your schedule looking this morning?"

Serafina grabbed a pen from the nightstand drawer, took down the details for the surveillance on a Bed Bath & Beyond coupon flyer, and ended the call to get ready.

After showering, she exited the bathroom with a towel wrapped around her body and another wrapped around her hair, ready to dress and head out for the job, when she heard her phone ringing again. Hoping it wasn't Larry cancelling the job, she raced across the floor to the nightstand where her phone remained in the charging position.

"Hello?" She paused and then remembered to finish her greeting. "Metro Investigation Services Agency."

"Hi, Frank Hollis please," the woman said.

"This is his assistant. He's . . ." Serafina thought about what to say next. "He's unavailable right now." She held up her hands to Datson and mouthed, *What?* Technically, what she said was true. Datson just needed to stop judging her, if only in her head. Hollis wasn't available, and that client didn't need to know why. "Is there something I can help you with?"

"Oh. Well, we usually have him work for us with this particular case we have. Do you know when he will be available?"

Serafina felt panic bubble up. "I'm afraid he is not well . . ." She stopped herself short of saying anything more on Hollis's condition.

It occurred to Serafina that this was the corporate client that Hollis had been providing investigative services to solely—their biggest client, the reason Serafina was hired in the first place. Hollis had wanted to make sure he could always be available for their jobs. He had explained enough in their time together about how important even one job of theirs was, that declining one meant a much larger loss in the grand scheme of things. If he let another investigative service agency take even one job, that could mean losing the whole client and subsequent jobs. He needed another person to tag team the jobs with him. Which is what she *thought* Hollis was doing the night he . . . *No time to be upset.*

"Hello? Sorry, you cut out." Good save, she congratulated herself. "Oh, there you are. Yes, I was saying that even though he isn't available right now, I'm sure we can cover the surveillance. When are you thinking you'll need our services?"

The woman hesitated and then answered, "Actually, now."

Fuck! Serafina wasn't sure how she could commit to this job, yet she knew she needed to. "Oh?"

"Are you, or rather, do you have anyone available right now to do the job?" the woman asked.

Without hesitation, Serafina committed them to the job. "Yes. Yes, we do."

Serafina took down the details for the surveillance.

She felt immediate despair as she ended the call. She'd already committed to doing the job that Larry Parson called about earlier. With no one to tag team the jobs with her, she would have to call and cancel the first job. Even though she and Larry had good rapport, she wasn't sure how much she could lean on that relationship. Would it also pose risk and have them losing future business? It was the risk she had to take. It wasn't like she had a choice. She couldn't be in two places at once.

Serafina worried about letting Hollis down. He'd always been able to depend on her. She liked that too. To be needed. Valued, even. So then why was he investigating her past? How could Hollis have hired

Cole to do that to her? She felt betrayed by the whole thing and wanted to not care about what happened next as an act of retribution. But she couldn't *not* care. She cared very much about it all, which made her want to just cry.

She started to call back Larry when it occurred to her that maybe Cole could help. Aside from how much it irked her to have to reach out to Cole for help, she couldn't let Hollis down. And maybe, just maybe, Hollis might realize her worth and stop investigating her if she regained his trust. But what did she do to even lose his trust to begin with?

Serafina didn't have Cole's number though. With her phone in hand, she quickly looked up the online phone account for the agency to find a number that could be Cole's. There were a lot of phone numbers with the 313 area code. She tried one of the more recent 313 area code numbers in the call history.

"Hello?" A woman with a familiar voice answered.

Serafina listened silently for a second and then responded, "Hello? I'm not sure if I have the right number. I'm trying to reach Cole . . ." She thought quickly about his last name and then continued, "McDermott."

"Sorry, wrong number."

Serafina recognized the woman's voice for sure, but she couldn't figure out the connection. "Maybe you know Frank Hollis then?"

"Sorry, no. You have the wrong number."

Serafina was positive she'd heard that woman's voice before; she just couldn't remember how. "Okay, thanks."

After ending the call, Serafina looked at the number she had just called. She didn't recognize the number, but she was sure she'd heard the woman's voice before. She thought back to all the dancers she had known that had come and gone at Planet Janet, but no one came to mind.

Serafina looked through the online call history some more. With Cole working as a police officer in Detroit, it was likely he had a 313 phone number, but there were no guarantees. There were quite a few 313 numbers to go through and even more with area codes that were 810, 734, and 586. She noticed Hollis's cell phone account listed on the site, and there were just as many numbers to go through on that call history as well.

She started to succumb to the feeling of deflation when she remembered the report Cole had dropped off. Maybe it had information. She quickly threw on some clothes and ran down the stairs, with Datson trailing slowly behind. With a quick and orchestrated movement, she opened the back door to let Datson outside and then headed to the front office area to find that report.

Serafina hoped with all her might as she opened the envelope for the report that the letterhead would have Cole's contact information. Pure elation came over her when she saw a phone number for Cole in the header. She immediately called the number.

She heard it ringing.

Please answer. Please answer.

It rang again.

Please, please, please!

It rang again. Then, the standard voice recording came on. *Fuck.*

Serafina wasn't sure if she wanted to leave a message. She wasn't sure what she would even say. Now, she wasn't even sure if she should have called Cole to begin with.

Serafina let it get to the point where Cole verbally inserted his name, "Cole McDermott," and then she hung up.

She would have to call the first corporate client back. Unless . . .

Maybe she could call Levi to help with one of the jobs. After all, he and Hollis went way back. Vietnam War buddies, in fact. And he *was* Hollis's silent partner. Wouldn't he have a vested interest in the business running smoothly? Datson barked from the backyard to be let back in.

She pondered that thought as she went to let him back inside.

Once back at the desk, Serafina realized there was no way Levi was going to cover. He wasn't even trained to do surveillance. Sure, he was a retired detective, but he was quite possibly Hollis-level in only knowing old-school technology. It would probably be more trouble than it was worth to train him, and he'd probably cause them to lose the client permanently. She didn't want to have to call the first client back, but she knew it had to be done.

She picked up the paper with the details she wrote down from her conversation with Larry Parson. Reluctantly, she put in his number and pushed send. She heard it ringing.

Just then, another call came through. Serafina recognized the number as Cole's. She hung up before Larry picked up, and she answered Cole's call.

"Hi, Cole?"

"Yeah, you called me?"

"Yeah." Serafina wasn't sure if she regretted calling him yet. "The reason I called . . ." This was her last chance to back out. But on the off chance she wanted to go through with asking for his help, she needed to figure out the best way to do it. She debated internally until the pause became uncomfortable.

"Everything okay?" Cole broke the silence.

"Yeah, kind of."

"Kind of?"

"Hmmmm." Serafina stalled some more.

"Okay, what's up?"

Serafina could hear Cole breathe in deeply on the other end of the call as he listened for her response. She committed to asking for his help, but how was she going to ask?

"Well, you do investigative work, right?"

Cole became quiet and reserved. "Why do you ask?"

Serafina realized he must be suspecting she looked at the report. She didn't want him to know she had read it. "I just figured since you said you are a police officer, that's all."

Cole remained silent on the other end.

In that moment, it felt like Cole was pulling away, so she blurted it out. "We have two clients—well, actually we have more than two clients, but these two clients in particular, well, they called this morning and they both want some surveillance done and both jobs are now. Normally, it's me and Hollis, and we tag-team the jobs, but, well, now it's just me and I don't know what to do. I can't be at two places at once, and I don't know anyone else I can ask. I was going to call the first client back and tell him we can't . . ."

Cole interrupted Serafina. "Don't."

Serafina stopped midsentence. "Don't what?"

"Don't do that. Don't call them and cancel the job."

"But . . ." Serafina felt she needed to explain.

"I'll do it," Cole said.

"You'll do it?" Serafina beamed with joy and resisted the urge to laugh. "You don't even know what I'm asking you to do."

"And?" Cole asked.

"And, what if it's not something you want to commit to?"

"Will it help you out?"

"Tremendously."

"Then, okay, on one condition."

Serafina sat thinking of what the condition could be, and felt guarded, as if she'd been tricked. "What's the condition?"

"The condition is . . ." Cole paused.

Serafina remained quiet.

"You stop looking at me like I'm some kind of asshole."

"Wha—" Serafina started to respond.

"Because I'm not. I'm not an asshole. I'm actually a really nice person."

Serafina felt unsure about how to respond.

Just then, Cole moved the conversation along to a more comfortable place. "So, tell me what I'm being asked to do."

Serafina put up her guard. "You know what? Nevermind."

"Don't be like that. I want to help. What do you need me for?"

Serafina resented the insinuation that she needed anyone. "I don't *need* anyone."

"That's not what I meant. Geez, woman! Can you put down your wall for just a second?"

There was silence between them on the line.

"Please?" Cole said softly.

Serafina wanted to trust him.

"So, you would *like* me to help be the backup for a job," Cole said, proceeding cautiously.

Serafina reluctantly responded, "Yes."

"Okay, and that means I will cover one of them while you do the other. Am I correct?"

"Yes." Serafina was quicker with that response.

"I got you covered."

This doesn't mean we're friends.

• • •

Serafina sat in the Explorer on a residential street, watching for her subject to appear from within his home. The visor cam was facing that direction and recording without audio. It had been such a relief to have Cole's help. Although, she wasn't about to admit it.

As Serafina homed in on the subject's front door, she looked through the pile of mail left on the passenger side seat from the other day. She noticed the phone bill for the agency still in the pile and remembered she never got a chance to pay it. She picked it up and looked it over.

Instinctively, as if an internal alarm went off, Serafina glanced up at the subject's front door. There was no change in status, so she grabbed her iPad from the equipment bag. She clicked on the Verizon app and logged in.

While keeping her eyes locked in the general direction of the subject, Serafina looked through the call history of Hollis's old cell phone to check on who he'd been in contact with recently. One number looked familiar. She wrote it down on the printed copy of the phone bill with a pen from the center console.

Serafina noticed some movement in front of her and looked up to see that it was the subject's neighbor pulling into their driveway. She watched the neighbor grab their mail from a mailbox right outside their front door before going inside. She looked back over to the subject's door again. Nothing notable.

Serafina looked on the call history of her own cell phone account for the number she had called earlier that day. *It was the same number.* The woman who said she didn't know Hollis actually spoke with him last Friday night for exactly nine minutes and thirty-six seconds, according to the call history of Hollis's old cell phone. How do two people who don't know each other manage to converse for almost ten minutes and not remember? There is no way that woman doesn't know Hollis, she thought.

Serafina looked at the subject's door. Still no movement. Then she looked back at the woman's phone number still in her call history. This woman clearly lied to her. But why? Serafina couldn't make sense of it.

Serafina continued to take quick glances at the subject's front door. Each time . . . nothing. She went back to the online account and looked at the call history for Hollis's cell phone again. That woman's number was on the bill at least four times spread out over the month. It looked like they talked at least once a week during that billing cycle.

She repetitively tapped the pen against the steering wheel. *That was it*. She went to her call history, selected the woman's number, and pressed send.

The phone rang. Serafina expected the woman to answer any minute, but instead, the phone just rang. Serafina let out a huff in frustration and then looked back up at the front door again. "This is a waste of my time."

She picked up the iPad again. "All right, lady. You wanna play? Two words: Reverse search."

Instantly realizing how corny that sounded, like some sort of catch phrase in a movie, she shuddered in embarrassment.

Serafina pulled up the background searching program and logged into her account. She looked at the woman's phone number on her phone several times as she typed the number into the search field. *Search*.

The search immediately resulted in a name. "There you go. Ms. Erika Santiago."

Serafina wrote down the address on the paper copy of the phone bill and then typed it into Google Maps on her iPad. Once the location was up and showing, she zoomed in on it. The location was near the Springwells Avenue and Vernor Highway area, just a short distance from Clark Park. Serafina's brows furrowed as she pondered its distance from the crash site.

This woman spoke with Hollis last Friday night, essentially right before he was shot. *She's got to know something*.

Focused on the mystery woman now, Serafina grumbled at having to continue looking up at the front door of the subject again, but she wasn't about to lose him either. If he happened to leave while she wasn't looking, it would make the whole morning a complete waste. Not that it wasn't already, but she'd have some explaining to do if she wanted to be paid for the time.

With nothing changed, Serafina went back to another section of the program and clicked on the car registration option. She typed Erika Santiago's information into the fields. The search revealed Erika to be registered as driving a 2012 white Ford Fusion.

"See you soon, Erika," Serafina said as she wrote the description of the vehicle on the printed copy of the phone bill.

Serafina's phone began to ring. She grabbed it and looked quickly at the caller before answering. "Hey, Cole."

"Hey. So . . . just wanted to let you know this guy just finished doing his grocery shopping for the month. A lot of food, that's all I gotta say. Wow."

"That much, huh?" Serafina stared at the subject's front door before putting Cole on speaker phone so she wouldn't have to hold the device.

"Yeah, looks like he is heading home. It's already been three hours. How much time did they want to dedicate to this guy?"

"Usually, three hours is around the limit."

"Why three hours?"

"Not sure. Maybe they figure that if a person is going to abuse their FMLA or whatever, then they'd do it sooner rather than later? Plus, there's gotta be a limit at some point. I don't think it's a hard stop at three hours but like a general benchmark or whatever." She realized she said "whatever" a few times and felt self-conscious. Was she being too casual with him? Would he appreciate it or start to see her as less than and not respect her?

The subject's front door opened, and the subject stepped onto his front porch. He looked around. *He's up to something*, Serafina thought.

She continued to watch him. "Hey I gotta go. My guy's up to something."

"Okay, sure thing."

Serafina picked up her camera and began taking pictures of the subject on his front porch. She was about to hang up when Cole stopped her. "Oh, wait! Hey . . . so, should I drop the surveillance?"

Serafina was hyper-focused on the subject now and only half-listening to Cole. "Yeah," she responded as she watched the subject prop the storm door open and then reenter the dwelling.

"Okay, I'll have the report and footage ready later today or first thing tomorrow."

"Okay, thanks," Serafina said without much thought while she watched for her subject to reappear.

"No problem." The call ended on Cole's end first.

Serafina realized that she should have been more attentive, and she regretted having been distracted—even if it was just Cole.

Serafina wondered what this guy was being investigated for because he was definitely about to do something he shouldn't. She could just feel it in her gut. Was it for misuse of FMLA, or ADA, or Worker's Comp; or was it something else, like theft? She figured it would probably be easier if she knew what someone shouldn't be doing to catch them doing something they weren't supposed to be doing. Did this guy have intermittent FMLA for vertigo or migraines, and he wasn't supposed to be doing anything other than resting? How about anxiety, or stress? That's a more difficult one—what if the doctor told them to go do that one thing they're doing because it helped ease that? How about care of a parent, where the parent is nowhere in sight? Was it for an injury he claimed to have sustained, yet didn't seem to have when he thought no one was looking?

Whatever the reason, Serafina needed to record his actions. She double-checked to make sure the video camera on the visor was positioned to get the footage.

The subject came back shortly with a heavy box and carried it down to the driveway. He then went back inside several more times to retrieve four more boxes. From the way he carried them, they appeared to be heavy.

"Hmmm. Whatcha got in them there boxes, huh?"

The subject locked up the front door and then released the pin stop for the storm door and let it slowly close shut.

Serafina continued taking numerous photos with her camera as the subject walked down his driveway to his vehicle and backed it up to where the boxes were stacked at the edge of the driveway near the front porch.

The subject loaded the boxes into his vehicle, and Serafina prepared to turn on the engine as soon as he was done.

After loading the boxes, he backed out onto the side street and began driving toward the main street.

"Where are you going?" Serafina said under her breath.

She followed the subject to a storage facility a few miles away and parked a half block down the street as the subject pulled up to the entrance. He put his code into the security system, the gate opened, and he drove through.

After about fifteen minutes, the subject reappeared at the exit gate. When the gate opened, he drove through and then headed the opposite way back home. He pulled into his driveway, parking in the backyard just as he had before, and then he went inside the house through the front door.

"Four-and-a-half hours just for that. You suck, dude."

Serafina waited another twenty minutes, losing all patience. She was dying of thirst and had to use the restroom something fierce. "That's it," she said. "I'm calling it. Done for the day." She started up the Explorer. "Now, where the hell's a bathroom around here?"

Chapter 17

Nothing fitting the description of a white Fusion was anywhere in sight as Serafina neared the location shown in Google Maps. "Erika San-ti-aaaaaaagooooo . . . where arrrrrrre youuuuuu?" She slowed the Explorer for the last block and looked at the addresses on both sides of the street to gauge how close she was, knowing that the GPS could sometimes be off.

Passing the searched address on the righthand side, Serafina looked down the long driveway of the upper and lower flat to the detached garage in the backyard. No white Fusion. She continued to drive down the block and then turned around and parked so that she could face the apartment building and have the advantage of seeing the white Fusion drive down from the main street.

Serafina felt uncomfortably exposed just sitting in the Explorer in broad daylight. After waiting a few minutes, she determined that that feeling was not going away anytime soon, so she decided to drive the short five-minute distance down Vernor Highway to Clark Park to see if Gill was around to pass some time. It would be nice to have a respite of sorts and engage in some interesting conversation with someone from her past who knew her parents and worked at their store. Maybe she would recall moments from her forgotten past, she thought.

At Clark Park, a few vehicles caught Serafina's eye, as they somewhat looked like the mystery vehicle in the ATM footage—the rust-colored Chevy Impala. Was it close? And was this some sort of instinctual, Spidey sense she had from being in close proximity to it? Without overthinking things, she began driving the perimeter of Clark Park to see if it might show up. She drove past the basketball court on the left, which was just as heavily occupied as the other day but now had a different mix of basketball players. As she rounded the park next to the freeway and looked over at the Ambassador Bridge to Canada, she saw a white car, and even though it wasn't a Ford Fusion, she now had Erika's vehicle as part of her mental search.

She came back around to Vernor Highway and waited for traffic to clear in order to turn left, focusing heavily on any vehicles looking anything remotely like Erika Santiago's or the mystery vehicle in the ATM footage. *White Ford Fusion. Rust-colored Chevy Impala. White Ford Fusion. Rust-colored Chevy Impala.* Nothing matched.

After making a quick left onto Vernor Highway and then another quick left onto Clark Avenue, Serafina made her way down to the basketball court again. Down aways, a dark blue Jeep Liberty with at least ten years on it pulled up to the left side of the street next to the basketball court and momentarily parked. She cautiously slowed down, noticing that the two individuals in the front seats were looking in her direction and talking with one another. With the engine still on, the driver's side door opened and a Hispanic man in his forties got out. He motioned to her to come over.

Okay, Weirdo Alert. Not knowing the man's intentions, Serafina wasn't sure what to do. She was too close to make an illegal U-Turn on Clark Avenue, and she was too close to park. As she neared them, she concluded the best course of action was to simply ignore the man and continue on.

"Hey, Serafina!" someone called out to her.

Immediately, Serafina took notice of her name and briefly met eyes with the man standing outside the dark blue Jeep Liberty. Her focus then went beyond him to the man in the passenger seat. *Gill?*

A white vehicle of some make and model was coming on the opposite side of the street and slowing down to a complete stop behind the dark blue Jeep Liberty, as it watchfully passed the man standing in the street. It wasn't a Ford Fusion.

Serafina motioned to the man that she would be parking to the right-hand side of the street, and he responded with a nod. She turned off the Explorer after pulling over and walked across the street once a few other vehicles cleared their pass through.

Gill leaned over toward the driver's side window and looked out at her. "Well, well, well." He beamed.

"Hey, there! I thought that was you calling my name." Serafina beamed back at Gill and then looked at his companion, the driver of the dark blue Jeep Liberty, who was guarded yet smiling at her.

"What brings you 'round?" Gill asked.

Serafina refocused her attention to Gill. "I was in the area."

"Yeah? So, what you been up to?"

"Nothing, really. Thought I might see you here, so figured I'd stop and say hi."

Gill laughed. "Is that why you nearly drove past us?"

Serafina's face felt exceptionally warm with embarrassment. "I . . ." She looked at Gill's companion.

"I'm messing with you!" Gill laughed even harder.

"Oh." Serafina blushed.

Gill's companion interrupted. "Hey, I'm Renzo."

"That's my brother," Gill added.

"Oh!" Serafina just realized Gill had a brother. She looked at Renzo, "I thought—"

"That I was some sort of creep hitting on you?"

"Kind of?" Serafina sheepishly admitted.

"It's okay," Renzo said.

"Naw, you had it right! He actually is kind of creepy," Gill blurted and then bellowed out in laughter.

Renzo didn't even try to defend himself. He smirked and nodded with admission, almost like a confession.

"I remember you mentioning him last time. I didn't realize he was your brother." She looked briefly at the ball players, distracted by some loud, boisterous bantering, and then resumed her attention on Renzo and Gill. "So, which one of you's the oldest?"

Without hesitation, Gill jauntily coaxed her. "Guess!"

"Not that game. Come on!" Serafina lightheartedly opposed, looking to Renzo for support. "Seriously—how's that gonna end for me?"

"All right, all right." Gill chuckled. "I'm the big brother."

"Really?" she asked.

"You act surprised." Gill questioned her.

"You wouldn't think so with the way he acts, would you?" Renzo joked.

"Very funny," Gill said to Renzo,

"No, I just . . . never mind, I don't know what I was thinking. See? This is what I mean—how is this gonna end for me?" Serafina laughed.

Gill continued. "Yeah, I'm just a few years older."

"And is it just you two? Or are there any more siblings I should expect to meet soon?"

Renzo held up his hand as if to say "one minute" to one of the basketball players who'd caught his attention. "I'll be right back," he said to Gill and Serafina, and then walked over to the basketball court.

Serafina watched Renzo strut over to the basketball court where a player was waiting for him. From the look of it, their conversation was nothing serious, so she resumed her attention to Gill. He was looking hard at her, which made her blush.

"What?" she asked.

He shook his head. "Nothing."

She tilted her head, waiting for him to admit that it wasn't her imagination that he was staring hard at her.

"Okay, fine. It's just wild!"

"What is?"

"When I look at you, I swear I can remember you as that little girl. You couldn't have been more than . . ." He thought about it. "Four?"

She assumed he meant when they last saw each other. "Yeah, I was four."

He smiled and nodded, as if remembering.

"What do you remember? I mean, I don't remember much. I remember some things here and there, but it's not like any of it makes sense."

"Yeah, I know what you mean."

Gill sat quietly while staring off at the young men balling on the court. Serafina watched the dribbling, passing, and hooping too, pretending it wasn't awkward in that moment and wondering if she should break the silence first.

"I remember they were good people." Gill turned to Serafina and locked eyes with her. His eyes seemed to say their own words. He tightened his lips together as if he wanted to speak and then simply nodded his head in agreement with himself.

Serafina felt compelled to say something; she just wasn't sure what that something was.

Gill continued, "I'm sorry for what happened to them. To you."

Serafina replied, "I know. It's not your fault."

Gill just nodded, accepting the past.

"Hey, so, where were you two off to?" Serafina asked.

"Home, actually. We live right over on the other side of the park, over there." Gill pointed in the direction beyond the basketball court. "This is on the way home when we get off the freeway."

"Oh." Serafina felt that the energy between them was now off somehow. She noticed Renzo finishing up his conversation and heading back over. "Looks like he's done now."

Renzo must have felt the weird energy too because he immediately looked at both of them with a questioning look. "All good?"

Serafina was hoping for Gill to respond first. She wasn't sure if things were "all good."

"Yeah! Of course! All good in the hood," Gill gleefully responded.

It was a little over the top for an answer, but she'd take that over the weird energy.

"So, how do you know each other?" Renzo asked as he readied to open the driver's side door. "Serafina . . . right?"

"She's *the* Serafina." Gill emphasized "the" as if she were famous but not necessarily in a good way.

Renzo looked confused for a split second and then his facial expression changed to reveal myriad thoughts and feelings. It caught Serafina off guard at first, but then Renzo's face softened.

"Hey, I'm sorry. I didn't put two and two together. I mean, Gill yelled your name when you were about to pass us, but it didn't register . . ."

"It's okay. Really, it's fine." Serafina reassured them both. She already felt bad about how it made Gill feel. She wanted to move past it as quickly as possible. "So . . ." she thought how she might change the subject. "Gill mentioned you're on your way home. I won't keep you."

"No worries. I had to stop and see my boy real quick anyway," Renzo said.

"It's been a long day. We'll catch up next time, okay?" Gill reassured her with a softer—almost apologetic—tone.

Serafina waved them off from the driver's side door of the Explorer and then exhaled as if a heavy weight had come off her. That visit was not what she had expected, not that she had been expecting anything in particular. She refocused on her plan to learn more about Erika Santiago and proceeded back over to the address on record.

Halfway down the block, after pulling onto the street where Erika supposedly lived, Serafina noticed a Hispanic woman roughly in her late twenties to early thirties getting into the driver side of a white Fusion parked in the street in front of the address on the GPS. Instantly, a rush of adrenaline kicked in as Serafina prepared herself to follow the woman. She decelerated and pulled to the side of the street to wait for the Fusion to drive off.

The woman put her visor down and looked in the mirror on the opposite side. She put lipstick on and then closed the visor.

"Hurry the fuck up," Serafina said, sure that the woman was Erika.

The woman pulled out and began to drive away. Serafina followed the woman, but then the woman pulled into a driveway to turn and go back up toward Vernor Highway.

Shit. Serafina needed to turn around too if she was going to follow the white Fusion, but she didn't want to be too obvious. Instead of turning into a driveway to turn around, Serafina continued past the Fusion and drove around the corner at the end of the block to head back up using the street one over.

At Vernor Highway, she looked over to her right just as the white Fusion pulled up to the stop sign on the corner of the other street. With a quick look for any oncoming traffic, the woman in the white Fusion pulled out onto the main street. Serafina turned left also, squeezing in at the last minute before traffic on the left completely closed the window. She proceeded to follow behind the woman a few car lengths back.

As she approached Springwells, Serafina started to pass a dollar store, liquor store, and laundromat set back from the street in a strip mall much like any other. She paid little attention to the vehicles and patrons until a rust-colored Chevy Impala caught her eye. She took a second look and immediately recognized it as the mystery vehicle from the ATM video footage.

There was a guy leaning into the driver's side window talking to the driver, with his back turned so Serafina couldn't see what he looked like. She could, however, see the driver, and as the traffic slowed down momentarily at the traffic light, she took the opportunity to get an even better look at him. His clean-shaven face sported a low-profile goatee, and he wore a white hoodie with a black trucker cap. She guessed him to be in his thirties.

The white Fusion was the first to approach the traffic light just as it was turning red, then the car in front of Serafina. With a few moments to spare, Serafina grabbed her phone off the passenger seat and took a quick picture of the driver. Within seconds of the traffic light changing back to green, the person behind Serafina honked.

"Impatient, are we?" Serafina said. "Geez, gimme a second."

Serafina looked back at the Impala before driving off. The person talking to the driver of the Impala looked over in her direction to see where the honk came from and then immediately leaned back over and continued to talk with the driver. He looked a lot like the speaker at the mentorship program. *Was that Xavier Palo that she saw?*

The woman in the white Fusion was far ahead now, and there was risk in losing her. Serafina had to drive away at that moment, but her mind was going a mile a minute.

Was Xavier Palo responsible for the attack on Hollis? That wasn't his Impala, though—or was it? Maybe it was Xavier's, and he was selling it to the dude in the driver seat?

She imagined how the conversation might have gone between them, with Xavier pointing out all the great aspects of the vehicle and the driver feeling it out, envisioning himself taking it for a spin. That's dumb, she told herself. Or is it?

She wavered on all possibilities. One such thought was that Xavier might have had the driver of the Impala shoot Hollis. But why would he do that? Think! Think! Xavier *was* a suspect of her parents' murders, which already made him somewhat suspicious. And Hollis was possibly investigating him for her parents' murders. Did Hollis get too close to finding out about Xavier, so then Xavier tried to take him out? Maybe he wanted to make sure Hollis couldn't bring any unwanted attention on him after all these years.

Serafina kept a steady pace—mostly, staying behind by a car or two—as she followed the white Fusion, making sure she stayed close only when there was risk of being separated by a traffic light. She didn't want the woman, presumably Erika Santiago, to suspect that she was being followed.

At Springwells Avenue, the white Fusion turned left at the traffic light and headed toward I-75. Serafina sped up her pace to make the turn at the intersection before missing her chance.

Several blocks down, Serafina watched a green car pull out from the Dairy Queen parking lot and move into the available space in front of Serafina, closing the gap and forcing Serafina to slow down to let it in. It drove excessively slower than traffic, causing the white Fusion to gain distance.

"Seriously!" Serafina admonished the green car with exasperation.

The Fusion went under the viaduct just before I-75 and then immediately pulled into the McDonald's parking lot on the right side. The black car behind the white Fusion and the slow-ass green car continued on.

As Serafina came out from under the viaduct, she pulled into the parking lot and scanned the area for the white Fusion. It was at the menu board where the woman was now placing her order. The food smelled incredible coming in through Serafina's slightly opened window. Her stomach growled as she imagined tearing up some warm, salty fries. She couldn't risk grabbing something to eat and losing the trail though. She'd have to wait until later. Instead, she just watched, patiently waiting for the woman to pull away from the drive-thru window, ready to trail behind her again.

Serafina followed the white Fusion out of the McDonald's parking lot, all the way back up Springwells, past the Dairy Queen, to where it made a right on Vernor Highway and then a left on Central Avenue, and another left on Dix Street. Serafina continued following the white Fusion past the point where Dix Street turned into Dix Avenue and down the street some more, all the way to a building on the right that had all the signs of being a strip club, especially with the name Tamale Girlz. Serafina quickly took notice that there wasn't any traffic on the road before slowing down and pulling over to the curb.

"All right, Erika. Guess we know what you do." Part of Serafina subconsciously knew all along, knowing Hollis.

Serafina felt it in her gut that this dancer knew something. But what? She definitely knew Hollis—despite acting like she didn't. Why lie about knowing Hollis? Did Hollis meet up with her the night he was shot? Serafina looked at the clock on the console of Explorer as she thought about people that she could ask who worked there—the valet guy, the bouncer, the bartender. It was 6:20 p.m. Serafina squinted her eyes as she thought it all out. Somebody would surely recognize Hollis if she pulled up a picture from her phone.

Assuming this strip club was like most others, she figured it wouldn't be opening until 7:00 p.m. and that Erika was just early to get herself ready for stage review. Maybe there was time to go grab some food and then come back.

Serafina was about to head back to McDonald's when she remembered a Burger King was on Vernor Highway if she wanted to backtrack that way and see if the rust-colored Chevy Impala—and Xavier—was still parked in that strip mall.

As she passed the spot just outside the dollar store, liquor store, and laundromat where the Impala had been, she envisioned Xavier and the other guy as if they were still there. Mexicantown was a small community, but not that small. It seemed like more than just a coincidence that Xavier would be seen next to the same vehicle in the ATM footage—the one having suspected involvement in shooting Hollis—especially when Xavier was a suspect in her parents' murder. Maybe she should pay Mr. Xavier Palo another visit.

A group of teens were hanging out near the entrance when Serafina pulled into the Burger King parking lot. She considered the drive-thru option but wanted to take the opportunity to use the restroom. With her adrenaline calming down, her bladder had awakened, and she didn't want to have to scarf down her food. Plus, where else was there to go to the restroom? She was decidedly against using a gas station restroom, even if they had one available to use, so she followed around the drive-thru, exited on the side street, and parked next to the alleyway. It was a short walking distance to the building, but she got to avoid being a potential target to obnoxious behavior.

When Serafina came out of the Burger King restroom, she could see the teens still doing their thing in the parking lot outside the entrance to her left. She proceeded to order some food and then poured herself a fountain pop as she waited for her food to be bagged. Afterward, she slipped out the other side door toward the Explorer parked on the side street, munching on a few French fries from the bag as she walked. *Heavenly!*

Serafina opened the driver's side door and was preparing to get inside when she noticed that the passenger-side window had been busted out. Everything she'd had on the seat and the floor were missing—her equipment bag, iPad, camera, notebook, even the video camera clipped to the visor. Gone.

. . .

"The report should be ready in a few days." The police officer handed Serafina his card. "If you think of anything else, call me."

Serafina took his card in her hand. "Thanks."

She got into the Explorer and watched as the police car drove away from the site. With the plan to go to the strip club to confront Erika still lingering over her like a dark cloud, she reluctantly looked at the time. It was almost 8:00 p.m. She withered at the thought of having to speak to anyone—or do anything that required energy. The only thing on her mind was getting home, putting comfy clothes on, getting in bed, and resting her head on a cold pillow—in that exact order. She remembered that Datson would be there hungry and wanting to be let back inside, so she put those on her list, assuring herself in the process that there would be nothing more added.

. . .

Serafina looked out at Datson from the back door, and while she waited in the doorway, pressed her fingers against the pressure points on her forehead, temples, and sinuses.

Datson relieved himself on a bush and then started meandering around the backyard, sniffing the ground.

"Datson!" she called to him.

Datson stopped in his tracks and stood looking at her.

"Come on, boy." She opened the door for him to come back inside, but he ignored her and went back to sniffing the ground.

She noticed he hadn't touched his dry dog food, so she brought the bowls inside and grabbed a can of dog food she knew he'd appreciate, peeled off the metal top, and dumped its contents into Datson's food bowl. She refilled his water bowl with fresh water.

When she went back to the back door, Datson was there waiting to be let in. She expected Datson to scarf down his food, but he just sniffed it and lay down as if not interested.

"Not hungry?" she asked him.

Serafina poured herself a glass of iced tea and opened up the cabinet where they kept the medicine. Unsure if she had a tension headache or sinus headache, she pulled out both the Sudafed and Aspirin bottles.

"One of you better work on this headache," she said as she took a mixture of both in her hand and swallowed them down with a swig of iced tea.

She left the light on above the stove and walked upstairs to the loft. She could hear Datson drinking his water as she climbed the stairs, feeling the weight of each step. As she came through the door for the loft, Datson pushed past her and jumped on the bed.

"Excuse me?" she said to Datson and then closed the door to the loft and locked it behind her.

Datson laid his head down, watching her every move, as if expecting to have to jump off the bed upon command. Serafina just smiled at him and went over to the windows to close the blinds. The sun was going down but still shone through the exposed parts of the window. She walked over to the bed, undressed to panties and a T-shirt, and climbed under the covers. The cold pillow on her head never felt better.

Her phone dinged with a message. She turned her head on the pillow and looked out of one squinting eye at the sender's name on the screen of her phone. She groaned when she saw it was Randy.

9:39 p.m.

Randy Staszak: *Any update on Hollis?*

It occurred to her that she hadn't spoken to Randy since Monday—

probably one of the longest times she'd gone without hearing from him. She told herself it was his doing but felt a deep sense of guilt in the pit of her stomach. She wasn't ready to be accountable for anything though. He'd hurt her with his nonchalant comments, and she didn't want him to think that was okay. But here he was acting like he actually cared. She didn't have it in her to leave him hanging. She started typing out her message, knowing at that moment that he'd see she was typing on his end. She was committed to sending something now, because if she didn't, she'd be paying for it with escalated angst.

9:41 p.m.

Serafina: *He woke up last night.*

She watched him texting back right away on the other end. There was a slight pause, and then his message came through. Without much thought, she responded right away.

9:43 p.m.

Randy Staszak: *Well, that's hopeful, right?*

Serafina: *Yeah*

She knew she couldn't leave it at just that. She needed to say more than that or Randy would read into it and take some sort of offense.

9:43 p.m.

Serafina: *Not feeling well. Going to bed.*

Serafina could see the dots as Randy was typing something. She waited for the message to be sent. The dots stopped. Then the dots restarted.

9:44 p.m.

Randy Staszak: *Hope you feel better.*

Something about his message felt constrained, like he was holding back. She had no energy to deal with his many moods. She waited a second more and then put the phone down on the mattress again.

Serafina's phone dinged again. Certain it would be Randy, she braced herself for him unleashing his thoughts.

9:46 p.m.

Cole McDermott: *I was going to stop by the agency if you're there. I have the report for you.*

Hmmm. Cole. That was new. And unexpected. Serafina wasn't sure how she felt about Cole texting her. She needed to respond to him though. She had no energy to talk. At least he was texting and not calling. Otherwise, she'd have to ignore his call. She sent him back a text.

9:48 p.m.

Serafina: *Can we meet tomorrow instead?*

There was a pause, as if Cole was thinking of how to respond.

9:48 p.m.

Cole McDermott*: Yeah, no worries.*

Chapter 18

Hollis heard familiar voices around him, but he couldn't register what they were saying. He tried lying still in his hospital bed, listening, but his body ached with a dull throb in the region of his shoulder that intensified in spurts—first, tolerable and then intolerable.

The intolerable spurts were like the rising tide, swelling in size as they came in, lingering, bubbling on the edges. As another wave came in, he held onto the lightweight hospital blanket that covered him, tightening his grasp, groaning as he rode the pain like it was a fierce, wild animal.

Levi shuddered as if recognizing his friend's groans as those from another moment in the past. "He needs pain medicine," he ordered as he walked over to Hollis.

"I'm getting the nurse. You stay here with him?" Suong swiftly exited the hospital room, not waiting for a response.

"Yes, of course," Levi said, not noticing Suong had already left the room.

Hollis looked up at Levi's face looking down upon him. So weary were Levi's eyes, as if weighted down by a troubled mind. Hollis resisted the vulnerability he felt. To have so much attention—to be a burden—was humiliating. If he hadn't been stuck in that bed, immobilized, he would have done all he could to make those feelings go away.

But since he wasn't able to escape in any fashion, he succumbed to the comfort of his friend's face, allowing himself to be soothed in the moments between the waves, loosening his grip on the blanket when the intensity of the throbbing subsided to dull aching.

Levi's face kept going out of focus. Hollis closed his eyes and then reopened them to see if that would improve his vision. It helped some, so he closed and reopened them a few more times. With each time, he had to will his eyes back open from a state of rest.

The nurse came into the room with Suong following behind and approached the hospital bed with a syringe in her hand. "How are we doing, Frank?" she asked and then inserted the syringe into the IV attached to Hollis's arm.

Frank watched her on his right side, waiting for whatever she put in his IV to alleviate his pain. The nurse began taking his vitals, methodically and without emotion. As he became less tense, he looked around the room. Levi was on his left side. Suong was also on his left, but closer to the foot of his hospital bed. Serafina was nowhere in the room from what he could see. He closed his eyes, disappointed.

"Come on in, son," Levi said. "No need to hang outside the door."

"Sorry, I didn't know if I was interrupting anything," Cole said as the nurse left the room.

Hollis breathed through the last bit of throbbing as the pain medicine started to ease his pain and then looked to see that Cole had entered his hospital room.

Levi reassured Cole. "No, no, you actually came at a good time. Hollis is awake."

Hollis focused his energy on keeping open his increasingly heavy eyes.

"Hi, I'm Cole. I'm a friend." Cole addressed Suong's questioning look of who he might be.

Suong looked surprised. "Oh?"

Levi cut in. "He's a police officer. He's doing some side help for Hollis."

"Hmm." Suong thought more on the matter. "You're a police officer?"

"Yes, ma'am," Cole said politely. "For Detroit."

Suong continued her questioning. "And you help Hollis?"

Hollis was too tired to be annoyed by Suong being Suong as he listened to their exchange.

"Yes, ma'am." Cole attempted to disengage with her by not looking at her directly.

"With side help?" she asked.

Dismissing her interrogation, Cole looked to Levi for help. Levi moved over to allow Cole next to Hollis's side and then gave Suong a look.

"How are you feeling?" Cole stood, looking down at Hollis.

Sore as a boil. The throbbing had subsided to a dull ache, enough for Hollis to relax his breathing. He licked his dry lips and spoke with a scratchy voice. "Better now."

Suong pushed past Levi to sit in the chair in the corner. Levi moved next to Cole. Looking over the left side of the bed, he asked Hollis, "Is there anything I can do to help?"

Hollis felt a sudden drowsiness take over him. He closed his eyes to rest them and attempted to speak but felt himself sinking into a deep, restful state.

"He's going again," Levi said.

"Yeah, looks like it." Cole stepped back from the side of the hospital bed, allowing Levi closer access to Hollis.

"We're going to get going now. Get some rest, my friend." Levi touched Hollis's arm, and then turned around and sighed. "I suppose I should give Serafina an update on how he's doing."

"Why?" Suong said curtly.

Levi didn't respond, but Hollis imagined him giving her the look he often gave her when she was crossing lines. *Good! That judgmental bitch needs to be put in her place.* He let go and allowed the sleep to take him.

Chapter 19

It was close to 10:30 a.m. Thursday morning when Serafina woke up. If it weren't for the fact that she felt like crap, she might have felt guilty about sleeping in that late, especially on a workday. But her head hurt—possibly worse than the night before. She wondered if it was from a tension headache or the usual sinus pressure. Either way, she needed something for whatever was causing the pain.

She went down to the kitchen, with Datson trailing behind her. She quickly let him outside, leaving the main door open to keep an eye on him. She opened up the cabinet where medicine was stored and pulled down sinus pressure medicine and aspirin, still unsure which would help best. She took both pills with a swig of water she cupped in her hands from the faucet.

She considered having coffee, but the thought of it sounded unappealing. After finding some teabags, she started to make herself some tea instead.

She grabbed a can of dog food for Datson from the pantry and began to scoop the contents into his food bowl when she noticed he hadn't touched his food from last night.

That's odd.

She picked up the dog food bowl and dumped the old food into the garbage can. After wiping down the bowl with a wet paper towel, she served him fresh canned dog food and continued to make her tea.

With her tea in hand, she opened the back door and called to Datson.

He resisted coming inside, so she closed the door and started to the front office area to check the desk phones. She hadn't had any calls from the office forward to her phone, so she wanted to make sure it was still set to forward.

On her desk, she could see the light for messages was not lit. She turned to leave the room and head back to bed but heard a knock at the front door as she did. When she turned back around, she saw Cole looking at her through the glass part of the door. *Great. Just what I want, to have Cole see me look like this.*

She reluctantly walked over to the door and let Cole in.

"Sorry about just stopping by."

But are you, really?

"Is this a bad time?"

And what if I said it was? "As good of a time as any. Come in." Serafina went to sit on the couch, placing her tea on the side table. She crouched her legs up under her and rested her head on the back cushion of the couch.

Cole stepped inside and looked at Serafina, visually absorbing her physical appearance.

"You okay?" Cole closed the door and stood awkwardly near the couch.

"No, my head is killing me."

"You take anything for it?"

"Yeah, nothing is working. I just want to lay my head down."

Cole didn't say or do anything in response.

Serafina looked up at Cole still standing there. "You can sit down."

Cole sat down stiffly on the opposite side of the couch.

"What you got there?" Serafina looked at the manila envelope Cole held in his hands.

He looked at the manila envelope then back at Serafina. "Just the report and pics from the other night. There's an invoice in there too for the billable hours."

Of course there is. She knew he was justified in billing his hours, that it wasn't a favor. She just wasn't in the most positive mindset, and she knew she wasn't being fair with that stance.

"Okay." Serafina closed her eyes and breathed slowly.

"I stopped by the hospital and saw Hollis."

"Mm-hmm." Serafina acknowledged Cole the best she could.

"He's more responsive than yesterday."

"Uhn." Serafina grunted.

"I couldn't stay long. He needed to rest."

Serafina opened her left eye slightly and looked at Cole. Then she nodded slowly.

From outside, Datson could be heard barking.

"I think he wants inside," Cole said, looking at Serafina with concern. "I can let him in."

Cole got up and walked to the back door while Serafina melted into the couch more.

• • •

"Hey!" Cole frantically nudged Serafina awake, causing her to jump out of a deep sleep. "The Explorer got broke into!"

"I know."

"You know?" Cole seemed confused.

"Yeah, please don't say anything to Hollis."

Cole nodded, waiting for more information.

"It happened yesterday." Serafina started to nestle her head back into the pillow on the arm of the couch. Her head started to hurt more just thinking about it. The tension peaked and started to spill out of her. She covered her eyes and let out all she'd been holding in.

"I was doing a job and stopped in Burger King to use the bathroom, and when I came out, the window was smashed out and my bag with all my equipment got taken! My cameras too. All the surveillance I did for that job is gone now. I don't know what to do. What am I gonna tell that company? That's one of the agency's biggest clients. What happens if they never want to hire us again because I had to be so stupid . . ."

"Wait, hold on. Hold on." Cole stopped Serafina midsentence. "You are *not* stupid."

"No?" Serafina looked at Cole with puffy eyes. She wiped the tears that had gathered near her nose.

"No." He sat looking at Serafina. They just looked at one another for a moment. Cole reassured her with a comforting grin. "Where are the keys?"

"To what?"

"The Explorer, silly."

"Why? Where are you going with it?"

"Up Woodward to Henderson Glass. Probably take an hour or so for them to fix the window. At least that's how long it took when I had to get my windshield repaired. Everything will be fine. You get some rest. I'll even take Datson. Get him out for a bit."

"You sure?" Serafina pushed her hair back and wiped her face where tears had started to dry.

Cole looked at Serafina as if he was really seeing her and nodded. She imagined him kissing her forehead as if she were a little girl who'd skinned her knee, and in that moment, she wanted to be that little girl getting kissed on her forehead. She wanted to be held and hugged and comforted. And what's more, she wanted to be held and hugged and comforted by Cole.

"Okay, if you're sure." She avoided looking at him further until she could understand the feelings she was having. "They're in the front pocket of my jacket upstairs."

Cole patted Serafina on her lower leg. "Okay. Do you need any medicine before I go?"

"No, thanks. I already took some before you showed up."

"Anything to drink then?"

Serafina shook her head and looked at her cup of tea on the side table.

Cole looked at the cup of tea. "Oh yeah, right."

"You could give me that blanket though. If you don't mind." She reached out and pointed to the throw blanket hanging over the side chair.

Cole grabbed the blanket and opened it up to place on Serafina. She took it from his hands and placed it on herself.

As Cole started to head out, she called to him, "There's glass on the seat—the driver's seat, I mean. Obviously, there's glass on the passenger side seat."

When Cole turned around, Serafina cautioned him. "Be careful when you get in."

Cole nodded. "I'll clean it up. You said the keys are in your jacket?"

"Yeah, front pocket." Serafina started to get up.

Cole insisted she not get up. "It's okay, I can get them. You said they're upstairs?"

Serafina nodded. "I think on the counter, or the chair near the door. I can't remember."

"No worries. I'm sure I'll find the jacket."

Serafina was resting deeply and on the verge of being asleep when Cole returned with the keys to the Explorer. He sounded like he was about to say something but stopped himself when he saw her. She let him believe she was asleep, and she listened as he softly walked back out of the room.

• • •

Serafina woke up to silence. She sat up on the couch and looked around the office of the agency, remembering that Cole had taken the Explorer to get the window fixed.

Her mouth was parched, so she went to the kitchen and pulled a can of iced tea from the fridge. As she opened it, she noticed a note on the counter from Cole.

Datson didn't want to come.

She didn't see Datson, but the door to the loft was open, so she assumed he would be upstairs on her bed. He seemed to like that bed a lot.

She looked out the kitchen window into the backyard. Her Jeep was parked in its usual spot. Next to it was an empty spot where she'd parked the Explorer the night before.

How was she going to tell Hollis? About the Explorer? About the stolen camera? The equipment? All her work—lost. She didn't want to worry him . . . or disappoint him. But there just didn't seem to be a way around this mess. She was going to have to tell him.

What would she even tell Hollis? That she parked in a neighborhood she knew wasn't safe? That she was investigating things no one even asked her to investigate? That she risked their livelihood to do . . . what? To follow a woman who Hollis may or may not know, but even if he did . . . really, was it any of her business anyway? He might understand, but she couldn't bear to see him deflated when he found out it was a job for his main client. He could end up losing their business after this. Who would believe that she actually did the job and that she had no proof because everything was stolen from the vehicle? And even if she showed them a copy of her police report, it's not like it would make a difference. She had let everyone down. Without the pictures as proof, whatever report she wrote up would be useless.

What do I do? Hollis would know . . .

Serafina went up to the loft to peruse the stack of papers she'd brought in the other night from the Explorer. On the bed, Datson was sleeping well. She could see his feet moving as if he were walking in his dreams. She refocused her attention on the loose mail and whatnot on the counter that she'd picked up off the floor of the passenger side, notes and such that must have fallen when the equipment bag was grabbed. Hoping she could salvage something and not have it a total loss, she laid everything out. She read some of her scribbling, but nothing helpful to the job assignment was among the notes. What's the use? she thought.

Between several sheets of paper was the phone bill she never paid. Her internal nagging system told her to pay the phone bill already. No more delaying. She took out her phone and walked over to the couch with the phone bill. *It's the one thing I should be able to do without fucking up.*

As Serafina logged into the online phone account, she thought about how she was supposed to question Erika Santiago after going to Burger King and how she missed that opportunity. *Yep, I managed to screw that up too.*

After finally paying the phone bill, Serafina started scrolling through the call history of the agency's office phone, wondering if there might be calls between Erika and Hollis there as well. "She thinks she's fooling my ass, but she's not."

When her scrolling for the agency only revealed the one call, she moved on to scrolling through the call history for Hollis's personal cell phone again, down to the most recent calls. The very last call was him calling her phone number. The time of the call was 12:39 a.m.

Serafina sat at the counter-height chair and processed what that meant. Immediately, her mind went to the voicemail she'd received Saturday morning, the one she'd thought was some drunk guy calling to say he loved her—*the Whack Job*. That was Hollis? Hollis had called her to say he loved her?

The door downstairs in the kitchen opened and then immediately closed. Datson moved his ears but had no plans on getting up. Serafina shook her head. *What a good watchdog you are.*

She started down the stairs to the kitchen. "Hello?"

"Hey, you're awake," Cole said gleefully, as Serafina appeared. He turned around and placed medicine on the counter. "I stopped and got you some medicine. I wasn't sure what you had here, but this always helps me."

"Thanks," Serafina said, as she looked out of the back door window. The Explorer was parked in its usual spot with a new passenger window. Already knowing the answer, she asked, "They were able to fix the window?"

"Yeah, it took just a little bit longer since apparently they permanently closed the location on Woodward. Luckily, they have a location in Troy, so it wasn't much farther to drive. And there wasn't too much of a wait."

Serafina turned to face Cole standing at the counter, maintaining eye contact. "Thank you."

Her sincerity caught Cole off guard and he softly replied, "You're welcome."

"No, I mean it. You have no idea how much I appreciate you getting that done. How much did it cost? I can reimburse . . ."

"No rush. I know you're not feeling well." He took the receipt from his wallet and placed it on the counter. "Oh, I almost forgot . . ."

Serafina smiled with anticipation.

"So, after I left—you fell asleep, and I didn't want to disturb you . . ."

Serafina nodded, following along.

He continued, "I was backing up down the driveway, and this bum was snooping around . . ."

"Bum?" Serafina was both confused and concerned, as if she could anticipate what he'd be saying next. Could he be talking about her foster brother, DeMarcus?

"Yeah, it's okay. I told him to get the hell out of here."

"What?" Serafina erratically paced around the room.

With Serafina getting agitated, Cole tried to calm her with reassurances. "He was a bum. He was insisting on coming inside to talk with his sister."

"What!" Serafina stopped abruptly and stood before him.

"Relax. I wasn't about to have him come in."

"How long ago was it?" Serafina asked.

"It's all good. He's not around anymore."

Serafina repeated herself, this time with urgency, "How long ago was it?"

Cole responded quickly, "Right when I left. Maybe a couple hours ago?"

Serafina put her head back with closed eyes, as if pleading with God.

The seconds afterwards might have even been minutes while both just stood there not saying anything. Then, Serafina asked, "Did he have burn marks on his face?"

Cole's eyes showed concern. "I don't understand. Is everything okay?"

"Did he have burn marks on his face?" she enunciated the words.

Cole stumbled on his words. "I don't know, I mean, yeah, I think so."

Serafina started crying. *Yes, it was DeMarcus.*

"What am I missing here?" Cole asked, confused.

Unable to find the words to respond, Serafina shook her hands and head side to side.

"Hey, I'm sorry. I thought he was some bum. How was I supposed to know you knew him?" Cole said, as his eyes sought out hers.

They stood in the kitchen saying nothing to one another while Serafina calmed her breathing, and then Cole broke the silence. "I *am* sorry, Serafina. I didn't know you knew that guy. If I'd known, I never would have told him to go away. You do know that, right?"

Serafina didn't respond either way.

Cole took the Explorer keys out of his jacket pocket and gently placed them on the counter, and then quietly left out the back door.

Serafina closed the back door and went upstairs to the loft where Datson was still sleeping on her bed. She went over to her bed and lay next to him, curled up and crying.

She'd left her contact information with numerous people and agencies in an attempt to locate DeMarcus. She wondered which one of them pulled through for her. Now she would have to recontact them to let them know it was a big mistake that he was told to go away, that he actually found the right place and she was inside sleeping, sick, and really wanting to reconnect after all those years.

Her phone dinged. She thought it might be Cole apologizing again. Part of her felt bad for reacting like she did with him, but she was just so disappointed. She would need to tell him that when she saw him next. She looked at the sender and saw that it was actually Randy. He was checking in after last night when she told him she wasn't feeling well.

3:38 p.m.

Randy Staszak: *You still sick? I can bring you something after work if you want.*

Him reaching out to offer anything comforting just made everything feel worse for Serafina, and she cried harder. She wanted to tell Randy that DeMarcus had stopped by, that after all these years, she had managed to locate him through her street connections. She was both excited about the progress of her search as well as hurt, disappointed, and frustrated. And lonely. And empty. How could she be honest about it all to Randy? He had already made his feelings known when she first brought it up last Friday night that he was not in agreement with her reaching out to find him like that. She doubted he would be supportive.

She didn't want to withhold information about DeMarcus, but she also didn't want to deal with Randy's reaction either once she opened up about what happened. He would be more focused on how it impacted him—as usual. Not about her. Not about her feelings about it all. No, she couldn't depend on him to be there for her in that moment. She would need to depend on herself. He needed an answer, though, so she texted back that she needed to rest.

3:39 p.m.

Serafina: *I just want to rest. Thank you though.*

Randy didn't respond right away. Knowing Randy, he was probably overanalyzing her text, misinterpreting her intentions, and getting Nick's stance on the whole thing.

3:39 p.m.

Randy Staszak: *Okay. Let me know if you change your mind.*

Yup, clearly he got Nick's input. Totally a Nick thing to say. She put down her phone and decided to go sit on the floor where the stack of Hollis items waited to be sorted, but first she needed to make herself something to eat. The medicine was starting to sicken her stomach.

She went to the kitchen and heated up the easiest thing she could find to make—Hot Pockets. The supply was quickly dwindling. She reminded herself that she'd need to go grocery shopping once she felt better. As she microwaved two of them, she looked at the time on the stove. It was hard to believe it was almost 7:00 p.m. She grabbed another iced tea from the refrigerator and took her dinner upstairs to the loft.

Serafina took several photographs out from the stack and held them all at once. One loose photograph escaped her grip and fell as she held the others up, one in each hand. She placed the one in her right hand down to better examine the one in her left hand.

The photograph was Hollis in a tuxedo, looking surprisingly dapper. He was standing in front of a three-tiered wedding cake with a beautiful blonde woman in a bride's dress, and they were both cutting the wedding cake with a special cake knife. Hollis looked so young! And he was happy—not like his normal happy but, rather, beaming with joy. They both were!

Serafina stared for moments on end at this photograph, wondering how she had not known that Hollis had been married. Surely, the topic must have come up at some point. At the very least, the topic might have been broached, or even alluded to at some given time. Serafina tried to recall previous conversations with Hollis, or anyone who knew Hollis—even Levi. How was it that she was just finding out about it at that moment? After years of knowing Hollis and Levi, and even Suong—like, how was that even possible?

Serafina noticed the date written on the back: June 1, 1974. It was written in cursive, along with the words "Lizzie and Frankie" in bubbly handwriting not typical of Hollis. She guessed it had been written by the woman in the picture—Lizzie.

Serafina set the photograph aside and picked up the one she'd placed down earlier from her right hand. It was Hollis and that same woman, Lizzie, both much younger, standing side by side, like . . . childhood sweethearts.

She looked closely at the two of them, wondering how old they were. Lizzie—apparently, Hollis's wife—must have been about sixteen years old when the picture was taken. If they were the same age, then that would make sense, because they were standing in front of a pickup truck as if Hollis was going to drive it somewhere. Was it his pickup truck?

She chuckled at seeing Hollis in a slim-fit, chartreuse-colored mock turtleneck and plaid, bell-bottom slacks that had an orangish-tan hue.

Great color combo. She laughed to herself, half-wishing someone was there with her at that moment to show the photograph to and share the humor with. It made her sad that there wasn't.

Lizzie wore a shapeless, drop-waist dress in sky blue with a white collar and matching white cuffs. Her shoulder-length hair was pulled back in a hairband, and the ends curled up. She was actually *very* pretty. She had a wholesomeness about her. Even Hollis looked innocent, although she guessed he wasn't that innocent if he was a sixteen-year-old boy with a pickup and a very pretty girlfriend.

Serafina set the photograph aside with the other and picked up the loose one that had fallen.

Oh, wow! They had a baby? From the looks of that photograph, it had been taken the day Lizzie gave birth. Wearing a hospital gown, Lizzie sat in the bed holding a newborn swathed in a neutral, white blanket. Hollis sat next to her wearing flared trousers and a velour V-neck shirt, smiling proudly. Serafina turned the photograph over to see if anything was written on the back. As suspected, bubbly handwriting. It read, "Our beautiful baby girl, Tracy," with the date of "4/7/1976."

Serafina turned the photograph back over and studied it. Hollis looked the happiest she'd ever seen him. It felt almost as if she were witnessing something she shouldn't be seeing, like a secret side of Hollis. His past marriage and daughter had been a secret, but the secret she felt most uncomfortable with was this happy side of Hollis. That wasn't to say he wasn't ever happy. He was happy at many times, but not like this. This was different somehow.

She took the photograph over to the bed and lay down next to Datson to study it more. She was beyond tired. Her body sank into the coziness of the mattress. Outside, she could hear rain start to fall. As she pulled the blanket over her and eased into slumber, the photograph loosened from her grip.

Chapter 20

When Serafina woke up the next morning, her headache had mostly gone, and she was ready to knock out whatever work requests clients had emailed. As she got her coffee and let Datson back inside from doing his business, she thought about how her day would unfold.

She definitely had slacked off that week on the investigative research part of her job, where she had to sit at her laptop for hours looking up information about employees. To say it was tedious work would be an understatement. It was a real yawner. But with some coffee, who knew? She might knock it all out more quickly than normal and still have time to . . .

Part of her wanted to go visit Hollis, but she couldn't bear to see him in that condition again. Plus, she wasn't sure she could hide her hurt feelings. Or hide that she was conducting an investigation to find out who shot him. He'd know something was up.

He'd find out eventually, but not until she was finished. Not until she spoke with Erika Santiago about her connection with Hollis and find out if she knew anything about what happened last Friday night. *Wow, was that really a week ago?*

She'd also want to speak with other people working at Tamale Girlz. Probably the bouncer and the valet, and most certainly the bartender. Hollis typically sat at the bar and tipped very well, almost excessively, so bartenders always remembered him. Then again, he tipped that way for bouncers and valets also. Heck, they all should remember him.

She thought about seeing Xavier and that other guy with the rust-colored Impala—the mystery vehicle from the ATM footage that may or may not be connected to Hollis being shot. Nothing was seen from the ATM video footage except for it driving down the street around the same time. And just like the bank manager had said, that wasn't the only street, so some other vehicle could have been the real one. But it had to be the rust-colored Chevy Impala. *She felt it in her gut.*

Would she want to plan another drop-in visit with Xavier? But what would she even say? Would she lead him down the path by getting him to talk about cars or something? *That was lame.* She'd need a better way to approach the topic with him. Or would it be better to befriend him, like a mole? She imagined herself getting caught up in some gang where she'd wear their gang's colors, like a bandana on her head, and be forced to commit some crime as part of an initiation and . . . she stopped herself right there. *Okay, you're being dumb.* Part of her suspected that was mostly made up for movies, but another part of her feared getting caught up in something she couldn't escape from. Either way, she'd need a better plan than that.

She thought about how she'd left things with Gill. She liked having that connection to her life before Randy and Wanda, before foster care, when she was part of an actual family. She chastised herself for even saying that, as if Randy and Wanda weren't her family. They *were* her family. She just longed for that something she was missing, even though she wasn't quite sure what it was.

In a way, Gill was the brother from her former life. He was her connection to all those mixed-up memories. If only she could ask him questions, she'd be able to know what were actual memories versus false memories that she'd made up in her head to fill the void. Then maybe she could finally piece together all the truths so things would make more sense. She just didn't want to hurt him by bringing up the past like last time they spoke. Clearly, she'd said something that upset him. She just wasn't sure what.

There were certainly many other things she still should do, but none of them sounded very appealing, at least with only having had one cup of coffee. It was probably too soon to have another cup already, but she told herself she was making up for not having any the day before.

The second cup of coffee was a gateway to continuing her procrastination. She reasoned with herself that she would make the time. And, as a bonus, she would go to Tamale Girlz too.

But first, she was going to finish cleaning up the stack of paperwork, photographs, and whatever else was on the living room rug upstairs in the loft. She took her second cup of coffee upstairs and sat down crisscrossed on the living room rug.

The discoveries Serafina had made the night before about Hollis still lingered. She told herself that the items really needed to be put away, but she also knew she was curious about what else she might find. She knew there was more to be discovered about Hollis's past, and she just couldn't help herself from wanting to know more.

She would have continued looking the night before, but she had been exhausted—mentally, physically, and emotionally. The last thing she remembered was going to bed with that photograph of Hollis and Lizzie in the hospital with their "beautiful baby girl Tracy."

The whole thing just seemed so odd to her. How could she have known Hollis for *that* many years and never have a clue about any of it? Surely, she would have asked something at some point, and if so, did he lie to her? Her quick scan of memories came up with nothing, so maybe he didn't lie because he never had an opportunity to lie. But what if she flat-out asked him? Would he lie?

What about Levi? Was she open to asking such personal questions about Hollis to him, knowing that Lizzie and Tracy weren't part of

Hollis's life for whatever reason? *Or were they?* No, because Levi would have asked Lizzie or Tracy to watch Datson. Would Levi even know about Hollis's wife and daughter? Of course! Levi and Hollis were in the Vietnam War long before Hollis married Lizzie. But would Levi tell her anything if she asked him? Probably not. He didn't want her getting involved with the investigation—basically telling her to stay out of it. She doubted that he would be forthcoming about them. And then, what if he told Hollis that she asked about them? Would he be hurt that she was asking about his personal business behind his back? Maybe.

She thought about how hurt she had been when she first discovered that Hollis had been investigating her. How she went for that drive to the Nautical Mile to clear her head. She'd been standoffish to Cole as well. How much of that was her own insecurities? Or did he really deserve that kind of treatment?

He *had been* a bit pompous and arrogant when she first met him, she thought, remembering him coming in with that damn envelope, and even when he had met Levi, acting all, "Yes, sir. No, sir." *Gimme a break!*

But, the other day, he was actually caring and sweet. She thought about how he had taken it upon himself to get the Explorer's window fixed, and how he was thoughtful in picking up medication for her. Maybe she had been too hard on him about DeMarcus, but she was just so disappointed. Maybe he would understand if she told him the next time she saw him.

While taking a swig of her coffee, Serafina noticed a few more photographs intermixed with paperwork just out of reach. She attempted to grab ahold of them with crisscrossed legs, but they were too far, and she caused her coffee to spill slightly onto her hand in the process. She placed the mug down, wiped the drips of coffee onto her sweatpants, and tried again, this time crawling several paces and stretching her right arm out the rest of the way to grab the small stack of photographs, then crawling backward to her original spot.

One of the photographs showed Hollis holding Tracy on his lap. She must have been about a year old in the photo. *Aww.* Hollis looked like such a good father, the kind she imagined her own father must have been.

Part of Serafina imagined herself as that baby, like she was looking back at her own family album of pictures. She was embarrassed about the thoughts she was having, glad no one else could hear them. She sunk into that feeling more.

It felt good thinking about how her father would pick her up off his lap and throw her up in the air and catch her, and how she'd bellow out gleeful laughs. How he'd rock her in his arms and smoosh his face into her bare stomach and blow air onto it, and oh, how she'd scream out in joy. And then her mother would come into the room because of all the commotion and tell him to be careful with her, and how it was time for her feeding. Her mother would be holding a bottle of formula in one hand and a spit rag in the other, and she'd be motioning to her father to give Serafina to her. He'd kiss her on her baby head and she'd be whisked away.

A newspaper clipping caught her attention, so she reached for it on the floor. It was an obituary, and the picture of the deceased woman was Lizzie in her mid-thirties.

Oh, fuck. Did she die? Is that why he doesn't talk about her?

The name "Elizabeth Lawson" was written above Lizzie's picture.

Why wasn't her last name Hollis? Did they get divorced? Was Lawson her maiden name, or did she get remarried? Where was Tracy then?

Right next to the obituary were some other newspaper articles. She pulled one out from the stack that was old and tattered. At a quick glance, she saw that it was a Texas newspaper, dated November 26, 1988, and that there were no survivors of a car accident off a major highway that happened the day before. At the top of the article was a picture of a pickup truck and a car, both mangled and contorted. Stuck to the bottom of the article was a canary yellow Post-it note with the words, "The Lord took 3 angels that day."

What did the note mean by "3 angels?" Three people died? Is that how Lizzie died? In a car accident?

Serafina continued to read through the article, skimming for important details to understand why Hollis would have it.

"accident involving two motorized vehicles"

"heavily intoxicated driver kills family of three"

At the bottom of the article was a photograph of a bunch of people holding a vigil. Serafina tried to process the details she'd read without having to actually read the article.

"no survivors"

Did "no survivors" mean the drunk driver died as well? It appeared so. And it looked like a separate memorial service was being held for him.

"memorial services for Steve Lawson, Elizabeth Lawson, and Tracy Hollis"

Lawson . . . Steve Lawson. Where had she heard that name before? Then it hit her. *Was he that guy . . . ?*

She went to the stack of photographs she'd looked at the other day and quickly sifted through them. She found the Polaroid of a very young Frank Hollis fishing with another little boy with whitish-blonde hair, where they could have been best friends. There, on the bottom, it was written, "Frankie and Stevie."

She found the photograph of Hollis and "Stevie" as young adults standing in front of a slate blue Dodge Charger, next to two young ladies who could have been their girlfriends. There, next to Hollis, was Lizzie.

Then, as if she needed any further confirmation, she found what she'd been looking for: the announcement for the graduation of Steve Lawson, with the photograph of him wearing a cowboy hat. Right there, plain as day, was his name: *Steve Lawson.*

Serafina could barely wrap her head around all the information she'd just discovered. This was supposedly Hollis's best friend growing up, and he ended up marrying Lizzie? And now he was dead? And so was his ex-wife—his childhood sweetheart—and their child?

Serafina did the math in her head: Tracy was born on April 7, and this happened on November 25 . . . 1988 minus 1976 equals twelve, so then, Tracy would have been twelve years old?

The whole thing was heartbreaking to find out, and it left her with so many questions that she knew she'd never get the answer to because Hollis wouldn't be bringing any of it up unless she flat-out asked him. She wasn't about to ask him about his past, knowing how painful it all must have been.

She picked up the photograph from the other night—the one of Hollis and Lizzie in the hospital room the day Tracy was born. She soaked up that look on his face, wondering how he could go from that happy to losing all those important people in his life. And not just through divorce but forever. How did that happen?

It was so much to take in. Serafina grabbed a pillow off the couch and lay down on the floor with her eyes closed.

She had always sensed Hollis was holding back a flood of emotions, but never understood there was something deeper going on. Now she could grasp why. Clearly this Steve guy betrayed Hollis and stole his life. What other explanation was there?

An overwhelming sadness for Hollis came over her. She really wanted to hear his voice, to feel connected to him. She didn't even care what they talked about. Was it too early to call him though? She grabbed her phone to see the time. It was barely 9:00 a.m. She found his contact information and called before she could overthink the gesture.

Hollis answered in his usual, hospitable way, "Mornin'."

Serafina gulped. "Hey, there. How are you doing?"

"Been better," Hollis said. "Everything all right?"

Serafina thought about everything that had happened since Hollis had been shot. No, nothing was all right. She was being pushed out of her home with Randy and Nick, and she was struggling to keep the business running by herself. Thank goodness she had Cole to help her, but how could she ask for Cole's help again after what happened yesterday with him shooing away DeMarcus . . . God, she hadn't seen him in years. They used to be so close, and she worried about him out there on the streets without anyone to help him, and how many more years would she have to wait to see him again this time?

She needed answers too. She needed to know why Hollis had Cole investigating her, and whether he was investigating her the night he got shot. And who shot Hollis? Was it the person in the rust-colored Chevy Impala? Did he know Xavier Palo? Was Xavier Palo involved somehow? He was a suspect in her parents' murder. Was that the murder Levi said was connected to Hollis being shot? Levi had said it was a store robbery in the '80s and that it had involved a gang member. Did that not fit the description of her parents' murder?

Somebody had to know something. But why was Hollis keeping it all a secret? Why not just tell her he was curious about her past? Was there something about her past she should be concerned about? Was he protecting her from some sort of danger? If so, maybe those people knew and broke into the Explorer to get information. How could she tell Hollis that she allowed the camera, equipment, and all her notes to get stolen? That's not something she could worry him about right now, not while he was in recovery and unable to help. That would make things worse. She needed to figure this all out on her own. She needed to get answers and get them now.

"Serafina?" Hollis asked, disrupting Serafina's train of thought.

"I'm sorry," she blurted in response. "I've just had a lot on my mind."

"I know. Been that way as long as I've known you," Hollis said. "Life's too short to worry so much, you hear?"

Serafina thought about how short life really was. That last newspaper article kind of proved that. Emotions rushed to the surface as she thought about how she'd almost lost Hollis. She blinked, and a few tears started to flow from the corner of her eyes. She quickly wiped them away with her left middle finger.

"How long do they think you're going to have to stay in the hospital? I can help you get around if you need me to."

There was a delay in Hollis's response. "Not sure yet. I appreciate your offer. I'll let you know if I do, hon."

"Okay." Serafina wondered if Hollis would take her up on her offer. He wasn't one for accepting help easily. Never wanting to be a burden.

There was a moment of silence between them, letting her know she wouldn't be able to keep him on the other line much longer. She accepted that the call would have to end soon.

"I'll try to come visit soon, okay?" She thought about visiting that day, but there wouldn't be time to finish up all the work assignments she had let pile up and have enough time to grab dinner before heading over to Tamale Girlz. She'd have to make a visit tomorrow instead.

"That'd be great."

They said their goodbyes, and Serafina ended the call. She stood there looking around the loft.

Datson had managed to come upstairs while she was on the phone and now slept on the floor near the sofa. Having sensed her staring at him, he opened his eyes slightly with his face still resting in its position on the floor.

"Let's get to those work assignments, shall we?"

Chapter 21

Evening had already set in when Hollis woke from his long afternoon nap after talking with Serafina that short while. As he lay in his darkened hospital room, his thoughts drifted back to a week prior, when he'd been shot on that dark, desolate street not even a mile from the Ambassador Bridge. In what he had thought were his last moments alive, he'd been really honest with himself.

As if taking inventory of his transgressions, his regrets, his disappointments, his fears, his feelings, and everything else he'd been stuffing away inside and denying himself all these years, he checked them off one by one.

Datson. He still had that handwritten letter that Datson had pulled out of his jacket, the one written in cursive, "If I die." *Well, he died.* And he probably died because of Hollis. If Hollis hadn't been shot, then Datson never would have tried to save him, and who knows? Maybe he wouldn't have been shot at all, or maybe the injury wouldn't have been so severe and killed him. And Hollis just left him like that, carried off to care for his own wounds, leaving Datson behind. Forgotten. Although, if he was really being honest with himself, Datson had never really been forgotten, because Hollis thought about him every single day. Caring for Datson reincarnated as a dog was his own weird way of making it up to his war buddy. But he still had that letter in its unopened envelope that he was supposed to give to Datson's girl. Hollis didn't even know if they had been married, engaged, or just seeing one another—spoken for until he returned. His guilty conscience told him he really should find this person and give them the letter. Even after all these years.

Not that it was any excuse, but he'd never handled death well. It probably started when he lost his mother at five years old, although he might have always been that way, and his mother's death was his first experience with it. Sammy had recovered from it relatively quickly, or at least he had seemed to. Hollis struggled after that. Even fishing with Daddy and Sammy afterward was difficult as he started to understand the permanency of death. Even for a fish.

Sammy. He could never expect forgiveness from Sammy after what happened. How he ignored Sammy's pleas to come back home, to Texas, when Daddy got sick that February in 1989 and needed to figure out how to keep the farm running. Maybe he should have gone then. Maybe he should have responded. But he didn't. He couldn't. Three months hadn't been enough time to process the loss he'd borne in November 1988. And going back to Texas to really deal with the pain had not been something he was prepared to do either. Even as Daddy's health had worsened, and the letters had kept coming, letting him know that time was about to run out, he wouldn't respond.

Then, in April 1989, right around when it would have been Tracy's thirteenth birthday, he'd received the news that Daddy had gone to be with Momma. He couldn't go then either. By the time he had mustered up the will to go see Sammy, so much time had gone by that he wasn't sure he could ever go back home to Texas and face Sammy. That's why he hadn't told Sammy he was even coming that fall of 1989. He had intended to surprise Sammy. But as he had walked that gravel road toward the farmhouse and had seen the cropless fields and the property development sign, he had remembered Daddy holding dirt in his palm, telling him how it was land and that it would be his and Sammy's to pass on.

That land had meant so much to Daddy. If he had been able to pull himself together during that time and help Sammy with the crops that year Daddy was sick, then they would have been able to pay the property taxes, and they wouldn't have lost the farmland to bank foreclosure. Even though he didn't hold the same perception of value on the land, he could have given up his share to Sammy.

To make matters worse, what Hollis had done to his older brother was essentially—he tried recalling the term used by the younger folks—"ghosting." He mentally affirmed it to be the correct term. How many years had it been? The last time they actually spoke was when Sammy had called Hollis to tell him about the car accident. He had insisted that Hollis make a trip to Texas for the funerals, and when Hollis said he wouldn't be coming, Sammy blew up at him over the phone, telling him to get his head out of his ass and do the right thing for once. Sammy didn't understand that Hollis couldn't face the reality of that loss. Not then, not ever.

Come to think of it, was Sammy even alive still? Who was there to tell him if Sammy did die? Maybe it wasn't too late to make things right between them. His guilty conscience told him he really should reach out to Sammy and apologize. Even after all these years.

Lizzie. He could have done a lot of things differently. She'd been the love of his life since they were in grade school, and it wasn't right the way things ended. They were supposed to grow old together. But she chose Stevie. And why wouldn't she? He drove her to leave with all his drinking. She had stayed as long as she could, dealing with his antics. What a sweet soul she was. All he did was take her for granted, thinking she'd never leave.

He thought back to that last night in October 1978 when he passed out on the front porch and Lizzie had finally had enough, walking out on him and their marriage, taking his sweet baby girl Tracy away from him.

He never really saw Tracy after that. He lost the opportunity to be a father to her, and whose fault was that?

It wasn't surprising that Lizzie moved back to Texas when she left him. She didn't know anyone besides him in Michigan, and there was no bonding with Suong. How she hooked up with Stevie, he'd never know. And he probably didn't want to know either.

Stevie. He'd dodged the draft with college as his shield. He only saw what was in the papers, not firsthand. He didn't have the agonizing nightmares that disturbed his sleep and made the waking hours intolerable. There was no escaping for Hollis, not like Stevie.

Hollis never held any animosity toward Stevie until the draft. And it wasn't fair because, really, he wouldn't want Stevie fighting in that worthless war anyhow. Stevie was too good for this Earth. So maybe it was better off that the two found each other. And maybe he shouldn't be so sore about it.

There was no better person he'd want to raise Tracy than Stevie either. He always knew how to comfort you when you needed it the most. *Shame on me for not being receptive to Stevie after the war.*

Hollis thought back to when Momma died. How Stevie was there helping him approach the casket to say his goodbyes. There every step of the way. How could Hollis blame him for letting go of their relationship after the war? Stevie graduated in 1973 and moved on with life. Hollis was stuck on the battlefield. His guilty conscience told him he needed to make peace with Stevie, but how?

That had been the worst call he'd ever received. The day Sammy called him to tell him they'd all died in a car accident by a drunk driver. A nightmare he kept hoping he'd wake up from. Unbearable pain. He tried numbing it the best he could, and when he couldn't, Levi stepped in—despite Suong's reluctance.

With six months to live, give or take, he needed to figure out how to depart this world in peace. He didn't want to leave things as they were.

Serafina. He should find a way to tell her he was dying and that he loved her. Immensely. Like a daughter. He wanted nothing more than to make her life wonderful. She'd been dealt a bad hand, but that didn't mean she had to continue to eat the crap sandwich. He still hadn't read the report from Cole and wondered what it would reveal about Serafina's past.

Hollis turned onto his right side and stared at nothingness—the metal side bars of his hospital bed and the IV tube that hung over it, the semi-closed curtain partially covering the door to his room, the annoying light from the hallway shining into his room.

It was too late for him to be a father to Tracy, but not too late for him to be a father to Serafina. Even if it were for only six months. He felt an overwhelming need to start that goal immediately.

Hollis leaned over as far as he could to reach his phone on the table to his right but found resistance from the IV tube. He picked up the IV tube and gave it more slack so that he could.

The last call on his phone was from that afternoon when Serafina called. He had hoped to see her. He wondered what she might be doing. He sat and looked at her number when he was startled by a knock at the door. Cole poked his head in.

"Well, how the heck are you!" Hollis said, placing his phone down on his lap.

"I should be asking you the same," Cole said, as he grabbed one of the chairs and moved it closer to Hollis's bed. "I know it's getting late. I meant to call earlier too, but—"

"Don't you worry none. It's all good." Hollis adjusted his bed upward.

"So, what are the doctors saying? Have they given you any idea on how long you'll need to stay here in the hospital?" Cole noticed Hollis looking parched. "Here, let me get you some water."

Hollis watched Cole go over to the side table and pour him some water from the plastic jug the nurse left him that morning.

In taking that first sip, Hollis realized how parched he'd become. He took a longer drink than normal, and then proceeded to respond to Cole. "Shouldn't be much longer. That's about all I know. They're already talking about outpatient care."

"That sounds hopeful." Cole sat back down in the chair.

"Yeah, but I'm surprised about it. Whatever happened to people staying in the hospital until they're completely better? Nowadays there seems to be such a rush to get folks out the door." Hollis adjusted himself in the bed, trying to get comfortable.

"Insurance companies," Cole said, shaking his head with disbelief.

"Exactly—and it's a sham!"

"I imagine you'll be starting physical therapy for your shoulder soon."

Hollis nodded but could tell that Cole had something on his mind that he was beating around the bush about getting out in the open. "Son, what's on your mind?"

Cole acted surprised but quickly succumbed to sharing his thoughts. "Serafina—"

Hollis bellowed out in laughter but caught himself. "Sorry." He snickered one more time. "She done got your ox in a ditch, huh?"

Cole looked confused.

"Tell it to me." Hollis encouraged him.

"Well, I stopped by and saw Serafina the other day."

"At the agency?" Hollis was interested but contained any expression either way.

"Well, yeah, I was just dropping off a report for her."

"Oh?" Hollis's interest piqued.

"She'd asked me to help on an investigation. There was a scheduling conflict with another, I guess?"

Hollis understood.

"Well, I think I may have upset her."

"How so?" Hollis asked.

"I shooed some guy away that apparently I shouldn't have."

Hollis listened intently. "At the agency?"

"Outside the agency."

"Serafina didn't want you to shoo him away?" Hollis asked.

"Well, no, but I didn't know it at the time."

"Where was she? What was she doing?"

"Resting. She was really sick."

Hollis thought about Serafina being sick. She hadn't mentioned that to him, only that she had a lot on her mind.

"He said he was looking for his sister," Cole said.

"Might have been her brother, Randy. And you chased him away?" Hollis sat up a little straighter in his bed.

"I didn't exactly chase him away, and I really don't think the guy was her brother Randy."

"Did he look like he, uh, goes the other way?"

"I'm sorry, come again?"

"Gay, son. Did he look gay?"

"I don't believe so, sir."

"Ex-boyfriend, maybe?"

"Doubt it." Cole was quick to respond. His response was one of disgust.

"Why do you say that?"

"Well, for starters, he said he was looking for his sister."

"Oh, yeah, there's that." Hollis chuckled. "You think he was talking about Serafina?"

"I kind of doubt that." Cole shook his head.

They sat quietly for a moment while Cole replayed it in his head.

"I just didn't think she knew this guy," Cole said defensively. "I mean, he looked like a bum."

"You sure she knew him?"

Cole nodded emphatically. "She was upset about it enough, so yeah, I think so."

They sat quietly a moment more, contemplating who it could be.

"But also . . ." Cole hesitated.

"What?"

"Well, not to sound racist, but . . ." he paused for a moment. "The guy was Black."

"Maybe he really was looking for his sister and Serafina thought he was someone else?" Hollis tried his best to make sense of it.

"No, she *knew* him." Cole insisted. "She knew this guy had burn scars on his face."

"Burn scars, huh?" Hollis processed this information. *Could that have been Serafina's foster brother she lost track of years ago? What was his name again?*

Hollis continued, "Did you find anything out from the investigation that might shed some light on who this fellow is? Or are you still working on it?"

"No, sir. Not that I can think of offhand." He paused a moment before speaking. "And actually, I finished my report up last week. I dropped it off at the office last Saturday. I suppose you haven't had a chance to read it yet."

That concerned Hollis. "Did you leave it with Serafina?"

"Well, yeah, but it was sealed in an envelope. I made it clear it was for you."

"Hmm." Hollis wasn't so sure she wouldn't open it. That wouldn't be good if she had opened it. She would certainly not understand why he had Cole looking into her past.

Hollis wasn't quite sure of the reason himself. Even though he felt like he knew Serafina as a person, he barely knew anything about her life. He just knew bits and pieces that gnawed away at him, and his hope was that Cole could help clear up some of the missing pieces. He knew he had no right to know private things about Serafina that she didn't herself share, but there might be things she'd want to know that he could help find out for her.

"Well, hey, I gotta get going now, but I'll check back with you later." Cole stood up from the chair.

"You take care now, okay, son? And don't you worry none about Serafina. I'm sure it'll all blow over soon."

Cole gave a hard nod as if to say, "Yes, sir."

Hollis watched him leave the room, and then picked up his phone to scroll through the news. That's when he noticed he had a missed call and voicemail message from Wednesday. When he listened to it, he immediately recognized the caller.

"Hey. It's Lexi. I couldn't find your new number the other day, so I left a message on your other phone. Some lady kept calling me back though. That your wife? Hope I didn't get you in trouble. If I did, sorry. Call me."

This isn't good.

He knew Serafina well. For her to keep calling Lexi—or rather, Erika Santiago—back, she was definitely fixated. When that happened, Serafina didn't let go.

Right then, Hollis saw his nurse pass by his door from the hallway.

"Miss! Excuse me, miss," Hollis called to her.

She poked her head in after passing by the door. "Was there something you need?"

Hollis didn't want to be rude, but he wanted to catch Cole before he got on the elevator. "The young man that was in here just a second ago, is he out there?"

"I apologize. I didn't see anyone in your room. What does he look like?"

"There was young man who just left my room. He's got blonde hair. He should be heading to the elevators."

The nurse looked down the hall. "There's a man with that description getting on the elevator right now."

Dagnabbit.

"Did you need my help?

Hollis shook his head. "No. Thank you anyhow."

He sat in his hospital bed. Maybe it wasn't the best idea to have changed his cell phone number after all. It had been a spur-of-the-moment decision to even upgrade his cell phone, let alone change his number. There was nothing wrong with the old number. In fact, his old number was like an extension of himself, like his arm, or leg. Part of his identity. Who he was. But lately, all the calls were from doctors and treatment centers—cancer, cancer, cancer. He was just so fucking sick of even thinking about his few options. *What options? Stage 4, they said.* Well, so then, what was the point? He wasn't going to spend the rest of his life, what little he had left, thinking one more second of his cancer. No more reminders. He had so little control over the cancer in his body, but he certainly had control over hearing about the cancer from his cell phone. It didn't have to make sense to anyone else. It made sense to him.

He looked at his recent calls and tapped on Cole McDermott's name. The phone rang once and was picked up on the other line.

Chapter 22

The parking lot at Tamale Girlz was mostly full when Serafina pulled up to the valet booth at 6:45 p.m., and she was highly apprehensive about going in. She'd worked at Planet Janet, but that was a high-end, reputable establishment, not sleazy like this place. She was used to businessmen on their lunch hour—*not this*. She watched the men in front of her exit their nondescript vehicle. They looked like locals of a shady neighborhood. She might have taken notice of the make and model of their vehicle had she not been enthralled by all the dents and dings.

The valet guy pulled forward with their vehicle and drove it to a parking spot in the back. Serafina pulled forward in the Explorer and waited. When he returned, he opened the driver's side door to assist her in getting out.

As Serafina stepped onto the cement slab, she handed him a twenty. "If you wouldn't mind, could you park it up front?"

He was a young Hispanic man in his twenties. He looked curiously at Serafina. "You new here?"

"Nope. Paying customer," Serafina said.

His eyes widened. "For real?"

Serafina smiled back. You wish, she thought.

He held one of the double doors to the entrance open for her to enter the bar.

The lighting was dimmed. On the left was a coat check booth. There was an empty bowl on the counter with a sign that read, "Tips."

A bouncer stood next to the unmanned coat check. He looked at his watch and then at Serafina. "Cutting it close, don't you think?"

"Excuse me?" Serafina gave him her slow-blink look.

"It's almost seven. Cutting it close."

"Close for what? From what I understand, the bar opens at 6:30 p.m.," Serafina said, eyeing the barstools to her right.

He shook his head in annoyance. "You gonna be ready for the stage in five minutes?"

Serafina scoffed. "Nope." She scoffed some more. "I'll be at the bar. Thank you." She walked over to the bar and pulled out a stool to sit on.

The bartender was a Hispanic woman in her thirties, possibly the same age as Serafina. She was talking with a cocktail waitress near the end of the bar, next to the fountain pop squirters and ice. When she finished, she approached a man at that end of the bar and placed a napkin in front of him. Serafina watched them briefly converse about what he'd like to order, and the bartender poured him a drink from a bottle and delivered it along with a tab.

When the bartender noticed Serafina, she went back over to the ice cooler where the cocktail waitress had just returned. They spoke briefly, and then the cocktail waitress left while the bartender waited. When the cocktail waitress returned with a paper form in hand, the bartender took it and headed over to Serafina.

"When you're done filling it out, let me know, and I'll let the manager know." The bartender placed the paper down in front of Serafina along with a pen and started to walk away from Serafina.

Realizing it was an application, Serafina called out to her, "Excuse me."

She turned around nonchalantly and slowly came back over to Serafina. "Yeah?"

Serafina gave her a twenty. "I'll have a pinot grigio. Keep the change."

The bartender took the twenty in disbelief.

"I won't be needing this but thank you." Serafina pushed the application away on the counter.

The bartender took the application, looked at Serafina, and pulled a wine glass off the shelf behind her.

Serafina took in her surroundings while she waited for her glass of wine. Two men sat at a small round table near the end of the bar in her direct line of sight to the stage, making it hard not to look their way. One of the men winked at her and then turned and laughed with his friend. Serafina ignored him and scanned the club.

In the middle of the club was an oblong-shaped stage with a pole on each end and one in the middle. Stairs to the stage were set off to the side. One long couch lined the perimeter walls of the bar. Square tables and chairs took up the space in the middle. Each table had a candle on it. To the right of the bar was the DJ booth and a hallway that led to the dressing room. A few customers were already seated and getting their drinks. The music playing was standard background music at a lower volume.

The bartender placed a napkin down in front of Serafina and positioned the glass of wine on it. "My name's Christine. Would you like me to get you a menu?"

Serafina thought about it. "Thanks, Christine. Maybe in a bit."

The voice of a female DJ came on the loudspeaker. "Welcome to Tamale Girlz! In a few minutes we'll be having our lovely ladies out and getting started."

Serafina took a sip of her pinot grigio. One of the men seated at the table near the end of the bar stood up and began walking toward her. Serafina placed her glass back down and anticipated his arrival.

"My buddy and I have a bet against each other on whether you're here to dance or be a waitress."

Serafina blankly looked at the guy, debating on what she should say versus what she wanted to say. "Why wouldn't you bet on me being a customer?"

The man's eyes widened, and he snorted with laughter. He turned around and went back to his seat. A few seconds later, he and his friend were laughing it up.

The Pretenders' song "Brass in Pocket" came on the speakers at a volume higher than it had been. The show had officially begun. One by one, the dancers followed each other out of the dressing room and up onto the stage. They gathered around the poles or just stood in the middle of the stage for the song. Serafina spotted Erika Santiago right away—there on the pole to the left. Her makeup was more dramatic than when Serafina had seen her last time, but it was surely her.

Serafina counted twelve young women on the stage, all appearing to be in their early twenties. A few of the dancers showed interest in Serafina's presence. They made comments to the dancers next to them while keeping their eyes directly on Serafina. Erika was busy talking to another dancer and didn't seem to notice Serafina.

When the song ended, most of the dancers headed back into the dressing room. As the next song started to play, the DJ announced three dancers to take over each pole on the stage. Diamond, a short-haired blonde wearing a white skintight dress and clear heels stayed on the stage and danced around the middle pole. Brittany danced on the left side of the stage in a red bikini. Nikki danced on the right in a black mini skirt and bra ensemble.

One dancer went over to the bouncer and showed him pictures on her cell phone. Another dancer went up to the two men seated at the table near the end of the bar and wrapped her arms around the one who had approached Serafina. The two of them briefly conversed and then the dancer looked directly at Serafina and smiled as if something funny was said. Serafina caught herself tapping her foot and tried not to be agitated.

A group of five men came through the door, and the bouncer pointed to various places in the room. The leader of the group gave the bouncer some cash, and the bouncer led the group to a corner table. They all took seats, and a waitress headed over to take their orders.

As the song playing over the speakers faded out, another faded in, and the DJ announced Summer as the next dancer. Brittany came down off the stage, and Nikki moved to the left pole. Then, as Diamond moved to the right side of the stage, the rotation sequence became clear. The first dancer went to the main stage, and then to the right side of the stage, and then to the left side of the stage, and then came down off the stage to try to get dances until they had to go back onstage.

The dancer at the end of the bar left the two men and headed toward Serafina. She placed her glass of wine on the bar counter next to Serafina and said, "My friend wants to buy you a dance," as she started taking off her bikini top.

Serafina looked at the guys at the end of the bar staring back at her. "I'm good."

The dancer looked back at the guys, smiled, and then looked back at Serafina. "Would you mind letting me give you one anyway? He already paid me."

Before Serafina could say, "No," the dancer placed her bikini top on the bar counter and stood between Serafina's legs at the barstool.

"What's your name?" Serafina asked the dancer.

"Jasmine," she said, holding her breasts in her hands, and pushing them slightly together to create cleavage. She leaned her head near Serafina's neck and let her long brown hair hang down to the side.

Jasmine turned around, leaned forward, and twerked her ass. The guys at the end of the bar stared and laughed together. She then leaned back into Serafina and pressed her breasts together again. When she turned back around again, Serafina took the opportunity to get information about Erika.

"Who was the girl in the red dress and red heels?"

Jasmine thought for a moment.

Serafina noticed Jasmine's uncertainty. "She was to your right on the stage."

"Oh!" Jasmine's interest piqued. "Lexi?"

"Real name Erika?"

"Yeah. How'd you know?"

"Mutual friend."

"Let's give a hand for the tantalizing Tawnie!" the DJ announced as the next song came on.

Jasmine stopped dancing and began to put her bikini top back on. "Thanks."

"Yeah, no problem," Serafina said. "Oh, hey . . . when does this place get really busy?"

"In about an hour?" Jasmine took her glass of wine and walked away.

Serafina could see the guys at the end of the bar were now talking and didn't notice the song was over. She caught Christine's attention.

"What'll it be?" Christine asked Serafina after walking over.

Serafina kept her lips closed as she smiled, her eyes holding a fixed and unnatural position. "I'd like to buy a drink for Lexi."

"You know what she wants?" Christine asked.

"No, she's in the dressing room. Can you have someone go ask?" Serafina knew from experience that this was a tactic customers would use to get a dancer over sooner rather than later, especially when dancers would hide out in the dressing room between sets, calling in their regulars.

Christine didn't verbally respond but walked over to a waitress at the station for the ice and fountain pop. Serafina could see her talking to the waitress. They both looked back at Serafina, and then the waitress nodded and went in the direction of the dressing room.

The entrance door opened and a few more customers entered. Most of them took a seat at one of the various tables the bouncer pointed out, rather than paying him a substantial tip for a private booth.

The waitress came back from the dressing room and gave Christine the order. Serafina watched her take down a wine glass and wipe it, and then open up a wine cooler and take out a bottle of merlot. A few moments later, Christine placed the wine glass on a circular tray for the waitress to carry to the dressing room.

"Get ready for the beautiful Brandy—center stage!" the DJ announced as another song came on.

As Diamond stepped off the stage, she bent down to grab her drink on the top step. Brandy allowed her to pass before climbing the steps to the main stage. Summer had already taken her position to the left as Tawnie moved to the right stage. A few customers who'd been eyeing Brandy came over immediately to tip her. When they were done, Brandy's G-string held up single dollars folded in half longways all along every available space.

Serafina watched the happenings around her while she anticipated Lexi's appearance. With her eyes in the direction of the dressing room, she noticed three dancers come out and congregate at the bar on the end closest to the DJ booth. One went over to the DJ booth to tip the DJ in advance for the day and go over her music selections. The two that stayed behind talked about the other dancers, particularly those already getting attention or hustling, like Brandy and Jasmine. It was too obvious in the way they spoke closely with one another while staring at the others.

The entrance door opened to let in more customers, with the valet attendant following behind to grab a fountain pop. When the valet guy walked past the dancers, they stopped him to discuss something. He laughed and then got his pop and headed back outside. As he passed by the coat check, Serafina noticed the customers tipping the coat check girl for taking their coats and discussing with each other where to sit.

"Let's hear a round of excitement for the luscious Lexi!" the DJ announced, fading in the new song.

Brandy moved to the pole on the right side of the stage, Tawnie to the left side, and Summer stepped down the stairs of the stage and beelined over to the corner table, where a guy who tipped her was sitting. The waitress who took Lexi's order went over to the corner booth and took more drink orders.

Just then, Lexi placed her glass of merlot on the stairs to the stage and walked onto the stage.

Lexi held onto the pole as she walked seductively around it. Then she leaned her back against the pole, and with her right arm stretched up above her head, held onto it and slid down slowly.

A guy from the group in the corner booth walked up to the stage and tipped Tawnie on the left, and then walked over to Lexi at the center stage and tipped her. Brandy tried to get his attention from the right, but he just turned around and walked back to the corner booth. Serafina looked back and noticed one of the guys in the group was already getting a double from two of the dancers. Upon looking more closely, Serafina realized the two dancers were the ones who'd been congregating at the end of the bar bad-mouthing Brandy and Jasmine. Clearly, they had influenced the guys not to tip Brandy.

Serafina looked back at Lexi and Tawnie, both vying for attention from the guys in the corner booth. They might get dances; they might not. Or they might have just been tipped as a way to exclude Brandy and lower her self-confidence. It was an effective mind-fuck game from what Serafina could remember of working at Planet Janet. Make the dancer think they're not worthy of a tip, that there's something wrong with them. Send them to the dressing room to "improve" themselves for thirty minutes once they got off stage. Get rid of the competition.

Serafina wanted Lexi to come over so they could talk, but purchasing Lexi a glass of merlot wasn't going to do the trick when the group of guys in the corner booth had just tipped her. And the attention she was giving them from the stage made it clear where she'd be going once she got off stage. Who knew how long Lexi would be over there—hours? It was just like the "hawks" at Planet Janet would always say, "It only takes one customer." And then there was the possibility that Lexi might have regulars come in after that. Serafina needed to make her move now. She took out a hundred-dollar bill from her pocket and stood up from her seat.

As Serafina walked up to the stage to tip Lexi, she could see in her peripheral vision that Christine, Jasmine, and the two guys at the end of the bar were all watching her. At the main stage, Serafina held the hundred-dollar bill in her hand and waited for Lexi to come and get it. Lexi slid down to the floor with her back against the pole and crawled to the edge of the stage. Serafina folded the hundred-dollar bill in half the long way as Lexi situated her right hip forward, allowing Serafina to place the tip in her G-string. As Serafina slid the bill under the string, she told her, "I just want thirty minutes of your time. If you give me that, I have another hundred for you."

Lexi looked down and realized she had a hundred-dollar bill on her hip. She nodded to Serafina. Heading back to her seat at the bar, Serafina noticed Jasmine making her way over to the corner booth to join in, welcomed by the other dancers or not.

Serafina continued past the two guys at the end of the bar. The one guy who spoke to her earlier tried to stop her with his arm. "Hey, you into girls?"

Serafina resumed walking to her seat. By the look of it, he had downed a few drinks and was now entering a new level of obnoxious. *Ignore him.*

Serafina noticed a few dancers she hadn't seen during stage review, who were possibly freelancers. At Planet Janet, the freelancers would pay the club a freelance fee of $20 to come in whenever they wanted but had to stay the whole shift. These freelancers must have arrived after stage review when Serafina wasn't looking, or they had still been in the dressing room getting ready for stage review.

Over the speakers, the DJ announced the dancer for the next song. "Let's hear some noise for the captivating Crystal!"

Noticing that the dancer coming to the stage was one of the two who had been badmouthing Brandy and Jasmine, Serafina thought, More like "Catty Crystal."

Tawnie on the left side of the stage bolted over to the corner booth as Brandy moved to replace her. Lexi moved over to the right side of the stage as Crystal put her wine glass on the top step before going on stage.

While Serafina waited for Lexi, she kept busy noticing more of her surroundings. Having noticed Crystal's almost empty wine glass, Serafina wondered why she didn't leave it at the corner table since, typically, dancers leave their glass at a table whenever they want to make it known to the other dancers that they've claimed a customer. Maybe she had a regular waiting for her? Serafina looked around, and no one seemed to be interested in Crystal. Plus, Crystal didn't seem to be eyeing anyone in particular. She actually seemed like she might go back to the corner table from the way she kept looking over there.

Got it! It was probably because she didn't want the waitress to take her glass away. Apparently cocktail waitresses were known to take glasses away when there was barely anything left. Serafina remembered her dancer friend Coco bitching about a particular waitress who always did that. Coco had been even more upset when the waitress minimized it with a comment about Coco wanting to drink spit. Without that glass as a prop, she'd have to pay for another drink if she wanted one. Plus, Coco had a tendency to pace her consumption by making her drinks last.

Serafina looked over at the corner booth guys. They were starting to slow down the dances, which meant they might be leaving soon. Her theory just might be correct. Or maybe Crystal wasn't one to claim customers. *Nah!* She laughed to herself.

While all the details of this bar were interesting to Serafina, she remembered that she was there for a reason. *Lexi.* Serafina needed to prepare herself for their talk.

Serafina motioned to Christine. "I'll have another pinot grigio, and I'm thinking I'd like to order an appetizer."

Christine brought over a menu. Serafina picked up the menu and glanced over it quickly, deciding on chicken tenders. *Can't go wrong with chicken tenders.*

"Chicken tenders?" Serafina said to Christine. "And do you have honey mustard?"

Christine nodded and took Serafina's tab to update it.

The DJ announced Jasmine on center stage. Serafina knew Lexi would be off stage next song. She flagged Christine. "Also, can you keep my drink back there for a minute? I'll be right back. I'm gonna run to the restroom real quick."

Christine nodded and went to pull the bottle of pinot grigio out of the wine refrigeration cooler.

Serafina looked at her watch as she stood up from her barstool. She couldn't remember what the visiting hours were for the hospital, but she was sure it would be too late by the time she left.

She thought of Hollis and what he might be doing. She could call him instead, when she was on her way home, but then, neither of them was much of a talker.

When Serafina exited the restroom next to the front door, she looked over at Lexi, now on the left side of the stage. Lexi was on her knees letting another guy from the group in the corner booth tip her. As the guy walked back to the corner booth, the DJ announced Taylor as the next dancer.

Lexi looked over at Serafina as the dancers rotated again with Crystal moving to the left side of the stage, Jasmine moving to the right side, and Lexi coming off the stage. As Taylor took center stage, Lexi began walking toward Serafina. Two of the guys in the corner booth called for her. Lexi smiled and gestured one minute with her index finger to Serafina, and then proceeded over to the corner booth and began talking with the guy who tipped her.

Serafina watched from her barstool, hoping Lexi wouldn't sit down, that she'd tell him she'd be over in thirty minutes. The waitress went over to their table with a bill and then started grabbing drink glasses off their table and placing them on a round tray. Lexi gestured one minute with her index finger to Serafina again and started dancing for the guy. *One for the road.*

Serafina looked back up at the stage and realized that Taylor was the dancer who'd been bad-mouthing Brandy and Jasmine with Crystal at the bar. She was already scanning the bar for her next dance.

In Serafina's peripheral view, she saw Christine placing her glass of pinot grigio on a new napkin.

Serafina was startled when Lexi sat next to her, not realizing the next song had started. Serafina had been mesmerized by all the different liquor bottles on the wall of shelves behind the bar.

"Hi, I'm Lexi. And you are?" Lexi placed her almost-empty glass of wine on the bar.

"A friend of Hollis," Serafina said.

Lexi looked confused but proceeded to sit down.

"It's Serafina," she said, pointing to Lexi's almost empty wine glass.

"You want another?"

Lexi looked at her glass and then at Serafina. "Sure."

Serafina caught Christine's attention and then pointed at Lexi's glass. Christine nodded and retrieved the bottle of merlot from the wine cooler.

"Look, it's roughly seven thirty right now, right?" Serafina twirled her wine glass lightly.

Lexi nodded slightly, watching the bouncer seat a new group of guys in the corner booth.

"I know your time is valuable, so how about you sit and talk to me, and I give you another hundred in thirty minutes? Sound fair?"

Lexi tried to contain her excitement over the money. Serafina knew that it would be a good night for Lexi regardless, but to get two hundred dollars within the first hour for basically doing thirty minutes of talking was an excellent start to the night. In addition, if the timing was well planned, Lexi would be deemed *that* much more desirable by the new group of guys in the corner booth and could easily squeeze another fifty to a hundred, depending on how many breaks they took between dances. So far, it looked like the ratio was one dance for every three dances sat out. It was sure to increase as business picked up.

With fourteen dancers, and three on the stage positions, that left eleven songs for a dancer to try to get dances between sets before having to go back onstage. With that rate, Lexi would be extremely lucky to get a hundred dollars in an hour, let alone two hundred. She was getting a very good deal. No seductive dancing in heels. No schmoozing. No party-girl acts. Just a relaxed conversation. *Under the spotlight.*

Since Serafina needed to make the most of their time, she allowed the songs and DJ announcements to become background noise and just focused on getting all the answers to her questions within the thirty minutes she had with Lexi.

Christine brought Lexi her second glass of merlot. Lexi took a sip and then said, "I'm not sure who you're talking about though. What's his name again?"

"Probably easier if I show you his picture." Serafina took out her phone and showed Lexi a picture of Hollis.

"Oh! Shoot! Yeah! I know him. He said his name was Frank," Lexi exuberantly said when she saw the picture. "He your friend?"

It surprised Serafina to hear Hollis had introduced himself as Frank instead of Hollis.

"How long have you known Hollis?" It was too weird for her to refer to him as Frank.

"Maybe a month," she said. "Why? Did he do somethin'?"

"When was the last time you saw him?" Serafina asked.

Christine placed Serafina's chicken tenders appetizer on the bar between her and Lexi with several plates and ranch dressing.

"Excuse me," Serafina called out to Christine. "I asked for honey mustard."

"Sorry, I'll get that for you right now." Christine motioned to the guy at the bar several stools down that she understood he wanted another drink. He must have caught her eye in that moment.

"Help yourself." Serafina got a small white plate for Lexi to have some chicken tenders.

"Oh, no thanks." Lexi said, keeping the plate close by.

"So, as you were saying? When was the last time you saw him?" Serafina nibbled a small piece on the end of her chicken tender while she waited for her honey mustard dressing.

"Shoot, maybe a week ago? Last Friday, I think." Lexi took a moment to remember, and then confirmed, "Yeah. Last Friday."

Serafina swallowed her bite of chicken and then washed it down with a swig of pinot grigio. "He came in here?"

"Yeah. Why?"

"Just trying to figure something out. That's all," Serafina said.

Christine placed down the honey mustard dressing and poured more merlot from the bottle of wine into Lexi's glass.

"Do you know when he left?" Serafina asked.

"Oh, yeah, like around midnight? Why you aksin'?" Lexi pulled a chicken tender off the appetizer plate and dipped it in the ranch dressing.

"He's my friend, and he was shot last Friday night. He's recovering in the hospital right now."

Lexi's face lost all its expression, and her eyes widened. "That must have been right after he came to see me."

Serafina nodded her head slowly. "Look, I know my friend Hollis doesn't get dances, but he does pay for dancers to sit and talk. What did you all talk about?"

"Nothing really, but this last time . . ." Lexi dipped her chicken tender into the ranch dressing, took another bite, and with a mouthful of chicken, said, "He just wanted me to find out some things about a guy who comes in here."

"A customer?" Serafina fired off her questions in the interest of time.

"Yeah."

"Do you know his name?"

Lexi sat thinking. To Serafina, it was clear that if Lexi gave a name, it may or may not be accurate.

"Is he a regular?" Serafina quickened the pace.

"He don't spend a lot of money, but yeah, he a regular."

"Your regular?"

"Not really. Just whoever sit with him. He ain't really worth sitting with unless it slow 'cause he only buys about four dances, but you gotta sit and talk a long time. Ain't worth it sometimes, ya know?"

"So then, he comes in a lot?"

"Yeah, kind of sad. Probably can't get him no girlfriend."

"How often does he come in?"

"Couple times a week."

"Does he have a usual day or time that he comes in?"

"Not really, but he be here almost always on Friday nights."

Serafina realized it was Friday night. "Is he here right now?"

"Naw." Lexi shook her head as she took the last bite of her chicken tender.

"Was he here when Hollis came to see you last Friday?"

"Yeah."

"When did he leave?"

"Maybe around eleven thirty?" Lexi took a small piece of chicken tender on the main plate, and Christine came to clear the empty dish.

"Was he alone?"

Lexi was starting to get distracted by dances at the corner table. Serafina could tell Lexi was getting agitated when she saw one of the guys from the corner booth tipping each dancer on stage a bunch of dollar bills on their G-strings.

Serafina had only brought two hundred dollars with her to the club, and on a Friday night. That wouldn't keep Lexi much longer. Lexi would have to do a set onstage soon, and that would also eat up their time.

Serafina rephrased her question. "Was anyone with him?"

"I was, for about an hour. Your friend paid me to sit with the guy and find stuff out."

"No, I meant, did he have a friend with him, or was he by himself?"

"Oh. No, he was by himself most of the time. Until his ride came to pick him up. They left together like thirty minutes after that."

"You talk with the friend too?"

"Naw, he wasn't much of a talker."

"What did Hollis want to know?"

"Like, really, whatever I could find out. Mostly about what he was like back in the day when he was normal."

"What do you mean normal?"

"Before he needed a wheelchair."

Serafina immediately thought of Gill.

"The guy in the wheelchair—was his name Gill?" Serafina waited in anticipation.

"I'm not sure. Think so."

"Were you able to find out anything for Hollis?"

"Not really. He wasn't in no gang. That was one of the questions I remember. Um . . . oh yeah, and your friend, Hollis, wanted to know if he knew a guy named Xavier Palo."

"You can remember the name Xavier Palo but not the name of the guy in the wheelchair?" Serafina tried to keep eye contact with Lexi to keep her from looking at the corner table.

"You know how people know people, like six degrees of separation an' shit?"

Serafina wasn't following her logic but agreed. "Sure."

"Well, my cousin and him used to hang back in the day. They DJ'd together at some house parties."

"You know him well?"

"Not really. He was a lot older than me and my friends. We just thought he was good-looking."

"So then, did he know Xavier Palo? And how'd you ask? Did he know that Hollis was having you ask these questions?"

"No, I did what Hollis said to do. Just find a way to talk about something and help the conversation move where I want it to go. I started talking about the music and then talked about house parties back in the day, then talked about DJs, and then I dropped the name."

"And he didn't know him?"

"Naw." Lexi eyed the customers coming through the double doors, lingering in the coat check area for the bouncer to seat them. "His friend seemed to recognize the name though."

"How do you know?"

"I don't know—the way he looked when I said the name . . . like he just knew the name."

"Did you ask him?"

"They pretty much left after that, so then I went over and told your friend what I found out."

Serafina thought about the information Lexi told her.

"Can you let me know the friend's name next time he comes in? Or if you find out anything else?"

"Yeah, no problem." Lexi took out her cell phone and prepared to enter Serafina's contact information. "What's your number?"

"You actually have it already." *It was the office phone, but whatever.* Serafina had the calls set to forward to her cell phone.

Lexi looked confused again. "I do?"

Serafina looked Lexi squarely in the face. "Yeah, I work with Hollis. I tried calling you back, and you said I had the wrong number, remember?"

Lexi thought hard. "Oh!" She laughed. "That was you?"

"Yeah, why would you tell me I had the wrong number?"

"I thought you was his wife or something. I didn't want him gettin' in no trouble. He was a nice guy."

The DJ announced Lexi.

"You still got the number?" Serafina asked quickly as Lexi stood up and grabbed her glass of merlot.

"Yeah."

Lexi began to walk toward the stage.

"Oh, wait," Serafina said. "On the message for Hollis, you said you forgot to tell him something. What was it?"

"Just that, you know how I meet a lot of people in here, and well, I've heard stories about him."

"Hollis?"

"No, the guy in the wheelchair. Wanna know why he in a wheelchair?"

Before Serafina could respond, Lexi continued. "Dude jumped off a building. Crazy, huh? Probably on drugs."

Chapter 23

When Serafina woke up that Saturday morning, she remained in bed, soaking up the silence and tuning into her thoughts. The vertical blinds covering the large loft windows allowed some sunlight to beam through the closed slats. On the bottom half of the mattress, Datson rested peacefully, giving no indication of getting up anytime soon. Instead of immediately jumping into her normal morning routine, she played back the past week's events.

With the night before still fresh in her mind, she thought of her time with Lexi and how exhausting it had been. But it had been worth it. Now, at least she had confirmation that Hollis knew Lexi and that he had been investigating Gill. Or, at least she assumed Gill since the person had been described as being in a wheelchair.

It made sense that Hollis would want to know more about Gill. After all, he had worked at her parents' store. But now, Hollis should have enough information to cross him off his list of suspects, shouldn't he? If not, maybe that's where Serafina could help clear things up. She could let Hollis know that Gill was cool, that he was kind of like family. And rather than being upset at Hollis for looking into her background, she should thank him for being the catalyst to her finding this special person who could fill in the blanks and bring some clarity to her puzzling past.

Hopefully Lexi—or rather, Erika Santiago—didn't give Hollis the wrong impression about Gill. It worried Serafina that Hollis had gone to see Lexi at Tamale Girlz more than once. But did Lexi really have much influence on him? After all, she only knew him as "Frank."

The things Lexi had said about Gill both intrigued and concerned her. Had Gill really jumped off a building? Was there any truth to that, or were they just rumors?

The more she thought about it, the more questions surfaced. Like, if he had done that—and she was noncommittal still about whether he had—then had he done it on a dare? Or an initiation, like *a gang initiation*? Lexi had mentioned that Hollis wanted to know if Gill knew Xavier Palo. Was he trying to see if there was a connection between those two? Was it because Xavier *had* been in a gang? Did that mean Hollis suspected Xavier of something? And how did Hollis even know about Xavier? Had he known something before Cole's report?

Xavier did seem guilty to Serafina, especially after she'd seen him standing next to the mystery car from the ATM video footage. Who was that person he had been talking to—the person in the driver's seat? Did either of them have something to do with Hollis being shot?

It was hard to believe that only a week had gone by since last Saturday. So much had happened in that short amount of time. And the scary part was that it felt like it may only be the beginning of what was to come.

She tried to shush the story in her head that Hollis was replacing her with Cole. But her insecurities were getting the better of her. Maybe it was for the best. She was starting to get tired of surveilling people anyways. Sitting for hours on end in anticipation of *anything* happening, but nothing usually did, and then she'd write up reports documenting all that nothingness.

Maybe she could take a look at what else was out there. See if another career path would be more suitable. Who knew? Maybe she would like it better. But what else would she do?

She hadn't really planned on any particular career path when she started her college program. It had been Hollis who convinced her to do the business administration program. She had just wanted a college degree so she would stop feeling like a loser, as if everyone was passing her by, all those people she'd known once upon a time advancing and going on with their lives.

Seemed like when she was growing up, the only choices were to be a doctor, nurse, teacher, policeman, or firefighter. No one ever talked about other careers. It wasn't until she'd already started her college program that she learned about other fields, like engineering and biotechnology. Now she was done with all her courses, and the graduation was set to commence in a few weeks. She let the possibilities of a new career churn in the background of her consciousness while she moved on to the reality that she was utterly alone.

How did that happen? She used to have friends in school, but it was always awkward bringing them home to meet her family and then having to explain away all their questions. *"Where's your mom?" "Who's she?" "Are you Black too?"* Then, as she got older, the questions turned to looks. Judgmental looks. Then the rumors and gossip would start. Cliques of mean girls excluding her from their precious groups, making her feel inadequate—like an outcast. As if she wanted to fit into their closed-minded groups. No, she was not a follower. She was a loner, one to set her own path.

Somewhere along the line, though, she had become dependent on Randy, like a crutch. But then again, Randy had been just as dependent on her. They kind of needed each other. Until Nick came along, that is.

Over the years, Randy had distanced himself from her and become one with Nick. *Surprised they're not married yet.* But hey, maybe that was in the works too, and she just wasn't told about that either. She digressed from her resentment and returned to wondering about a path forward. Maybe their codependency had run its course, and she was the last to know. Maybe she'd ignored all the signs. Maybe it was time for her to find a Nick of her own.

But was she even interested in a relationship? Not really. Most guys seemed desperate or obnoxious. Was it possible that she wasn't interested in men because she was interested in women? She thought about how Coco wasn't openly bisexual in high school but was now. Was she bisexual too?

She'd only been attracted to a few females in her life, and it wasn't in a sexual way, more like an admiration or an "I wish I looked like that" sort of way. No, she was definitely into men. She noticed them. A lot, actually. But it wasn't worth it. She didn't want to be told what to do, or be controlled, or be someone's property. Not that she knew any men like that. She was going off of what she'd seen or heard from dancers whose boyfriends were jealous and always thinking their dancer girlfriends were fucking customers. Actually, come to think of it, a few probably were. It always seemed suspicious when some dancers would see their customers outside of work. Like, what was the point of a stage name if they were going to tell customers their real names and let them into their personal lives? She digressed, refocusing her attention back on men she'd been attracted to.

As guys go, the only one who'd come close to being decent in a long time was Cole the other day. But then she had exploded on him about DeMarcus, and now he was probably like, "*What the fuck, crazy lady?*" But in her defense, she *had* been sick.

She tried to stay optimistic about DeMarcus. Maybe she would have to wait to reconnect with him, but on the bright side, he was alive. Unfortunately, he was a bum. At least, he had looked like one to Cole. But he was alive.

And maybe Randy was right on some parts. DeMarcus had disrupted their lives last time by stealing their belongings for drugs. If only she could get him into a drug rehab program. But she hadn't even researched anything about that. How much did something like that cost? It wasn't like he had health-care insurance. Was that something government programs covered? She had no idea where to start on that. She was very accustomed to conducting research, but this wasn't something she'd researched before, and she didn't know where to begin. She would need to be prepared better for when she did find him so she could get him in a program immediately. Maybe she could ask Hollis for some Boomer guidance, she suggested to herself jokingly. She smiled, thinking about him.

His friendship meant a lot to her, and in that moment, she was willing to be honest with herself about it. That he wasn't just her employer. She actually enjoyed his company. They were so similar in many ways. They *got* each other on a level others didn't. They could work in the same room for hours without saying a word and then instinctively know what the other needed. Like she'd offer him a Coke, and he'd offer her an iced tea when they went to the kitchen—and she knew that a Coke was any kind of pop except for Dr. Pepper, and that Dr. Pepper was in a category of its own. Either one of them would put on Pandora and stream a station they'd created, and it just felt right for the other. Sometimes they'd purposely annoy the other while working to get the other one to react, like, "Stop tapping that pen!" And the one tapping the pen would laugh. Okay, that was mostly her tapping the pen, but he did it once to her too, giving her a taste of her own medicine. God, she really missed him.

Back to Cole. He *was* very handsome. Even with her guard up, there was no denying that. And he seemed to genuinely care about her. But was it just as friends? Or was he setting the stage for more? Would that be too horrible if she found someone—like Cole, but not necessarily Cole, although it could be Cole—to be in an intimate relationship with?

She pondered the thought. Was she just being resistant to it? Could be.

Maybe on some subconscious level she was resisting the next step, which usually was settling down and having a family. Whether it be having children naturally or choosing to foster or adopt instead, or even if she chose to have pets as her fur-babies, she was resistant to the idea of being in the spotlight, having the world take notice of how *different* she was.

That was a part of her she didn't want the world to see, a part she kept hidden, but rather than delving deeper into that feeling, she joked to herself that if she did the whole children thing, then she'd have to join Mommy groups, and she definitely was resistant to that. There was some truth in that though. She tried her best to avoid catty women groups who badmouthed one another behind each other's backs. The kind who asked all sorts of personal questions to use later as a way to elevate themselves in the groups. And, of course, *she* would be a target. It's not like she couldn't tell how jealous other women were when they looked at her. She shouldn't have to downgrade herself or downplay her looks to being *blah*, but that's what it had come to over the years. That's the look she got from Suong too.

But Suong, she was more than just that. There was something more going on with her. To have such insecurities about whether her husband was at a strip club or cheating on her was something Serafina couldn't really understand. *Just leave the dude if you don't trust him.* But then again, maybe it wasn't that easy once you were married with kids and you had a mortgage, and your finances were tied up in a big knot. The unraveling took time.

Even if there was a part of her she didn't want the world to see, a part she kept hidden—so what! Lots of people did. Even Hollis. She'd always noticed his resistance to talking about Texas, or his past, in general. It had always been somewhat of an off-limits topic, where he'd change the subject or create a diversion, redirecting her to something else as if she wouldn't notice the sleight of hand, like a magician. Look over here, not there. Now she knew why.

Geez, she still couldn't believe he'd lost his wife, daughter, and best friend. And to lose them all so tragically. To think, he even had a brother. Who knew if he was still alive, but she was curious and wanted to find out. Part of her thought, It's none of my business. But her past was none of Hollis's business either, so he had no room to be upset if she looked into it.

Hollis had asked her to be his assistant so she could cover other jobs he couldn't, but here he wasn't even on another job. He had been out investigating her past—and why? Did he want to replace her and just wanted to dig up some dirt so he'd have a reason to? Her gut told her that she was telling herself a story there, but she couldn't find another explanation. None of it made sense.

She thought back to her reaction last Saturday morning when she'd listened to Hollis's voicemail and thought it was some drunk who dialed the wrong number. She felt horrible for referring to him as a "Drunk Whack Job," or whatever she had called him. It was a mistake she wished she could take back.

Last Saturday morning had been an especially harsh day. It had started with Randy exhibiting an extreme level of Randy-ness and had ended with her life completely upended. Actually, come to think of it, things started to go to shit the night before when she told Randy she had been searching for DeMarcus. Deep down, she had known Randy wouldn't be thrilled about it. She just hadn't expected that kind of response out of him. More like caution, but with kindness. Maybe what she was looking for was compassion, if not his approval, and understanding that she had good intentions. Instead, she got a little more than she'd anticipated, and it had caught her off guard. But, on some level, she knew he was right. Even if his main objective was to protect his relationship with Wanda against any potential threats.

And what was that again? *There's no rush?*

Serafina's thoughts became erratic, bouncing from one gripe to another. She started stewing over the thought of how she had been the one who'd found the house in the first place. She'd been the one who had convinced Randy to take that next big step since the apartment wasn't big enough for her, Randy, and Nick—not that Nick didn't have his own place, but he was there practically every night and any other time. Why couldn't they have looked at buying a bigger house instead of kicking her out? Like she did for them.

Then her griping moved on to the feelings of betrayal she had for not knowing that they were trying for a baby. Maybe it was a personal decision between the two of them, but they clued Wanda in. Okay, she didn't have proof of that, but there was no way Randy would have held in something that big from Wanda. Randy was very much TMI about everything else she didn't want to know about. This was something she actually would have wanted to know about. Then maybe she wouldn't have been caught off guard in such an awkward and rushed manner. She could have planned better. And how long exactly had they been trying? A month? Six months? A year?

Serafina thought about the people in her life, her main sources of friendship. Was it really just Hollis and Randy? She thought about it more, and then added Coco to the list so she wouldn't feel so pathetic. She scoffed at referring to Michelle as Coco, but she rarely saw Michelle outside of work anymore, so it seemed fitting to call her Coco. Plus, the whole Coco persona was more than just a stage name because Michelle was a completely different person when she used that name. It was as if Michelle was being transformed into an alter ego that, at times, was unbearable to be around.

Oh shoot! She forgot about Coco's birthday yesterday. She could always tell Coco that she and Hollis had to work. Coco should understand that not everybody had time to take off work to go to someone's birthday at a strip club and have them ignore you while they went to make money.

Back to griping. How could Randy have told Wanda and not her? She couldn't prove it though. If he did, then that was betrayal, for sure. She should try to get information from Wanda next time she saw her. When would that be though? Probably not for a bit. Maybe at the next holiday get-together, Serafina could pull Wanda aside and act like she knew long before last Saturday morning and get Wanda to admit that she knew too. Serafina couldn't just come out and ask Wanda, though, because then Wanda would automatically go on alert and shut off access to that information.

And was it really possible Hollis was trying to replace her? He needed someone to do the jobs he couldn't. Cole already had a job as a policeman. That would be a downgrade in pay and position for him. It wasn't like the salary Hollis paid her was substantial. It was enough. And it was reasonable for the work she did. There wasn't an abundance of work, and the jobs didn't pay a lot.

And this Samuel Hollis Jr. person—was he still alive? He could probably fill in the pieces of the Hollis puzzle for her. At least most of them. Like why did Hollis avoid going back to Texas? Or even talking about Texas. Did Hollis miss his father's funeral? If so, why? She knew why . . . the car accident. How did one ever get over something like that?

There was so much she didn't know about Hollis's past that she was dying to know. Would that be so wrong of her to seek those answers out? Wasn't that what he'd done to her? Not that two wrongs made a right, but how could he get upset and not be a hypocrite if she did?

The one topic she'd really avoided thinking about was where she would live now that Randy and Nick wanted her to move out. She thought about the first apartment she had moved into so many years ago. It had been hers first, and then Randy had moved in shortly after getting with Nick. It was a small two-bedroom, but it was cozy. She could afford something like that on her own again. She'd have to start over on some things, though, which could get expensive. All the stuff they'd had was moved to the new house and then replaced and donated over the years. There was barely anything left that used to be from that apartment. And not that she would get that exact apartment back—that would be amazing if she could—but maybe she could get a place above a store, like a loft or something, a place like this. She realized she was falling in love with the loft and her life at the agency.

If Hollis let her continue to live there, she would certainly be willing to pay him rent. It would be worth it. He'd have extra security at night, and it would help out with costs for the agency. She was already starting to plan out her argument for him to let her rent it.

She started thinking about how she'd decorate it. Maybe some houseplants and some lighting to enhance the ambiance. Maybe a few more throw rugs, not just the one in the open living room space. A few pillows for the couches and a throw blanket like the super soft one Hollis had in the main office area. Some pictures on the walls? But what would the pictures be of? Family? Fun things she'd experienced? Nope, she didn't have any of that. She really did need to get out and get a life. It was time.

Whether or not she would ever meet someone who shared the same interests, one thing was for sure—she needed to go make some memories, which wasn't going to happen by lying in bed wasting the day away. It was time to get up and get going. She wasn't sure where to begin, but she knew her agenda would include using the restroom, dressing for the day, letting Datson outside, pouring some coffee, and putting down some food and fresh water into Datson's bowls.

She came out of the restroom and went over to the bed, changed into regular clothes, then grabbed her phone and the can of leftover iced tea on her nightstand before heading downstairs. "Come on, boy!" she called to Datson.

Datson stirred as if thinking about getting up. Serafina headed down to the kitchen and poured him his usual amount of kibble. She rinsed out his water bowl and refilled it with fresh tap water. Then she pulled out a coffee mug, added the usual amount of cream and sugar, and set up a K-cup to brew a single cup of coffee. Still no signs of Datson. She took her cup upstairs to check on him.

As Serafina entered the upstairs loft from the doorway of the stairs, she immediately noticed Datson collapsed on the floor, halfway from the bed to the doorway, and he didn't look well. Serafina raced over to Datson to see what was wrong with him. He tried to get up several times, but his back legs were weak. She calmed him by stroking the fur on his head. She needed to get him in to see his veterinarian. They'd know his medical history and be able to provide him with the medical assistance he needed. Some medicine or shots. Hopefully not surgery. Thank God it was just a short drive to Woodward Avenue. How was she going to get him there though? She couldn't pick him up by herself. Without someone's help, she wouldn't be able to get him down the stairs and into the Explorer, or even into the veterinary hospital. She tried not to go into a full-blown panic, as she paced back and forth quickly, trying to figure out what to do, who to call.

Her first thought was Cole, but she wasn't sure if he would be available, and if he was, whether he would ignore her call. She had been kind of shitty to him. But she had planned to apologize at her first opportunity. She just hadn't known she would need him again so soon. Now would her apology come across as insincere or only because she needed him for something? There was always Levi. Or Levi's son, Brian? Would that be weird to ask Brian? She looked over at Datson. *Ah, fuck.* Okay, just call Cole. *Where's my phone?*

Chapter 24

Serafina picked up her phone and frantically fumbled for Cole's number. Without hesitation, he picked up right away and agreed to come over to help. When she heard him pull into the driveway seven minutes later, she raced down the stairs to let him in through the front door.

"Thank you, thank you, thank you! You have no idea how much I appreciate this." She let him inside and closed the door.

"No worries. I'm right on the other side of Woodward, so it's really no trouble at all."

In Berkley, she recalled from his address on the report he had dropped off for Hollis. She didn't want him knowing she'd read the report, though, so she acted as if that were news to her. "Oh, good."

Not waiting for directions, Cole made his way up the stairs to the loft, where Datson lay on the hardwood floorboards, and knelt down to his level. His cologne lingered in the air as Serafina walked behind him.

"Hey there, boy," Cole said softly, like a gentle whisper, as he lightly pet Datson's head.

It was heartbreaking to see Datson in the state that he was. And it made her feel like a horrible human being to have feelings for Cole start to surface right then—of all times. She tried to ignore his sensuous scent and calming voice, and when she couldn't, she chalked it up as evidence that she really needed to get out and meet someone.

"I think we should try to get him into the back of the Explorer. Might be easier than trying to get him in the back seat of my car." Cole looked up at Serafina from his kneeled position.

Serafina just nodded her head, imagining Cole kneeling before her with a ring in hand, asking her to marry him. An odd sensation came over her, and she reminded herself that it was neither the time nor place to be fantasizing about that sort of next step in her life, especially with Cole. *But why not Cole?*

"I can probably pick him up by myself if you can get the front door propped and open up the back of the Explorer."

"You sure? He's pretty big."

"No, but let's try that first. If I need your help—"

Serafina interrupted him. "Just let me know. I'll be right in front."

He redirected his attention to Datson. "It's okay, boy," he said, petting Datson.

"Give me a sec, real quick. I just want to unlock the back of the Explorer and get that ready."

As Serafina returned to the kitchen, Cole was already coming down the stairs with Datson held up against his body. She raced to the front door and opened it. Cole took Datson over to the open hatchback of the Explorer and laid him down.

"Let me grab my phone and lock up, and then we can go."

"Do you need to grab your purse too?"

"Naw. I have all I need on my phone case. It's got a place for cards and whatnot."

"Oh, okay. Just checking." Cole returned to comforting Datson while Serafina went inside to grab what she needed.

When Serafina turned around after locking up the front door, Cole's car was parked on the street, the hatchback of the Explorer was closed, and Cole was sitting in the passenger side of the Explorer. She got in the driver's seat, and they headed to the veterinary hospital a few miles away.

The veterinarian was speaking with one of the assistants when Serafina and Cole entered the lobby of the veterinary hospital with Datson.

Serafina spoke first. "Hi, I believe Datson comes here to see you, and I'm taking care of him right now . . ."

She thought about whether to mention, ". . . while Hollis is recovering in the hospital," but decided that was more information than they needed to know.

". . . for his owner, Frank Hollis."

"Oh, yeah, we know Datson very well, don't we, Dr. Paulson?" the assistant said, allowing the veterinarian to confirm.

Upon seeing Datson's condition, Dr. Paulson immediately guided them to one of the available rooms and directed them to place Datson on the examining table.

"Okay, let's take a look," Dr. Paulson said after closing the door to the examination room.

Dr. Paulson checked Datson's abdomen. "Hmm. Looks like he has some swelling of the abdomen." She then checked his gums. "His gums are pale too."

"What does that mean—the swollen abdomen and pale gums?" Serafina asked.

"Could mean anemia. Has he been lethargic?"

Serafina looked at Cole before responding. "Kind of?"

"When did he first exhibit lack of movement?" Dr. Paulson asked as she walked over to her desktop computer in the corner and opened Datson's profile in the system.

"This morning. Like not even an hour ago. He was sleeping peacefully on my bed, and I went to get him food and let him out. Normally he follows behind me, but this time he didn't, so I went upstairs to check on him, and he was in the middle of the floor, like he just collapsed there. And it looks like his back legs are weak."

Dr. Paulson had Serafina and Cole move away from the examination table so she could get a weight measurement on Datson. She then went over to the desktop computer again and recorded his weight.

"He's lost a significant amount of weight since his last checkup three months ago. Have you noticed any change in his eating?"

"Well, yeah." Serafina thought back to when Levi first brought Datson over to the agency for her to care for him. He'd been lively then. "He was doing well about a week ago, as far as I know, but his owner—Frank Hollis—he's been . . . away . . . and I just thought . . ." She looked briefly at Cole and then back at the doctor. "I thought he wasn't eating much because he missed Hollis."

"I thought the same thing the other day when I stopped by." Cole reassuringly rubbed Serafina's right shoulder blade with his left hand. "Remember how he didn't want to go to Henderson Glass with me?"

Cole directed his attention to Dr. Paulson who was now at Datson's side examining him. "How much weight has he lost?"

Dr. Paulson momentarily looked up. "We typically consider anything over 10 percent of their normal weight to be significant. So, three months ago, he was sixty pounds. He's now, well you saw on the scale, he's now fifty-one."

Ten percent of sixty pounds was six pounds. What percent of sixty pounds was nine pounds? While Dr. Paulson continued her examination of Datson, Serafina did the math in her head. *Fifteen percent.*

"When did he first experience a loss of appetite?" Dr. Paulson asked.

"Like a week ago?" Serafina said, fearful of where the questions were leading them.

"I'd like to do a blood analysis and urine sample analysis." Dr. Paulson hesitated and then continued. "I also think we should perform some medical imaging of his chest and abdomen. He'll need some light anesthesia for that." She paused to get Serafina's acquiescence.

Having no clue how much all of that would cost, but knowing Hollis wouldn't hesitate on giving Datson whatever medical care he needed, Serafina agreed. "Okay, yeah."

"It could be up to an hour," Dr. Paulson said before leaving.

Within a few minutes, Datson was taken out of the room by a few of the staff, leaving Serafina and Cole alone together next to the examining table. Each took a seat at the two available chairs next to one another and waited for Dr. Paulson to return with news. They sat quietly for a few moments before Serafina broke the silence.

"Oh, my goodness! I just realized I didn't ask if you were able to stick around with me. I just assumed—"

Cole interrupted her. "It's fine." He patted her hand briefly. "I'm yours for as long as you need me."

Both of them sensed the awkwardness in the air, so Cole clarified what he meant.

"I mean, I don't have to work today. It's my day off, and I wasn't really doing anything. I can stay."

Serafina wasn't sure what to think about Cole or their relationship. Did he like her, or was that her imagination? She wasn't ready to put a name on it. Whatever it was between them, she was just grateful for his company.

After another minute of silence, Serafina decided that *that* moment was as good a time as any to apologize to Cole about her reaction to him shooing DeMarcus away when she was sick.

"Hey." She turned slightly to face Cole better.

Cole remained in his forward-facing position, looking as if he was expecting to hear bad news from her.

She wasn't sure how best to approach him with the apology, and then decided she should just say it, lay it all out. "I owe you an apology."

Cole perked up and turned toward her.

"I'm really sorry, Cole, about the other day when I was sick and got upset at you about DeMarcus—not that being sick is any excuse."

"DeMarcus?" Cole asked.

Realizing she owed him an explanation, Serafina thought about where to start. It wasn't like Cole didn't already know most of her past. It shouldn't come as a shock who DeMarcus was.

"DeMarcus is . . ." She paused to inhale and exhale deeply first, and then continued. "He was my foster brother growing up. I guess he still is, but I haven't seen him in years."

Serafina looked at Cole, who listened intently, without judgment. She still didn't want him to know she'd read his report, so she decided to tell her story as if he didn't already know many of the details.

"When I was about four years old, my parents were murdered in their store on the southwest side of Detroit. The Department of Human Services couldn't locate any relatives, so I was placed in foster care. My foster mother is Wanda Price. She's a teacher in Detroit and lives in Hamtramck. Anyway, when I got there, she was already fostering my foster brother, Randy, who I currently live with, but not for much longer—that's another story."

Cole coaxed her with a questioning look.

"They just dropped the news on me that they're adopting and want me to move out, so now I need to find a place to stay."

"I thought you were living in the loft above the agency?"

"It was just to care for Datson." Serafina tightened her lips and nodded. "But, whatever. Anyway, so where was I?" She brushed it off.

"You were telling me about how they couldn't find relatives for you, so you went to live with Wanda and Randy?"

"Right." Serafina mentally retraced her story back to where she'd left off. "Anyway, she was also fostering her two grandchildren, DeMarcus and DeShawn. They were older than me by a few years."

Serafina was debating on how much more she should mention, but then Cole spoke up. "That was DeMarcus that showed up at the house that day, wasn't it? Geez, I should be the one apologizing to you."

Serafina smiled as she teared up. "You actually did. I just wasn't being receptive to it, and that wasn't fair to you."

"Hey, hey, it's okay. We're good." Cole reassured her.

Serafina wiped her eyes before any tears could escape.

"You said you hadn't seen him in years?" Cole asked.

Serafina sighed heavily.

"I'm sorry. I didn't mean to pry. You don't need to tell me."

Serafina reassured him. "No, it's okay. It's just hard to talk about because, well, it's complicated. My brother Randy—foster brother, whatever—he doesn't approve of me trying to find DeMarcus."

Serafina looked at Cole, who was looking right back at her, intently listening. His eyes were a striking blue color. "Last time DeMarcus was in our lives was years ago. He disappeared after stealing a lot of belongings from Randy and Wanda—my foster mom. Oh yeah, I already said that."

"Nothing from you?" Cole inquired.

"No, not me. Just them. It was back when I had just moved out and got my own apartment—before Randy moved in with me, and then he bought a house with his boyfriend, and I moved in with them, blah, blah, blah. You're not interested in all that."

"I actually find it fascinating. You're a very interesting person." Cole smiled genuinely at her.

Serafina tightened up. "Interesting as in *different*?"

Cole reassured her, as if worried he'd offended her. "Oh, no, well, okay, yes—but in a good way."

Serafina side-eyed him, with a smirk.

"I mean it." Cole turned toward her more. "I really do."

Serafina nodded.

"So, why did he steal their belongings?" Cole kept the conversation going.

"He was on drugs. Probably still is, considering you thought he was a bum."

"Hey, he might not be anymore."

Serafina nodded. "Thanks, but no, I'm pretty sure he's still on drugs. I was hoping to get him into a drug rehabilitation program."

"Oh?" Cole looked as if the topic had sparked something within him.

"Yeah, I had reached out to a lot of organizations and contacts to try to locate him. I wasn't expecting him to show up that fast before I'd had a chance to research options for him. I don't even know what he would qualify for without medical insurance or how to maneuver through that."

"I could help with that," Cole offered. "If you want."

"Oh, I couldn't." Serafina resisted. "Plus, it may be a while before I get in touch with him again. I don't know which one of them relayed my message to him, so I'll need to reach out to all of them again."

"Oh, Serafina. I'm so sorry. I totally get why you were so upset at me."

"It's okay. Hey, it is what it is. I wasn't prepared with a place to take him anyway. Next time, hopefully, I'll be prepared."

"The burn scars . . . What happened—if you don't mind me asking?"

"It's really sad, actually. He and DeShawn had to go back to their mom after she got out of rehab—court-ordered and all—and shortly after that, he returned with burn scars on his face, and DeShawn was dead. So was their mom. I could never get a clear answer about it when it first happened."

"From Wanda or DeMarcus?"

"Both. So, I had always assumed that they—not the mom, obviously—were playing with fire."

"Maybe it was?"

"Even then I knew something was off because when we went to the funeral, DeShawn had an open casket, and he didn't have any burn marks."

"Maybe it was smoke inhalation?"

"See, that's what I started to think too as I got older, still trying to make sense of it all, ya know?"

Cole nodded.

"It wasn't until years later—last time he was around, actually, DeMarcus—that I flat-out asked him, and he told me what happened."

"What happened?"

Serafina shook her head side to side, as if trying to say, "Such a shame." "So, they went home to live with their mom in her apartment, and things were good for a while, but then she started using again. Staying out for days, never coming home."

"Geez, how old were they?"

"Hmm." Serafina thought about it. "Let's see, it was about a year after I came to stay with them, so I was about five years old? DeShawn was a year older, so he would have been about six years old. DeMarcus was about three years older than DeShawn, so he would have been nine years old at the time?" She nodded in agreement with her results.

Cole shook his head with disbelief.

"So, yeah, they were left to care for themselves," Serafina said.

"And nobody from their schools reached out?"

Serafina shook her head. "No, it was in the beginning of summer, right after school had let out."

"Wasn't Wanda around to check in on them?"

"Apparently, from what little I know from Wanda, she fought hard to keep them, but the court cleared them to go back to their mom's. And she—Wanda's daughter—was upset at Wanda for, I guess, fighting her in court? Keeping her kids from her? Who knows. But basically, she made it so Wanda only got visitations every other week, something like that."

"Not once a week?"

"No, because I guess they had to be supervised, and Detroit DHS was short-staffed?

Cole seemed to be getting angry. "That's unacceptable."

Serafina nodded her head in agreement. "Yep."

"Okay, so then what happened?"

"Their mom had been gone for days, so they were having to take care of themselves. Apparently, DeShawn kept crying that he was hungry, so DeMarcus boiled up some water to make him some macaroni and cheese. Their mom came home after being gone for days, and she went to the bedroom for something. While she was in the bedroom, DeMarcus heard DeShawn say something about finding candy, but he didn't look to see what DeShawn was talking about. Well, what he thought was candy in his mom's purse or bag or whatever was actually drugs. When she came out, DeShawn was having a seizure, and she got all upset that her drugs were gone and then started attacking DeMarcus in the kitchen for not keeping an eye on him, saying things like, 'I needed those, and now they're all gone! Now what am I going to do?' And I guess the pot of boiling water fell on his face during the struggle? She just left after that with DeShawn foaming at the mouth, going into cardiac arrest, and DeMarcus's skin falling off. Not sure how one of the neighbors found out, but I guess they called 9-1-1."

"That's horrible!" Cole was visibly upset by what he was hearing.

"He was the sweetest kid growing up. I suppose he just never recovered after what he experienced. I just wanted to get him the help he needs, so he can fight this drug addiction and get his life straight."

"I feel sick thinking about how I treated him."

"Well, he was nine when that happened. He's an adult now and has to be accountable for his own life at some point."

"Still."

They sat quietly for a moment, and then Cole asked, "How long has it been? Since they left with Datson? Half hour?"

"Oh, no, longer than that. I believe it was shortly after ten when they took him back." Looking at the time on her phone, she saw it was close to eleven. "It's been at least forty-five minutes, possibly even an hour."

"You sure? Time went by fast."

Serafina nodded. "Mm-hmm."

They sat without talking for a bit, and then Cole broke the silence. "My older sister was a drug addict."

"Really? And the rehab helped?"

Cole shook his head. "No, she died."

"Oh, my goodness! Cole, I'm so sorry."

"I was in high school when it happened. They found her body in a drug house in Detroit. And you know what the worst part is?"

"Uh-uh." She shook her head "No."

"Well, okay, it's not the worst part, since dying is, but you know what I mean."

"Mm-hmm." She encouraged him to continue.

"Someone raped her postmortem."

"What!" She was unsure of what to say next. The thought left her speechless.

"Yep. At one point they thought it was part of a gang initiation, but then the whole investigation went stale."

"Seriously?"

"Mm-hmm. That whole thing is why I went into law enforcement."

Serafina had always detested the police. To her, they were hypocrites by acting above the law and putting their sirens on to go through traffic lights when there was no emergency just because they didn't want to have to wait. They looked down on regular citizens when they talked to them, and that was just the beginning of her disdain for them. How about all the profiling and attacks on the African American male population? The thought of being associated with a cop was cringe-worthy to her, but she was starting to see a different side of Cole, one that made her want to make an exception to her anti-police stance and give him a chance.

The door to the room opened, and Dr. Paulson came in, closing the door behind her. Serafina and Cole were about to stand, but she motioned for them to remain seated. She grabbed her stool in the corner and rolled it away from the computer desk over to where they sat.

"Datson has what is called visceral hemangiosarcoma. It's a highly invasive, aggressive type of cancer that's inherited. It begins in a blood vessel and spreads readily throughout the body. It causes tumors to grow rapidly in internal organs like the spleen, liver, heart, and sometimes the skin. And it causes hemorrhaging and bleeding. That's what we're seeing in Datson right now. His enlarged abdomen is from hemorrhaging. So is the weakening in his back legs and the sudden collapse he had this morning."

"Are you sure?" Serafina asked.

"Yes, the results confirm what we suspect."

"But he was fine last week," Serafina insisted.

Dr. Paulson gave a pause before responding. "It often goes undetected in its early stages. It's not until it has advanced that it becomes noticed."

"So, what does he need? Medicine? Surgery?" Serafina started to turn to taking action.

"It's not that simple. Depending on the size and extent of the tumors, treatment could be surgical removal along with chemotherapy. That might give him four months more to live. But what he has is incurable, so the condition *will* continue. To give some perspective, when the cancer is localized to the spleen, and there's no signs of rupture, only 10 percent make it more than a year. His has gone beyond his spleen, and he's *already* bleeding out."

"What are our options then?"

"I'm afraid his prognosis isn't good. Even if we were to surgically remove whatever tumors are present, this type of cancer is almost always fatal in the long run. And he'd be living in considerable pain for the short time he has left. He's fifteen years old, right?"

"I think so."

Dr. Paulson just nodded, allowing Serafina to come to the conclusion on her own.

"So, then, what? We just let him bleed to death?"

"I'm recommending euthanasia, rather than have him endure pain in his final hours. He may not even have that long. He's sedated right now but awake enough if you want to say goodbye to him."

Serafina started crying. "I'm gonna have to call Hollis and let him know. Oh God, he's going to be crushed. I can't do this."

"I'll handle that. Go be with Datson. I'll be right there." Cole took out his phone and motioned for her to go with the veterinarian.

The room where Datson lay sedated was dim compared to the other room she and Cole had sat in. Dr. Paulson guided Serafina to Datson's side. His back leg had an intravenous cannula inserted into it, and the area around it was shaven. That was probably how they sedated him for the medical imaging procedure. She looked over at Dr. Paulson, who was starting to prepare the euthanasia solution.

"Will it hurt him?" Serafina asked.

"No. It's kind of like general anesthesia in the sense that he'll lose consciousness and won't feel any pain. The difference, though, is that his cardiovascular and respiratory systems will be suppressed and will stop functioning altogether within a few minutes."

Emotions overwhelmed Serafina as she stood by Datson's side, knowing his life was ending in just a few moments. Knowing that Hollis would be getting bad news in the other room from Cole. Knowing how much that loss was going to hit Hollis. All the loss he'd had in his life, and now to lose Datson. Things would never be the same for him. Or her. Or Datson. She gently stroked the fur on Datson's head and then kissed his forehead and snuggled her face into his. She could tell he knew she was there. There wasn't anything specific he did to let her know, but she knew.

"Are you ready?" Dr. Paulson asked softly, ready to inject the euthanasia solution.

Serafina looked at the door hoping Cole would walk in. Just as she thought she'd have to do it on her own, Cole opened the door and walked over to Serafina's side. She looked at him, and he nodded to indicate he'd told Hollis. Unable to contain her grief any longer, her face contorted as she tried to hold in her sobs. He pulled her into his arms and held her while she sobbed quietly, her body convulsing.

His embrace felt incredibly comforting, and she didn't want to let go in that moment. But she knew it was time. She pulled away from his arms, wiping any tears before they could fall, and nodded to Dr. Paulson. Within seconds, the solution had entered Datson's body and was beginning to take effect.

The room was quiet as they stood at Datson's side, waiting for him to pass. Both Serafina and Cole comforted Datson with petting. Within a minute, Datson lay still with his eyes open.

Dr. Paulson checked Datson's heart with her stethoscope. "His heartbeat is slowing."

Serafina could no longer control the tears that flowed from her eyes. Even her nose was running. Cole quickly found a box of Kleenex on the counter next to the sink and handed some available tissues to Serafina. She wiped her face with the tissues and continued to pet Datson as Dr. Paulson periodically checked for the absence of a heartbeat.

"It's over. His heart and lungs have stopped functioning." Dr. Paulson put her stethoscope away and turned to both Serafina and Cole. "I'm so sorry for your loss."

Serafina remained focused on Datson. She imagined his soul leaving his body and dissipating before her eyes while Dr. Paulson continued to speak.

"I've known Datson for a good portion of his fifteen years of life. He'll be missed by all of us here at the clinic."

Serafina heard Dr. Paulson and Cole continue to talk. On a subconscious level, she knew what they were saying, but she didn't want to disconnect from Datson just yet.

"I'm going to step outside now. Take as long as you need."

Cole stopped Dr. Paulson before she left the room. "I spoke with his owner, Frank Hollis, and he asked to have the invoice and crematory options emailed to him. I have his contact information for you if that's all right."

"Sure," Dr. Paulson said sympathetically.

• • •

It was a quiet drive home, with Cole driving and Serafina staring out the passenger window, processing it all. When they arrived back at the agency, Cole parked in the driveway, shut off the engine, and turned toward Serafina, who was still looking out the window.

"Did you want some company? I can go get us some breakfast—or lunch if that's what you're in the mood for."

Serafina slowly shook her head. "I'll be fine."

"Are you sure? I really don't mind."

Serafina slowly shook her head again. "No, thanks."

Cole gave her the keys and they exited the Explorer together. After opening the front door, Serafina looked back at Cole, who was now in his car. He put his hand up as if to say goodbye, so she returned the gesture before going inside.

As soon as she entered the front office, she wanted to leave. It felt completely wrong to come back to the agency without Datson. She closed the front door and curled up on the couch with the throw blanket.

Her whole life felt like it was falling apart, and she had an intense urge to take action, to fix everything. But how? Where would she start? Datson wasn't coming back. Randy and Nick still wanted her to move out. Now they might lose their biggest client because all her video footage and notes from that last job had been stolen out of the Explorer. Maybe she could recover something from the break-in of the Explorer? She remembered the alleyway next to where she had parked that day. If she had been the person to break into the Explorer, she certainly would have run down the alley. Maybe the thief tossed an item or two if they got in the alleyway and realized it wasn't worth anything to them? It was worth checking out. Even if it resulted in nothing, it was her doing *something*.

Chapter 25

Serafina parked the Explorer just outside the Burger King where it had been broken into, but this time, she made it a point to park closer to the main street. As she got out of the Explorer, she paid special attention to her surroundings before heading to the alleyway, scanning all directions for anyone and anything remotely suspicious.

Although she was apprehensive about going in the alleyway alone, it was her best chance to retrieve any of her stolen belongings. She just needed to be extra cautious and prepare to run out at the very first sight of danger. She stiffened herself as she walked over to it.

A stray dog meandered down the alleyway to the left, sniffing the ground along the way. It stopped at a garbage bag that had been torn open and started digging at it. Serafina decided to check out the alleyway to the right first.

Off in the distance, she could hear a basketball hitting the pavement in one of the adjacent backyards. She diligently scanned the sides of the alleyway for any remnants of her stolen items, anything that might have been tossed as worthless. A few times, she thought she saw something, but they were just false alarms. After a few blocks of turning up nothing, she turned around and headed back to check out the other alleyway.

Before venturing down the other alleyway, she quickly glanced over at the Explorer to make sure it was still intact. Noting nothing amiss, she continued to where the stray dog had been. She was immediately disgusted by the putrid odors emanating from the torn open garbage bags. Inside one of the houses, she could hear a hungry baby being comforted and guessed the smell was from dirty diapers. With stifled mouth-breathing, she hurried her search.

Down a few blocks and back, she'd resolved to the realization that there was nothing to find. If she recovered anything, it would be a miracle. It was all gone. And now there was only one thing left to do, and that was to accept it. Move on and move forward.

Before leaving the vicinity, Serafina decided to use the Burger King restroom while she was there. She'd come to know in her line of work that restrooms were hard to come by. *Use it while you can.*

As Serafina headed to the side door of Burger King, she couldn't help but look over to the parking lot on the other side, half-expecting to see the teenage miscreants from the last time she'd been there. She hadn't expected to see the rust-colored Chevy Impala there instead. It was parked facing the gas station, making it so she couldn't identify the driver, but from what she could see, the driver appeared to be the same guy from the day she'd seen Xavier standing next to it.

Without being too obvious, Serafina went around to the front of Burger King and approached from the other side to get a better view. Just then, someone started to get out of the passenger side. They wore a Burger King uniform as if they were just starting their shift. Serafina hung back a moment to keep a low profile. They closed the car door and turned around, and that's when Serafina saw her. *Pregnant Tammy!*

Tammy was starting to walk toward her but was so focused on other things that she didn't seem to notice Serafina standing on the sidewalk leading up to the side door. Serafina looked back at the Impala, still parked with its parking lights on. There was no time to use the restroom. She needed to head back to the Explorer as quickly as possible so she could follow the Impala.

Serafina swiftly walked back to the Explorer, picking up the pace as she got closer to it. Halfway to the Explorer, she noticed the Impala reversing out of its parking space, so she increased her speed again. When she looked back and saw it waiting at the exit of Burger King, ready to enter onto the main street, she began to run the rest of the way to the Explorer. As Serafina opened the Explorer door, she looked back and saw that the Impala wasn't there anymore. She immediately turned on the engine and sped to the main street to try to catch up to it.

Serafina spotted the Impala up ahead. It didn't appear to be much in a hurry, which helped her close the gap relatively quickly. Just three cars ahead.

Just then, Serafina's stomach growled. *Seriously*?! It had to have been the smell of Burger King aromas that woke it up. No time for eating now. She needed to keep up with the Impala heading toward Springwells as they passed store after store. Normally, she would be taking in the scenery, noticing things like the Spanish words that kept her an outsider to her own culture. *Restaurante. Super mercado. Pollo.* But in that moment, Serafina could only see the Impala.

They passed Springwells Avenue, Holy Redeemer Church, and what used to be her parents' store. She was keenly aware of her surroundings, but nothing mattered. Her heart raced as the three-car length became two.

Unexpectedly, the Impala turned right just before getting to Clark Park. Serafina had been so used to driving all the way up to Clark Avenue that this surprised her. She slowed down before turning, and then proceeded down the side street.

The Impala was almost at the stop sign at the end of the block when she completed her turn. About a third of the way down on the second block, she watched the Impala pull into a driveway of a house with an upper and lower flat. Serafina slowed down and parked roughly five houses away to make her presence less obvious.

The driveways all went alongside the houses into the backyards, right up to the detached garages. Serafina couldn't see much from where she was parked and had no idea of the driver's whereabouts at that point. This wasn't going to work.

She considered whether she might be able to capture the license plate and address if she walked slow enough past the house and aimed her phone's camera at just the right angle in that direction. It was worth a shot.

As she readied herself to get out of the Explorer, she felt pressure in her bladder. She knew it wouldn't be long before she'd need to find a restroom again. She could make it though. Not that she wanted to drive all the way back to Burger King, but that was always an option after getting the license plate number. She tried not to think too much about it, but that didn't seem to help. She started thinking about how she might crouch down in the back of the Explorer and pee into something as a worst-case scenario, but there was nothing to pee into even if she became that desperate.

It's now or never. Serafina wrapped her hair up into a messy bun, threw on a jacket, and exited the vehicle. She checked that the Explorer doors were locked, and then opened up the camera function on her phone and began walking toward the house where the Impala had pulled into the driveway.

She approached the driveway of the house just as the driver of the Impala was coming out of the front door. The two briefly met eyes before he turned around to lock the door. *Damn, he's leaving.* Could she remember the license plate? Maybe, she thought. Probably not though.

Serafina stood to the side of the driveway and held the phone as if she was texting someone. Positioning her body so that it wasn't obvious, she acted as if the sun glare was affecting her as she texted. Then, when the license plate numbers came into view, she quickly snapped the picture.

She glanced up at the address numbers and recited them in her head repeatedly until the driver had completely backed out into the street and driven away. Then she typed the address numbers into the Notes app on her phone.

Even though she really needed to use the restroom at this point, she knew it would be too obvious if she turned around and started walking back to the Explorer, so she continued to the corner and came back on the opposite side of the street, like a regular person going for a casual stroll might. During that walk, she thought about the driver's connection to Xavier and Tammy, and Tammy's connection to Gill. Was it possible that Gill knew Xavier too? She didn't want to jump to conclusions about Gill, though, especially since Lexi—or rather, Erika Santiago—had said he didn't know Xavier.

She was eager to look up this mystery person the second she returned to the Explorer, but she needed to find a restroom first. *Non-negotiable.* Unable to hold on any longer, Serafina decided to head back to the bathroom she knew of, back to Burger King.

She drove down the block to the stop sign and turned left on the one-way street over to Clark Avenue and up to Vernor Avenue. As she was about to turn left onto Vernor Avenue, she noticed a man wheeling himself down the sidewalk and quickly realized it was Gill. *Speak of the devil.* She rolled her window down and yelled to him, "Hey, stranger!"

"Oh, hey!" he said enthusiastically. "What brings you over to this part of the hood?"

"Just checking on some things." It wasn't exactly a lie. "Where're you off to?"

"Heading home. You should come hang out."

"Right now?" Serafina tightened her pelvic muscles as the need to pee worsened.

"Well, yeah, unless you got something else going on?"

"Naw, it's just I have to use the restroom so bad!" Serafina laughed.

"Well, come on now! Let's get you to my place. It's right up here on the next street." Gill motioned ahead.

Serafina contemplated the offer with extreme brevity, as her bladder would not allow her to wait much longer. "Yeah, okay. How do you wanna do this?"

"Just unlock the door. I can pull myself in. I just need you to collapse the chair and put it in the back."

Serafina did as Gill instructed and then headed in the direction he motioned.

"Turn here on the left. It's a few houses down on the second block. On the right. Yellow house. Can't miss it."

Serafina turned left as instructed.

"Sorry I didn't have much time to talk the other day." Gill pointed to the house up ahead on the right.

Serafina pulled up to the house and parked in the street. "Here okay?"

"Yeah, it's good."

As Serafina turned off the engine, she realized she had only got the address numbers for the Impala, not the street name. *Might have to circle back later.* Regardless, she had a good picture of the license plate, and that was something. She assisted Gill back into his wheelchair, and they headed up the ramp to the front door.

"I try to keep the place clean," Gill stated apologetically as he opened the door before they walked inside.

Inside the house, Gill pointed to the hallway opening. "Turn left and go down the hallway. Bathroom's first door on left."

Serafina bolted toward the hallway opening.

"I'm gonna get myself a nice cold pop. You want something to drink?"

"Same!" Serafina called from the hallway.

When Serafina returned to the living room, she could hear him moving about in the kitchen on the other side of the wall. "You need any help?"

As soon as she asked him that, she immediately second-guessed whether it would be taken the wrong way. Her offer had nothing to do with his disability. She would have asked Randy, Nick, or even Hollis the same thing.

"Naw, be right there."

Serafina took the opportunity to check her phone and noticed she had a missed voicemail from a familiar phone number. *Hmm. Whose number is that?*

The message was forwarded from the agency landline and was left sometime around 1:00 p.m. that day. She played the message as she began wandering around the living room and glancing at the framed pictures on the wall.

The first picture to catch Serafina's attention was of a young Gill before he needed a wheelchair. He couldn't have been more than seventeen years old. He had a basketball in his hands and was standing next to his brother, Renzo, and some other kid; both looked to be about fifteen years old or so. They looked so young with their peach-fuzz mustaches with Gill towering over them. Good for Renzo to have caught up in height! The other kid looked familiar. Either he was the one that Renzo had walked over to that day when they stopped her at Clark Park, or she must have seen him up at the court playing ball. Upon recognizing the voice on the voicemail as Erika Santiago, or rather Lexi from Tamale Girlz, she instantly put all her focus into listening to the message.

"That guy you was aksin' me about—the one in the wheelchair? Gill? Well, he come in 'bout an hour after you left. He left behind some prescription he must'a picked up before comin' in. I looked up the name of the drug before he came back in for it. It's for schizophrenia. Fucker's crazy . . ."

Schizophrenia? Could this be why Gill ended up in a wheelchair?

She'd once read about a guy with schizophrenia who heard Mother Mary tell him to poke his own eyeballs out after looking at pornography and ended up blind from actually doing it. Was it possible he experienced something similar? What other reason is there for jumping off a building?

Serafina could hear Gill rolling his wheelchair into the living room, so she turned around. Gill maneuvered his chair toward her, balancing two cans of Coca-Cola in his lap.

As he extended his hand out to give her one of the cans, her phone dinged. She glanced quickly at it. Seeing that it was just a long rambling text from Randy, she put the phone in her jacket pocket and accepted the can from Gill.

"I'm glad we crossed paths today. I been needing to get something off my chest. Somethin' I been carrying with me too long." Gill pulled an old, brown leather wallet from his hoodie pocket and gestured for Serafina to take it from him.

Serafina skeptically accepted the wallet. "What's this?"

Gill positioned himself before her. He started to speak and then paused, as if trying to select the perfect words.

Serafina's phone dinged again. It was probably Randy again, she thought. It can wait.

"Look, what I'm about to tell you . . . I just want to say I'm so sorry."

"Sorry?" Serafina repeated his last word. Sorry for what? she wondered. Her instincts told her to back away, but she stood there frozen to the ground. What would she find if she opened up the wallet?

"Open it." Gill maneuvered his wheelchair so the sun from the window wasn't in his eyes.

"Whose wallet is this?"

Ding. Either another text message came through, or it was the same one notifying her again. Serafina ignored it.

Gill nodded his head for her to go ahead and open the wallet. "Look, I know you're looking for answers, but I wanna be the one to give them to you. Not Lexi or anyone else."

"You know I went to see Lexi?"

Gill nodded. "Look, I'm not mad about it. I understand why you did it. I just want you to hear my side before you decide I'm this terrible person."

Serafina's phone dinged again. *It's got to be another text message from Randy.*

Serafina's face tensed, and she felt the urge to run out of the house. But he was right. She had been wanting some answers.

"Did she tell you I have schizophrenia?"

Shit.

"I left my medication at the bar," Gill said. "I'm sure Lexi told you. She done told everybody there."

Serafina's phone began to ring, jolting her. She contemplated how she should respond to Gill, but she was distracted by the ringing as if it were a crying baby.

"Did you want to get that?" Gill looked in the direction of her phone, still in her jacket pocket.

Serafina could only shake her head "No." She inhaled a deep breath as the ringing stopped.

"Anyway," Gill said, "I can't tell you enough how sorry I am for what I did. I didn't know that the voices I was hearing, telling me to do stuff, confusing me, that . . ."

Serafina's phone rang again. She reached inside her pocket, felt for the switch to turn off the sound, and silenced it.

". . . that those voices were just my schizophrenia. Hell, I didn't even know I had schizophrenia at that time. Just started happening all of a sudden."

Serafina's heartbeat raced, and she began to perspire.

"That night, the night at your parents' store . . ." Gill paused and looked regretfully at Serafina. He breathed in a few deep breaths and continued, "Well, that was me. I'm so sorry. I didn't know what I was doing."

Serafina felt more than uncomfortable; she felt unsafe. She needed to process what she was hearing, but at the same time, she began to take notice of her surroundings, assessing her exit strategy.

"It was me. If it means I go to prison, then so be it. I'm tired of carryin' this. Don't you see how much I regret what happened?" Gill rolled a small step toward Serafina.

Serafina backed away and began to turn around. She put the wallet in her other jacket pocket and readied herself to sprint past Gill and out the back door, but there, in the door's entryway was Renzo, pointing a handgun at her.

Gill rolled his wheelchair toward Renzo, only a few feet from Serafina. "Renzo, there's no need to be concerned. I have it handled."

"Oh, I see how you have things handled. I think I heard just about enough," Renzo countered.

"She was gonna find out anyway."

"Maybe about your schizophrenia, but you had to go tell her everything. Why? Now, how am I supposed to protect you?" Renzo shook his head.

"That's what I'm trying to explain to her right now. That it wasn't my fault. That I wasn't right in the head. But I am now. Been taking my medicine—"

"Don't be stupid. You think she would just up and forgive you for killing her parents?"

"Don't you want to stop hiding the truth about what happened? I do," Gill pleaded.

"And then what? Spend the rest of our lives in prison?"

Gill held both hands out as he tried reasoning with him. "Renzo, put the gun down. We still have a chance to change how this turns out. You shoot her, then you definitely goin' to jail."

Renzo repositioned the handgun in his hands, taking better aim at Serafina.

"Renzo!" Gill shouted, insisting this time. "Let's just sit down and talk this out."

"What's there to talk about? You don't think she's going to go to the cops? How do you know she's not a cop herself? She sure been snoopin' like one!"

"I'm not a cop," Serafina said in defense.

"Why were you at the field where that guy crashed his motorcycle? Snoopin' around an' shit?"

Gill was confused. "What field? What're you talkin' about?"

"He's a friend of mine." Serafina held her hands out, reassuringly. "That's all."

"Naw, I think you was snoopin'," Renzo insisted.

"What friend?" Gill asked.

Still pointing the gun at Serafina, Renzo reached down from the corner of the entryway, beyond Serafina's view, and pulled out a small, white, kitchen garbage bag full of items. He swung it toward Serafina, letting it drop to the ground in front of her feet. Items crashed out of the bag's opening—all belongings that were stolen out of the Explorer.

Serafina's mind raced for a response. "I just wanted some answers. Like, who shot him? Why?"

"Oh, I think you know who shot him. I saw your notes. Rust-colored 1978 Chevrolet Impala in ATM video."

At that very moment, Serafina realized the young kid next to Renzo in that picture was the driver of the rust-colored Impala, and she remembered Tammy had said her boyfriend's name was Manny. She used the information to reason with them. "So, look, I know Manny's your friend and all, but believe me, you don't want to be involved in this.

"You think Manny shot your friend?" Renzo exclaimed.

Serafina was unsure as she examined the expression on Renzo's face. If it wasn't Manny's, then whose was it?

Renzo pointed the gun toward the wall with the pictures on it. "Saw you looking at the pictures. Take another look."

Serafina didn't want to take her eyes off the gun being pointed at her, but she felt she had no choice. She looked at the pictures on the wall. There was the picture she'd looked at earlier of Gill, Renzo, and Manny when they were younger. She then glanced at the other pictures, and immediately one stood out. How did she not see this picture first? There, as clear as day, was Renzo leaning against the Impala she'd been following.

"It's your car?" Serafina slowly turned around.

"Not anymore. I sold it to Manny."

"So, people would think Manny did it?"

"Naw, that deal was in the works long before your friend showed up. Me and my boy already had it worked out that he was gettin' the loan an' all that week. What happened to your friend wasn't planned, but hey, he just wouldn't stop diggin' up the past. I saw him that night at the bar, askin' all these questions about Gill. That shit's in the past. What's diggin' up the past gonna do for you or your folks? What's done is done. Move on already."

"*You* shot him?" Serafina realized she had been holding her breath and took in a long-awaited breath.

Gill immediately wailed out. "No! Aw, man. Renzo. Don't tell me you shot her friend?"

"I had no choice. He was going after you. I'm not gonna lose you over somethin' that wasn't your fault."

Renzo then turned his attention to Serafina. "Look! You think he wanted to be in a wheelchair? That's the crazy shit schizophrenia makes you do."

Renzo was visibly agitated, and his agitation was escalating quickly. Her escape options were dwindling the longer she stayed there. With no time to really think things through, Serafina bolted past Gill, toward the entryway to the bathroom. As she did, a loud shot pierced her ears and stunned her nerves to the core. She instinctively prayed that the bullet had missed her. Unsure if she'd been hit, she quickly inspected her chest and arms. Right then, Gill fell to the floor a few feet from where she stood.

"No!" Renzo screamed as he raced toward Gill.

Serafina darted to the bathroom and locked the door. She considered calling 911 but realized there was a window to escape from. She opened the window, pulled up the glass insert, and scrambled out the window. Her feet thudded on the ground beneath her, and without haste, she scurried down the side yard toward the street. Another loud shot went off, and this time she immediately felt the force penetrate through her left thigh as she fell to the ground. She used all her strength to get back up, but a foot kicked her to her side, and she rolled over. Serafina looked up to see Renzo hovering over her. She was already losing a lot of blood and felt faint.

"You know, I didn't wanna have to kill you, too, but you gave me no choice." He pointed the gun at her head and positioned himself to pull the trigger. Serafina closed her eyes.

The dreaded bullet was shot. The sound jolted Serafina, causing her to momentarily open her eyes. No Renzo. She closed her eyes again.

"You're gonna be okay. Stay with me, you hear!" A familiar voice soothed her as she drifted into an unconscious state.

Chapter 26

"I imagine it must feel strange to be getting out of one hospital just to turn around and go see Serafina in another," Cole said as he parked his car at the agency's curb to drop Hollis off.

"That it is," Hollis said, taking off his seatbelt.

"Half hour sound okay?"

"That'd be fine. I won't be long. And you're sure this won't be too much trouble?" Hollis asked.

"Not at all," Cole said. "I have time before my shift, and I planned on stopping by the hospital to see Serafina anyway, see how she's doing."

"And you said earlier, you moved the Explorer over to the hospital already?"

"Yes, sir. I managed to have a buddy from work help me yesterday after Serafina came out of surgery."

"That's good." Hollis thought about it. "That's real good. Thank you, son."

"I suppose you still need to get your motorcycle, too, huh?"

"Unfortunately. But I have a minute to get that. Getting the Explorer back was a little more urgent. So, I appreciate your help with that."

"Of course."

Cole waited for Hollis to open the front door and then drove off just as Hollis stepped inside the main office and closed the front door behind him. Hollis hadn't stepped foot in the agency in just over a week, yet it felt much longer. One of the first things he noticed was Datson's bed against the wall with a chewed rawhide in it. Hollis sighed, taking in the emotions and letting them settle there in the pit of his stomach. He wasn't ready to discard Datson's belongings. Not yet.

Everything in the main office looked the same, yet the temperature felt warmer than usual. He walked over to the thermostat and checked the setting. Sure enough, it was set slightly higher than he usually kept it. Knowing Serafina liked it warmer, he shook his head in disagreement but accepted it as it was. He hated to admit it, but it *did* feel cozier.

It had surprised him to hear from Cole in the car that Serafina had to find a new place to live. She hadn't mentioned that to Hollis. He had no idea that Randy and Nick were even thinking about adopting. When Cole realized Hollis hadn't known about her living situation, Hollis had to promise not to let Serafina know that he knew. Cole had been quite adamant about it, too, saying something about how she'd be upset that he shared something she told him in confidence. It made Hollis wonder, *Just how close are these two getting?*

He went into the kitchen and noticed a piece of paper on the counter with a list of grocery items. One item was Hot Pockets. He looked in the freezer and laughed when he saw most of his stash had been depleted. He grabbed the list and stuffed it into his jacket pocket. He decided right then and there that he would stock the kitchen for her, like a real apartment, and tell her the upstairs loft was hers to stay in for however long she wanted. There was no reason to keep that loft empty and unused anymore. And he had no plans for it otherwise.

Hollis stood at the kitchen counter looking around, beginning to see the agency in a different light. When he had first moved there, it had just been a landing spot in his mind. Nothing long term. He had just wanted to get out from under Levi and Suong's roof after being laid off from the Fisher Body Plant in Detroit when it had closed its doors for good in 1984. A lifetime ago. His memories of working there as a machinist had all but faded, but he could still remember—clear as day—all those people he'd worked with ten or more years saying goodbye after that last shift. A couple years later, when he had found permanent work in Rochester Hills, he'd decided to get a house out that way but keep the agency as a business expense. That's when Levi stepped in and became his silent partner. Hollis couldn't have afforded both places without it.

Neither property was considered desirable at the time, but that was then. Both properties were worth something now. He had no intention of moving though. His property in Rochester Hills was perfect for him. The house itself was set on a nice, deep lot with fifteen acres, give or take, and the property backed up to the Clinton River. Adjacent to his lot had been a similar property, but it didn't back up to the Clinton River like his. It had been sold to a development company and over the years had become a well-established subdivision that affluent C-Suite execs devoured at first chance. He knew what his property was worth. It wasn't like he hadn't ever been approached to sell it. But he wasn't about to give up the convenience of fishing for bass, carp, and steelhead from his own backyard.

His transition from machinist to semi-retired and working at the agency happened a couple years after Serafina had started working for him. Since then, he'd find himself fishing and think about just retiring altogether. Both mortgages had been paid off years ago, so he didn't really need to continue working if he didn't want to. But if he did retire, what would become of the agency? Or Serafina?

He could easily convince Levi to sell the business. Levi had always been noncommittal about his involvement in the business, anyway, saying maybe once he retired . . . But that had all changed once Levi left the police force and developed other interests. It was just as well too, since Suong would have never trusted Levi to be around Hollis for anything more than a quick visit, as if Levi was susceptible to indiscretions. Levi didn't need Hollis for that, apparently. Suong's unannounced drop-in at the agency that one time was plenty enough proof that something was going on in their marriage, something he preferred not to be sucked into.

At one point, Suong may have thought Levi was hanging out with Hollis at strip clubs, but the truth of the matter was that in all their years of knowing each other, Levi had never gone to the strip clubs with him. Hollis liked to keep his worlds separate like that. Plus, he didn't want anyone, Levi especially, changing the dynamics or having a loose tongue after a few drinks and divulging anything personal about him. And he didn't trust the people he knew from the outside to treat the dancers right. It gave him too much anxiety thinking about how they'd offend the dancers or take advantage somehow. Then Hollis would be put in a situation where he'd feel guilty by association, and things would be awkward thereafter. Or that the person would continue to come in afterward and change the dynamic that way. And worse, somehow make him an accomplice to infidelity. He wanted to avoid complications. That's why he avoided people. Serafina understood him like that. She avoided all the drama too.

With his own mortality knocking at the door more and more every day, he couldn't help but wonder about the kind of legacy he'd be leaving behind, and to whom. It wasn't like he'd invested much of anything he'd made over the years. There wasn't much to his name aside from the two properties in Royal Oak and Rochester Hills. That was it. *Well, that and a bunch of unsorted regrets up in the loft.* He looked upward from where he stood in the kitchen and decided to take a look upstairs.

Hollis was surprised by the loft's transformation. The faint smell of Murphy Oil Soap lingered in the air. The hardwood floorboards glistened with the reflection of the sun shining off them, no longer dull and dingy as he remembered them being. The windows were void of the dust that had caked on over the many years of being closed up. The items he'd had out on the living room area rug were now stacked and sorted, ready to be boxed up.

Clearly, Serafina had seen it all. Part of him had angst over his past being known like that, but he couldn't blame her. He should have put it all away—not just years but decades ago. Plus, having her stay up in the loft had allowed her to care for Datson.

He went over to the stacks for a closer view. The floor could easily be cleared if he could find a box for the items on the floor and get someone to help load them into the Explorer. Once he had the boxes home, that would be another story since, technically, he was still recovering from his wounds.

Most of the items didn't need to be kept anymore, so for those, he had half a mind to burn them in a pit out back. But there were a few items, like the photographs, that he wanted to keep. Even the ones of Lizzie and Steve. For the first time in a long time, he thought about Tracy. She'd be in her forties now if she hadn't died. He might have even had grandkids or great-grandkids if things had been different. He let the emotions in, no longer resisting, and allowed them to join other emotions that had settled in the pit of his stomach.

As he looked at the stacks more closely, he noticed the envelope from Datson. *Yep, that too.* He knew he needed to get closure on that, or else he'd have some explaining to do once he got to the Pearly Gates and saw Datson. *That is, unless Datson reincarnated again.*

He couldn't change the past. There was no use in beating himself up about it anymore. What was done was done. It was time to have some compassion for himself and the person he had been. After all, he was just a kid at the time. A kid going to war. So was Datson. And what happened to Datson was not Hollis's fault. He knew that. But he *did* owe it to Datson's girlfriend, fiancée, or whomever, to give her the letter in the envelope. He reassured himself that it wouldn't mean he was to blame for Datson's death. How he would find the person and give them the letter, he wasn't sure. But a decision was made to give himself closure, and that's what mattered.

Just then, Cole texted him to let him know he was about to leave and head back over. Hollis "liked" the message and then took one last glance around before heading back downstairs for Cole to pick him up.

The middle of the floor caught his eye, and he thought about Cole saying Datson had collapsed there. How scared Serafina must have been. She handled it well, though, calling Cole for assistance, driving to the veterinary clinic. He understood why she had asked Cole to call him instead of her with that difficult message. Knowing Serafina, she had probably felt like she let him down. She'd be wrong though. She had stepped up when he had needed her the most. If anything, he felt bad that she was even put in that position. But he was also glad that Levi had asked. It gave him great solace to know that, in his absence, Serafina had been there to comfort Datson as he left this world.

It was still so hard to believe that Datson was gone. The veterinarian's assistant had told him over the phone that the decorative canister he'd selected had been ordered, that the cremation would take a few days, and that they'd give him a call when Datson's remains could be picked up. To be over like that . . . it just seemed so quick.

He'd struggled with knowing what to do with Datson's ashes, but then, right before being discharged from the hospital, the perfect spot came to mind—the spot right under his favorite "fishing tree." It was a tree on his property they would sit under for shade when he fished. Having closure on that felt good and gave promise for other closures he was now willing to confront.

Hollis passed the nurses' station on the right and continued down the hall, glancing at the room numbers along the way. At the end of the hall, he heard voices, and after turning right again, he saw Randy, Nick, and Wanda leaving a room on the left. Randy lingered in the doorway, continuing to talk into the room. Nick was holding their jackets, looking at Randy. Wanda met eyes with Hollis, smiled softly, and held her hand up to say hello. It was a courteous gesture, one that made Hollis feel both welcomed and awkward.

Hollis approached the doorway to Serafina's hospital room. "I hope I didn't come at a bad time."

Both Randy and Nick turned around when they heard Hollis.

"Not at all," Randy said. "We're actually on our way out. You came at a perfect time."

Nick smiled and nodded at Hollis. "You seem to be recovering nicely."

Hollis nodded in agreement. "I'd say so."

"That's good to hear," Nick said, with Wanda gesturing for Randy to move out of the doorway to let Hollis pass through.

"We'll check on you later, okay?" Randy called out to Serafina before moving out of the way.

Hollis watched the three of them head down the hallway before poking his head into Serafina's hospital room.

"Hey, there." Hollis walked over to the foot of Serafina's bed. "How you feeling?"

"Eh." Serafina wavered her hand back and forth. She winced and held her left thigh as she adjusted herself in the bed.

"Hurts?" Hollis felt like he should say more but wasn't sure what to say.

Serafina nodded, still wincing.

A call came through Hollis's cell phone. It was a number he didn't recognize, but with the 248 area code, he suspected the caller was someone local to him. He silenced the ringer without answering the call and put the phone back in his jacket pocket. "They give you anything for the pain?"

"Yeah, just before you got here. Should be kicking in soon."

Hollis knew from experience that it wouldn't be long after the pain medicine kicked in that she'd be getting tired. Then their visiting time would end. He'd get behind the wheel against doctor's orders and drive the Explorer back to his place in Rochester Hills. Even if he decided to sleep on the couch at the agency, it'd be weird now that the loft had kind of become Serafina's place. He just needed to officially let her know it was hers to stay in.

"Loft looks nice. Are you thinking you want to move into it?"

"I'm sorry, Hollis. I was just staying there while—"

Hollis interrupted. "No, no. That's not what I'm saying. I'm asking because I'm offering it to you for as long as you need. Or want."

"You mean you don't mind?"

"Naw, it's a nice space up there. Be nice to have it put to good use."

"You sure? I saw you had some stuff stored up there."

"Yeah, I'm sure," he said, nodding. By "stuff," Hollis knew she meant the personal items he'd left out on display. How many years had he held onto those items, as if punishing himself with the burden of their emotional weight? No more. With the little time he had left, he was determined more than ever to let it all go and give himself the closure he needed. "It's time," he said.

Serafina held back her happy tears the best she could and said, "Thank you."

Looking at Serafina lying in that hospital bed, Hollis couldn't help but feel responsible for what happened to her. She wouldn't have put herself in danger like that if it hadn't been for him looking into her past and getting shot. It was then that Hollis felt he should be up front with her about it all. She deserved an explanation, and he knew she was expecting one.

"Serafina—" he began.

"Hey, real quick, sorry to interrupt," she said, "but could you pour me some water, please? Sorry, go ahead."

"Yeah, yeah, sure." Hollis went over to the side table and poured some water from the small plastic pitcher into a clear cup and then gave it to her before resuming his seated position.

All right, back to my explanation. As he thought about where to start, he realized how difficult it would be. Not because he didn't want to tell her but because there wasn't just one clear reason.

He'd been telling himself all along that he had done it for her, to give her understanding of her past. But really, he knew there was more to it. If he was truly being honest with himself, part of it had been curiosity getting the better of him. He had questions, like why did she have to go into foster care long term? Was she really an orphan? Was it true they couldn't find relatives for her? So much didn't add up or make sense.

Just then, a nurse came into the room. Hollis scooted over to let the nurse by so she could monitor Serafina's vitals. Hollis and Serafina just sat there looking at one another, waiting for the nurse to leave.

Just like that, it was as if an epiphany had bubbled up to the surface. On a very subconscious level, he had known what he was thinking about doing, but it had never made its way into his awareness until just then. *He wanted confirmation he was making the right decision to leave his life's accumulations to her.* That's all they were to him—accumulations. Things he had to give away. And part of that act involved deciding *who* to give them away to.

Hollis had come across estate paperwork shortly after his diagnosis while researching end-of-life preparation materials—even bookmarked the site to go back to when he had read something about how it would save your loved ones from having to go to probate court to get their inheritance. Looking back, it had clearly planted a seed in his mind.

The only other person he could see leaving his estate to would be

Samuel, but that presented even more for him to confront. Was Samuel still alive? Would Samuel's health even permit him to deal with the sale of the two properties, and what would Samuel do with the money when *he* passed away? Leave it to a girlfriend Hollis didn't even know? Someone Samuel picked up at the local watering hole? No, thank you. Hollis wanted his life to truly count for something. He knew it all could make a huge difference in Serafina's life.

The nurse finished looking over Serafina. "The doctor should be in shortly to speak with you."

Hollis watched the nurse leave the room. The moment had come. He knew he owed her an explanation, but he wasn't prepared to tell her about his cancer, even though, in his gut, he knew he needed to.

"You okay?" Serafina looked inquisitively at him.

Her question had caught him off guard, and it must have shown.

"You just look sad," Serafina said. "Everything okay?"

Hollis readied himself to lay it all out, that he had been curious about her past because he was thinking about leaving everything to her. "Serafina—"

"Oh good, you're awake," Cole said, entering the room. He looked at Serafina, then Hollis, as he walked over to the foot of Serafina's bed.

"Hey," Serafina said, smiling at Cole.

Hollis noticed how her eyes sparkled when she looked at Cole. She had always been a tough nut to crack, having her guard up and suspicious of everyone's intentions. It was nice to witness her open herself to someone other than him. That gave him hope for her.

"Oh, there's my jacket." Cole motioned to his light gray zip-up loosely folded on the wide window ledge.

"You were here earlier?" Serafina asked, her eyes squinting.

"Yeah." Cole picked up his jacket. "I stayed until they had you out of surgery. I'm sure you don't remember."

"Cole's the one who dropped me off so I can drive the Explorer back when I leave here," Hollis said to Serafina before directing his attention to Cole. "Thank you again for coordinating that."

"Don't worry about it. Glad I could help." Cole reached into one of the pockets of the jacket he was holding and pulled out an old wallet. "I saw this on the ground next to you when the ambulance came. It must have fallen out of your pocket when you fell."

"You were there?" Serafina looked confused as he handed it to her.

Cole hesitated and then nodded. "I was the one who called the ambulance."

Serafina thought for a moment, putting the wallet down next to her. "That was you? After I got shot?"

Cole nodded again.

"I don't understand. What . . ." Serafina became agitated. "Wait, were you following me?"

Hollis spoke up for Cole. "That's on me. Serafina, I was worried about you. One of my sources left me a voicemail that you kept calling her. It made me concerned you might've read the report Cole dropped off. I didn't want you retracing my steps and having the same thing happen to you. And look, I was right to worry."

Cole lowered his head. "Look, I'm not proud of this, but I saw your notes that day you had me get the Explorer key from your jacket. I didn't think much about it until the other night when Hollis called me."

Serafina looked at Hollis, then Cole, then back at Hollis with angry hurt in her eyes. "So, you asked him to follow me?"

Cole jumped in again. "He just wanted me to keep you safe—"

"You mean keep an eye on me?" Serafina blurted.

Cole knew she was upset, so he didn't argue. He just continued. "He filled me in on some of the things he'd found out, and that made me remember some of the things you wrote down in that notebook."

"Like what?" she asked.

Cole started to respond, but Serafina cut him off. "No, you know what? That wasn't cool. Both of you."

"You're right. It wasn't cool," Hollis said. "But please don't blame Cole. This is all my fault. I should never have started down the path I did in looking into your past. It was wrong of me to do that."

Serafina's tears let loose, one after another. "So . . . what? You don't trust me? What is it? What did I do?"

"No, no, no, dear. You didn't do anything wrong. Don't you think for one second you did anything wrong." Hollis patted her lower leg.

"Then why?" she asked.

Hollis shook his head in shame. "I'm sorry, Serafina. I don't have a good reason."

"And you hid it from me too."

"I *am* really sorry," Hollis said remorsefully.

Hollis and Cole waited for Serafina to respond. After a moment of silence, she breathed in deeply, exhaled, and then nodded her head as if to accept his apology.

Serafina wiped her face of loose tears and asked Cole, "How long have you been following me?"

"Look, it wasn't my intention to follow you at all. I just knew you weren't in a good place after we . . . after *Datson*." Cole turned to Hollis. "I'm so sorry, again."

Hollis accepted his condolences.

Cole continued. "I was coming back to see if I could persuade you to go get lunch with me when I saw you leave. Something just told me to follow you. I don't know what it was—gut instinct? All I know is that I found myself following you to Mexicantown. When you left Burger King, though, I wasn't able to keep up, so I lost you for a bit. I drove down to Clark Park and parked there, hoping you might show up since your notes seemed to reference it a lot. I was about to give up and head home, but then I saw you pick up a guy in a wheelchair, and I got scared thinking that was the guy Frank—er, Hollis—was investigating."

That was the first time Hollis had heard Cole call him "Hollis," and it must have been Serafina's first time as well, because she gave him a look of recognition when he did.

Serafina turned to Hollis. "How did you even know about Gill? I mean, he wasn't even mentioned in Cole's report."

"I was looking at your birth certificate one day, and it just dawned on me how strange it was that you went into foster care because they couldn't find any relatives for you. So, I searched their names, and that's when I came across the address for the store. Then I started searching information on the store and came across Guillermo Vargas."

"But why did you suspect him of having something to do with my parents being killed?"

"I didn't actually. But I had a feeling something more was there, especially that first time I followed him to Tamale Girlz and asked one of the dancers about him. You met her the other night. Lexi?"

"Why'd you go back though?"

"Lexi'd already given him a couple dances, and he was getting ready to go. But she mentioned he was a regular, so I asked her to call me next time he comes in—which she did, but I was always too late by the time I showed up."

"But you had me cover for you that last night you went there. How'd you know he would be there that night?"

"I didn't. But I had a feeling he would be."

"How'd you know to have Lexi ask him about Xavier Palo? Cole hadn't dropped that report off yet."

"Cole called me a few days prior about some of his findings. I already knew most of what was in that report."

"Yeah, about that," Serafina redirected her questioning to Cole. "Why'd you drop that report off anyway? Most people would have emailed it."

Hollis thought about it, and yes-siree, Serafina had a point. Even *he* would have emailed the report. He waited for Cole to respond.

Cole blushed. "I . . ." He looked at Hollis, and then back to Serafina.

Hollis remembered back when he had hired Cole. He'd acted weird when Hollis had given him a picture of Serafina. Almost like he had been shocked by her beauty, that she looked like a Brazilian model out of a Victoria Secret catalog. *Did Cole have a crush on Serafina?*

Cole just shrugged at her question.

"So hey, that was you that kept texting and calling me, wasn't it? When I was in that house?" she asked him.

"Well, yeah. I was trying to warn you when this other guy showed up. He was looking at the Explorer for a good minute, and he just had this look on his face. I can't explain it, but it set off all kinds of alarms for me." Cole began to get choked up; his eyes reddened as he held back emotions. "But then, when you weren't responding, and I heard that gunshot, I knew you were in danger. That's when I called 9-1-1 and ran to the side of the house to try to find a way in. But then you came out from the side yard, and I saw him pointing that gun at you and . . ." Cole paused as if still processing it all.

"*You* shot him? Renzo?" Serafina pulled herself into more of an upright position.

Cole looked straight ahead.

Hollis hadn't known those specifics. "I'm sorry, son."

"Is he dead?" Serafina asked.

Cole slowly took a deep breath and then nodded.

"You did what you had to do. There wasn't a choice," Hollis said to reassure him, and then turned to Serafina. "Have the police questioned you yet?"

"Yeah, but I didn't know who shot him. I just knew Renzo had shot my leg and was standing over me about to shoot me in my head."

They all exchanged looks, as if coming to a consensus that everything should be all right.

"What about Gill?" Serafina seemed concerned.

"They rushed him here to Detroit Receiving too." Cole seemed unsure of how to interpret Serafina's concern. "I'd be surprised if he pulls through though. He was in bad shape when the ambulance took him."

"He did it," Serafina said, matter-of-factly.

"Did what?" Cole asked.

"Killed both of my parents."

"How do you know?" Cole asked.

"He told me."

"He flat-out told you?"

"Yeah." She recalled the moment as it happened. "He was apologizing for it, actually, saying he wasn't in his right mind at the time, that he didn't know he had schizophrenia, that it just came out of nowhere but that now he's on medication."

"He must have kept the gun; it was the same one used to shoot Hollis." Cole looked at Hollis.

"No, Renzo did *that*," Serafina said. "Renzo's his brother. The one who shot me. It's actually Lorenzo, I guess, just like how Gill's real name is Guillermo."

Hollis realized that Renzo must have been the person to pick up Gill from Tamale Girlz the night he had been shot.

"Ahhhh. Okay, that makes sense," Cole said.

"Renzo said Hollis was snooping around and asking too many questions. I suppose, in his own way, he was trying to protect Gill," Serafina said, as if recalling the last moments in that house. "But then Renzo ended up being the one to harm him."

"I thought for sure that Xavier was involved," Cole said.

"I thought so too," Serafina said. "I saw him leaning over the Impala with Manny in the driver's seat on Wednesday."

"Manny?" Cole asked.

"Renzo's friend that he sold the Impala to."

"The Impala in the ATM video footage you mentioned in your notes?" Cole asked.

"Yeah, near where Hollis was shot. But I'm sure Xavier knows a lot of people. He's like an icon in the community." Serafina took a deep breath. "Sorry, I think my pain medicine is starting to kick in."

She nestled her head into her pillow and shifted her body to get more comfortable. "It's making me a liiiiiiitttle bit drowsy." She held up her hand and gestured "little" with a small space between her thumb and index finger.

"I'll let you get some rest. I gotta get ready for my shift anyway."

"Oh, wait!" Serafina called out to Cole before he could leave. "Did you happen to see a white trash bag at that house with notes and a bunch of equipment in it? In the living room?"

"Yeah, it had to be admitted into evidence, but I worked it out to get it back for you right away. I can drop it off if you'd like."

Hollis was confused. Did he miss something?

"I'm sorry I kept it from you, Hollis," Serafina began explaining. "But the Explorer got broken into, and I didn't want to tell you because they stole my surveillance on that one case we were working on. I was so afraid that that client would be upset since I had nothing to report on. I just didn't want to let you down. That's why I went back to the Burger King where it got broken into. I was trying to see if anything could be recovered. Turns out, it was Renzo who did that." Serafina redirected her attention back to Cole. "If I can get that surveillance footage, then I should be able to get that report to them on time."

"It should all be there. Everything that you reported missing on that police report was recovered." Cole's eyes locked briefly with Serafina's. "All right. Well, I'm gonna head out now; let you get some rest."

"Cole." She stopped him.

He turned around.

"Thank you."

"Uh-huh." Cole smiled sincerely at Serafina.

"I mean it. For everything. Thank you."

After Cole headed out the door, Hollis raised his eyebrows and smirked.

"What?" Serafina asked.

Hollis looked in the direction where Cole had stood and smirked even more.

"What?" Serafina insisted defensively.

"Oh, nothing." Hollis continued to smirk.

"He's a nice guy." Serafina blushed.

"I didn't say he wasn't."

"There's nothing there, so you can stop with the smirking."

Hollis noticed the wallet on the hospital bed next to Serafina's hand. "What's with the wallet?"

"I think it was my father's. Gill had it."

"Gill had it?"

"Yeah." Serafina nodded her head. "Oh, wow, I really need to go to the restroom."

"You always do." Hollis laughed.

"Hey! I can't help it. They have this IV pumping a ton of fluids in me." Serafina positioned herself on the side of the bed.

Instinctively, Hollis moved the walker closer to her bedside.

"Oh, yeah! What were you about to tell me? Before Cole came in?"

Hollis reflected on what lay before him: *six months waiting to die.* There was no denying it. She would know soon enough when his fatigue worsened and he was forced to rest all the time. This wasn't fair to her—not to tell her. She might not want to be a private investigator anymore. But maybe it was better she didn't know. Not until it was really time to tell her.

Hollis tried not to make eye contact. "It's nothing."

She stood at the bedside and gave him an insistent look.

"Go use the restroom." Hollis tried to change the subject. He moved the IV stand closer to Serafina.

"Okay, but when I get out . . ."

Serafina slowly and steadily made her way to the restroom using her walker, pulling the IV stand along with every step.

Hollis listened to the voicemail on his phone. It was Levi's son, Michael. "I stopped by your room, but you had already been discharged. Can you give me a call when you get this? I'd like to speak to you about some of your lab results."

Dagnabbit. He knew Michael was an oncology doctor and what he'd be wanting to discuss. Changing his phone number wasn't enough to escape the reality of his cancer. He couldn't avoid facing it.

Serafina's doctor entered the room just as Serafina came out of the restroom.

Hollis felt the need to get as far away from all hospitals as possible in that moment. "I'm gonna head out now. You do what the doctor tells you."

Serafina looked like she wasn't ready to have Hollis leave. He gestured goodbye and headed for the door without looking back. Behind him, he could hear Serafina responding to the doctor's questions, and he knew she'd acquiesced to his departure.

Chapter 27

Serafina was glad to be out of the hospital and far away from everything that reminded her of it. But now she was having to do her own wound care. And it meant a temporary stay with Randy and Nick, at least until she could get her doctor's okay to go up and down stairs again. She was counting down the days until her next doctor appointment, when she would just about beg for that clearance.

It's not that Randy and Nick were pressuring her to move out anymore. It was actually more like incessant hovering and lack of privacy driving her away now. Plus, she had become used to the loft at the agency as being her place. Hollis had already given her the go to fully move into the loft but had stressed that the doctor had to clear her first. That wouldn't stop her from moving everything there, keeping only what she absolutely needed at Nick and Randy's.

She wanted to stop feeling like an extension of others' lives and start to really live her own. That's basically what it all amounted to.

There were other things she looked forward to being cleared for as well. Operating a motor vehicle, for one. But also taking a hot, high-pressured shower instead of having to settle for a sponge bath, because getting herself clean was proving to be an arduous process that left her exhausted and ready for a nap before she'd even dressed the wound.

She removed the splint, revealing where the bullet had been lodged into her femur, fracturing the bone. As she dressed the swollen and stitched area, she winced in pain. She started to think about how many more hours she'd have to wait before she could take any more pain medication, and suddenly panic crept in. She'd need to take something, even if it wasn't time. The pain was too unbearable.

After undergoing a blood transfusion and several surgeries, the doctors were able to repair most of the damage to her leg's tendons, ligaments, muscles, nerves, and major blood vessels. The rest of the healing was just going to take time. That included her mental health too apparently.

PTSD was one of the things the hospital therapist had warned her about as a side effect of having a gunshot wound. Handing her a pamphlet, he'd explained how it was traumatic to be shot and that she may feel a multitude of things afterward. The inside page listed the side effects: shock, panic attacks, anxiety, depression, feeling down, becoming withdrawn, feelings of isolation, loss of appetite, lethargy, irritability, disruption in sleep, nightmares, mentally replaying the event. She'd read each of them, one by one, with her mind confirming. *Yup. Yup. Yup.* She was suffering from most, if not all of them.

"These feelings are not signs of weakness," he'd emphasized, claiming the caption on the pamphlet as his own words of wisdom. She played back the conversation in isolated moments, things that had resonated with her. "*Get support.*" "*Treatments are available to help you.*"

Before leaving, he had recommended she see a therapist to process the event and her associated feelings about it. She'd agreed to then, but she wasn't holding herself to that promise. She didn't owe him shit. She would process everything however she saw fit.

She zipped up her special wound-care pouch, put it in a duffle bag that was resting on top of the stacked boxes in her soon-to-be old room, and looked around. There wasn't much else to pack, and soon, folks would be wondering when she'd be arriving at the agency for her graduation party. Just a few more moments, she thought. A quick rest was in order.

She lay still on her mattress, staring at the ceiling. The house was quiet without Randy and Nick there.

Cole had kept her apprised of everything going on while she was in the hospital—that Gill was recovering from his equally life-threatening wound and had been sent to a county jail to await trial for his involvement with her parents' murder. Everything she had explained to the police about what transpired was still being sorted out, like how Gill had admitted to being involved in her parents' murder but hadn't explained what happened. Or how Gill had yelled out when he'd found out that Renzo had shot Hollis.

No! Aw, man. Renzo. Don't tell me you shot her friend?

Since the moment she had regained consciousness in the hospital, those words repeated in her head. She was stuck reliving that waking nightmare. In her mind, it was on an endless loop. It replayed the event in Gill's living room again and again. It just wouldn't end. Which is probably why she felt tense all the time. And why she often caught herself holding her breath.

It was hard enough accepting that Gill had killed her parents. Not knowing much about schizophrenia, was it possible that Gill's condition might have made him confused to where he didn't know what he was doing when he did that? If that was the case, would he get off on temporary insanity or something like that? She felt horrible for him, despite what he'd done. It was painfully clear now why he had avoided telling her too much about their time at the store.

He was the only link she had left to her past, though, and so she couldn't help but mourn the loss of the relationship they could have had. Who else was there to tell her stories about her parents so that maybe she could begin to remember them? Or let her know whether she had lived at the store—which was something she had started wondering about recently. Perhaps they'd lived in an upstairs apartment of the store, or maybe there was an area beyond the main part of the store, but now—how would she find out? She had zero memories. All she had was that wallet. And from the moment Cole gave it to her in the hospital, she couldn't stop looking at it. She pulled it out from her nightstand drawer and looked at the contents inside.

Inside one of the laminated sleeves was a photograph of her father, her mother, and what appeared to be Serafina as a baby. Serafina was now about the same age as her mother in that photograph—maybe thirty years old or so? Her father might have been a few years older than her mother.

Pushed partially inside one of the deeper slots was her father's Michigan driver license. Both her parents had kind eyes, kind expressions—what you'd expect in one's parents. But nothing about either of them really looked like her. Her father was clearly Caucasian, and even so, none of his features resembled hers. Her mother appeared to be Hispanic like Serafina, but again, none of her features had any resemblance. How was that possible?

Serafina's phone dinged, interrupting her thoughts. She put the wallet in her hoodie pocket for safekeeping.

Seeing the message was from Randy, she read it and responded to each text as they came through.

10:28 a.m.

Randy Staszak: *I'm gonna have to send over Brian to come pick you up whenever you're ready. I'm dealing with a cake situation right now.*

Serafina: *Okay*

Randy Staszak: *So then are you ready yet? Or do you need more time?*

Serafina: *Now's fine.*

Randy Staszak: *You sure? Not trying to rush you.*

Serafina: *All good. I just finished getting ready.*

Randy responded with a "like" to her last message.

With her mind replaying the event in Gill's living room, she thought about the text message that had come through before all of Cole's attempts to warn her—the long rambling one from Randy that she had chosen to ignore in the moment. She scrolled up to see it, to read it again.

10:39 a.m.

Randy Staszak: *Hey, this isn't how I wanted things to go. I know us keeping the whole adoption stuff from you hurt you. I had Mom and Nick sworn to secrecy because I really wanted it to be a surprise for you. I had it all planned out in my head how I was going to have you open a wrapped giftbox and there'd be something like a bib or baby shirt inside saying something about how they love their aunt. I'm angry at myself for allowing what you said about looking up DeMarcus to get me all sideways to where I ruined the whole surprise and hurt you in the . . .*

As she scrolled down to read through the message, she found comfort, knowing that Randy had been thinking of her all along.

Randy Staszak: *. . . process. You are very important to me and I can't imagine not having you in my life. I know I treated you unfairly. You deserved better than that. I really hope you'll forgive me. Because I really am sorry. I miss you.*

Of course she had forgiven him. It hadn't been their first time being on the outs with one another, and it wouldn't be their last. The important thing was that they always made up. They were family in every sense of the word, and she felt bad for ever doubting that.

While laid up in the hospital, she'd missed her graduation ceremony. This graduation party was supposed to be a way to cheer her up. Something concocted by Hollis and Randy. Framed to be a simple barbecue with friends and family. It was hard to be cheered up these days, but she was going to do her very best to be in good spirits, so they wouldn't be disappointed. Plus, it might just be what the doctor ordered—literally.

She thought back to when she'd asked her doctor how long her recovery would be, and his response had been, "Depends." Her gunshot wound wasn't exactly minor, so it wouldn't just be a few weeks. "Up to a year to completely recover," he'd said, adding that having a good support system at home would be key and that even a few friends and family members could make a huge difference . . . and isolating herself from others was something to avoid. Okay, okay, doctor—I got it, she'd thought as she'd listened to him lecture her. Then he had ended the whole thing with how she would need to follow up with a few months of physical therapy. *At least*, he'd emphasized.

As she mentally prepared herself to be picked up for her graduation party, she decided to take something for the pain before it got too severe. She had pain-relieving medication, but nothing like what she would have expected. The hospital staff, concerned about her developing an opioid addiction more than her being able to manage the pain, had taken her off the hydrocodone within the first week, ensuring her that Motrin was enough. *Nope, it's not, motherfuckers.*

Using her crutches, she got up and went into the kitchen to grab some tequila from a top cupboard. Next to it were shot glasses purchased as souvenirs. She poured herself a shot glassful, swigged it, poured another, swigged again, and then rinsed the shot glass out with some dish soap and put it back up in the cupboard with the tequila.

So far, she knew the invite list to include Hollis, Randy, Nick, Wanda, Cole, Levi, Suong, their youngest son, Brian, their son—*the doctor*—Michael, Michael's wife Kendra Hill—who had been mentioned on several occasions as being an attorney—and their seven-year-old daughter, Maya Hill-Nestor.

Having met Michelle only a handful of times over the past nine years, Randy had asked about inviting her as well, but Coco hadn't been *Michelle* to Serafina in a long time, and Serafina could do without the awkwardness and drama. It would already be awkward enough if Suong showed up, although Hollis had said he had a feeling Suong wouldn't be showing up because when he'd mentioned the get-together to Levi, he had seemed off, like there was something going on between him and Suong. In true Hollis fashion, he hadn't pried. He wasn't about to be sucked into whatever was going on in their marriage.

Hollis had seemed resistant to having Michael come to the party, but she might have misinterpreted things, because when she had inquired more about it, Hollis had reminded her that Michael was a doctor and might have to work. Still, something seemed off with that.

Serafina heard the front doorbell ring.

Chapter 28

Serafina lifted herself up off her bed, placing a crutch under each arm, and carried herself to the back door. She opened the door and yelled for Brian down the driveway. "Hey! Back here!"

Brian Nestor, the youngest of Levi and Suong's sons, was Serafina's age and surprisingly handsome. She wasn't quite sure what she had expected him to look like, but she hadn't expected him to be so attractive. He had Suong's eyes—absent of judgment—and Levi's jawline.

"Sorry about that." Brian rubbed his shoes off on the doormat of the back door stoop.

"No worries," Serafina said, letting him inside and leading him across the kitchen to her bedroom. "Randy's just funny about walking across the carpet in there with shoes on. So, we all use the back door." Serafina realized the sexual inuendo in what she'd just said and shushed her dirty mind. Tequila did that to her sometimes.

As they stood in the doorway of her bedroom, she noticed how much taller he was than her. It made her stomach flutter.

"Just these boxes?" he asked, pointing to the ones next to her bed.

"Yeah. You might need to make several trips. I'm not able to help on account of these crutches." In her side view, she noticed the toned muscles of his arms. *Damn!*

Brian knelt down to test out their weight, and then picked up several at once, leaving the larger one for a second trip. As he did so, Serafina got a whiff of his scented antiperspirant spray, a real manly-man fragrance she found irresistible. *Fuck me!*

"I'll be right back for the other one in a sec. Let me just run these out to my truck."

Serafina watched him as he carried the boxes out of her bedroom, across the kitchen floor, and out the back door—the whole time appreciating his athletic physique. She took a moment to sit down while she waited for him to return and made sure nothing else needed to be packed up. All that was left was the cheap bed and nightstand she had bought at Ikea when she had first moved out on her own. She had no use for it now. The bed in the loft, along with all the other furniture up there, was much nicer than anything she could afford.

Within minutes, Brian had returned and slung the duffle bag over his shoulder and picked up the last big box. Waiting patiently in the kitchen, he asked, "Was this all there was?"

Serafina took one last look around the bedroom and then pulled herself back up onto her crutches to follow him out. When she finished locking the back door, Brian was already loading the box into the back seat of his slightly lifted, black Dodge Ram. She made her way slowly down the driveway, wondering the whole time how she'd get herself up into the passenger seat.

"Ummmm," Serafina said, smirking as she stood in front of the passenger side door.

"I can help lift you up, if you're okay with that," Brian said as he opened the passenger side door for her.

Although it wasn't the most sexual of encounters one could imagine, it had been a long time for Serafina. Something about his strength in guiding her up into her seat made her tingle all over and instantly want him. There was definitely chemical attraction. Or maybe it was the tequila. She couldn't decide what it was, but she liked it.

After placing the crutches in the back seat, Brian pulled himself up into the driver's seat and drove them to the agency. Most of the conversation had been about Brian, but it wasn't really his fault. She'd led the conversation that way by asking him questions so that she wouldn't have to talk as much. She wanted to savor the tequila's numbing effects for as long as she could, and talking would have brought the pain back in full force.

On the way there, Serafina learned that Brian was a chemical engineer for a tier 1 supplier for the big three automakers. He was only living with his parents so he could pay off the last bit of his student loans and save for a down payment on a house. And he worked out at the gym a lot in his spare time. At one point, he did pause long enough to ask Serafina what happened with her leg, and when she said someone shot her, he simply responded that she might want to find a new line of work if she was getting shot at. "Just sayin'."

The shooting part had been a fluke, the result of her doing extracurricular work that wasn't part of her job description, but she nodded in agreement. Her reasons for considering a new line of work had nothing to do with getting shot at. She was ready for something new, something not so boring. Something with health insurance and a 401k. Something that felt like it had a future where she wouldn't feel so stuck and stagnate.

But here she was moving into the agency. Was it really the time to be thinking about a new career choice? She wondered how Hollis would feel about that. Well, she thought, maybe she could rent from Hollis and help out as a side hustle? At least until he could find a replacement. And with a new job, maybe she'd make enough money to buy herself her own house?

At the agency, Brian helped her out of the truck and then opened the back door to retrieve her crutches. As he handed them to her, she leaned up against the passenger seat with the truck door open, situating a crutch under each arm.

"These boxes all go up to the loft, right?" he asked, as he grabbed a few and pushed the doors closed with the side of his forearm.

"Yeah, keep the duffle bag downstairs though. I'll need that later on." Serafina began walking up the walkway to the front door with Brian beside her. "You know how to get up there?"

"Oh, yeah, I helped Hollis take out a lot of boxes from up there this morning, and we loaded them into his Explorer." He gestured, as if pointing his head to the Explorer in the driveway.

There, parked in front of the Explorer, was Serafina's Jeep. She couldn't remember if she had parked it there in the driveway two weeks ago when she'd taken the Explorer—the day she'd been shot—or if someone had moved it. But as she looked at it, she felt a moment of realization that she was officially moved out from Randy and Nick's house, and while it was all new and a bit uncomfortable, she felt free and excited. It was a new beginning for her, and she was more than ready to fully embrace it.

"So, then next Friday night?" Brian asked.

Serafina realized she had been on autopilot while he'd been talking, nodding in agreement without being present about what she was agreeing to. "Next Friday?"

"Yeah, but if you prefer Saturday night, that's cool too. I like this one place because the food is unbelievably good, but it doesn't give off that air of being too fancy like some restaurants do. But if you prefer a different place, I'm good with that too. Birmingham has lots of great places. Just let me know, and I'll get us a reservation, okay?"

As they entered the front door of the agency, she realized that she had just signed herself up for an actual date. Serafina felt both nervous and excited, but with her senses dulled by tequila, she gave little reaction. "Yeah, yeah, for sure."

A banner with the word "Congratulations!" hung from the ceiling above the hall entryway. It was a small touch that made her smile.

"I believe most folks are outside in the backyard," Brian said in the kitchen. "I'm gonna run these upstairs and bring in the other boxes."

Serafina stood at the backdoor, peering out. "Okay, thanks."

Everything looked perfect. Daylilies and sage plants were in full bloom all along the fence, and black-eyed Susan wildflowers burst out from the corner of the yard.

Hollis was the first person to catch her eye, standing next to the gas grill, grilling what looked like hot dogs and burgers and swatting at a yellow jacket.

Next to the grill was a table with all the food and fixin's. One glance and she knew Randy had tended to it. Everything looked orderly and followed a proper sequence—the first section being paper plates, plastic silverware, and a paper towel roll on a stand that folks could get 1/3 sections off instead of full paper towel sheets. The next section had mustard, ketchup, white onions, relish, pickles, tomatoes, and iceberg lettuce near the hamburger and hot dog buns. Proper serving utensils lay next to the baked beans, Caesar salad, veggie tray with ranch dressing, and potato salad.

Knowing the potato salad was from Costco, she already knew how the conversation would go. Someone would mention it, and that would turn into a whole conversation where Wanda and Randy would go on and on about all the deals they got at Costco. Oh boy, she thought jokingly.

On a small, separate card table, she spotted a red velvet cake with cream cheese frosting, some small paper plates, and some plastic forks. It was all so very nice.

As Serafina stepped outside into the backyard, she noticed Levi and Wanda sitting at one of the foldable tables. It was decorated with a disposable plastic tablecloth and situated on the freshly mowed lawn away from the grill. Her first reaction was one of relief because Suong was nowhere in sight. Her second reaction was one of shock because there, on Wanda's lap, was an infant girl who couldn't have been more than seven months old.

Wanda noticed Levi's distraction and turned around to see Serafina standing there. "Hey, there you are!"

"Um," Serafina said with bewilderment, "you have a baby on your lap."

"I know! And isn't she so precious?" Wanda pretended to nibble the baby girl's fingers.

As Randy slid up next to her, she turned to face him. "I didn't think you'd have your baby that quickly!"

Randy shook off the notion that the baby was his. "Oh no, no. Mom's decided to be a foster parent again."

"For real?" Serafina turned to Wanda. "But, what about work? Won't that be difficult to manage?"

"You want to tell her?" Randy asked Wanda.

"I've decided to retire."

"Oh, wow. I didn't even know you were thinking about it."

"It's time. And plus, all this talk about adopting a baby made me start thinking about fostering again."

"A baby's a lot of work."

"Tell me about it. Two-year-olds are even harder."

Serafina looked confused.

Randy interjected. "They often come in sibling groups, so she has a little brother. Nick took him to go potty."

"So, what is this? Practice?" Serafina asked Randy.

"This is just as much a surprise for us as well. She literally just got them yesterday.

"Yesterday? Wow."

Randy nodded in agreement.

"What are their names?" Serafina asked both Randy and Wanda.

"Darius and Cashmere." Wanda wiped some spit up from the infant's mouth with a white spit cloth.

"Cashmere?" Serafina clarified, as it was clearly a "stripper name" to her.

"Cashmere," Randy affirmed with a head nod.

Serafina gave the look of questioning.

Randy gave the look of affirmation.

Serafina gave the look of shaking out crazies from her head.

Randy gave the look of "I'm with you, girl!"

Serafina gave the look of "Okay, well, if you say so."

Randy gave the look of "It is what it is."

Serafina gave the look of "I know what you're saying."

Wanda interrupted their silliness. "What are you two doing over there?"

Randy and Serafina both laughed.

"I've really missed you." Randy leaned into Serafina for a hug.

"Me too." Serafina repositioned her crutch to the side so she could truly embrace Randy.

"So, then what's the plan with your baby?"

"Oh, I thought I told you."

"Told me what?"

"That we're putting that on hold."

"What! Why?"

"It's complicated," Randy said. "Let's go grab you some food, and we can talk."

"So, I want to hear more about this change in plans," Serafina said as Randy handed her some plastic silverware to hold.

"We just decided to get married, ya know? Not keep holding off on it." Randy picked up a paper plate and pointed at the burgers and the hot dogs that were fresh off the grill.

Serafina pointed at the burgers. "But what does that have to do with adopting a baby overseas?"

"We can't adopt if we're married." Randy pulled a hamburger bun from the plastic bag and placed a burger on top of it, making sure to leave room on the paper plate for other food.

"Wait, what? I thought Taiwan was LGBTQ-friendly. Like, didn't they recently legalize same-sex marriage?"

"They are, but their law is funny around adoption." Randy pointed at the condiments as a whole.

"How so?" Serafina leaned one of her crutches up against the table and then placed a single slice of Kraft cheese on top of the burger patty.

"Well, so I can adopt as a single gay man, but we can't adopt as a gay married couple." Randy stood holding Serafina's plate up for her as she squeezed some ketchup and Miracle Whip on top of the cheese slice on her burger patty.

"Huh? That's weird." Serafina scooped a small spoonful of potato salad next to her burger. "So, then why don't you just get married after you adopt the baby?"

"Nick wouldn't be able to adopt the baby."

"Not even as a stepparent?" Serafina asked, opening one of the ice-filled coolers at the end of the table. She looked at the various cans of Coca-Cola, Sprite, Dr. Pepper, and A&W root beer, and then closed the cooler lid to see what was in the other cooler.

"Nope. Only if the baby were my biological child."

"But heterosexual married couples can, right?"

"Yup."

"That's bullshit!" Serafina said.

The other cooler was filled with ice, water bottles, and White Claw hard seltzers. She grabbed a mango-flavored White Claw and closed the lid to the cooler.

"Yup." Randy sighed.

"You'd think there'd be better equality around those things by now."

Randy just nodded. "Here, let me get that for you," he said, taking the White Claw hard seltzer from her so she could use both her crutches as they walked back to the table.

Randy continued, "We thought about delaying getting married, but who knows how long the adoption process will take. We just don't want to wait anymore."

"How long does the process take? The way you made it sound with that letter, I thought it was only a matter of weeks."

"I was being shitty to you. It's actually a long process. We only completed the application. There's a lot more to it, like the USCIS filing and fingerprinting, dossier preparation, and home study. And it's super expensive."

"Like how expensive?"

"Mmmm . . . upwards of twenty-five thousand. There's tons of fees, and they add up."

"Oh, man. I had no idea. I'm really sorry to hear that," Serafina said as they both sat down at the table.

"I don't know. I guess there's a lot of research we have to do, and it feels like we'd just be having to spend a lot of time and money with no guarantees just to adopt a child rather than a baby."

Serafina gave him a judgmental look.

"Well, not to sound shitty, because, yeah, we weren't babies when we entered the system, but I just really want a baby. I want the whole experience: the baby shower and the waking up in the middle of the night for feedings and getting them on a regular sleep schedule. I want to be a part of the *whole* story of our child, not just appear in Chapter 5."

Serafina took a bite out of her burger and opened up the can of hard seltzer.

Randy reached across the table to grab his water bottle and pull it closer for a sip. "I started seeing my therapist again."

Serafina hadn't expected Randy to jump from the topic of babies to the topic of therapy. "Yeah?" she asked with a mouthful of burger.

"Yeah. I probably should have never stopped going. It's just that memories from my past keep showing up, you know? You'd think with all those years of therapy that I'd have finished processing everything from my childhood, but it doesn't ever seem to just go away. Little bits of memories pop up more and more, and I can't make them stop. I don't want that shit messing up my future. And the more I try to control it all, the more I feel out of control. It all seems so chaotic at times, ya know?"

This was the *real-ist* Randy had been in a long time. Or could it be ever? He was never this open and deep. He was always superficial in anything he discussed. Always for show. Name dropping and trying to impress with one ups. But here he was being real, like never before, and she wasn't quite sure how to respond.

He continued, "Mom is thinking about selling her house and moving in with us."

"Seriously?" Serafina nearly choked on the food she was chewing.

"Yeah, I know what you're thinking. It'll be interesting, for sure."

"No, no. I think it's a great idea," she said, thinking what a horrible idea it was—especially for Nick. "But what about not having enough rooms? I mean, she's starting to foster again, right?"

"We had a contractor come out and turns out we can convert the upstairs attic space into a nice room with dormers, which would be perfect for Mom."

This peeved Serafina. Just a few weeks ago, they were essentially evicting her, but now they were . . . *You know what? Whatever!* Now that she had a taste of being on her own again, she wanted nothing more. "Still don't want to move?"

"We'll see. We've been considering it more and more. It would be nice to have more bedrooms for little ones or guests."

"Guests? Who's going to come visit you?"

"You won't come and visit?"

"Sure, but why wouldn't I just drive home after visiting?" Serafina took the last bite of her food and finished it with a drink of hard seltzer.

"I don't know. What if we have a game night and you drink too much?"

"Why do I sound like a lush in this scenario of yours?" She laughed, setting the hard seltzer can down. "And when have we ever had a game night?"

"Fine, but regardless, converting the attic space only increases the value, so we're moving forward with that. And with Mom there fostering, we get to see for ourselves if a baby is what we're ready for. But either way, we're getting married, and that's that. No more waiting."

"Hey." Serafina stopped Randy and looked him in the eyes. "I'm really happy for you. You deserve all good things in life."

Randy smiled. "Thank you. And so do you."

They both noticed Cole coming outside from the kitchen's back door. He walked toward them looking exceptionally handsome, with his slim fit T-shirt accentuating his toned physique.

"Speaking of all good things in life," Randy said.

"Shhh!" Serafina stifled Randy.

"Hey," Cole said, standing at their table.

"Hey, you made it." Serafina smiled, blocking her eyes from the sun with her hand.

"Of course." Cole looked around and then waved at Hollis over at the grill.

"Why don't you grab yourself some food and come over?" Serafina offered.

"Yeah, for sure," he said, his blue eyes meeting hers and holding their gaze for a moment. Then he tapped the table twice and said, "Okay, I'll be right back."

Chapter 29

Everyone was enjoying one another's company. Michael sat next to his wife, Kendra, at the table with Levi and Wanda, each admiring Cashmere. Brian stood on the lawn talking with Nick as Nick blew bubbles from a wand for Darius and Maya to catch. Cole had joined Serafina and Randy after grabbing some food, and they were deep in conversation.

Just then, Hollis returned from inside the house and got everyone's attention. "Okay, well, y'all know I'm not one for many words. But today might just be the day ya catch a rooster wearin' socks." He waited a second to make sure all eyes were on him. "First, I want to say thank you to everyone who helped make this special day come together. As you know, Serafina wasn't able to make it to her graduation ceremony, so we are going to stage our own ceremony of sorts right here in this backyard."

"You're kidding." Serafina blushed.

Hollis opened his phone and clicked play on the classic graduation ceremony song he'd downloaded off iTunes. He stood away from the grill, facing the tables. In his hands, he held a piece of paper rolled into a scroll. He motioned for her to come up.

"Seriously?" She laughed it off.

Positioned there like a soldier, Hollis stood, waiting. As he remained committed there to his post, his emotions got the better of him, and his eyes began to get teary.

Cole assisted Serafina with her crutches, helping her up. As she began walking with her crutches toward Hollis, he held out his hand to shake hers and then handed her the piece of paper scroll.

He stopped the song. "Serafina, you may not be my daughter by blood, but in every other respect you are. I couldn't be prouder of you if I were your actual father. Go ahead and read the paper."

Serafina opened it and then took a moment to examine its contents. "It's a quitclaim deed. To this property." She stood there, stunned.

"I want to thank Kendra for helping me draw it up." He faced Kendra. "Thank you."

Kendra gave a courteous wave. Her husband, Michael, sat next to her, and appeared to be restraining himself of emotion.

Hollis continued, but with his focus on Serafina, "Levi sold his share of the business back to me, and that includes the property. I'm giving it all to you."

Serafina could hear the murmuring among folks. *Wow, did you know? No, I had no idea. So, what will you and Suong do?*

Hollis was starting to get choked up, his eyes holding back tears. "It's up to you what you do with it. You can continue the business or not. Sky's the limit."

"What are you gonna do?" Serafina asked.

"Fish full-time of course!" He laughed.

Serafina hugged Hollis, and as they held their embrace, she whispered to him, "This is too much!"

"Says who?"

"Are you sure?"

Hollis pulled away to an arm length and looked her in the eyes before kissing her on the forehead. "Never more sure in my life."

Serafina gave him one more big hug. "I'll go put this inside, so it doesn't get damaged."

"I can do that for you," Hollis offered, taking hold of the scroll.

She nodded and then headed back over to the table to sit with Cole and Randy.

"What an amazing gift!" Randy exclaimed.

"Yeah," she said, feeling like the whole thing was off somehow. The gift was too much, even if Hollis said it wasn't. Plus, it wasn't like Hollis to willingly put himself on display like that. To be so open and public about anything was unnatural for him.

"He can adopt me too, if he wants," Randy joked. Noticing Nick was calling him over to the lawn, he added, "I'll be back. Nick wants me for something."

Cole could see something was bothering Serafina. "Are you okay?"

"Yeah. It's a lot to process, I guess."

"I bet," Cole said, and then went on to ask her, "So, then what do you think you'll wanna do?"

She shrugged, not knowing what she wanted to do. She had never really ever been given the opportunity to have choices like that.

"Well, if you ever need another person to help run the agency, I'd be happy to provide my services—if I'm not working, of course."

They talked about how the property was close enough to the main strip to make it into another business of her choosing or rent out to a CPA firm, a chiropractor, or something like that. But she also liked the idea of living there in the loft, so maybe she wouldn't rent it out. The more they talked about it, the more her tequila buzz fizzled away, bringing forth subdued pain. She refrained from thinking much more on it.

"Lots of options," she summarized. "I think before I go commit myself to a nine-to-five job, I might want to get some more answers about my past."

"Yeah?" Cole asked, excitedly.

Serafina nodded. "Yeah, I do."

"Like what more are you wanting to find out? Maybe I can help?"

"Not really sure, but yeah—maybe."

"You still got that wallet? I didn't mean to snoop, but I saw it might have been your dad's."

She took out the wallet. "This?"

"You carry that thing wherever you go?" His eyes expressed amusement.

"Haha—no. I was looking at it just before I headed over here."

Serafina handed Cole the wallet. "There's nothing in it except for that picture of my parents and me when I was a baby, and his old Michigan driver's license."

"Sometimes people write things on the back. Do you mind?" he asked, indicating he intended to take the picture out from its slot.

"Yeah, sure."

Cole looked at the back of the picture. Nothing was written on it. He looked at the picture for a moment and then proceeded to put it back. When he did, the picture seemed to get stuck, as if something else occupied the slot. He tried to wiggle his finger inside the slot but had difficulty. "Something's in there. A laminated card, I think."

"Here. Let me try." Serafina took the wallet and dug her index finger into the slot. She rubbed her finger against the surface of the laminated card, moving it back and forth with her finger until it had some give to it. Then she resituated her index finger on it and pulled it out. There in her hands was an old taxicab license from Texas with her father's picture. After giving it a good look, she handed it to Cole for his inspection. "Maybe I have relatives in Texas."

"Ever think about doing a 23andMe test?" he asked, examining the taxicab license.

"Oh my God. You're brilliant! Why didn't I think of that?"

"Are you being facetious?"

"No, no. I'm being serious. I think that's probably a great place to start."

"Hey, I'm gonna grab a hard seltzer." He pointed at her empty can of mango-flavored White Claw. "You want another?"

"Yeah. If you don't mind."

Not two seconds after Cole got up from his chair, Brian sat in it. "So, hey, I gotta get going now." He gave her his phone. "Why don't you send yourself a text, and I'll text you later about our plans for next Friday."

After Serafina texted herself from his phone, he quickly got up. "Okay. See ya."

Serafina looked up to see where Cole was, but she didn't see him. Off to the side of the table though, she spotted two cans of White Claw hard seltzers. Cole must have stopped by while Brian was there, she thought. Was he upset about that? Did he even like her in that way?

She grabbed her crutches, put one under each arm, and ventured toward the back door, passing Randy along the way. "Have you seen Cole?"

Randy looked around. "No. Everything okay?"

Serafina shrugged. In that moment, her heart ached for Cole to return. She went inside to catch up to him.

As she went to the front room to look outside, she noticed the main front door was open. Beyond the screen door, she could hear Michael and Hollis engaged in a heated discussion on the walkway.

"There's no point in fighting it. My cancer is terminal."

"But we're seeing really positive results with this new treatment. Why wouldn't you at least give it a try?"

"Michael, I know you have good intentions, but this is my decision, and I'd appreciate you not telling anyone either."

"Well, you know I can't anyways because of HIPAA."

Their conversation got really quiet. When Serafina peeked out, she could see them hugging. Kendra and Maya were waiting for Michael in their dark SUV parked across the street.

Serafina sat on the couch and got very still. Her mind raced with thoughts. She felt the need to take action, as she often did, but this time her inability to process what she'd heard kept her in place.

He's got cancer? Terminal cancer? Like how long were they talking? Six months? A year? How long had he known about it? Why wouldn't he fight it? Why was he keeping it a secret? Especially from her! Is that why he seemed so out of character? She knew he'd been acting weird!

The tequila was wearing off, and with that, pain was reemerging in full force. She hadn't even had an opportunity to process everything else. A date with Brian. Wanda retiring. Wanda fostering. Wanda moving in with Randy and Nick when they were so quick to make her move. Upsetting Cole. And now this? Hollis dying of cancer? It all felt like so much, and she was feeling herself begin to implode.

As Hollis entered the front door, Serafina stood up. Unable to contain her emotions any longer, she exploded at him. "How could you do this, Hollis? How could you tell me I'm like your daughter and not tell me you have cancer? When were you going to tell me? You don't think I have a say in you getting treatment? Well, I do, dammit! You're getting the treatment. So, don't you argue with me about it, because you're getting the treatment!"

She broke down crying hysterically. "You're getting the treatment. You hear me?"

Looking at him, she wiped the flood of tears pouring out down her cheeks. "We're fighting this."

Hollis took her in his arms and held her tight as she let loose her emotions. "All right, baby girl. All right."

In that moment, Cole came into the front room from the hallway.

"Sorry, I was in the restroom. Randy said you were looking for me?" He stopped in his tracks when he saw Serafina crying.

Hollis held up his hand and waved Cole over.

Once Cole was next to them, Hollis asked, "Can you help her upstairs to the loft to rest while I try to clear folks out?"

Cole nodded and then took Serafina's arm over his shoulder.

Hollis took Serafina's face in his hands and kissed her forehead. "Let me see folks out and then we can talk, okay?"

Serafina wiped her face of tears and nodded.

Cole helped Serafina to her bed, and then sat quietly on the mattress's edge, available but also giving her space.

Serafina looked up at Cole. "Did you know?"

"Huh?"

"Did you know he has cancer? That he's dying?"

He looked surprised to hear the news. He'd walked in when she was crying and must not have heard their conversation before then. He shook his head and vehemently insisted, "No, I swear. I didn't."

A few minutes passed, and then she spoke up. "I feel so stupid to have you see me like this." She wiped mascara smudges from under her eyes.

"No, don't be."

"It's hard for me to process it all." She swallowed. "And I'm in a lot of pain."

He leaned in. "Can I get you anything to help with that?"

"Yeah, some Tylenol? We should have some in the kitchen cabinet next to the microwave."

Cole nodded. "You got it."

Serafina grabbed his arm before he stood up. "Oh, and some iced tea, too, please."

He nodded again.

Returning with a Tylenol bottle and a can of iced tea, Cole sat beside her and assisted with opening the bottle, taking out several pills, and handing her the opened iced tea to take a swig.

"I just don't get it," she said, meandering in her thoughts. "I mean, why wouldn't he try to fight it? So what if they say it's terminal—he should still try!"

Cole sat silently listening, affording her the space to process.

"He probably needed that treatment months ago." She sighed. "All those afternoon naps on the couch he's been taking recently —it was probably because of the cancer."

She started crying again, which prompted Cole to grab some Kleenex off the nightstand and hand them to her.

"How could I have been so oblivious to the signs?" She wiped her eyes with the Kleenex, and then slightly blew her nose. "It's just like with Datson. Apparently, I'm just *that* fucking clueless."

"Hey, no self-deprecating talk." He stopped her. "And if you remember—I had no idea either."

Serafina nodded, feeling exhausted and defeated. She really wanted to rest, but she didn't want to be alone. "Will you stay awhile?"

"Mm-hmm."

"Thank you, Cole."

"Of course."

She settled into the silence and allowed her thoughts to surface as they came. It felt comforting to have Cole there. To have someone care about her needs. And in that moment, it dawned on her that Cole was becoming a very good friend. More so than Randy had ever been. She wasn't even sure if Randy was capable of selfless acts. But then again, with Randy, there had always been a bit of sibling rivalry over Wanda's love. Serafina, not being one for competition, had bowed out from that contest long ago. Distancing herself.

She knew deep down that her relationship with Randy wasn't healthy.

But for so long, he had been all she'd had. So, in the interest of not being completely alone, she'd learned to tolerate his treatment of her. But now, just maybe, she could find true friendship with Cole.

Feeling safe in Cole's company, Serafina closed her eyes and willed the best possible outcome for Hollis. *Everything is going to work out.*

About the Author

J.P. Zeigler is a Detroit native, born and raised, who proudly attended Detroit Public Schools. She earned bachelor's degrees from Oakland University and University of Michigan-Dearborn, and an M.B.A. degree in human resources management from Baker College. When J.P. Zeigler isn't working her day job as an HR Director, she is writing, hiking, and exploring all there is to do in the San Francisco Bay Area where she lives with her family. Her debut novel, *Hollis and Gray*, is the first book of its series. Her website is www.jpzeiglerbooks.com.

Made in United States
North Haven, CT
24 May 2024

52885701R00221